The Last
Message

D1135825

Catherine Hope's love of reading began at a young age. Her parents always had a book close by, although they read vastly different genres, which rubbed off on her as she devoured everything from romance to espionage. She fondly remembers her mom with a book propped against her cosy-covered teapot at lunchtime.

Catherine started telling stories as a child, and it naturally grew into a passion for writing. Her goal is to breathe life into her characters and worlds, and transport her readers into the pages of heartache and triumph.

When Catherine's not writing or thinking up fresh stories, she spends time with her family, friends and menagerie of pets. But she's always ready to jet off to explore the world, where many of her experiences find their way into her books. Catherine lives in a small town in Ontario, Canada.

The Last Message

Catherine Hope

HEADLINE
ETERNAL

Copyright © 2023 Catherine Hope

The right of Catherine Hope to be identified as the Author of
the Work has been asserted by her in accordance with the
Copyright, Designs and Patents Act 1988.

First published in 2023
by HEADLINE ETERNAL
An imprint of HEADLINE PUBLISHING GROUP

1

Apart from any use permitted under UK copyright law, this publication may
only be reproduced, stored, or transmitted, in any form, or by any means,
with prior permission in writing of the publishers or, in the case of reprographic
production, in accordance with the terms of licences
issued by the Copyright Licensing Agency.

All characters in this publication are fictitious
and any resemblance to real persons, living or dead,
is purely coincidental.

Cataloguing in Publication Data is available from the British Library

ISBN 978 1 4722 8617 8

Typeset in 11/14 pt Minion Pro by Jouve (UK), Milton Keynes

Printed and bound in Great Britain by Clays Ltd, Elcograf S.p.A.

Headline's policy is to use papers that are natural, renewable and recyclable
products and made from wood grown in well-managed forests and other
controlled sources. The logging and manufacturing processes are expected to
conform to the environmental regulations of the country of origin.

HEADLINE PUBLISHING GROUP
An Hachette UK Company
Carmelite House
50 Victoria Embankment
London EC4Y 0DZ

www.headlineeternal.com
www.headline.co.uk
www.hachette.co.uk

Moving on from tragedy and heartache is one of the most challenging things I've had to endure. I/we are left with an aching hollowness, which at least for me, remains as a hole in my heart. There are days when the memories are not as painful as others or I have the ability to "forget" for a little while, but then a tiny reminder can so easily knock you off your feet. Even years later. This book is dedicated to all those suffering from the loss of a loved one as you try to rebuild your life around the hollow.

I hope you love Lizzie and Nick as much as I do and treasure their journey.

xxx

Chapter One

My phone spun through the air and down toward the blue waves. How on earth I'd managed to send it flying out of my hands was truly an accomplishment. But then I'm talented that way.

I shrieked and leaned over the rail, balancing on the slippery rung, as I watched my lifeline gracefully spiral down. The sun striking off the face in staccato bursts with every revolution was like a movie reel.

For the briefest moment, I almost panicked at all the images I could have lost forever. Thank goodness for the cloud.

But not everything was saved there. Tucked in the phone case were a few precious photos of Rob, my twin, in his final days. I'd used our parents' old Polaroid, for nostalgia's sake, to take the photos, and they were irreplaceable,

It was gone, out of reach and forever to rest at the bottom of the Strait of Juan de Fuca. All because of a whale. A stunning whale and her calf, but still, a whale.

I curled my arms over my head and watched the waves devour my phone.

I'd desperately wanted to see whales when I'd decided to come to the Pacific Northwest. Everyone told me how fabulous it was if you were lucky enough to catch sight of them. Go whale watching, they'd said. You'll love it, they'd said.

To be fair, I'd been excited to get so lucky and actually see the two whales. Perhaps too excited. In my haste to get the right shot for my next article for Condé Nast, the phone slipped in my fingers, the PopSocket popped off and, like a juggler, I played hot potato with it until—poof!—it was gone.

I was still standing at the damp railing, tottering on my tip-toes, staring at the swells that fanned out from the hull of the ferry. Suddenly, my feet slipped and I flung my arms around the railing, narrowly avoiding following my phone into the abyss.

Strong hands gripped my shoulders and hauled me down.

"It's not worth it, ma'am." A man's voice, just behind me, was edged with alarm.

I glanced at him and realized he thought I was a jumper.

I widened my eyes and shook my head. "Oh, n-no, I wasn't going t-to, it's just that my phone . . ." My voice caught when the reality of my loss hit home. I closed my eyes. "So much was on it." My voice croaked in barely a whisper. I was religious at backing up my phone. It held so much of my work and personal info, but those Polaroids were gone.

"I'm sorry," he offered. "Maybe it's up in the clouds."

Up in the clouds.

Despite everything, that almost made me giggle and I opened my eyes. I didn't want to correct him, and forced a smile at the elderly man. "I'm sure you are right."

He wagged a finger at me. "Be careful next time, no leaning over railings."

"I promise. And thank you." Turning away, I pushed through

the other passengers, the joy of seeing the whales, just moments before, now faded.

If I hadn't been such a procrastinator, I'd have scanned the last photos of Rob on my external hard drive and Carbonite. But I hadn't. I chastised myself now. I knew better than that, having lost a lot of work a few years ago when my laptop crashed. But I never thought about those last few images in my phone case. Regret pierced me.

I found a bench away from the passengers, and sank down on to it, feeling drained all of a sudden. Absently, I rummaged through my bag, in search of the tissues I knew I had in there somewhere.

Emotions I'd been able to manage, for the most part, since Rob died were rushing back. I didn't want to cry here. In public. Or anywhere, for that matter. I'd done my share of crying in the months following his death.

Memories rolled over me. Rob had teased that I spent too much time *behind* the camera rather than living *in* the moment. I'd argued back that it was important to have photos, both for my job and memories.

But he'd laughed, leaned forward to gently touch me on the head, and then tapped his chest.

Memories live here, Lizzie, he'd said.

I could still hear his voice, soft and low but weak as the cancer ravaged him.

I drew in a ragged breath, my throat and lungs tightening. I pulled a bottle of water from my bag and took a long drink. My hat, or rather Rob's hat, blew off my head, landing on the bench beside me, and started to skitter across the wood. I grabbed it before it could fly off in the wind and shoved it in my bag. If I ever lost his hat . . . well, I couldn't bear to think about it.

As time went by, it was getting more difficult to visualize

Rob's face, and that hurt so much. How could my twin's face fade? Out of habit, I reached for my phone, wanting to see a picture of him, and moaned.

"No, Rob, faces and voices fade. Photos are always there," I murmured.

He'd made me promise not to wallow after he was gone. It had been the most difficult time in my life, somehow worse even than when our parents died. One from illness and the other soon after from a broken heart.

But, damn it, it wasn't easy!

I was taken back to his room.

Rob lay so wasted and pale on the hospital bed set up in his house. Rather than keep the draperies closed, they were open so the atmosphere wouldn't hold the weight of being a sickroom. A snowstorm painted the old Georgetown street into the perfect Christmas card. But Christmas this year hadn't been festive, even though I tried to brighten it up with sparkly lights. I crossed my arms and shivered.

"Lizzie, come here," Rob's voice rasped.

I turned from the window to see his hand stretched out to me. I rushed to him and took his chilled fingers in mine, gently rubbing them. But they wouldn't warm up, his skin dry and thin. His breathing had changed and deep in my heart . . . I knew.

"Shh, save your energy." I brushed my knuckles softly across his sunken cheek.

I wouldn't cry! Couldn't. I'd save that for after.

"No, I-I need . . ." He swallowed and closed his eyes for the briefest moment before fixing them back on me. Eyes so like mine. And a brightness filled them. "To say . . . tell you . . . after I die—"

"Rob, no, don't say that!" My eyes prickled and I blinked, but it didn't stop the tears that spilled down my cheeks.

"Lizzie, come on." He drew in a gurgled breath.

I was shaking my head. I simply couldn't believe we were here.

"Everything is arranged. There's nothing you h-have to do. You know that, s-so . . . promise me." His voice faded and his eyes fluttered shut.

I leaned over him, suddenly panicked, and whispered, "Rob, Rob, promise what?"

His eyes opened and they had a faraway look in them, but his voice was suddenly strong. "P-promise me you won't stay here. Go and follow your dreams. Don't let go of your dreams." I held my breath as he took another slow one, before continuing, "I've tied you down for too long. You must live your life. Promise me."

I nodded and tears almost blinded me. "I'll try."

"No, don't try. Do. It's important you leave here and move on." He lifted his hand and touched my cheek. "Go and do the things you've always wanted to do. Stop being so cautious, and live on the wild side. Life is short. Do it for me." He closed his eyes and whispered. "I need you to promise me this."

"I p-promise." I didn't know how I'd manage to keep this promise, but I had to. For him. "Rob? Did you hear me?"

His mouth moved slightly. "Yes. So tired."

"You sleep, I'll get you some fresh water." I placed his hand under the covers and pulled them up to his chin. My once big, strong, full-of-life brother was now so frail and small on the bed, it was shocking. I still couldn't believe this was happening.

Taking the empty glass from the bedside table, I smiled at the Polaroid we'd taken yesterday. He'd had a good day and he'd told me a joke as I grabbed a selfie. I'd treasure that image forever. I quietly left the room.

The ferry horn went off, loud and mournful. It snapped me back to the present. In a way, I was glad, because reliving going back into his bedroom, only to find he'd slipped away in the short period of time I was gone, wrecked me. I hadn't been by his side when he died. I'd never forgive myself for that.

I straightened my shoulders and stood, pulling the strap of my bag over my head. And now that special photo was with my phone under the waves. I exhaled, doing my best to bring back my happy thoughts. I much preferred them over the soul-sucking despair of grief.

Rob would've thought it hilarious that I'd lost my phone. I knew exactly what he'd say.

You're an accident waiting to happen, and it makes being your twin so freaking exciting.

And here I was, in the Pacific Northwest, working on my next blog, and half of it was now among the fishes and bottom feeders. Well, I'd had to rewrite before and, while it was annoying, usually the rewrite was better. I should still be able to make my deadline.

With Rob's encouragement, I'd followed my dream of becoming a freelance journalist a few years ago, making the leap from the dog-eat-dog corporate world. I'd picked up some regular commissions from lifestyle magazines, and had found my happy spot doing travel writing.

Then Rob had fallen sick.

His illness grounded me. No way was I going to leave him alone, and my blossoming new career was put on hold until . . . well . . . until. I'd refocused, declining opportunities that would take me abroad, and accepting those that kept me close to home. Rob had to be my main priority.

But over the last year or so I'd been able to put myself out there again and find editors interested in my free-wheeling adventures. Then my foray into blogging, with a Mardi Gras article from New Orleans, became a huge hit. I'd been shocked, and pleased, and the next thing I knew I was in demand. A total one-eighty from where I'd been a few short months ago, and the pressure was on. So I'd upped my social media presence, but was still careful to keep my journalism jobs at the forefront.

Out of habit, I went to post on Insta, then fisted my hands. The first order of business was getting another phone. Pronto.

The ferry arrived in the port and people moved like a pack of sheep to the exit. I let myself be carried along with the flow off the boat. Then, extricating myself from the herd, I found a spot by the sea wall. If only I hadn't decided a little ferry trip was a good idea. Then I'd still have my phone and not have to go through the irritation of replacing it. I'd still have my precious photos, be able to dive into my next job without the rewrite, and not be in this predicament.

Savage Cove was small, quaint and historic, with a very pretty waterfront and marina, shielded by a spit on the west side that kept the sea relatively calm. Despite everything, I was glad I'd chosen to settle here for the next six weeks.

I wandered along the seafront, awestruck by nature's beauty. The salty tang on the air was invigorating, and my nose was tickled by the mouth-watering aroma of fish and chips carried along by the sea breeze. I knew exactly what I'd be having for dinner later.

Beginning to feel a little bit better, I enjoyed watching the birds soar on the wind, calling to each other with sounds akin to laughter. Blocking the sun with my hand, I didn't recognize the species. I remembered seeing a bird book at the beach cottage I'd rented. I'd look them up when I got back.

The air was delightfully fresh, and I lifted my face to the sun's warmth, closing my eyes. I was *in the moment*, just as Rob had instructed. Live life. Enjoy every moment. Grab adventure with both hands and hang on tight. Don't dwell on the past or that he was gone. Our time together had come to an end, but I was still here.

"Right then. On to more living, and finding a phone."

I strolled a little further along Wharf Street, past a row of beautiful and obviously very old wooden buildings. They'd been lovingly cared for and looked like they'd been converted into very high-end B&Bs and restaurants. The location was prime, and I was inspired to plan a future article. I enjoyed history and learning about town origins. A story focusing on these lovely buildings would be interesting.

At the intersection of Wharf and Lincoln Street, which ran away from the water, I stumbled across a market with vendors selling a variety of wares—from art, to baked goods, cheese, crafts, and numerous other items. A particularly interesting metalwork booth caught my attention.

It was selling handcrafted metal sculptures in all sizes. I found a lovely pine tree statue and a little heart made of steel. I was always on the lookout for hearts, and this one had to come home with me.

Nick was glad to be back from his latest business trip. It was a great day in the PNW and the top was down on his Jag. He needed the fresh sea air to clear away his travel hangover, and it had him seriously thinking, yet again, about scaling back the trips. It was definitely a baseball cap and sunglasses kind of day.

He was coming home, although it didn't really feel much like home anymore. The last few years had been especially difficult, and he'd thought that working hard and traveling often was the way to keep his mind sharp. He'd been to some pretty fantastic places, though always alone. He doubted there would ever be a time he would have a travel companion, but he couldn't deny it would be nice to share the adventures with someone who appreciated them.

He let out a sigh, and squinted, cursing that he'd packed his sunglasses and cap in his carry-on bag, which was in the trunk.

The good weather had brought out all the tourists. He liked to see his town hopping, but he also preferred to keep his distance from the crowds. Normally, he'd bypass Wharf Street to avoid traffic and tourists, but today he hadn't. He didn't know why and was a bit startled when he found himself driving through town.

His timing lined up with the docking of the ferry, and the street was crammed with pedestrians. None of whom were being particularly traffic savvy.

Nick rested his elbow on the door and watched the people spill along the waterfront, keeping his eye on the road in case someone simply walked out from between the parked cars.

Creeping forward, he didn't think he'd ever seen it so busy. Savage Cove had changed a lot in recent years. He still hadn't decided if he was adapting, or just ignoring the changes, by staying at his beach house most of the time when he wasn't away.

He had no reason to leave the house, other than for basic necessities, and most of the time his dad handled that. Which Nick appreciated. Other than working, walking Houdini on the beach, spending time with Dad, his life had become uneventful.

Nick supposed that, after the drama of three years ago, uneventful wasn't all that bad. He didn't think he was lonely. No, not at all. He kept himself occupied well enough. Yet, watching the couples and families stroll along the seafront, he felt a little twinge in his chest.

He'd almost had that.

He thrummed his fingers on the steering wheel, making slow progress along Wharf, and turned his attention to the tent tops of the market. The market was a new attraction, in only its second or third year.

The place was a zoo. A car suddenly stopped in front of him and he had to put on the brakes hard.

"Geez. I really should have taken the bypass," he muttered.

Nick looked back at the market, forcing down his impatience as the car in front unloaded, the passengers taking their time to get out and move along. It was like a competition to find how many clowns could fit in a Volkswagen.

A flash from one of the tents made him blink. Refocusing, he saw a woman holding something that caught the sun. It glinted in the sunlight. The woman's back was to him, and he was struck by the shimmer of her hair under the sun's rays. Almost as bright as the flash that had nearly blinded him. He tried to focus and saw her hand gripping a metal object that looked like a heart. The seller put it in a paper bag and he watched as the woman exchanged money for the item.

She was tall, slender, and moved with a willowy grace. He caught his breath, wanting to see her face.

He was so intent on waiting for her to turn around, that he didn't see the car in front had driven off. Until the sound of a loud horn behind him snapped him out of his trance. Nick lifted his hand in acknowledgement and drove forward.

Finally, he was moving. He glanced back at the market in the rear-view mirror, trying to find the woman again. But he couldn't see her through the crowds, and then the market disappeared around a bend in the road.

The image of her stuck with him all the way home.

* * *

Crossing the street, I walked up Lincoln, the gentle incline following the contours of the landscape. In the background the mountains rose, their peaks making smudges of inky blue and white on the horizon.

Looking into the store windows as I passed by, I was focused on one thing only. The other stores, while tempting, would have to wait. I'd prefer to avoid driving to Seattle and, while I could order online, I wasn't confident next-day delivery to the cottage would be without further drama. In-store shopping seemed to make the most sense to me at the moment. I really wasn't ready for big-city chaos right now. I'd only just begun to feel settled after my cross-country drive, before my arrival here a few days ago. All I wanted right now was quiet time, with only the sea, me myself and I, and my work.

There was a lot to discover about Savage Cove. Originally, it was the name that had caught my attention. I just had to visit a place that named itself "Savage" and find out why. If I were to hazard a guess, from what I'd seen so far, it would have something to do with the ocean. I stored away a note to myself to dig into this and turn it into a blog post or article for my editor, Kate.

A cozy little side street leading back to the seafront veered off to my right, lined with more of the older buildings of brick, stone and wood. All were carefully maintained, and many had window boxes overflowing with colorful flowers. An appealing-looking café a few buildings down caught my eye. My stomach growled, reminding me I hadn't eaten anything since breakfast— and that had just been a dish of yogurt. After getting a phone, I'd come back and see what they offered.

A few storefronts later, I saw a sign blinking at me through the display window. Leaning closer, I cupped my hand over my eyes to look deeper into the store. A neon sign at the back was flashing. *Electronics.*

"Thank God." I pulled the door open and wandered down the aisles.

It was a hodge-podge, a little bit of everything, from touristy stuff to groceries, magazines, books, and a wall cooler loaded with beverages, ice cream, and other frozen items. But what I needed was at the back.

I beelined to the counter.

"Can I help you?" A red-headed young man popped up from behind a display case, startling me.

"Oh! Uh, yes, I'm looking for a cell phone." I continued looking for a display, but there wasn't much inventory. "I need an iPhone, please."

"We are limited with stock. But I can order anything you want, it'll just take a few days to arrive."

My heart sank. But I was here now, and I decided at least I knew one would be on the way soon. It wasn't that long to wait. "Okay, let's place an order. Can I get a cheap phone to use in case of emergencies until the new one comes in? Something basic will do."

'Sure." He placed a few on the counter and nudged one toward me. "This one. Super cheap, refurbed number, and you can toss it once you get your new phone, if you want."

"Okay, deal."

I filled out the paperwork for my order, and gave it to the store clerk. He looked at the paper.

"Right then, this is all good, Lizzie," he said with a smile. "I'll call the new—well, old—phone you got today when your iPhone comes in."

I thanked him and left the store with a phone in my bag. I'd have to pull out Old Faithful—my SLR camera—if I wanted to take any photos in the next day or two.

"Now," I said to myself, "let's go check out that coffee shop."

I set off with a fast-paced stride and quickly found myself in front of the café, peering in through the tall windows. A simple word was etched on the middle, arched windowpane in a hipster-style font. *Sol.*

The aroma of fresh roast drifted on the air, and my tension floated away. I hadn't realized just how stressed I was until now.

I pulled open the door, the tinkling of bells announcing my arrival. My frayed nerves were already beginning to calm.

Chapter Two

Inside, I inhaled blissfully. The scent of coffee, baking, and wood smoke wrapped around me like a warm and comfy blanket. I'd found my place.

The café was welcoming, with honeyed wood accents, a high, silver tin ceiling, old chandelier lighting, and intimate table lamps. The side and back wall appeared to be original deep-red brick, adding to the ambiance.

A fireplace, a remnant of days gone by, was to my right. A cheery fire crackled behind an old, intricate iron screen. Beside it was a grand staircase. Wood and black iron climbed the wall to a landing where the stairs turned ninety degrees and rose to a second level. On the first step, a red velvet rope hooked to brass stands barred the way ahead of anyone going up. I was super curious to know what was up there. Had this been a saloon, boarding house, mercantile, or brothel in days gone by? I could almost see the ladies from bygone years standing at the railing, teasing the men below. The history this place held was almost tangible.

This café was an absolute treasure. It wasn't so much a coffee shop as a homey gathering place and an eclectic mix of styles. Its location was perfect, with its tall windows affording a view of the water framed by old and renovated buildings.

I sniffed the air again. My mouth watered as I walked across the old wooden floors, scattered with colorful rugs, past snug seating areas and booths clustered between potted plants. Intimacy and coziness embraced me and I smiled, pretty sure I'd just fallen in love.

Next time, I'd bring my computer and work here.

I paused in front of the antique display case with a beautiful curved glass front, chock-full of the most mouth-watering bakery treats I'd ever seen: sandwiches wrapped in waxed paper, tempting donuts dripping with icing on cake platters, loaves of bread in baskets, pies and tarts artfully arranged on beautiful old bone-china cake stands, and a hot section which held deep-dish meat pies, sausage rolls, sliced prime rib and more.

I felt like I'd struck gold and tapped my fingers happily on my thighs, letting my eyes wander over the delicious-looking food. How on earth could I decide?

One of everything, please.

Needing to rest my feet, I glanced around to find an empty seat and spied one at the end of the counter. Sliding on to the high stool, I hooked the heels of my shoes on the brass rail running the length of the bar and let out a sigh. I was shattered.

I watched the staff serve the guests with friendly efficiency as I waited patiently, despite my stomach loudly protesting the delay.

A young woman approached from behind the bar. She had her hair pulled back with a tie-dyed scarf keeping the long dreadlocks off her face.

"Afternoon, would you like to see a menu?" She placed a napkin in front of me.

"Is all that made on site?" I pointed at the curved glass display.

"It sure is." I heard the pride in the barista's voice. "Every day, plus we do have some day-olds for discounted prices."

"It all looks delicious. What would you recommend? I can't decide." I smiled at the woman and was rewarded with a smile in return. Maybe I could strike up a conversation and find out some information about the café.

"Depends if you want sweet or savory."

"Hmm, I think sweet today."

"Then the maple bacon donut," the barista suggested. "Totally."

"Oh my God, maple bacon? How did you come up with that combination?"

"The last owner visited Whistler, and a hotel up there had them. She recreated them and they are a hit. Can I get you one?"

"Yes, please. No arm twisting needed here."

The barista laughed. "A drink too?" She glanced at the door as the chimes tinkled again.

"Yes, I'd like a large coffee."

"Drip or special?"

"Oh, drip, please, with three cream. Thanks." I sat against the backrest of the stool, feeling right at home.

"Great, I'll be right back."

I pulled out my replacement phone and looked it over. It was a blast from the past, before the days of smartphones that held your entire life on them. It would do until the new one came in. I sent up a silent wish for it not to take too long.

The barista came back with my donut and coffee, and I put the phone down.

"That's a rather ancient device." She smiled, and I laughed.

"Yep. Only temporary until my new one comes in. I was brilliantly coordinated on the ferry today and managed to lose my phone over the side while taking pictures."

Rolling my eyes, I picked up the mug and inhaled the delicious scent.

"Ouch, that's gotta hurt." Amanda (according to her name tag) winced in sympathy.

I took a sip and closed my eyes in delight. "It did, but . . . wow! This coffee is wonderful. Helps to ease the pain a little bit."

"Enjoy! I'm sure the donut will too." Amanda moved along to serve some new customers sitting in a booth.

The wall in front of me was lined with a variety of photos, some old, some new. One in particular caught my eye. It showed an outcrop of rocks by the seaside, capturing a wave crashing in a fan over the rocks with perfect timing.

I took a bite of the donut and almost moaned in delight. The flavors of the maple cream, icing and bacon were divine. I wasn't at all ashamed to take such enjoyment in this decadent treat.

Squinting, I looked again at the photo. It seemed familiar. The rocks were similar to those just down the beach from where I was staying. But then it was a craggy coastline. It could be anywhere.

I put the donut down. "Amanda, where was this photo taken?" I pointed to it.

Amanda walked over and her lips pulled down in a frown. "I'm not too sure, but it looks like Bicker Beach."

"What a coincidence, I'm renting a house on Bicker Beach."

"It's really nice out there. Oh, excuse me." Amanda hurried off to take the orders of the crowd of people coming in the door.

Turning my attention back to the photos, I speculated about

the history they must hold. I pulled my Moleskine out of my satchel and scribbled down some notes. Mainly about the photos on the wall, and the disastrous ferry trip. Nothing too in depth, but I needed to regroup, and writing had a way of calming my mind.

With a pen in one hand, I held the donut between thumb and forefinger of the other, savoring every morsel of the deliciousness until it was finished. Absently wiping my mouth with a napkin, I glanced up from my journal to study each of the photos on the wall. The stories in those old pictures made me even more curious to discover the history of the town and its unusual name. Faces from the past looked back at me, calling to me to dig into bygone years to find all the answers.

I folded the napkin and tucked it under the plate after finishing my afternoon treat. I settled the bill and left the café with a wave to Amanda, heading out to wander the town for a while. Later, I planned to hunt down the fish and chips I'd smelled earlier.

Long after I had written up my daily notes, created an Instagram and TikTok post about my mouth-watering dinner, and enjoyed my nightly glass of wine on the patio looking out over Bicker Beach, I was curled up in my bed reading the next book in my TBR pile. The pages were lit by the book light attached to the headboard, leaving me in a small glow while the rest of the room ringed my bed in darkness. The sheer curtains lifted in lazy waves with the sea breeze, giving the impression of ghostly visitors coming through the open window. I jumped when a branch knocked against the outside wall.

I slid down into the pillows a little more and pulled the covers up to my chin, telling myself I wasn't spooked. Finally, I reached over to flick on the bedside lamp.

"That's better." It was reassuring to speak out loud, even to an empty room. "Dumbass, there's nothing to be frightened about. Since when did I become a fraidy cat at night?"

I sucked in a deep breath of the ocean air blowing through the open window. Snuggling under the thick comforter, I sighed and forced myself to relax, deciding I'd never been more comfortable than I was right now.

My eyes grew heavy and my thoughts drifted. I had almost six weeks ahead of me in Savage Cove. It was a lovely blank page I could fill with whatever I wanted.

I drifted off to sleep, cozy and warm . . .

I was awoken by a loud buzzing and vibration on the bedside table. Startled out of sleep, I reached out and knocked something to the floor. The buzzing went off again.

"W-what?" I threw off the quilt and shivered in the chilly room. The lamp was still on and I blinked while my eyes adjusted. I glanced at the clock and saw it was 2.45 a.m.

Another buzz. I reached down to the floor and fumbled around until my fingers touched the phone, knocking it so that it skittered away as if it was coming to life with each buzz. Stretching further, I finally caught hold of it.

I looked at the face of the phone and rubbed my eyes to clear my vision. There was a message. Who on earth would be texting at this time in the morning? Nobody I knew had this number.

I opened the text. I needed to read it a couple of times, as it didn't make any sense to my sleepy brain.

"W-what . . . who . . .?"

Marissa, this year I am sending my last message to you. I don't know if I'll ever be able to forgive myself, and I will never forget you, but I have to find a way to let you go.

19

"Huh?" I blinked and ran my fingers through my hair. Marissa? I checked the time again. Only a few minutes past the last time I checked. I squinted to read the text again. There was no number showing who sent it.

Unknown caller.

Even if my first instinct was to reply, I wouldn't be able to. There was no way I could let the sender know the message had gone astray. I gently put the phone down on the bed and sat there, thinking about it.

The message was raw. Emotional. Soulful. I kneaded my chest with my knuckles, surprised how affected I was by the despair the words conveyed. They were meant for someone else, and I couldn't help feeling I'd intruded on someone else's pain and heartache.

It took a moment for my heartbeat to settle down. After a quick trip to the bathroom, I shut the windows, turned off the light, and crawled back into bed. I yawned and snuggled into the pillows, desperately needing more sleep.

But I lay there, sleep now firmly out of reach. I couldn't get the text message out of my head. I groaned and fished for the phone tangled in the sheets. I read the illuminated message again.

Either someone had made a mistake, or this number used to belong to somebody else.

Despite my curiosity, it was none of my business, but there was something so heart-wrenching about the message.

I put the phone down and fell back into the pillows. I finally nodded off again, but it was a rough sleep. I floated between waking and drifting off, constantly thinking or dreaming about the text. I couldn't shake off the words or stop them running like a reel of ticker tape through my brain.

Finally, I gave up trying to sleep and got out of bed. I padded into the kitchen and made a cup of tea. Sticking my arms into the cable-knit sweater I'd made, with tea in hand, I grabbed a throw blanket from the sofa and went outside.

I slung the blanket around my shoulders and sat on a lounger, tucking my legs under me, hands cupping the hot mug.

The moon was full and its reflection glittered off the waves. Stars were out, but they paled in the moon's light. I stayed, thinking and planning, until the sun rose, bathing the shore and water in gold. It was too beautiful for words. Exhaustion finally overtook me and I snuggled back into bed, knowing exactly what I was going to do about the text.

Chapter Three

I stood at the edge of the waves on the empty beach, watching the sun sink toward the horizon. Sunsets and sunrises drew me like bees to honey. The shifting colors, sense of completeness, and awe of nature moved me deep in my soul. It was so easy to get lost in the moment and forget what had brought me here. I cleared my throat, wiping the back of my hand across my eyes. Tears. Tears that crept in at the most unexpected moments, ever since Rob had died.

I wasn't a crier. Normally. I'd always been steadfast, sturdy and optimistic. And he'd made me promise not to be sad. To be brave and live life. But it was so damn hard.

I lifted my face, loving the feel of the wind on my skin. It would be sticky from the sea spray but I didn't care. I drew in a deep breath and rolled my shoulders, cramped from being hunched over my laptop most of the afternoon.

Waves washed up across the sand. The sun was at the perfect elevation on the horizon to create an almost blinding haze from the spindrift. I stepped closer to the water. Waves splashed over my ankles, sucking the sand from around my feet when the water receded, back to the sea. I sank in the soft, warm sand as if greedy fingers had risen from the earth and curled around me.

Distant barking reached me over the sounds of the sea and wind. I raised my hand to shield my eyes and turned. A streak of gold came from around a bend in the beach. There weren't many houses along this stretch, and I wondered where the dog had come from.

Within moments, the golden retriever was at my side, barking and jumping around me.

"Who are you, buddy?" I reached down and patted him.

The dog found a stick and tossed it in the air. I laughed and picked it up, throwing it back. The dog was wet, clearly having had a swim. He was relentless with the stick and we played for a couple of minutes until he stopped, standing alert, his attention focused on the direction from which he'd come.

A figure rounded the beach, distorted in the miasma hanging over the sea. It was difficult to see the shape of the shoreline, with its rocky outcrops and trees. I squinted through the bright haze, and watched for a moment as the figure grew more defined the closer he came.

The dog barked and then turned back to me. He still wanted to play.

I assumed the man approaching was the dog's owner. If he was calling the dog, I couldn't hear, and the pup seemed very content to hang with me. Moments later, it bolted off.

I turned.

The man was standing about twenty feet away, with the dog jumping around his legs. He had the strangest look on his face, like he'd seen a ghost, and then he glanced down at his dog and petted him.

He was barefoot, the bottom of his jeans damp, and his

untucked shirt billowed out on the gusts, outlining a muscled chest. I shifted on my feet. His hair was just long enough to blow around his collar. He walked out of the mist and his features became clearer.

He was tanned and athletic-looking. As he approached, I could see his face more clearly. His eyes drew me in. For a moment, I almost forgot to breathe. Green, flecked with gold, rimmed with thick dark lashes below equally dark brows. They were the most beautiful eyes I'd ever seen.

He seemed to falter a step when his gaze met mine, and stubbed his toe on a rock in the sand. He did a little hop before catching himself.

"Oh, are you okay?" I reached out instinctively and then pulled my hand back, pressing it to my chest.

"Yep, no problem except a bruised toe—and maybe a bit of bruised pride."

He smiled back and I bit the inside of my lip to stop from laughing when he grimaced.

"Hi," I said, and then asked, "is he your dog?"

"Hi." He nodded and approached me. "Yeah, he is."

"What's his name?" I asked while leaning over to pick up a few smaller pieces of driftwood.

"Houdini."

Houdini jumped around me, waiting for me to throw another stick.

I laughed. "Does he live up to his name?" I drew back my arm and pitched the stick. It sailed through the air with Houdini racing along behind, watching it until it dropped into the waves, where he pounced on it.

"You bet he does. He pulled a disappearing act and ended up here," the man said, and crossed his arms. He watched Houdini's antics with a smile curving his lips.

I had to admit he was a damn fine-looking man.

I pushed hair out of my eyes. "Well, we found each other and then you found us. It all worked out."

"Yes, it did." He turned and faced me. "I'm Nick."

He reached out a hand and I took it. His fingers, firm, strong and warm, curled around mine. For a moment, I couldn't look away from him. We stayed frozen, touching, as the waves lapped around our feet. The wind blew my hair over my face and ruffled his.

"Ah, and I'm Lizzie." Tingles rippled up my arm and bloomed across my chest. I let go of his hand, confused by the power of my reaction to him. I turned my face to the sea so the wind could blow its cooling breeze over my heated cheeks.

We were quiet and I took the opportunity to gather my thoughts. After brushing the wind-whipped hair from my face, I cupped the back of my neck and watched Houdini play in the waves. He was soaked.

"Nice to meet you, Lizzie."

I turned and our eyes met again.

His voice was just as warm as the expression in his eyes. "Are you new here? Visitor?

I cleared my throat. "Yes. Visitor." I glanced back at Houdini, who was now happily sniffing the sand, then back at Nick.

"Nice. Renting for the summer?" he asked, looking out over the water to the setting sun.

"Yes, I'm staying at a cottage on the beach. It's heaven." I reached up to pull my hair into a pile on the top of my head, holding it off my neck for a moment, before letting it fall down my back. "I've been here a few days, and have it booked until the end of July."

Houdini started to bark and jump about in front of us,

tossing sticks in the air and catching them. I laughed, grateful Houdini's playfulness had shifted me out of feeling flustered.

"Clever boy!" I cheered him on, which only excited the dog more and he raced around. "Houdini has the zoomies!" I called and picked up more sticks to toss. I turned to Nick. "It looks like it's going to be a beautiful sunset."

"It does. When the sky is clear and it's not raining, the sunsets are spectacular here." Nick looked out over the waves.

"Feel free to watch with me if you like." I glanced at him.

Nick looked down at Houdini, and then at his watch.

"I mean, no pressure, just a thought . . . you know, since you're here is all. And the sun is going down."

"Sounds good. Just looking at the time. I flew in yesterday morning, and jet lag is starting to take hold."

I tried to hold back from showing how thrilled I was that he'd decided to stay. I didn't want him to think I was some kind of weirdo. "Great!" Without a second thought, I grabbed his arm. "Oh, look at the colors. And, so you know, I don't normally do this sort of thing. Hang out with some random dude on the beach. But . . ." I tilted my head and felt I was looking right into his soul. "You don't seem the serial killer type. Plus, you have a dog."

He shook his head, looking a bit dumbfounded. "No, I'm not, and yes, I have a dog. Although I'm not sure how that would make a difference."

"Well, I think it does." I turned back to the sea and lifted my face, feeling the curve of a content smile on my lips. I tipped my head back, enjoying the way the wind tugged on my hair, billowing it out behind me.

"If my word means anything at all, I can assure you I am not a serial killer, or any other kind of bad guy."

I glanced at him and we smiled at each other. He turned to watch the sun on the horizon.

"Then, I guess that settles it." I flickered a glance at him, smiled and then pointed to the sunset.

He chuckled and returned his attention to the fiery sky.

I folded my hands together, tightening my fingers to stop them from trembling. I couldn't believe I was nervous. Even if Nick didn't exude any kind of warning signals, I still was on edge. He was a total stranger, after all, but there was something magnetic about him. And the expression in his eyes made my heart turn over. They seemed to hold a sad wariness, and I wondered what had happened to him for such a shadow to be reflected in his gaze, but intuition told me I had nothing to fear from him.

Cautious by nature, being watchful of others was a by-product of the corporate world I'd immersed myself in before Rob pushed me to take a chance on writing full time. He'd believed I should trust my instincts, had made me promise to do so. My chest tightened, as it did whenever I thought of him and the promise I'd made to him.

Staring out across the waves, I could almost hear him, his voice weak and raspy. I blinked the threatening tears away, not wanting to cry in front of Nick.

Lizzie, once I'm gone you need to live on. Feed your wander-lust. Travel. Write. See the world. It's what you've always wanted to do. Explore, and don't let anything keep you from your goal. You can take me with you in your thoughts. Okay? Promise?

And I had. A deathbed promise was powerful. I lifted a finger to catch a tear that spilled on to my cheek. Of course, I would honor it. I wouldn't let anything stand in my way of my promise to my brother.

Houdini started barking and I snapped myself out of the rabbit hole I'd just fallen into. I shot Nick a glance. He didn't seem to notice and was staring at the horizon. His dark hair blew off his strong forehead and the sun was reflected in his eyes, giving them a golden, almost mystical, appearance. His legs were spread wide, his feet bare, and I realized I found him exceedingly sexy. My heart galloped like a racehorse. I hadn't felt this giddy since high school. Could he be feeling the same?

He caught me watching him, and smiled.

"Ah, um . . ." I couldn't find any words to say, so I just looked back to the ocean.

The wind gusted in from the sea, churning up the water. It was a sudden change from moments before. The sky darkened with the dipping down of the sun, and a bruised smudge along the horizon made it difficult to tell the difference between sky and sea.

I was intensely aware of Nick standing next to me and did my best to focus on the shifting colors in the sky. I'd never experienced this immediate sense of electricity before, but it was exhilarating. I steadied my breathing.

"So lovely." I wrapped my arms around myself, unsure what to do with them as a wonderfully weightless feeling swept over me.

"It is," Nick replied, his words faltering.

I pulled my attention from the horizon to glance at him again.

Our gazes clung to each other for the briefest second. I felt heat rise again in my cheeks and looked back out over the water.

Houdini broke the moment when he pushed his way between us, his tail thumping a tune on the sand.

"You're wet, boy. And smelly." Nick stroked the dog's head.

"Nothing like the *odeur de puppy*."

He laughed and I joined in.

"No, there isn't," he agreed. "He'll be ripe when I get home."

The sunlight quickly faded and dusk descended on us.

We turned back to each other. It was a pleasant change to have to tilt my head to make eye contact with him. I closed in on five foot eight and, in my experience, I was usually at eye level with most guys.

"That was a gorgeous sunset," Nick said. "It was nice to meet you, Lizzie."

"Yes, it was spectacular. And a pleasure to meet you too. We can thank Houdini for that." Did I sound lame? I hoped not. I didn't mean to, but I was thrown a little off balance. I didn't want him to leave, but it didn't feel right asking him to stay longer.

He crouched down and petted Houdini after he hooked the leash on to his collar. "We sure can thank him. For once, his running off ended up being a good thing." He stood.

We stared at each other.

"Right, then." He nodded and gathered up the dog leash in his hand. "See you on the beach?"

"Yes, see you on the beach." I lingered, waiting for him to walk away.

"I look forward to it." Nick smiled and lifted his hand in farewell.

"Me too." I shifted on my feet and then headed back to my cottage.

At the wooden path that led from the beach to the porch, I turned and watched him walk down the beach with Houdini leading the way. He glanced back and raised his hand before they were both swallowed up by the growing dark.

I stood for a few moments, then walked up the path and into the cottage. I grabbed Rob's hat from the bench and took it inside. Holding it in my hands seemed to bring me closer to Rob. It was the essence of him, well worn, frayed in places, with hints of pin holes where I'd removed all the hooks, flies and buttons Rob had collected and displayed. He'd worn it practically everywhere.

I sighed, and fingered the brim of the Tilley. Yes, Rob's hat. The one thing I carried with me all the time that I couldn't bear to ever lose, like I had the photos in my phone case.

After closing and locking the door, I rested my back against it and sucked in a steadying breath, thinking of Nick. Why did I have the oddest sensation that something wonderful had just happened?

Chapter Four

Sol had already become my favorite café. It was packed again, but I found a stool at the bar and had a lovely chai tea.

While I drank, I turned my focus to the photos on the wall again, scanning them for something to jump out at me.

Many were faded or yellowed with age, and some had slipped down in their frames. I had the urge to straighten them. They showed Savage Cove's past, much of which probably wouldn't be in the history books. I yearned to learn more about the town, curious and moved by their silent stories. My eyes slid past the image I'd seen the other day of Bicker Beach, which reminded me I still hadn't been out to find those rocks. Note to self: do it today or tomorrow.

A photo on the wall next to the coffee machine—one that I hadn't noticed the other day—caught my attention. It was at an awkward angle to my seat at the bar, but there was a *mood* to the black and white image. It struck a chord with me.

I slid off my stool and walked a few feet closer to see it better. I was spellbound. A woman with long dark hair sat on a

31

rocky outcrop, the sea wild and just as untamed as she appeared to be. The image seemed to shift and change as if it was alive. I could almost feel the wind off the sea, blowing the woman's hair around her face and whipping it into a dark cloud, concealing her features. Through the strands, her eyes, just as dark as her hair, seemed to look beyond the person holding the camera. She wasn't smiling, nor was she frowning, but her face had a Mona Lisa expression that held an essence of mystery, sadness, and something more.

I was intrigued. Who was this woman? Underneath the image was a simple black inscription, but I couldn't make out the etched letters.

"Excuse me, are you using this stool?" A couple stood behind me and they indicated the stool next to me.

"No, sorry, just looking at the photos." I went back to my seat, but my interest was piqued and I was repeatedly drawn back to the photo. The background looked similar to the other landscape photos I'd been told were of Bicker Beach.

The barista on duty today came over to ask if I wanted anything more. It was the perfect opportunity to inquire.

"No, thank you." I checked her name badge. "But I was wondering, Wendy, that picture by the coffee machine of the woman, where was that taken?"

"That was out on the coast, close to Bicker Beach," she answered sharply.

Despite her tone, inwardly I smiled. I'd been right.

"And the woman? Who is she?"

The barista's face clouded and looked sad for the briefest moment, before continuing as she retrieved my mug and plate. "Marissa . . . she used to own this café."

Light exploded behind my eyes. Marissa! The name in the text. What were the odds that they were the same woman? It wasn't possible, was it? I had to fight to keep my voice calm. "Oh? What happened to her?"

Wendy hesitated before answering. "She passed away. Three years ago."

"Oh, I'm sorry." The journalist in me jumped with excitement, this was getting too spookily interesting. I had so many questions. "Did you know her well?" I gently prodded.

If the Marissa from the text was the same woman as in that photo, then I'd found a needle in a haystack. Marissa was the recipient of the text. Marissa had owned this café. Marissa was dead. What had happened to her, and why was someone texting a heartfelt message to her number?

"We were friends. I've worked here since her husband bought the café for her." She looked up to see more visitors arriving. "Excuse me."

"Of course." I looked at the photo. Eager for her to come back and tell me more, my imagination took flight. I wasn't entirely convinced all this was a coincidence. Pulling out my Moleskine, I made some notes. My gut told me there was a story here.

Marissa
Café owner, husband purchased
Died 3 years ago
Photo taken at Bicker Beach
How did she die?
Are the Marissas in the text and photo the same woman?

I finished my drink, and saw Wendy was busy with a rush of guests. Disappointed, I decided to leave. Hopefully, I'd be able to ask more questions the next time I came. I gathered up my belongings and slung the strap of my satchel over my head.

I glanced at the photo as I walked by. The woman in the image appeared to be looking at me through the strands of blowing hair, her eyes following me as I passed by. A thought whispered through my mind like a chilly mist off the ocean. I was hesitant to give it life, but it persisted. Her eyes held a darkness that felt so suffocating, for a moment I had difficulty drawing breath.

"Don't be silly," I chastised myself. Even so, I was unsettled. I wanted to learn more about Marissa, the mysterious woman by the sea. I pulled my attention from the photo and shook off the sense of foreboding that had settled on my shoulders.

As I wove my way through the tables, an older woman reading by the window glanced up from her book and we made eye contact. I smiled and she nodded, returning the smile.

The woman was tanned and elegant, with short platinum-blonde hair, and gave off an air of approachability. Was she local? If she was, maybe she would know the deeper and unrecorded history of Savage Cove. I hesitated a moment and was going to say hello, but I was jostled by a group of teens coming in and, when I extricated myself from the group, she had returned to her book.

Next time.

I glanced back at the photo on the wall, becoming more intrigued by the minute. The questions were endless.

Even in the photo. I could see that Marissa looked . . .

Restless.

Back outside, I looked around for a library sign. Without my new phone, I couldn't pull up a map and search for it, so I wandered around Savage Cove. There was no harm in getting to know the town, and I did love walking. Striking out, I just followed the streets, discovering that most roads led to the waterfront. I would use it as a homing beacon if needed.

I was charmed by the town. I felt the history of it oozing from the buildings. I tried to imagine what it had been like fifty, one hundred, or more years ago. My imagination ran to the past and easily distracted me as I walked the pretty streets.

Passing the lovely buildings and walking under the old trees filled me with a sense of well-being. Something I hadn't felt in a long time. I drew in the tang of the sea and scent of the flowers. There was a tangible sense of nature here that I was fast growing to love. And the feeling of belonging—a sense of kinship to the streets I was walking along—startled me.

As a pre-teen and teenager, the library was always my go-to place, to while away the hours. We library geeks had found each other in the rows upon rows of books. I found comfort and inspiration within the walls of knowledge, and contentment in knowing that learning was at my fingertips. It was heaven for me.

I stopped to get my bearings and realized I must have walked in a circle because I could see the waterfront again. This time, being further along, I saw the tourist information center; small and cute, just like the rest of the town. I scanned the brochures on the shelves under the awning. Maybe there would be one for the library. I noticed a few brochures that interested me for future stories. There was so much to choose from, it was rather overwhelming. I knew the Pacific Northwest had a lot to offer, and that's why I came, but, wow, there was so much to do and see, it would take forever to accomplish my mile-long list. I selected a few, knowing I'd want to do a road trip to round out my blog, social media posts, and the articles due to my editor. I picked Rialto Beach, Forks, and Hoh Rain Forest. I was pretty sure they would spark more interesting locations to visit.

"Aha, there you are." I spied a leaflet and added it to my selection. Savage Cove Library. I looked at the address and at the simple map on the back. I got my bearings and then turned around to walk along the wharf until I came to Lincoln.

Ten minutes later, I climbed the steps of the beautiful old building. Inside, I just had to pause and inhale. There was the smell I'd been waiting for. Books, papers, ink, wood, and leather. Every library I'd been in over the years had that same special scent.

Even though the interior of the building had all the character of the 1800s, the old had been seamlessly merged with the new. There was a bank of computers and tablets set up on stands in various positions, and a business area with scanners and printers.

I was thrilled to see a section under the lovely, curved stone ceiling with antique wooden filing cabinets housing the cards for the Dewey Decimal System.

Books were checked out with a bar code scan, and electronic scanners were positioned at the exit turnstile to catch any books that may have found their way unscanned into bags. I pushed through the entry turnstile and went to the counter where some staff were working.

"Excuse me? I was wondering if you could point me in the direction of old newspapers?" I put my satchel down on the counter and waited for directions.

A young woman with black heart-shaped glasses and streaks of pink hair looked up. "We keep about five years of newspapers in hard copy. The rest get scanned and are available online," she said, coming forward. "How far back do you want to go? Also, our internet is down today, so it's old-school research only." She smiled apologetically.

"Three years, please. And no worries on the net."

"I'll show you where they are." The librarian came around the counter. "Follow me. Unfortunately, we have to keep them in the basement because they take up lots of space."

"That's fine." I smiled and strode along behind her, down the main aisle to a set of wide stone stairs.

At the bottom, the librarian pointed. "In here. We're in the process of further organization, but everything is separated by year and by month. Do you know which month you're looking for?"

The woman pushed open the door and I was assaulted by the scent of newsprint and an underlying whiff of dampness. It wasn't an offensive smell, but rather one I found comforting, and I was eager to get started.

"Not really. I know it was about three years ago. I'm looking for information on the death of a local woman named Marissa. Maybe you know the name?" I walked over to a wide table that held a book of enclosed newspapers dated last year.

"I don't recall that. But then I've only been here about two years. I came from Seattle, wanting a more small-town life." The woman walked to the back of the room where there was a wall of drawers. "Is that why you're here in Savage Cove? Needing a bit of coastal life and quiet quaintness?"

I smiled, thinking about the question. "Not exactly, but the town is lovely."

"Well, your research sounds very interesting. I hope you find what you're looking for."

I looked at the bank of drawers, itching to dig in. The woman pulled one open, and I peered in.

"Now, here is the first quarter of the year you're looking for, and then the others will be in the respective drawers. You know, you'd probably get quicker results searching for articles online?"

I nodded. "I know, but there's something about a library, plus it gets me out of the house. I'll see what's here first, and then I can follow up with some online research." I lifted the first book of newspapers out.

"I understand. It's kinda nice to go back to basics, now and then. I still use a day planner. I've tried to get used to using calendars online, but I just can't make it work." The woman laughed and I joined in.

"Me too! I try to keep my calendar on my phone and sync it to all my devices, but I wind up just putting everything into a month-at-a-glance planner anyways."

"You and me both. Well, if you need anything else, I'm just upstairs. Don't hesitate to ask. Good luck on your hunt."

"Thanks. How long is the library open?" I inquired.

The woman checked her watch. "Only another forty-five minutes."

I grimaced.

"Sorry, we close early today."

I waved my hand. "It's okay. Thanks very much for all your help."

I was excited to look through the papers. A mysterious death was sure to make the front page of the *Savage Cove Gazette*. It would be easy to flip through and look at the headlines first, before diving deeper into the newspapers.

My curiosity was piqued, and who knew, perhaps there'd be enough intriguing information for an article about Marissa? Maybe I'd title it "Lady of the Sea".

I took a big breath, looked at my watch, and began.

It was starting to rain again, and I was glad to be back at the cottage.

The heart-wrenching text I had received still weighed on my

mind, and the strange coincidence of the woman in the café photo also being named Marissa really was too intriguing to ignore. I couldn't shake the feeling that the text and the photo were connected and, for some reason I couldn't quite explain yet, I was drawn to Marissa's story.

I was keen to start searching online. Not all the newspapers had been stored at the library, and some dates were missing altogether. Searching through the papers, I had finally found reference to a Marissa Wright who had disappeared three years ago. Other than that, there was very little information about her.

Who was this woman, and what had she done with her life?

But the only mention I could find online was a column recording her death. She had gone missing one day, and her husband's crashed sailboat was discovered on the rocks.

"Hmm, there should be more." I kept digging and discovered Marissa was a local business owner, which had to mean the café. Just as I was clicking open a new window on my computer, the power went out.

"Damn! Why now?" I had a charged laptop but no power to run the Wi-Fi. I sat back and looked out the window at the pouring rain.

It was getting dark quickly, and I got up to look for candles with the aid of a flashlight. Finding a bunch, I lit a few between the kitchen and living room.

I didn't like losing power. It made me feel helpless and very much alone. How had pioneers done it?

An hour passed and still not a flicker of electricity. The cottage was chilling off a bit. I could have started a fire, but it was getting a little late and I was tired. Instead, I decided my warm, cozy bed was where I wanted to be.

I blew out the candles, got ready for bed, and crawled in

with a flashlight on the bedside table. Thankfully, my Kindle was charged and I opened a Jill Shalvis novel.

But I couldn't focus on the words. My brain was racing. Was there a connection between the text and the Marissa from the café? And if there was, surely the only person who could have written the text was her husband.

Chapter Five

The next morning, I was up early to find the power had come back sometime in the night. It was misty and I longed to get out on the beach. I filled my to-go mug with freshly ground, perked coffee, and pulled my sweater on. I wanted to do some dictating while walking along the edge of the surf. It seemed the perfect place to let my thoughts wander and summon up the words I needed.

Barefoot, I let the waves splash up around my feet. With every step I imagined the water cleansing me, and drawing my discomfort and anxiety down through the soles of my feet into the sand. The waves swept in, swirled around me, and retreated back to the sea.

Mist wreathed itself around me. The visibility was low, and it felt as if a great, grey blanket had been dropped over the world. I drew in a deep breath, feeling invigorated.

Continuing along the beach, pretty soon the light linen fabric of my white pants was wet and sandy, slapping around my ankles with every step. I didn't care but continued dictating thoughts about the mysterious text and the "Lady of the Sea" into my recorder. If I could discover more, then it might be possible to find the sender of the text.

I simply couldn't imagine how he must feel.

My heart swelled with pain for him. Was losing a wife any different than losing a twin brother? It had been devastating for me. Even though I'd had time to adjust to the inevitable, it hadn't made it any easier. My chest pained, thinking of Rob and the hole his death had left in me. No one could ever fill the void created by his absence.

A sibling's love was different than romantic love, of course. Both important, and each having a significant impact on a person's life. I'd had boyfriends—some I liked more than others—but I'd never felt the romantic love that would rip my inside to shreds should I lose that person. So I guess that meant I couldn't truly comprehend how a husband would feel losing his wife.

I tried to understand it now.

Did he have as big a hole in his soul as I did? Had he filled it? The text I'd received left me wondering about the intent behind it. He said he was letting her go and I assumed that meant . . . What exactly did it mean?

Could he have fallen out of love?

Had time healed his wound to a degree that he could move on?

What would make him send a text like that, long after her death?

So many questions. And answers that I would probably never get. But I wanted to try. The urgent need to find the sender burned inside me.

My thoughts were coiled into a tight knot, and I realized I needed to put away the recorder and allow myself to be here in the moment. *Grounding myself*, as my therapist said, and I had worked so hard to learn. Running my hand over my forehead, I put the recorder in the large pocket of my sweater. I bent to pick up a stone and rubbed my thumb rhythmically across the smooth surface, soothing my mind.

My coffee was still hot. The mug promised to keep contents piping for hours, and it appeared to live up to its sales pitch. I sipped and stopped to look out over the lazy waves. They were gentle today, rolling slowly and quietly over the sand before retreating. It was hypnotic and I let myself become mesmerized.

I'm not sure how much time had passed when the faint sound of a dog barking found its way through the mist.

I continued along the beach, hoping I'd see Nick and Houdini, and stopped near a craggy outcrop of rocks that spilled into the ocean. I'd have to climb across them to get to the other side. But there was no need. At that moment, Houdini came racing over the top of the rocks, which meant that Nick wasn't far behind.

Excitement lit me up. I felt my stomach fill with butterflies. My mouth dried and I was suddenly nervous. I climbed up on the lower rocks to look over and, sure enough, Nick was coming toward me from the other side.

"Well, good morning!" Nick called, and lifted his hand in greeting.

"Hello. We finally meet again on the beach." I felt the smile widening on my face, and I jumped off the rock on to the sand.

Without the golden glow of sunset and approaching dusk, I was able to truly see him. He appeared from the mist as if he was a ghost. A very attractive ghost. I gave a soft sigh.

He was barefoot again, and I smiled, wiggling my own bare toes in the sand. He wore shorts, and his legs were tanned and muscular. His hair was darker than I'd remembered and blew in the wind around his head. He had loose curls that I found entirely appealing. Girls would kill for hair like that.

"Yes, we do finally meet on the beach."

He jumped off the last big rock to stand beside me.

I glanced up at him. He was the most attractive man I'd ever seen. Today, he had on a Seahawks T-shirt which fit him nicely. He curled up Houdini's leash, which made his muscles flex in his arms. I blinked, shocked at the sudden rush of desire he provoked in me.

We glanced at each other, his smile wide and easy, and the color of his eyes vivid in this light. I dug my toes into the sand and looked away, still shaken by the intensity of my reaction.

"Houdini insisted it was time for a walk. I think he's the one who has me trained," Nick said.

I smiled and petted Houdini, who pushed against my legs. "They do keep you on a schedule, no doubt about that." My hair fell over my face when I leaned down. I flung it back and glanced up at Nick. "I suppose there's no being lazy when you have a dog."

Nick glanced down at me, and I stood up, our eyes still locked. He shook his head. "Nope. That's for sure. I knew he wouldn't settle and allow me to get to work until he had a bit of a run."

He picked up a rock and threw it into the waves. Houdini raced after it.

I had a tinge of disappointment. He was just out for a quick walk today. It would've been nice to be able to stroll along with him a bit.

"He chases rocks?"

"He does, and he'll dive for them too. I just have to be careful they are out of his reach so he won't catch one."

"Yeah, that wouldn't be the best thing. Great way to lose a tooth. So you're busy today, then?"

He nodded. "You?"

"Yes, me too. Getting a little bit of exercise in before settling down to write is always good." I patted the pocket of my sweater. "I've been doing a bit of work while walking this morning."

His eyebrows raised. "You have? And how do you manage that when I don't see any pen and paper."

"I dictate. Walking along the beach lets my mind clear so the words flow."

"You're a writer?'

"Yes, a journalist, and I'm blogging too now. Travel mainly. I love discovering new places and sharing the stories I find."

"There certainly is something different about writers. I'm pretty sure you're born with a unique brain. Being able to craft the stories that you tell is exceptional."

"I guess it is, it's not something I've ever thought of that way. The words just come to me, same with ideas."

Houdini ran off to sniff around the base of the rocks.

"Have you thought about writing a novel?" he asked, turning to keep an eye on the dog.

"It's crossed my mind numerous times. I'm not sure I'm ready for that yet, though. It takes a lot of dedication."

Perhaps the story of Marissa could be my debut, I thought.

"Coming up with an idea for a book seems like a challenge. But writing articles seems even more so, because you have to find a different idea for each one."

It was very observant of him. Strange how I'd always thought plotting a novel would be harder, but he was right. Writing many different stories meant coming up with multiple ideas. Suddenly I felt rather proud of myself.

"I'm never short on ideas. They rush into my head and easily distract me from the task at hand, so I have to control them by noting them down in a folder on my laptop. No matter how many times I tell myself that the idea is so good, and no way will I forget it, I still do . . . hence a folder called *ideas*." I laughed and he joined in. It was a nice deep, shiver-inducing laugh that suited him to a T.

Nick checked his watch and frowned. "I have to be home for a video conference call soon. I have five more minutes before I have to turn back."

The rush of disappointment was intense. I didn't want him to leave.

"Please don't let me hold you up," was all I could say, though. "It was good to meet you on the beach again." I pulled my recorder out of my pocket and flipped it on. "I have more dictating to do, as well."

I looked up at him and, when our eyes met, I swore I could physically feel the connection between us, it was so powerful.

I was lost in his gaze. It sounded so stupidly clichéd, but I was. His eyes were hypnotic, and I was unable to look away. All I could do was stand there, mesmerized. Did he feel it too? Slowly his mouth turned up in a grin and I was enchanted, smiling back at him.

"Ah . . . well . . ." I stammered, so shaken by the moment passing between us that I couldn't find any appropriate words. I wished I could tell what he was thinking.

I stood frozen, unable to make a move, until he shook his head slightly and then glanced at his watch. "Yes, well, duty calls."

I cleared my throat and pushed the hair caught by the wind out of my face. It broke the moment, and it was like the invisible connection I'd felt between us abruptly snapped.

"Yes, well, it was nice to see you again." His voice sounded a little forced.

I furrowed my brow. "It was," I said. "I hope we meet again."

"I'm sure we will." He turned and hopped back on to the rocks. 'Houdini, come."

The dog was at his side in seconds. I watched him climb back the way he'd come, over the rocks, and then he was gone.

I wasn't sure what to think of our meeting. On the one hand, it had felt so powerful to me. But on the other, there was a hesitancy about his words that made me doubt my own reaction. It deflated me, and I shrugged my shoulders.

"Stop, it's not like I came looking for a connection. A man," I scolded myself. "I'm here for me and Rob. I won't be staying, so it's pointless to look for something that can never be."

But something had brought me here to Savage Cove. And I'd met Nick pretty much right off. I trudged back along the beach and wondered if Destiny was playing a cruel joke on me.

The feeling hung with me most of the day as I worked on the articles that were due. I spent some time on social media, checking my profiles to see the level of engagement. Views and likes were up across the board, and while I was thrilled to see the growth, it also meant new challenges. I'd learned you're only as good as your latest article or blog, and each one needed to be better than the last. My editor, Kate, always said I was a perceptive and intensely sensory writer—I made my readers feel as though they were in the place I was visiting with me, or eating the food I was writing about. She said that was why they responded so well. I think it was because I imagined I was writing for Rob, describing the experiences as though he was living them with me.

I checked my emails to find one there from Kate. I opened it.

Hi Liz,

I hope you're having a great time on your adventure. Thanks for keeping me in the loop, sorry to hear about your phone. The "Lady of the Sea" idea is intriguing. Let me know when you have worked out more details on it and can send an outline.

Remember too, we discussed the possibility of you doing a piece on loss of a twin or loved one. What you are doing, the promise to Rob, and embarking on your journey, I think it would be a wonderful outlet for you, and interesting as well. Please think about it.

Best,
Kate

I sat back in my desk chair and puffed out my cheeks. Yes, we had talked about it. But I wasn't sure readers would want to read something like that. Isn't life tragic enough as it is, without reading about more grief and loss?

I wanted to share happy, fun, inspiring stories set in faraway places. I closed the email without responding. If I answered her now, it would be with a huge NOPE.

I drew in a deep sigh and looked out the windows on the beach side of the house. A postcard-perfect view of the sea was framed beyond the panes. It would be so very easy to stay longer. I had no ties to anywhere. I was a free spirit and could go whichever way the wind blew. All the belongings that I hadn't sold, or was keeping for sentimental reasons, were in storage back east. It was just me, my vehicle and a couple of suitcases.

I had no roots anymore, but there was an end date on my time here in Savage Cove. My thoughts went to Nick and I suddenly felt lonely.

And just like that I was uninspired.

I pushed back the chair. It was hard to write when you started overthinking. Wondering about choices made and to be made, not to mention letting a man you'd just met take up space in your brain.

Yes, wondering if maybe I'd made a mistake embarking on this road trip. It wasn't because I was doing it alone, I was fine with that. It was . . .

I chewed my thumbnail and stared out the window. What was it, then? I had no *home* to return to. Friends had fallen by the wayside when I'd dedicated my time to Rob. My job was mobile—I could do it anywhere, as long as I had access to Wi-Fi.

In just under six weeks, I'd be heading out again. So putting down roots and making connections wasn't ideal. I tried to make myself feel better about the present and rekindle the excitement about future trips.

I sighed. I'd been on the road for almost a year now, and found my way here via New Orleans with lots of stops along the way. I'd enjoyed it. Living on the road had seemed perfect. I had no one to account to except myself. No schedule. No expectations other than making my way to Savage Cove. Deciding to settle here for a period of time hadn't really been on the cards, but when I'd seen the cottage on an online rental site, I surprised myself by booking it for all the available days until my next adventure. Even more surprising was discovering I liked it here. A lot.

My next trip was by plane, which meant storing my vehicle and reducing luggage to one smaller bag.

I'd started out being excited, eager to explore and fulfill my promise to Rob, so why did it suddenly feel like a huge headache? All this only served to compound my feelings of disquiet.

I walked into the kitchen; pulling open the fridge, I stared at the shelves. Nothing appealed to me, even though it was well stocked. I pushed some items around and then shut the door.

I groaned, then grabbed my keys, wallet and left the cottage.

I climbed into my car. "I'm fine," I told the empty vehicle.

Was I really?

I realized I needed the comfort of being around people. It was unlike me. I was good being alone. What had changed?

Maybe I'd just go into Savage Cove. Which reminded me, I needed to find out where the heck my new phone was. I'd stop by the shop to inquire.

Perhaps I would see Nick. For all I knew he lived in town and took Houdini to the beach by car.

I replayed our few minutes on the beach this morning as I drove, squeezing the steering wheel. Seeing him today had only heightened my feelings of loneliness. What had happened to the old me? I must get her back, if I could find her.

Maybe I wasn't as fine as I thought.

Chapter Six

It was a beautiful morning. Very different from yesterday. I felt a little better and was going to do my darndest to not let melancholy take hold of me. After all, I'd fought so hard since Rob's death to try and find my way.

So today, come hell or high water, I was going to find the rocks in Marissa's photo. I'd have to make do with my camera, since they told me yesterday the shipment hadn't come in yet. I was starting to think I should've just driven into Seattle after all, or ordered online.

I decided to head out in the opposite direction this morning. Away from the direction Nick had come from. Outside on the beach, it was glorious. The sun was rising and all clouds were gone. The sea was relatively calm. It was breathtaking.

"I could easily fall in love with this place," I said out loud as I stood at the edge of the surf and let the waves splash up around my feet. I stared out over the water, my eyes shielded by the brim of my hat, watching the sky change as the sun rose higher behind me.

I stepped back from the water and walked along the edge. Now and then a wave came up to swirl around my ankles.

Seabirds were still snoozing, propped on one foot. I skirted them, not wanting to disturb the resting birds, but most scurried off only to fluff their feathers and settle back into sleep mode once I'd passed by.

With every step along the beach, past the birds, around the rocks and through the gentle surf, the rugged and raw beauty was almost too much to absorb. It filled me with a wonderful sense of well-being. I was really glad the people I'd met in New Orleans during Mardi Gras suggested coming here.

My trip into town yesterday afternoon had been the right medicine. Unable to resist the fish and chips I'd smelled when I first arrived in Savage Cove, I got an order and sat by the seawall and people-watched while I ate. Of course, I had to go to the café on my way home and ordered a decadent hot chocolate with whipped cream and a combination of caramel and chocolate drizzle, topped with shaved dark chocolate. Comfort food.

I drew in a contented breath now, enjoying the easy breeze on my skin and the warmth of the sun as it rose higher in the sky, and promised myself I would enjoy the moment.

I swung my camera to the front and lifted it to snap an image. The light was perfect and the view was simply fantastic. I'd write a post about it for my blog, possibly include my fish and chip dinner. With the number of my followers still climbing swiftly, I felt increasing pressure to get posts up a few times a week, if not more frequently.

Rocks were everywhere, scattered on the sand and piled up in bunches, with some that spilled into the sea so I had to climb over them, but nothing yet that remotely resembled the formation in the Lady of the Sea's photograph.

Maybe I should go the other way. I stood with my hands on my hips and turned to look back the way I'd come. "Damn." Facing back the way I was originally walking, I trudged forward. "May as well keep going for a while."

I was worried if I turned around now, the rocks I was looking for would be just beyond the next curve of the beach. Much like when on road trips our parents told Rob and me we were almost there. *Just over the next hill.* Which usually ended up being many, *many* hills. I smiled, remembering those family trips and how Rob had told Mom he'd never believe her again, because it was never just over the next hill.

I sighed and wandered further down the beach. Around the next curve I spotted a pattern of rocks that looked just like those in the picture. A thrill rushed through me, and I glanced around to get my bearings.

I walked with a quicker stride over the sand, and stopped in front of them, certain I'd found what I was looking for. They jutted out into the sea, craggy and sharp, and were much bigger than they'd appeared in the photo. As I started to climb, I slipped, making my heart leap in my chest. This could be dangerous if the waves were high.

"Whoa now, no need to break a leg," I murmured and steadied myself, making sure I had good footing before continuing.

It would be super easy to get hurt here. I wondered if this was where the boat had crashed. I scrambled over the rocks to the one that appeared to be where Marissa's photo was taken. I stood with my feet firmly planted and imagined her here. The wind blowing hard, which it wasn't doing right now, and Marissa gazing past whoever took the photo, into the distance.

I turned my head to look back at where the person behind the camera had likely stood. Who had taken the picture? What had Marissa been looking at? I imagined her climbing over the rocks and stopping close to the edge. Had she been happy, sad . . . what? The photo of her at the café only heightened the mystery. I couldn't shake the feeling that there was something more to her disappearance. The mystery of this woman I'd never met had taken hold of me, and she had touched me in some way I couldn't quite define.

I sat on the rock and took in the scenery. Trees edged most of the beach, thicker in some areas than others. The wild rawness of sitting here, surrounded by nature, fed my soul and filled me with calm. The beach, in all its beauty, was a lonely one. Empty, with no houses along this stretch, unlike where my cottage was. Except for a figure coming my way.

My heart leaped. Could it be Nick? The sun was in line with the person and, though I raised my hand to shield my eyes, I couldn't tell.

I climbed carefully down from the rocks. Back on the sand, I walked toward the person silhouetted against the brightness. A dog ran around his legs. Suddenly, I was filled with excitement and realized I was smiling. It had to be Nick and Houdini.

A few minutes later, I was close enough to see the figure was an older man. I tried not to show my disappointment. He had to be in his mid to late seventies, but he looked fit and spry. He was good-looking, with a shock of grey hair and a neatly trimmed beard, and he seemed vaguely familiar. His dog rushed around us and then wandered off.

"Good morning," he called to me and lifted his hand in greeting.

"Morning! Beautiful, isn't it?" I wondered who he was.

He stopped. "It's always beautiful. Morning is my favorite, before the rush of the day begins."

I glanced at him and smiled. He was fairly tall.

"I agree."

We stood quietly together, looking out over the water.

"I haven't seen you before." He faced me. "New here?"

I laughed. "Is it that obvious? Yes, I arrived earlier this week."

"I know pretty much everyone around here, so yes. It's obvious." The friendly grin never left his face. "Us locals know when non-locals have landed."

"Oh dear, are you not particularly fond of non-locals coming to your little spot of paradise in the world?" I asked.

He laughed. "No, not at all. Please don't take it that way, we appreciate visitors. There's not many of us old timers left here." He shook his head and continued, "Most have moved away. There's not much here for the younger crowd. Bigger cities like Seattle have a powerful pull."

"Yes, I guess that's true. Sad, though, because it's so lovely here." I meant it.

"It's visitors, like yourself, that help keep us going. Are you here for long?" he asked and scratched the neat beard on his chin.

"Well, I rented my house until the end of July." I pointed the way I had come, and the man looked off in that direction. "But I'm quickly falling in love with the area."

He smiled and nodded. "Not hard to do that." He took a step back and hitched his belt. "Well, I guess I should get going, Candy has already got a good head start on me."

I turned and saw that his dog was walking along the edge of the surf, a little distance away.

"I'll let you be on your way," the man said. "Maybe I'll see you on the beach again sometime."

"Yes, that would be nice. Have a good day. I'm Lizzie."

He nodded. "Walter Charlton." He lifted his hand. "You have a good day too, Lizzie."

I watched him pick his way over the rocks with an energy

that belied his age. Meeting people on the beach—what a wonderful way to become familiar with Savage Cove. I headed back the way I'd come, ready for a late breakfast, coffee, and to settle down to work.

I spent a productive day focused on my writing. When I looked up from my work that afternoon, it surprised me how much time had gone by. I hadn't thought about anything but my deadlines and a few proposals I'd emailed to Kate.

I gasped at the stunning colors of the sky that filtered through the overhanging trees at the back of the cottage and danced in the window. I dashed outside and ran down to the beach. This was too beautiful to miss.

I couldn't help glancing both ways to see if anyone else . . . namely Nick . . . was on the beach, as well.

I was alone.

Rather than let myself be disappointed, I focused all my attention on the wonder of nature.

Nick leaned back in his leather chair, glad to be home. Business travel was really starting to wear on him. In the back of his mind, he'd been turning over the idea of cutting back.

He'd plunged himself into work after his wife died, but then he'd sold his network security company for a tidy profit last year, and invested it well. He consulted now, not that he needed the money, but it kept him busy with trips around the globe on a fairly regular basis. He was too young to retire and, if he was honest, he needed the distraction.

He looked around his office, which faced the ocean and led into the main living room. His dad lived on the property, in a boathouse he'd renovated years before, just after Nick's mom died. His dad was aging, even though he was still sharp as a tack and active for a seventy-seven-year-old. Nick was thankful he was close, but this house had become a shell, with no life inside. Nick still couldn't believe almost fifteen years had gone by since Mom got sick. He shook his head and tapped the end of the pen on his desk.

He'd hoped Dad would find someone for companionship. But he'd been so dedicated to Mom. Nick wondered if there was an element of grief that held his dad back, even after all these years.

No matter how hard he tried not to worry about his dad, he did, though Walter was wiry, still walking miles and miles on the beach every day. His health always had been excellent, and Nick wanted it to stay that way.

Nick swiveled his chair around and looked out the window again. The sky looked like it was on fire. He never tired of the view, and it never failed to lighten his mood. He had been doing a lot of thinking lately, and for the first time in years, he was truly beginning to feel like his old self. He spread his hands out on the old wooden desk. Carved from local wood over a century ago, when his great-grandfather had built this house. Not as grand then as it was now, after many renovations, but grand enough for his time.

Nick sighed. Another anniversary of his wife's death had come and gone. It still haunted him, and he still lived with the if-onlys and what-ifs. Could he have changed things? He would never know.

Nick had hoped to give his dad grandchildren, so he could dote on them and teach them all he knew about the sea, building boats, nature, their family history, and how the Charltons had made their mark in Savage Cove. That was just the tip of the iceberg of information packed into his father's brain. His dad was a fount of knowledge. He deserved to have grandkids at his knee, worshipping him.

Nick tossed his pen on the desk and frowned. Well, never say never, he supposed. Having kids, that is. He scoffed quietly, and Houdini raised his head from where it was resting on his front paws. He'd bought Houdini for his wife, hoping the lovable golden retriever would keep her company while he was away on business. Again, what he'd thought and what she'd thought were polar opposites.

Houdini put his paw on Nick's knee and curled his claws into his leg. "Hey, boy. I know what you want. You're enough of a handful to keep in check, let alone a bunch of kids too."

Houdini cocked his head to one side, his tongue lolling out, and Nick smiled at him. He petted the dog and asked him, "How many times have I taken you out already?"

Houdini tossed his head and backed up, his front paws springing in little bunny hops, his fluffy, golden ears bouncing, and his wagging tail turning into a full body wiggle.

Nick laughed. He was pretty sure if the dog could talk, Houdini would tell him walks were the best thing ever and that he never got enough.

"Okay, let's go. It's going to be a nice sunset, and maybe we'll see Lizzie." Nick pushed himself up from the chair with a groan. Yeah, he needed a walk.

Houdini followed him to the breezeway and sat waiting patiently for him to take his collar down from one of the many hooks on the shiplap wall.

"Come on then." Nick shouldered open the door to the side patio, where a stone path led down to the beach.

As soon as there was enough room, Houdini shot past him. Nick tried to grab him, cursing himself for not putting the leash and collar on him first. He shouted, knowing full well that once he got to the beach the dog would zone out completely, as if he'd suddenly gone deaf.

The golden retriever bolted down the path to the surf, launching himself into the waves. Nick ran after him, which Houdini took as being a wonderful game of chase. Off he ran, out of the water, nose to the sand.

"Damn dog, he sure lives up to his name," Nick muttered and jogged along the beach, knowing the dog wouldn't go far. Still, it was a pain in the ass to chase him down.

Now and then he shouted for Houdini. In the house, the dog was glued to his side, following him everywhere. The only place he seemed to lose his mind was on the beach.

He saw his dog running and jumping into the waves. Lifting his hand to shield his eyes, Nick stopped dead in his tracks. A woman was throwing driftwood for Houdini. It was a sight that made his heart stand still in his chest and his breath stop.

Nick couldn't move, frozen to the spot by a scene that so vividly recalled both the past and the moment, just three days ago, when he first saw Lizzie playing with Houdini in the waves.

He'd been holding his breath, and he let it out with a puff when he saw long blonde hair blowing from under the woman's hat, tangled in the wind. Of course it was Lizzie. His wife was gone. A multitude of emotions raced through him. Before he knew it, he'd called out to her.

She raised her hand, waving, and a smile widened on his face.

"Hey! This is a lovely surprise," she called to him as he got closer.

"Houdini was relentless, and I gave in," Nick replied.

"Ah, he's such a sweet boy."

She was stunning in this light. Her eyes were an almost translucent turquoise, like the waters of the Caribbean. The color of her top almost the same hue. Each time he saw Lizzie, he noticed something more appealing about her. Today she was laughing with Houdini, and everything about her was light. Free. Relaxed.

He wasn't sure what to do with the emotions rising in him. He'd done his best to shut them out after Ari died, but being with Lizzie challenged him.

"Want to move to my porch? It has a great unobstructed view," Lizzie suggested.

"Oh, sure." The invitation was a pleasant surprise.

"Great! I don't know about you, but I'm a little hungry and I picked up some yumminess at the market today. Are you hungry?"

"As a matter of fact, I am."

"Let's hurry before we miss it." Lizzie skipped and jogged toward her cottage, her long, tanned legs eating up the ground.

Houdini was hot on her heels.

Nick laughed and followed her. He couldn't remember the last time he'd run for pure pleasure.

Chapter Seven

The dash to the cottage felt awesome. I was breathing a little heavily, but energy raced through my muscles. It had been a while since I'd done any kind of exercise, except yoga and stretches. I pulled off my hat and shook out my hair.

"We made it." I panted and leaned on the railing of the porch, facing the sunset.

Houdini slid to a stop, his tongue lolling out and tail waving like a flag. Nick easily jumped up the couple of steps and stood beside me. He didn't appear winded at all.

"The sky is amazing," he said. "Just in time too."

"Mmm." I didn't have words for the view in front of us as we stood silently watching the glory of the setting sun.

Dusk came swiftly. Soft lighting from a lamp just inside the window cast a glow out through the glass and over the wooden porch. I turned to look at Nick, startled to catch him watching me. My mouth dried up and I couldn't look away from him.

Time froze for a beat. I shivered and he reached for a towel from the pile I'd folded and put on the chair by the door. Silently, he held it up for me and, not looking away from him, I stepped into the towel. He wrapped it around my shoulders, rubbing them gently. I warmed up, and not just from the friction of the towel against my skin.

Nick pulled the towel tight across my shoulders, and I curled my fingers into the warmth. "Thank you. Let's go inside." It seemed the perfectly right thing to say.

"Let me tie up Houdini. He's wet." Nick said.

"Why don't we just dry him with these towels? I don't want to leave him outside in the cold."

After giving the dog a vigorous rubdown, we went in. I was starting to shiver. It wasn't too chilly—I knew it was my emotions running amok, like a teenager after a first kiss.

"The living room is through there. I'll be back in a jiff after I put something warmer on."

"Thanks." Nick led Houdini over to the floor by the window and instructed him to lie down.

I dashed into my room and quickly pulled on a T-shirt, leggings, and woolly socks, before shoving my feet into my mocs. I rummaged for a sweater, slipped into it, and buttoned it up to my neck.

"Brrr." I shivered and tucked my chin into the collar. I began to warm up and caught myself in the mirror.

"Damn, girl, you are a wreck," I told my reflection. I brushed my hair and wound it into a topknot. Quickly dabbed on some lip gloss, smoothed my eyebrows, and patted my cheeks. There was no time to doll myself up any more than this. Next time.

I hurried from my room, turning on lamps and glad that I'd tidied up yesterday. I'd been getting a little lazy, being on my own.

When I came into the living room, Houdini looked up at me, with ears perked and eyes wide. Nick was sitting on a chair next to him. Houdini jumped to his feet, tail wagging, and did a nosedive on to the big oval rag rug with his butt in the air.

"What a fun dog." I laughed at his antics as he rolled on his back and snorted. "Now, what can I get you to drink? Warm, cold, hard, soft?"

"I'll have whatever you're having." He followed me into the kitchen, with Houdini right behind.

"I need something warm." I was still chilly. "Hot chocolate?"

Nick rubbed his hands together and glanced at Houdini as he sniffed around the floor at his feet. "Sounds perfect."

I put a pot on the stove and filled it with milk, cocoa powder, sugar, and vanilla.

"Think I'll put a shot of something in it. Would you like one too?" I asked, and continued to whisk the mixture.

"Tell me where and I'll get it for you," Nick offered.

"Over there, beside the window on the table." I watched him. He looked just as good from the back as he did from the front. I noticed his feet were bare again, which I found unbelievably sexy.

"Did you want a pair of socks?" I asked when he put the bottle of caramel cream liqueur beside the stove.

Nick looked down and wiggled his toes. "No, I'm fine." He gave me a cheeky smile, which I returned.

"Okay then, how about you stir this, and I'll whip up something to eat."

"Deal."

I handed him the whisk. Our fingers brushed, and heat flooded up my arm.

"Um," I cleared my throat. "I have some cheese, meat pies, pickles, fruit, and fresh bread, sort of like a plowman's platter."

"Sounds good," Nick replied, and poured a generous helping of the liqueur into the chocolate. "Mugs?"

I pointed to a cupboard and set up a grazing board, taking extra care to make it as visually appealing as possible with what I had. Loaded with drinks, plates and food, we went back to the living room. I organized the dishes on the coffee table before the white and blue slip-covered couch. It was a solid thing, with thick cozy cushions that gobbled you up.

"Mind if I start a fire?" Nick asked.

I sank on to the couch. "Mmm, not at all, that would be perfect." I curled my feet under me, snuggled into the corner of the overstuffed sofa and dragged a pink and lime-green quilt over me. "There's wood in the box."

"Do you have more wood stacked anywhere?"

"I'm not sure. I hadn't checked outside for any."

"There's enough here for a couple of fires. My dad always has cords of wood ready to go. If there's none around here, I can get you some."

I was touched by his offer. "Thank you. That's very kind."

Before long, Nick had a fire crackling in the hearth, and warmth spread into the room. The dark of the night outside the windows, facing the sea, reflected the coziness of the living room.

As I watched Nick poke the fire and set the screen in front, I was overcome with a sensation of utter contentment. It all seemed perfectly natural, me on the couch, Nick building a fire, hot chocolate and snacks on the pine coffee table.

Houdini finally settled, after exploring the cottage, and stretched out between the sofa and coffee table on the colorful rug. I leaned down to pet him and he didn't even budge.

"He looks exhausted."

"A good dog is a tired dog," Nick replied.

I nodded, closed my eyes and tipped my head back, resting

on a soft throw pillow. The fire crackled and Houdini's gentle snores made me smile.

The couch moved and I opened my eyes. Nick sat at the other end.

"You look very comfortable," he said, and handed me a mug.

"Thank you, I am. You?" The aroma of chocolate tickled my nose, and I took a sip.

"Yes, very much so." He leaned forward and selected some food from the tray. "I've seen this cottage from the beach. It never seemed to have any life in it, though."

"Really? I don't know why. It's booked right after me." I sipped again. "I do love hot chocolate."

"I can't remember the last time I had some. Maybe as a kid." Nick looked out the window. "Sun's gone now." He glanced back at me. "How long are you staying here?"

"Just under six weeks." I leaned forward for some cheese and grapes.

"Ah, then you're moving on?"

I nodded. "Yes." A tightness in my chest startled me when I answered him. Why? Because I'd just met this interesting man and my time in Savage Cove had an expiry date?

Silence, except for the sounds of the cottage moaning against the wind that had risen in strength, the crackle of the fire, and Houdini's gentle snoring, filling the room. Wind rushed around the chimney, making the fire jump and dance.

"Storm's coming," Nick said casually while he selected more food.

"Oh? I do like a good storm." I looked out the window but didn't see anything ominous.

"Me too. Do you know where you're headed to when you move on?" he inquired.

"Well, I have a flight booked, and the next stop is supposed to be Hawaii, before moving on to wherever the wind blows me." I had the urge to explain myself to him. "It's kind of a promise I'm fulfilling."

"A promise to travel? That's my kind of promise." Nick smiled and I found myself returning it. He had a way of easing the tension I hadn't realized had built in me.

"Yes, I suppose it is." I sighed and curled my fingers around the mug. "How about you? I'm hazarding a guess that you live in the area?"

"You guessed right. All my life." He sat back and rested his ankle on his knee. "I'm a local. Born and raised here. My family goes way back." He shrugged his shoulders. "However, I do enjoy travel as well." He lifted his cup. "This is good."

"Thanks, it was a favorite of mine . . . and my brother." My light mood of moments ago darkened, as it always did when I thought of Rob. Even though I was working hard to not let my grief drag me down. Reminders were difficult.

I was quiet for a moment, thinking of Rob and the memories a simple mug of hot chocolate could bring back. I shook it off. "I'm on a bit of an adventure, you could call it, and at the same time, working. I was told this area was worth the trip."

"I have to agree with whoever told you that."

"Fantastic. I'm ready to explore." Even as I said it, I still couldn't believe everything that had happened over the past year. I sighed. Being Rob's beneficiary had given me the funds to honor the promise I'd made to him, but it sure was a tough way to receive it. I'd rather my brother be alive.

"How about you? You said you like to travel."

He nodded. "I do. But a lot of it is for business, and I think I've forgotten what it's like to travel for pleasure."

"Maybe you should turn your business trips into mini vacations?" I suggested.

He raised his mug. "Excellent advice."

I tipped mine toward his in agreement. "You must know a lot about the area. Places to visit, tourist traps, hidden gems?" I let this new prospect excite me. It did good to help me tamp down my survivor's guilt. I shifted on the couch and looked at Nick, ready to pick his brain.

"You could say so." He put down his mug, leaned back on the couch, and crossed his hands behind his head.

His fluid movements captivated me. Power and strength came off him in waves, and I soaked them up.

For the next little while we chatted about places I should visit, and our peaceful presence together was nice. Houdini snored louder and made little yips and growls, his body twitching in his sleep.

I leaned over to watch him. "He must be slaying a dragon."

"He sometimes gets really into his dreams." Nick bent his head and looked at the shelf under the coffee table. "You do puzzles?"

I leaned over to look. "Oh, well, not in years. I didn't even notice them. Do you?"

He reached down and lifted the battered puzzle box, putting it on the table and removing the lid. "I do. I like the challenge. This one looks fairly easy. A thousand pieces is a breeze." He chuckled. "Give me three thousand pieces or more, anyday."

That did it for me. I was hooked on him. He did puzzles, for crying out loud.

"Easy! Holy cow." I swept my fingers through the jumbled jigsaw pieces. "I couldn't imagine putting this together. What do you want to bet there are pieces missing?"

"Maybe, maybe not. It would all depend on how careful the previous users were when putting them away. This one," he pointed to Houdini, raised his eyebrows, and continued, "is a puzzle-piece thief. I have a puzzle mat now so I can keep what I'm working on out of his reach."

"A puzzle mat? Now that's hardcore," I teased. I liked our banter. I liked him.

Thunder rumbled in the distance.

I looked out the window. "Oh, you were right about the storm."

Nick stood, and instantly Houdini was on his feet, wide awake. "And I see lightning. We should probably get going before the storm rolls in. I don't want to be on the beach if lightning is close."

"I could drive you home?" I offered, but he shook his head.

"I appreciate that, but we'll be fine." He held up the leash.

"If you're sure." I glanced out the window.

Lightning flashed in the distance. I was disappointed nature had brought our evening to an end.

I followed Nick out to the porch.

He turned and we looked into each other's eyes.

"Thank you. This was an unexpected evening, but very nice."

The low timbre of his voice made me shiver lightly, with a need I hadn't felt in years.

"Yes, it was." Part of me wanted to ask him to stay, and the words hovered on my lips.

"I'm sure I'll see you on the beach again." He stepped away from the door and I had the strangest sensation he was putting distance between us.

"I hope so." I lifted my hand and waved as he went down the path.

Lightning lit the night. One moment he was there and the next he was gone. My arms hung slack, and I couldn't place the feeling that took root deep inside.

I almost ran after him, but held myself back. It was surprisingly hard to do.

The sky held the heaviness of last night's storm. Gone was the blue sky and white fluffy clouds. In its place was a gloom casting day into dusk. The perfect day to stay home, build a fire and curl up with a book for a while. I called about my phone, and they apologized profusely. Promising soon. Surprisingly, I seemed to be managing quite well without it. And here I'd thought a smartphone was a lifeline I couldn't live without. Who knew?

I had to do work today, and would research Marissa as well. But first, it was indulgence time. Me time. And while I felt a little guilty, I told myself it was okay.

Even though it was late June, the dampness off the sea hugged the ground under the steel-colored clouds. I shivered and pulled some wood from the box. There were only a few pieces left.

I hadn't built a fire since I was a kid, but it was like riding a bike, right? I arranged scrunched-up newspaper and kindling in the grate. Put a couple of pieces of wood on top and lit the paper.

Success. I made fire!

I pulled the same quilt over me that I had last night when Nick was here, and snuggled into the corner of the couch. Balancing the Kindle on my knee, I sipped my hot coffee, and watched the fire for a moment before opening the book and getting lost in the story.

A while later, rain smacked the windows. My coffee was cold, and the fire needed another log. I fed it, and went into the kitchen for a pastry I'd bought at Sol.

I was restless and prowled around the cottage. I hadn't investigated it well, and this was as good a day as any. The owners had lots of books and games stashed on shelves. Most were nicely aged, and I smiled seeing the game Trouble. Rob and I had loved that as kids. Tucked into a corner were newspapers. I pulled them down and sat on the floor, looking at the dates. What was the chance the date I needed would be here?

I held my breath and quickly went through the pile. Some of the dates were old, but nothing in the last few years. Disappointed, I sighed and gathered them up to put them back on the shelf. One day, I'd go through them and dig into the history of the area. I didn't feel like it today.

I sat on the carpet in front of the fire and pulled out a drawer on the coffee table. Cards, poker chips and notepads for keeping score. Then I spied the puzzle box again.

Holding it on my lap, with my palm resting on the top, I imagined I could feel Nick. It was silly but it cheered me a bit. I turned and faced the fire, took the lid off, and dumped all the pieces on the wooden floor.

"Might as well give it a whirl."

I spread the pieces out and turned them all face up. Finding the edges and the corners seemed to be the best course of action, then I'd work my way in. The picture on the battered box showed me the puzzle was hard—a forest scene with lots of greens and a waterfall.

I imagined Nick sitting here with me, working on it together. It was a wistful thought, and I wasn't exactly sure what to make of it. How could a man I'd only seen three times have made such a profound impact on me?

Chapter Eight

My morning routine of walking early had become a staple, a great start to my day. After the last two days' mixture of cloud and sun, today there was a haze hanging over the water, blanketing everything in a soft silence. I loved the solitude of the beach, dictating when ideas popped up, and simply enjoying nature. Today was the furthest I'd ventured, and when I rounded a bend in the coastline I stood stock-still and gasped.

A magnificent house appeared through the trees. It was set back, facing a wide section of beach, ringed by towering pines, and artfully landscaped to echo the contours of the rocky coastline.

Built mainly of timber and stone, with soaring windows across the front and decking that ran the full width of the home, it rose in stepped levels, in perfect harmony with the surroundings. Almost as if it grew from the earth itself. I was in awe. Dare I take a photo?

It appeared empty at the moment. I didn't know if I should walk past it, unsure of the beach laws and if it was private property. I looked for "No Trespassing" signs and didn't see any. Still, I wasn't quite comfortable so I just stared at the house, wishing I could have a peek inside.

"Wishful thinking." I indulged myself a few moments longer before tearing myself away.

It had been a lovely walk, but I needed to get home to start working on my notes and create my fish-and-chip post. Just as I was turning, something caught my eye. I snapped my head back and spun around, stubbing my toe on a stone. I let out a gasp, and took a step forward—more like a hop of pain—before catching my breath. I thought I saw a person with a shock of silver hair, in dark clothing, standing further down the beach, past the magnificent house. When I looked back, the beach was empty. Had I really seen someone, or was it like Bigfoot sightings? I laughed at myself. No, I wouldn't submit this to the Bigfoot/Sasquatch Sightings Mapper website. It was the first time I'd seen anyone else on the beach apart from Nick and the older man, Walter.

I was disappointed I hadn't encountered Nick or Houdini on the shore for the last couple of days. I wondered why, and of course wasn't able to come up with a reason that made me feel any better.

I sighed, hoping we'd cross paths again soon. Nick had invaded my thoughts. This quiet, reserved, very attractive man was hovering in my subconscious, behind whatever I was doing.

I headed back the way I'd come, watching where I placed my feet. The air was getting hazier and I bet fog would roll in at some point today. Rocks littered the beach, and a yellow stone caught my attention. I picked it up and held it to the light. The stone was pretty, with what looked like stripes inside. With one last wistful glance over my shoulder at the beautiful house, I started to walk home, eyes on the sand, searching for more stones.

I heard my name on the wind, halted and listened. I shook

my head, I was imagining things. The mist continued to build on the horizon.

But I heard it again, distant and faint. There was nobody around, so who had called me?

"Okay, Rob, enough of freaking me out already," I said to the empty beach. "Pretty sure if I keep hearing you, I'll believe I'm going nuts."

I heard it again. *Lizzieeeee.*

This time, I turned around and peered into the mist. Where was it coming from? I still didn't see anybody.

"I'm overtired." I spun around, determined to head for home. The wind swirled around me and I heard a sharp whistle cut through the air.

"Okay, what the heck?" I stopped and turned again.

Houdini was racing in my direction. Nick was further down the beach and jogged toward me, his arm raised in greeting. I waved back and headed over to him.

"Hey, what a nice surprise." I was thrilled to see him.

"I saw you from the window." He pointed back to the beautiful house.

I grabbed his arm. "That's your house?"

He nodded. "Yes."

"Wow, I was admiring it but didn't feel right walking past it on the beach, so I turned around. The last thing I expected was for you to appear."

He gazed down at me. "It's good to see you."

I realized I was still holding his arm, and let go quickly.

"How have you been? I haven't seen you recently." I tried to keep my tone light.

"I was out of town for a couple of days." He shrugged his shoulders. "Unexpected business trip. And here we are, back on the beach."

"Yes, and here we are." The rush of relief at hearing he'd been away on business surprised me. It also lightened my mood. He hadn't been avoiding walking on the beach, or bumping into me. "Are you traveling a lot at the moment?"

"Enough. I probably will have to make a couple of trips over the next few weeks."

I nodded. The next few weeks were even closer to my departure date. I could feel myself getting confused and anxious, so I distracted myself by watching Houdini being his typical silly self, racing around, tossing driftwood he'd found in the air and catching it.

"Here, boy," I called him and he came at a run, tackling me to the sand. "Oww, you're too big for that." I laughed, and it made Houdini even more excited. He stood over me and licked my face.

"Houdini! Get off." Nick reached for the dog as I tried to push him off. I couldn't stop laughing and soon Nick joined in. Houdini was in seventh heaven.

"I'm so sorry."

"Don't be. I called him, and he was just being a happy dog."

"Go get the stick." Nick pitched the driftwood down the beach, and the dog took off.

I felt the dampness of the sand seeping through my shorts and took Nick's hand when he held it out for me. Before I could process the sensation of our palm-to-palm contact, he pulled me to my feet. I was unprepared and wavered a second, trying to get my balance back. I reached out with my other hand, catching him on the chest.

"Whoa, careful there," he said, and took my elbow with his fingers.

"Oh, thanks. Lost my balance." Reluctantly, I let go of his hand and chest so I could wipe off my shorts.

Nick brushed sand off my back. "He can be a handful. I should have stopped him."

"It's okay. He was excited, and I should have been ready." I slapped my hands together to clear the rest of the sand.

In the middle of pushing my hair back, I froze as Nick reached up. He brushed his knuckles across my cheek. I couldn't help it when my eyelids fluttered and I leaned into him slightly.

"There's some sand . . ." His voice was soft.

"Uh, th-thank you." I opened my eyes, and my fingers brushed his.

He drew his hand away when Houdini started barking.

What I wished he would do was pull me into his arms so I could feel every hard plane of his body. I wanted to tangle my fingers into his unruly hair while he kissed me senseless.

I couldn't remember the last time I'd had feelings like these. Had I been so focused on my grief that I'd forgotten who *I* was? A woman with wants and desires. It unnerved me a bit, and I needed to think about it. But later. I felt Nick was having a similar reaction, as he cleared his throat and reached down for a stick to throw for Houdini again.

"Do you have plans for today?" I asked, hoping to break the tension vibrating between us.

He faced me. "No, not really. How about you?"

I shook my head. "No, well, other than wishing my new phone would arrive. I have some outlining to do, but only self-imposed deadlines, which means I'm allowed to make any changes I wish." I smiled.

"Ah, the pleasures of self-employment. How would you like to come back to my house for some breakfast?"

His invitation pleasantly surprised me. "I'd like that very much. Thank you."

He nodded and called Houdini, who promptly ran ahead to lead the way.

"Now you can see the inside of my house. And it's my turn to feed you." Nick chuckled, and we fell into step.

"True." I laughed and juggled the stone I'd found earlier in my hand.

"You found some agate."

I held it out. "Is that what this is? I didn't know, I just thought it was pretty."

"Yep, common enough here because it's a volcanic area."

"What? Volcanoes?"

Nick smiled, and I wasn't sure if he was teasing. "Yes. It's an active area of subduction." He pointed to the horizon. "The Cascades has five active volcanoes."

I was horrified. "N-no! Why didn't I know that?"

He gave me a sideways glance. "Mount St Helens? And don't worry. They're quiet, and we're too far away to receive any damage from blast or pyroclastic flows."

"Oh my God. That sounds terrifying." I felt stupid now, and of course I knew about Mount St Helens.

He reached out and touched my shoulder. "They're sleeping right now, it's all good."

"Okay, if you say so. And here I thought there wasn't anything to be concerned about in this area. I hadn't factored in volcanoes."

"We live on a dynamic planet, with earthquakes, volcanoes."

"Don't remind me. A planet that spits and tries to shake us off."

He broke out laughing. "I'd never thought of it that way before."

Chapter Nine

Nick led Lizzie down the beach and they fell silent, both lost in their thoughts, until they reached his house.

"Up here to the side door." Nick looked around for Houdini, and whistled.

He appeared like magic at their side and raced up to the door, waiting for Nick to open it.

"Come on in." He pushed the door open.

Lizzie followed him into the mudroom. Houdini dashed by and nearly knocked them both down.

"Dog!" Nick shouted, and grabbed Lizzie's elbow to steady her.

"Whoa, that's twice. He is a fiend, isn't he?" Lizzie yelped. "Thanks, or that might have been rather ridiculous ... me sprawled out in front of you."

He smiled. "I bet you never look ridiculous. Even on your back on the floor."

"Ha! You don't know me well enough."

"Yet." His fingers lingered on her skin, and the moment drew out until he reluctantly let go of her arm.

"I can make you and your brother's favorite hot chocolate if you want. Do you see him often?" He pushed the door shut behind them and wiped his feet on the throw rug.

She was doing the same, her head down, suddenly quiet. When she looked up, pain was etched across her face.

"What's wrong?" Nick asked, concerned by her shift in mood.

Lizzie twisted her fingers together and drew in a shaky breath. She looked utterly vulnerable.

"Oh . . . he died." Her voice was small.

Nick was struck silent for a moment.

"I am so sorry. I didn't mean to upset you." He drew her into his arms, and she didn't resist.

Folding her into a hug seemed a natural thing to do. Nick understood her grief. It could come out of nowhere. A simple comment could strike and leave you in a state of shock. Her arms slipped around his waist and she rested her head on his chest. He caught the scent of her shampoo.

"You didn't know, please don't worry. Rob died about eighteen months ago. It was very hard, right afterward, and it took a while to find myself. Sometimes, I think I'm still looking for the old me." She drew in a shaky breath. "The last few months have been better."

"It's hard, I can understand." He lowered his voice.

She looked up at him. "You can?"

He nodded, and they stared at each other for a beat. He could relate to her grief and felt he needed to offer her an explanation. But Nick hesitated. He wasn't ready to mention his wife. He continued, "Yes, we lost Mom. It was fifteen years ago, but it never completely goes away."

"I'm sorry. It's like a huge void inside you, isn't it? Both my parents are gone too."

"I'm so sorry. Yes, it is, but you do find a way to live with it."

Nick moved around Lizzie and turned to her. "How about we change the subject to a less sad one? Let me make you that breakfast."

He walked down a short hall into the kitchen, feeling Lizzie's presence behind him.

"You cook too?" she asked.

He heard the humor in her voice and glanced over. He was glad her mood had lightened.

"I cook, clean, and do everything else that needs to be done. A necessity of solo life."

He hired some help throughout the year, mainly for the exterior of the house, and once a month he had a deep clean of the interior.

He watched Lizzie pull her hair back, as she had on the beach the other day. The movement stretched her shirt over her very enticing curves. Then she let her hair drop and shook it out. "It's all frizzy from the fog."

"What, your hair?" he asked, not understanding the problem.

She laughed. "Yes."

"I didn't notice." And he hadn't. She was beautiful.

Her vibrant personality filled the kitchen and, with her here, the house didn't seem so empty. It was a long time since a woman had been in his house—or in his life.

"So then, what's your morning drink of choice?" Nick pointed to the espresso machine. "I can whip up pretty much anything for you."

She glanced at the machine and raised her eyebrows. "Wow, let me see. That looks like it belongs in a restaurant." She tapped her chin and pursed her lips while she considered. "I can't decide. I'll tell you what, how about you surprise me? Make me something that you like."

Nick wasn't expecting her response, but he liked it. "Challenge accepted."

He felt the weight of her stare when he took his faithful old Moka pot out of the cupboard. He'd bought it in Italy, years ago, when he'd learned how to brew the perfect cappuccino from Fiorella, his landlady. He remembered her fondly. For an older woman, she'd been a firecracker. He kept the pot in memory of her and his time in Rome.

"My goodness, that pot looks like it's seen better days," Lizzie exclaimed.

"It has, that's for sure. But it makes the best coffee. I learned a lot from my landlady when I lived in Rome. Fio was an amazing cook too. She made everything old school and, to this day, I've never found Italian food to match it." Nick prepped the filter, set the pot on the stove, and reached for his Tuttocrema frother. He poured milk in and set it to warm.

"I've never made coffee like that. It's just plain drip for me. My friend has one of those fancy machines." She pointed to the espresso maker. "But she constantly bemoans the fact that it's a quest for the ever-elusive crema and she rarely achieves it."

"Ah, yes, the elusive crema." Nick nodded and tapped the frother. "I will do my best."

She waved a hand. "Pff, don't worry about that for me. I'm not a coffee aficionado, I just need my morning shot or two. Hang on, did you say Rome?"

"Yes, I did. Double challenge, then. To turn you into a coffee aficionado, and to prove my skill as a chef. Do you have a breakfast request?"

"Ah, nope, again, I'm happy with whatever you would make for yourself. Don't go to any trouble just for me. I'm still stuck on Rome." She laughed and spun on the stool at the kitchen island.

"I went years ago. It was a backpacking adventure through Europe." He looked at her and smiled. "You know, going cheap, staying in hostels and seeing the world."

"Well, not really, but Rome is on my list! Tell me more."

"I stayed in Rome the longest. The history and architecture overwhelmed me. I had to explore the city."

"It sounds amazing." Lizzie was listening to him intently.

He was eager to tell her more. "The catacombs and crypts were something else to see. I visited the Vatican, of course the Colosseum, traveled around, visited the Amalfi coast, Tuscany and stayed for a while in Positano. And the food." Nick kissed his fingertips.

"It must have been incredible. I'll have to pick your brain because you've convinced me a trip to Rome definitely has to happen."

She looked entranced, and he was sure she was conjuring up images in her mind. Lizzie appeared perfectly at home, relaxed in his kitchen. Nick decided he liked how she looked, sitting there. It wasn't hard to imagine her bathed in the morning light, sipping coffee he'd made for her, hair tousled after getting out of bed.

He dropped his chin to his chest and turned back to the Moka pot. Yep, his thoughts were running away with him. He remembered he had biscotti and put some on a plate, placing it on the island in front of her.

"Yum." Lizzie reached for one and munched happily.

"Okay then, give me a few minutes to get the coffee ready, and think on the eats. Feel free to wander around."

"Nick?" Her voice was soft.

He looked down at her.

"Thank you. This is sweet of you."

"You're very welcome. I like the company." He smiled, as did she, before sliding off the stool.

"Okay, I'll go in there and check out the view." She pointed behind her and turned on her heel to leave the kitchen. "Just call if you need any help."

He watched her until she disappeared behind the wall to the living room, and drew in a slow breath.

"Nick, this is spectacular," she called. "I can't believe the height of the windows. And the view overlooking the beach!"

He started to whistle. Something he used to do all the time, but hadn't done in ages. He realized he was happy. It felt good.

Nick decided he'd whip up some crêpes. He had some lobster in the freezer, which would be perfect. His dad had stocked his fridge with staples for him. For anything more elaborate, he'd have to go to the grocery store.

He heard Lizzie in the other room as he prepped the food. It was nice to hear life in the house again. Nick paused, shredding the Parmigiano-Reggiano. He knew he wasn't ready to talk about his wife yet, and he'd removed all her photos, so he had no concern that Lizzie would come across one and he'd have to explain. He started shredding again. His wife was a conversation to have in the future, if ever.

Batter mixed, he set it aside and returned to the coffee. "Coffee's ready," he called.

"Mmm, I can smell it." She came back into the kitchen and sat on the stool, taking the cup he handed to her. She raised it to her nose and inhaled. "Oh, my. If it tastes as good as it smells . . ." She sipped reverently, and closed her eyes in delight. "No words. No words."

Nick laughed. "I'm glad to get your stamp of approval." He set the cast-iron crêpe pan on the stove to heat, and whisked the batter again.

"You have some great volumes in your library," she commented between sips of coffee.

"I like to read when I have time, and I've become something of a collector." He poured his coffee. "If it was nicer weather, we could sit out on the patio, but we can eat here or next to the window."

"Perfect. There's still a great view from inside."

"Okay, the table by the window, then."

"What can I do?"

Nick told her where to find cutlery and table settings, and he liked the way she made herself comfortable. Again, he thought how nice it was to have Lizzie in his house. His wife hadn't been much of a housekeeper. She'd been the kind who preferred to be kept, and he'd done his best to keep her happy.

Nick didn't want thoughts of Ari invading his time with Lizzie. He pushed her out of his head, surprised it was easy to do. Guilt was never far away, and it had eaten him up for the last three years. It had been such a long time to carry it around. And if he wasn't careful, it would roll right back over him with Lizzie in the house. After a few painful early experiences, he'd resisted any form of dating, and he didn't look at breakfast with Lizzie as a date. He wasn't sure how to categorize it yet, but he was going to suppress the guilt that poked at him.

It didn't take long for him to make and plate up the crêpes. He put everything on a large tray, including fresh coffee, and carried it to the table she'd set up.

She was standing by the window. "It has changed out there. The fog is thick." He heard the concern in her voice.

"Breakfast is ready." Nick set the tray down.

She turned from the window. "I'm impressed. You *can* cook."

He pulled out her chair so she could sit.

"Gentlemanly, as well." She gestured to the chair, reluctant to tear herself away from the view.

He sat down across the table from her. "My mom taught me

well. Thank you, just a little something I whipped up. Enjoy."
Nick put a plate and a fresh mug of coffee in front of her.

Who would have thought he'd be cooking breakfast for this vibrant woman?

He wasn't sure how all this had happened in such a brief space of time, and he puzzled over what it was about her that drew him in. He watched her stand in front of the window, cradling the mug in her hands, the view behind framing her. And then he knew.

Her presence.

She gave him a feeling that was hard to pin down. The only way he could describe her was rather corny, but bang on. She filled the room with sunshine. Like a breath of fresh air. Not leaving any room for darkness.

Nick wanted to know more about her, what she liked, didn't like, her favorite color, food, and all the little things that made her who she was.

She turned and caught him watching her. The bridge of her nose crinkled when she smiled, and her eyes had a life of their own. They captivated him.

"What?" She sat down at last, put her mug on the table, and picked up her fork.

"Oh nothing, just thinking how nice it is to be sharing breakfast with you." He took a contented sip of coffee and silently thanked Houdini for taking off, the day he met Lizzie on the beach.

Chapter Ten

Later that morning, as I drove into town, I couldn't get Nick out of my head. I didn't mind the space he took up, and I was pretty sure he liked me as much as I liked him.

I smiled, and angled my car into a spot right across the street from the café. I had Nick on the brain, but I also had work to do. I grabbed my bags from the passenger seat, somehow got them jammed into the steering wheel, and struggled to free them. I finally scrambled out of the door, completely lacking any form of grace.

I reorganized my bags on my shoulder and puffed a strand of hair from my nose while I waited for the traffic to clear. There weren't a lot of cars—call it rush minute—but when it was safe, I ran across the street and pushed open the café door. Once again, tinkling bells above the door greeted me.

Still without my phone, and told it could arrive today, I'd decided it was the perfect excuse to spend a couple of hours at Sol. I could use their Wi-Fi and do some polishing on my article, which was due in two days, then pick up on the research for Marissa again.

This time, I hoped to get a comfy chair and table by the window or fireplace. My previous visits had been rather quick, but today I wanted to relax, put on my iPod while I got some work done. I'd been a terrible procrastinator since arriving in Savage Cove, and I was falling behind.

I found a small round table, tucked in the back corner. I put my bags on it and went to stand in line, keeping an eye on my stuff. I wasn't too worried about it.

I was a little surprised the café was so busy. I checked my watch: 10:30. Maybe it was always like this, all day every day. Most people looked like they'd been here a while, and I couldn't say that I blamed them.

The attractive older lady with short, sassy platinum-blonde hair was here again, reading a book in a chair by the window. She was absently sipping from a big mug, the string from the tea bag wrapped around her baby finger.

There was a different barista behind the counter today. Amanda was efficiently serving guests at the tables, with a constant smile. Her lilting voice was a delightful accent against the comforting backdrop of the café sounds. Quiet background music drifted from hidden speakers, creating a peaceful ambiance.

When it was my turn at the counter, the barista came over to take my order.

"Surprise me with today's special. And I'd like a cheese scone if you have one."

"Warmed with butter?" she asked.

"Yes, please."

I thought of Nick while I waited, and a feeling of warmth spread in my chest. He'd offered to drive me back to the cottage after we had breakfast, and I gratefully accepted, since the fog had rolled in. You could barely see your nose in front of your face. We'd arranged to meet on the beach the next day and go back to my cottage for breakfast. It was the first time we'd made plans, and I was excited to know I'd be seeing him again so soon. I doubted I'd ever be able to top the lobster crêpes he had made for me. Gazing at today's pastries, which were a feast for my eyes, I ordered half a dozen. Then I would at least have some reliably tasty treats on hand.

I took my mug, scone, and box of pastries back to the table. I sat down and lifted the drink, wonderfully chocolatey, blended into coffee, with a light foam on top, drizzled with a fruity sweetness. It reminded me of Christmas.

I pondered the situation with Nick. We had only just met, and were in the getting-to-know-you stage, so the possibility he could be uninterested or already entangled in a relationship crossed my mind. Maybe he only wanted a friend.

"Well, that would suck," I told my steaming mug, blowing on the hot liquid. I hoped he would have said something, if that were the case. But then I reassured myself: if he was in a relationship, I couldn't see him having breakfast with me, or suggesting meeting on the beach. I wouldn't do that. But what if he did turn out to be the type to have a string of women? He was attractive enough.

No. I decided he wasn't like that. He didn't give off those vibes. And, whatever happened, it would be kind of nice to spend time with him while I was here.

But now, time to get busy.

Opening my iPad, I started working on the article again. All I had was an opening line, and it definitely needed some work. I finessed it a little more.

Welcome to Savage Cove. Yes, that's where I am now, in the Pacific Northwest, and my own introduction to it wasn't entirely welcoming. Not Savage Cove's fault, but mine. I can be extremely talented, at times, and today I rose to the task.

Put it this way, ferries and me are not a good fit . . .

I sat back, looking at the words. It was a better start. I also wanted to tie this into an Instagram and TikTok post about the fish-and-chip dinner. People loved foodie posts. But I simply couldn't focus any further on writing new words or editing what I had.

I was drifting. Thinking about starting research into incidents that had happened in Savage Cove, linking to the name Marissa. Kate was waiting for this article and I *had* to focus, especially after the power failure the other night. I was looking forward to our Zoom chat later. Over the course of Rob's sickness and death, Kate had been there in the background for me. Patient. Encouraging. A rock. Suggesting little tidbits of what to write so as to keep my finger in the pie. Our editor-writer relationship had slowly morphed into a more personal friendship. I'm sure she would understand if I told her the article was going to be a few days late.

But I couldn't shake off the desire to research Marissa, and it made me pause. What was it about this woman that intrigued me so? The mystery about what happened to her was consuming me and . . . relatable. It was why I became a journalist.

I sighed and saved my work, promising myself I'd finish it later.

When I'd first searched for information on Marissa, I found very little, and I wondered if perhaps her death hadn't happened in Savage Cove. I broadened my search.

A few articles popped up, and one headline lower down in

the results mentioned a woman disappearing off the coast. I clicked on the article and read it.

A woman had disappeared. A sailboat was discovered. Crashed, up on the rocks, but no body was found. The owner of the boat was located and police discovered his wife, Marissa Wright, was missing. With no body, and Ms Wright unaccounted for, she was presumed drowned. An investigation was launched but ended inconclusively. The husband, Nicholas Charlton, while initially a suspect, was not charged.

I froze, my cup halfway to my mouth. One detail niggled at my brain. Hadn't I heard that surname somewhere before? I reread the article.

Nicholas Charlton.

Could this be my Nick?

I stared at the foam on my mug, and it reminded me of the coffee Nick had made in his kitchen. I closed my eyes and replayed our conversation at breakfast. We hadn't talked about anything that could make a connection between the two men. Still, there were so many questions.

Wouldn't it be too big a coincidence if Nicholas and Nick were the same person? If he was, that meant he was a widower. I sat back in my chair and thought about it. If foul play was investigated, and the findings inconclusive, that meant he would have been cleared of any wrongdoing. And that text to Marissa was heartfelt and sorrowful. Right?

I shivered.

I was being ridiculous and fanciful, but I wanted to get to the bottom of this. And the best way to do that now was to Google him. I held my breath, waiting for results. The only Nicholas Charlton result was an article about a minor league football star—I recognized his photo from Rob's sports obsessions. I sighed with relief. Okay, so that was settled, at least for now.

I looked around the café and wondered if anyone here knew the story. Then I switched my attention to the photos on the wall. There was only one portrait—the one of Marissa. The rest were visual documentation of Savage Cove's history.

I longed for someone to talk it all over with. Rob had been a great listener. I'd bounced a lot off him, over the years. Even if he was the wilder twin to my more cautious one, he gave good, sound advice. I smiled, remembering how he'd be the one who dragged me around on adventures, arguing about what she-nanigans he'd get us caught up in. A wave of longing swept over me. Time is supposed to heal all wounds, but time wasn't being kind right now. Even after eighteen months, I missed him so. He would have loved to help with this mystery.

I dropped my chin in my hand and stared at the screen, not seeing what was there. My thoughts cascaded back to three years ago, when he'd received the devastating cancer diagnosis. I'd dropped everything to be with him straightaway. His girl-friend had jumped ship, saying she hadn't signed up for this. I was so angry at her, but Rob had been stoic about it. As most of my friends fell by the wayside, and even the occasional texts to see how things were going faded away, I gave all my attention to Rob. Then I disappeared off on the adventure he had wanted for me.

Now I realized just how much I had isolated myself. But I'd been trying to heal the broken parts of me, and I knew I was still fractured. I fiddled with my pen and frowned.

My phone buzzed inside my bag and startled me. Was it another text? I fished through the satchel and pulled it out. My shoulders drooped. It wasn't a text, but a phone call. Who had this number?

Then it dawned on me. The person who sent the text! Maybe they were calling Marissa and I could find out more.

"Hello?" I listened and no one replied right away. "Hello, anyone there?"

I gave it another second and was about to hang up when I heard fumbling on the other end and the sound of breathing.

"Hello, hello," a male voice replied.

Was it him? The man who sent the text? I clutched the phone and my heart quickened.

"Hello. Who is this?" I held my breath.

Silence again. I waited, hearing only distorted sounds.

"Yes, sorry. I apologize. Is this Lizzie?" the man asked.

"Uh, yes, yes, it is. Who are you?"

It sounded like a hand covered the phone and I heard a muffled voice. "I'll be with you in a moment."

Getting frustrated, I was about to end the call when the person on the other end came back to me.

"I'm sorry about that. It's Keith from the store."

"The store?" I didn't know a Keith.

"You ordered a smartphone? It just came in."

"Oh! Yes. Thanks for calling." I packed up with my free hand. "I'll be right over."

"Great, then. See you."

I made sure I had forgotten nothing and cleaned up the table, carrying my cup and plate to the counter. I wove my way between the tables to the door and glanced at the woman with platinum-blonde hair. She looked up and we made eye contact. I smiled at her and wished this had happened earlier, because it would have been a great way to start up a conversation. She nodded and smiled back.

Damn, I would love to talk to her, but I needed my phone. I stashed my bag in the car, locked it and walked over to the shop.

A little while later, I was headed back to my car, pretty new phone in hand. I was ready to tackle the world.

Chapter Eleven

I took my hand-held voice recorder and strolled along the beach, dictating thoughts for future story ideas, and keeping an eye out for Nick. I couldn't get enough of these walks. I reflected on our breakfast at my cottage yesterday. Pastries from Sol had been perfect. The Breakfast Bomb, as they called it, was loaded with bacon, cheese, a bit of pesto, and all wrapped up in puff pastry. My mouth watered just thinking about it. We'd sat out on the porch, with Houdini at our feet, and watched the mist roll in off the sea, chatting about nothing in particular. It had been wonderful, relaxed, and not long enough.

Today, I wanted to get started on my Lady of the Sea story, article, whatever it turned out to be. Maybe even a book, I mused, as I strolled along the sand. Raising my recorder, I started to talk.

It all started with a photo on the wall in a cute café called Sol, in Savage Cove, Washington State. A windswept woman, perched on rocks that reached out into the sea. Tendrils of hair blew across her face, and her eyes, haunting and pained, seemed to stare out of the photo at me.

I was hooked and needed to know everything about her . . .

I was so engrossed, I forgot where I was. It wasn't until Houdini raced past me that I realized how far along I'd walked. I looked up to see Nick just down the beach. I waved. Warmth radiated through my body, and I clicked off my recorder.

"Houdini, come here, boy," I called, and he rushed up to me, pressing against my legs.

"Fancy meeting you here," Nick said with a smile.

"Yes, fancy that." I laughed and liked it when he pulled me into a hug. I could stay in his arms forever. It was so good to see him again.

"Are you working while you walk?"

I nodded and fixed my hat after it was pushed askew when we hugged. "Yes, making notes for future stories."

We fell into step and our hands brushed, then his fingers took cautious hold of mine. Heat flushed my neck.

"Nice hat."

"Thanks, it was Rob's."

Nick smiled and gave a gentle nod. "Do you always dictate?" he inquired.

"Not always, but it's a great way to multi-task. I can talk up a storm while I wander along, and then transcribe and edit when I get back." I laughed. "Sometimes the bloopers are hilarious."

"Bloopers?" He glanced down at me.

His eyes were smiling, and I felt like they could really *see* me. Me, deep, down inside, and I drew in a breath, completely distracted. I blinked, forgetting for a moment what he'd just said.

"Uh-huh, yes, bloopers. When I transcribe my words, sometimes I'm, like, what the heck was I trying to say?"

He threw back his head and laughed. It was a lovely deep sound that gave me the tingles. "I'd like to hear them sometime."

"Sure. I have a list of them on my laptop." His mention of the future made my heart swell.

We continued strolling along the sand, waves lapping at our feet. If I could suspend this moment in time, I would.

"Lizzie?" He stopped and turned to me.

I looked up at him, unable to decipher the serious expression on his face. "Y-yes?"

His eyes stared into mine and I held my breath, uncertain what he was going to say and suddenly worried I wouldn't like whatever it was.

"I was wondering if you'd like to go out to dinner tomorrow night?" he asked.

The breath whooshed out of me. "I'd love to." I realized how quickly I'd responded. "Well, perhaps I should check my calendar first. I'm in such demand, you know." I gave him a cheeky smile, hoping I hadn't appeared too desperate.

He grinned, and then we both laughed.

"Great, I know a place I think you'll like."

"Perfect, I look forward to it. Soooo," I drew the word out and twirled a strand of hair around my finger, "is this a date?"

He smiled slowly and nodded. "I guess it is."

I nodded and rocked on my feet, looking up at him. The wind blew my hair across my face and I pushed it aside, holding it back. I couldn't contain my smile as excitement for this shift in our friendship filled me with anticipation.

His phone buzzed. He dug it out of his pocket and frowned. "Damn." He looked annoyed.

"Is everything okay?"

He held up his phone and shook his head. "Yeah, work. I'm sorry, but I have to go."

"I understand." I tried not to let my disappointment show.

"Thank you. I'm glad we were able to grab these few minutes together."

"Me too. I'm looking forward to tomorrow." I tipped my head up.

"As am I." He wasn't frowning now, but his expression was intense.

I held my breath when he gently tugged my hand, drew me closer, placing his fingertips under my chin. My heart fluttered, waiting for the kiss I knew was coming. I raised my hand and rested it on his chest. Before our lips could meet, Houdini pushed his way between us and Nick stepped back.

"Well, then, tomorrow?" His words wrapped themselves around me.

I nodded. My face was hot, and I was pretty sure a blush stained my cheeks. A blush! Of all things.

"Yes, tomorrow." I couldn't believe I was at a loss for words, struggling to find something to say without sounding ridiculous.

"I'll pick you up around seven." He whistled, and Houdini ran to his side.

"I'll be ready."

We turned and went in opposite directions, but looked back at each other until we'd each rounded a bend in the beach.

I was going on a date. How long had it been since I'd last gone out with a guy on a legitimate date? Too long. Way before Rob had gotten sick. My step lightened. I thought about how events led you in a certain direction. Stepping on a path would lead you one way, and then forks in the road offered different possibilities. But you'd never know the exact destination until you took a chance.

Chapter Twelve

"Where are you taking me?" I murmured.

The winding drive from the main road took us under a canopy of trees. Twinkling lights, secreted in the shrubbery lining the laneway, created a magical aura. I rolled the window down and inhaled the scent of the forest air.

"It's so beautiful. I'm sure fairies are floating on the breeze," I said softly. I glanced at Nick as we arrived in front of the Crab Stone restaurant, a low building sitting cozily under the tall trees on the edge of the water.

By his wide smile, I could tell he was pleased. "Yes, it is. I had a feeling you'd like it here. It's whimsical, and the food is very good."

He pulled up to the valet, reached over, and touched my hand. "Please stay here for a minute."

Nick got out. He looked in through the windshield as he rounded the front of the car, and with my full attention on him I barely noticed the valet had opened my door. Nick nodded at the man and discreetly slipped a tip into his palm.

I swung my legs out of the car. How was I to rise gracefully from the low-slung vehicle in a barely knee-length dress? I glanced at my sandaled feet but I needn't have fretted. Nick extended his hand and I took it, gazing up at him as the exhilarating warmth of unsaid promises beat softly in my chest. He eased me up as if I were whisper-light, and I floated to stand next to him.

"Why thank you, kind sir." We faced each other, and I was thrilled when he kept his fingers entwined with mine.

We walked up a flagstone path, between more fairy lights, under arbors tumbling with flowers. At the main door, pale pink climbing roses clung to the wall, marching their way around windows and along the iron railings, also strung with lights. The roses were in full bloom and the fragrance was entrancing.

"I would die for a garden like this."

"I do think you would have to stay in one place to nurture it."

I glanced at him, wondering at his words and if he meant anything by them.

Nick ushered me through, with his hand at the small of my back, and I let the thought slide away, instead focusing on the warmth of his fingers. My breath caught and a sudden yearning trembled through my body, almost making me stumble.

"Steady on." Nick caught my elbow.

"I'm okay. Too used to being barefoot on the beach." I let him guide me through the door into the restaurant, his touch steady, comforting, and I loved how it made me feel.

"Can this get any more gorgeous?"

"I'm glad you like it."

"Oh, yes, I do."

There was no maître d' or host waiting to seat us. Just a sign at the front, with beautiful calligraphy, saying to please find the table of your choice. The restaurant was busy, and the aroma of the food promised a superb culinary experience. Tall windows framed the view of the harbor and boats beyond. The outdoor setting was breathtaking.

"This way," Nick whispered in my ear.

I shivered at the intimacy in his voice, and thought of our almost-kiss yesterday. I felt the looks from other guests as we walked past. I wondered why, and a rush of pride at being beside Nick filled me.

I was in tune with his nearness now, and it was intoxicating. Between this and the beauty of the restaurant, it was difficult to find words.

To help shake off my powerful reaction, I cast about for something to say. "Look," I leaned closer to him. "The view is stunning."

"It sure is." He smiled down at me, and I sighed.

The tables were set with beautiful blue and white gingham, fresh flowers, and candles. He led me past the inside tables, and out through an archway to a deck that overlooked the water.

I gasped when we stepped outside.

Tall plants and the ever-present fairy lights were strategically placed between the tables here, creating intimacy for the diners. They also helped to conceal the propane heaters to stave off the evening chill. All the tables were taken, except for a prime spot in the corner. It had a little sign. *Reserved.*

"You?" I looked up at Nick.

He had the biggest smile on his face.

My heart nearly burst. It was such a simple thing, but he'd gone out of his way for us to have a wonderful evening. I squeezed his hand.

He nodded. "Yes, I wanted to make sure we had the best table in the house."

He held the chair out for me and I sat, my eyes not leaving him when he took the seat beside me, both of us facing the water.

"Thank you. I'm touched." I reached for his hand.

"You're welcome." His fingers curled around mine.

"So picturesque. It could be a postcard." Boats bobbed at their moorings, and lights were beginning to flicker along the docks.

"Yes, I agree," Nick replied, his eyes meeting mine with an intensity that made the rest of the world disappear.

I was helpless to look away from him.

Nick abruptly cleared his throat and unfolded his napkin, his smile fading. His sudden shift in mood made me wonder if I had imagined the previous moment.

"This place has been here for as long as I can remember." He looked out across the water. I was rewarded with his sparkling eyes and warm smile, and gone was the moment of melancholy. "It has quite the history. Something that maybe you'd like to write about?"

"Mm, I do like finding little places like this. They're a dream. I could definitely build this into something."

We sat silently while the waiter filled our water goblets from the silver pitcher, making the ice clink against the turquoise glass. It had been a long time since I'd felt this content. It was easy being with Nick, and I loved talking to him. I felt myself breathe deeper, and be present in the moment, which was something I'd struggled with since Rob got sick. A sudden stab of regret passed over me, knowing how much he would have loved it here.

Shaking it off, I asked, "Did your work drama get resolved?" I lifted the goblet and examined the bee figures pressed into the glass.

"Yes, for now, but I think it's going to call for an onsite meeting."

"Oh, were you hoping to avoid having to travel?" I was intrigued.

He nodded. "Yes, I had put off a business trip, but it looks like it's going to happen."

It disappointed me to know he'd be leaving. "Will it be for a long time?'

"Not if I can help it." He met my gaze. "I'd rather spend time with you."

A thrill rushed down my arms, making my skin tingle, and I was momentarily lost for words. "Same here."

"Your time here will go quickly. Have you made plans for the rest of your stay?"

"Yes . . . and no, not really. Basically, I'm just mooching around to discover places of interest I can write about. I'm never at a loss for ideas, and I'm forever thinking about creating a series. If you have any suggestions, I'm all ears." I sat back in the chair and watched a sailboat come in, expertly maneuvering into a slip.

I pointed to it. "This, just this, look at it." I took out my phone to get a photo, it was just too pretty for words. "I think I've fallen in love."

Nick chuckled. "It's not hard to do. The problem, though, is when you live here all your life, you tend to take it for granted." He stared out at the water.

I wondered what it would have been like to grow up in a place like this. "I can understand that. Sometimes it takes a new set of eyes to help you see what's right in front of you." I put my phone back in my purse.

Nick looked slightly startled. "That's a very interesting comment."

We fell silent, each caught up in our own thoughts, watching the boats coming in as evening fell. I wondered what the future held. Nick had come into my life totally unexpectedly, and we seemed to be like two puzzle pieces that had gone missing from the box. Found and fitting together. It was utterly bizarre to jump to that analogy, but it simply felt undeniable. At least from my perspective. But what about his? I wasn't yet sure, but whatever this was turning into—friendship, companionship, summer fling, who knew?—there was no doubt I liked being with him.

A lot.

The shift in my world after Rob's death had been tectonic for me. The deathbed promise he had forced me to make set these wheels in motion. Me righting my world. Exploring. Experiencing.

Living.

Now it held an unexpected temptation that had come out of the blue. And one that could knock me off my rails, if I wasn't careful.

I observed Nick from behind my fall of hair, taking in his expression with a sidelong glance. He was concentrating on the menu, and I opened mine.

"So, what were you like as a kid?" I asked.

"Hmm, like any other kid, I suppose. I swam, fished, walked the beach, played football, rode bikes, went to school." He lifted a finger to get the waiter's attention. "Would you like something to drink? We have a lot of great microbreweries around here if you like beer?"

"Sure, something light. Do you mind picking for me?" I had no clue about beer.

"No problem." Nick turned to the waiter.

I turned to watch the water as the harbor lights were

reflected back in a kaleidoscope upside-down world. A feeling rushed over me that I hadn't experienced before. It pushed out the worry and concern that was ever present, even though I did my best to suppress it. Right now, I was feeling . . . elation. Yes, that's the word. Elation. In this moment, all seemed right with the world.

I came back down to earth in time to hear Nick ask about biscuits.

"Biscuits?" I inquired.

He nodded. "Their buttery cheese biscuits are well known. Famous even, and served since they opened, oh, about forty-five years ago. They're superb."

"Ah, another bakery treasure," I said, and looked at the menu. Too many delicious-sounding selections.

"How so?" Nick asked, also looking at the menu.

I put the menu down. "The café over on the side street off Lincoln. They have a wonderful bakery. I mean, everything in there is mouth-watering. We had them for breakfast the other morning." I sipped from the water glass.

His face darkened. "Oh. Yes."

"Is something wrong?" I asked, surprised by the sudden change in his expression. The look I'd seen there, just moments ago, had vanished. What had triggered the change? It couldn't be the mention of the café, or could it?

"No, it's all good." He glanced at me over the menu, his eyes no longer holding the shadow of darkness from moments before.

"Do you know which café I mean?" I prodded gently.

"Yes, I do. It's a nice place, but I haven't been there in years. What are you having for a main course?" he asked, giving me the impression he was avoiding the subject.

Gone was the elation of the moment before, and a little seed of doubt was planted. Trying my best not to water it, I focused back on the menu.

All the items made my mouth tingle with anticipation, so I asked Nick. "Help! I don't know what to order."

He chuckled. "That's always the problem here. You can't go wrong with anything, unless you dislike something. But I think I'll get the fish. Do you like fish?" Nick lifted the painted rock used as a paperweight and slid his menu underneath.

"When in Rome." I smiled and put my menu with his.

We sat back when the waiter brought the beer.

"Did you go to school here or away?" I lifted the beer glass.

"I didn't go far, just to Seattle, didn't want to leave Dad after Mom had died."

"I'm sorry." I felt a pang about Rob, and a wave of sadness rushed over me.

"Is something wrong?" Nick asked, sliding his hand over mine.

I nodded, blinked a couple of times, and glanced at him. "Yes, it's just that memories come back when you least expect it."

"I totally understand."

I waited, hoping he would share more about his past.

A basket of warm buns was placed before us, forcing a momentary pause.

"Here we go." Nick moved the napkin aside and inhaled the warm aroma. "Here, you've got to try these. They are so good."

I took one. Putting it on my plate, I broke off a piece.

"For some reason, my entire trip seems to be about food so far. I'm going to have to be careful or . . ." I puffed out my cheeks.

He laughed, and I joined in.

I popped the piece of the bun in my mouth and closed my eyes. "Oh my God, this is heaven."

"Right? I usually take a box home with me so Dad can have some as well." Nick finished his and reached for another.

"It sounds like you come here often." I chased the bun with some beer and put the glass down, waiting for his reply.

He drew in a deep breath. "I have in the past. Not so much recently. But it never seems to change."

I wanted to ask who he'd dined with, and bit my tongue to keep from blurting out the question.

"Taking a box of biscuits home sounds perfect, and I might even venture to ask for the recipe. Do you think they'll share it?" It was difficult to move past the question that burned to be asked, but I did.

"I doubt it. I know they've been asked to share it over the years, and they always politely decline. It's a secret family recipe. Many have tried to recreate it, but it always falls short."

"Oh, darn. I knew two brothers who owned a butcher's shop, they had their own smokehouse on the farm where they did their meats and cheeses. There was a fire and they lost everything, including the big ol' recipe book that had been brought over from Germany with the family . . . I think a hundred years ago. Or something like that anyway." I had another piece of bun and a good sip of beer.

"That's quite sad actually." Nick shook his head.

"Right. They were going to rebuild due to customer demand, but the brothers eventually decided not to. Without the recipe book, they'd have to start from scratch."

"You'd think they'd have the recipes memorized." Nick frowned.

"You would, but they only had a handful. It ended up turning quite ugly when one brother accused the other of being careless and setting the shop on fire." I looked at Nick. "I'm sorry, that was a completely random thing to say. I guess

I was thinking this biscuit recipe should be kept safe, just in case."

"It was an interesting story." He pointed his finger at me. "Now that takes the cake. Family is family. It's a shame they let a tragedy break them apart."

"I agree." I laced my fingers together and watched the lights shift and repaint the water's surface into a new abstract pattern. I wanted another bun. "I didn't realize how hungry I was, but those buns are calling my name."

"Then have one. Or not. The meals are generous portions, so it's a good thing you're hungry."

I unfurled my fingers, wiped them on my napkin, and picked up the menu to have another look. I knew I said I was going to get the fish, but one last peek wouldn't hurt. I sucked in my lower lip. "This is going to be difficult."

He shook his head. "I thought you were going to have the fish?"

"I think I've changed my mind, have you?"

"No, I'm not one to change my mind once I've made a decision." His eyes met mine.

I had a feeling there was a double meaning in there somewhere, which made me all but forget I was holding a menu in my hand.

Chapter Thirteen

The sun set and the candles flickered on the tables, shifting the mood to a much more intimate setting.

"These are so simple yet very pretty." I turned the Mason jar filled with sand, a votive, and a variety of pebbles and shells. There was one on each of the tables, and it was the perfect touch. Our table was bathed in a soft romantic glow from the candlelight.

"Coffee?" Nick asked me.

I shook my head. "No, but thanks, though. I've learned that coffee after a meal like this only upsets my tummy. And I usually have a rough night." He smiled, and I asked, "TMI?"

"No, not at all. You seemed to enjoy the coffee at breakfast the other morning, so I thought I'd ask." He folded his napkin and put it beside his plate.

"It was the best coffee I think I've ever had. And to think it came from that battered coffee pot."

Nick threw back his head and laughed. A carefree sound that sent rivers of delight running through me.

"Yes, well, I treasure that pot. It means a lot to me, and I can always count on a perfect cup of coffee from it."

"How did it get so beat up?" I asked, genuinely interested.

"I tipped it over on the gas stove. It didn't take long for the flame to attack the handle, melt it. And in my haste to right it, I sent the pot and contents crashing on to the tiled floor."

"Sounds like something I could do without any problem at all. Poor thing. And you still kept it. That says something." I appreciated that he was showing his sensitive side.

"I did, and it traveled all over with me after I left Rome. I often think of Fio, my Italian landlady." He was quiet for a moment. "I'd be surprised if she was still alive. She seemed ancient when I was there."

"You could always reach out? Maybe visit again?" I suggested.

Nick nodded. "I could and I should. I feel guilty not keeping in touch with her. That pot is irreplaceable, for many reasons."

"I get that. But don't forget, you have that fancy steam engine of a coffee maker that'll do everything for you—including making a sandwich."

"Hmm, that big coffee maker wasn't my idea." He frowned, and I wondered what had caused another shadow to cross his face.

"No? It wasn't? Then why did you get it?" I tentatively prodded, as my mind slipped unbidden to Marissa. My stomach knotted, waiting to see what he would say, and I played with the edge of my napkin.

"No, it wasn't my idea. The damn thing cost almost two thousand dollars. We used it for maybe a couple of months."

We.

"Then why don't you sell it? When was the last time you used it?" I thought that might give some indication of a time frame.

"Over three years ago." He sat back in his chair and stared off, over the railing, directing his gaze at the harbor.

"That's a long time. It might not even work anymore," I suggested. And it was the perfect time to ask. "Who bought it?"

He faced me, and I held my breath at the complicated look on his face.

"It was for my wife." He said the words as if they were painful.

I was careful not to show how hearing them upset me.

"I see. So am I the other woman?" It needed to be asked, even if the answer wasn't what I wanted to hear.

The waiter showed up, and the moment was gone. He took the plates, asking if we wanted anything else, and left when we both replied no.

I waited. If Nick didn't answer, I would ask him again.

He drew in a breath, leaned forward and rested his forearms on the table, folding his fingers together. He looked down at the table and then up at me from under his eyebrows.

"No, you're not. She died." He didn't elaborate.

I gasped softly. "I'm sorry. That must have been so awful." The shock of hearing him say he had been married was harder than I imagined it would be. I leaned forward and placed my hand over his, careful not to let my fingers tremble.

"It was."

"How did she die?" I asked gently, though my head was spinning. One question was answered, but now I had so many more.

Was he over her?

He drew in a breath. "She drowned."

I let out a hiss and sat up straight. Just like Marissa Wright. "Oh! How horrible, I'm so sorry." I could feel his pain, and I was trying not to be distracted by the similarities.

"It was horrible actually. We really don't know what happened. She disappeared, presumed drowned, and I had no definite closure." He pushed his hand through his hair and sat back in his chair. "It still left me with a feeling of helplessness . . . guilt . . ."

I was quiet for a moment, watching myriad emotions play across his face. He still grieved. While I understood, it left me with as helpless a feeling as he described. We both were dealing with death, grief, and the difficulty of moving on.

"Oh, Nick, I understand. You loved her. It's hard to lose a love. You know I'm alone now, with both my parents and my brother gone." I heard the pain in my voice, and my throat tightened. "I still find it hard to talk about it, but I know talking helps."

Nick placed his other hand over the top of mine. We looked into each other's eyes.

He squeezed my fingers, and it was as if he'd reached in and touched my heart. I was so moved, I couldn't hold back the little catch in my breathing.

"No, it wasn't an easy time. For you, either. But here we both are." Nick rubbed his thumb across my knuckles and then pulled his hand back.

"You still have your dad. And I want you to know, I'm here to listen. We both share a tragedy."

The waiter came back with the check and interrupted the moment. While Nick dealt with the payment, I was trying to sort out my feelings. Our conversation had been raw, and a heaviness weighed me down. Talking helped, but it also poked at the wound.

He'd told me he was a widower and his wife had drowned. I chewed on my thumbnail and ran through it all in my head. Could it just be a coincidence? I didn't know her name and it struck me I also didn't know Nick's last name. Our friendship evolved organically and it never occurred to me to ask him. His wife's name, and his last name, would be the defining factor.

The waiter left and I needed to move. Walk around. I was glad Nick had trusted me, told me about his wife, but I also didn't want to think about him being married to someone else. Could she have been his great love? A love that would never be matched? How did that bode for future relationships? I was getting way ahead of myself. Everyone had a past. I just was still hoping his didn't include one Ms Wright.

Nick stood and pulled my chair out for me.

I tried to let go of my agitation, and take each moment as it came. I smiled.

"Thank you very much for dinner, it was lovely. It's such a beautiful night, would you like to walk along the dock for bit?"

"You're welcome. I'm glad you enjoyed your meal." With his hand at the small of my back, he guided me into the restaurant. "Sure, we can check out all the expensive boats."

"It's so pretty," I said as we strolled between the yachts. I slipped my arm through Nick's unthinkingly, and he stiffened slightly. It was a habit; I would do it with Rob. When I realized what I'd done, combined with his reaction, I pulled my arm out quickly and looked up at him. "Oh, ah—"

But Nick smiled down at me, shaking his head. He offered his arm to me this time. "Don't be sorry, it was nice."

He took my hand and slid my arm back through his, but I could still sense the reservation I'd picked up on. It left me slightly unsettled, and I resisted the urge to lean into him. Where we touched flooded me with warmth.

"I used to walk like this with my brother," I explained.

"Tell me about him." Nick's deep voice held a comforting tone.

I glanced up, met his eyes. "Okay . . ." I paused and took a deep breath. "We were twins."

"Twins! I wasn't expecting that. How amazing." He was genuinely surprised—a response that was all too familiar.

"It was. And we were close, as twins are. For a brother and sister, we were joined at the hip. Mainly beginning to go our own ways in high school. We remained very close, especially after Mom and Dad died. We had our own lives, obviously, but lived not too far from each other, in DC." I tried to smile. "Then he got sick and gave his best fight."

"I'm sorry, Lizzie." Nick let go of my arm and put his around my shoulder, pulling me in tight to his side.

I wrapped my arm around his waist. We walked a few steps in silence.

"It's tough losing people," Nick said. "I'm thankful I still have my dad."

"Oh, you're lucky. I miss my parents and Rob terribly." I rested my head on his shoulder and didn't fight the wave of grief that suddenly consumed me. This time, Nick's body was far more welcoming than it had been when I slipped my arm through his.

"And there's nobody else?" he inquired.

Was he asking if I was involved?

I shook my head. "No, there isn't. There was, but then there wasn't. Not many people can be a good partner when there's life drama going on around them. Especially when the relationship is casual and not committed." I was vague, not wanting to dive too deep into any of my previous relationships. Mainly because they didn't matter anymore. "I put all my focus into Rob when he got sick." I shrugged my shoulders.

We turned down along a floating dock that formed a pathway between two others. It created an interesting sensation as it moved gently under our feet.

We stopped midway, the land on the other side of the water a dark smudge under the crescent moon. It hovered in the sky, a graceful beacon scattering its reflection on the water like a silver disc fallen from the sky.

Chapter Fourteen

"I adore watching the moon," Lizzie sighed.

Nick looked up. "I rarely pay attention."

He liked the way she leaned into him. At first, when she slid her arm through his, his response hadn't been overly welcoming. Lizzie sensed it too, and he was quick to smooth over the moment.

She understood loss. It was a kinship they shared, both living with the fallout of events neither had any control over. After losing Ari, he had no interest in dating. He'd had a couple of awkward set-ups, thanks to business friends who wouldn't take no for an answer. He hadn't been optimistic, for a few reasons—mainly the fact that he simply wasn't ready. The times he had gone out only resulted in him retreating more into his shell. It was all superficial. It wasn't until meeting Lizzie that he'd felt a slight shift in his thinking. Only time would tell. And that wasn't something they had much of.

"It's so magical, looking at the night sky. I imagine I might see an object drift past, or . . . something like that."

He glanced down at her. "I think that surprises me."

"What? That I keep an eye out for aliens?" She laughed, and he did as well.

"Nothing wrong with that," he reassured her. "What was the expression in the movie *Contact*? If it was only us, wouldn't that be a waste of space? Or something like that, anyway." He couldn't believe he remembered the line.

"It's one of my favorite movies!"

She smiled at him, and for a brief second his heart beat faster. He said softly, "There's something inviting about the path of moonlight on the water. Like we could step on it and walk into a new world."

Did I really say that?

"You're a romantic." She smiled and squeezed his waist. "I like it."

Her comment surprised him, and he was glad she didn't laugh when he said it. He'd never been called romantic before, and he rather liked it. Ari had said they were both compatible that way, with neither of them being romantic. He never really knew if that's how she wanted it to be, or not. He had failed her in so many ways, but he had to shake that off. He was here with a warm, responsive, open woman, so unlike Ari.

"I guess I must be," he chuckled. "Maybe you bring it out in me."

They moved on and stepped carefully along the floating dock as it shifted and swayed under them. He held her carefully after she stumbled a bit when the wake of a passing boat made the dock shift suddenly. Turning at another corner, they emerged on to a dock that led back to shore.

Nick wasn't ready for the evening to end, and that was unexpected. He slowed his step to draw out the next few minutes. Lizzie was silent, as was he. But he was enjoying having her beside him, their arms around each other, and their comfortable silence was a balm to his soul. She didn't make demands, or complain. With her, it was just . . . easy.

He didn't think he'd ever had that kind of quiet peace with his wife. Nick frowned, recalling their last conversation. Well, not a conversation, but an argument. It had been the worst feeling, especially as he was just leaving the house. His trip had been tainted by it, and he'd wanted to apologize as soon as he got home. But that hadn't been possible.

Lizzie rested her head against him. He looked down, and a rush of emotion nudged at the grief . . . and guilt . . . that touched him for the millionth time. Would he ever be able to get over it and move on? The moon's rays bathed them in silvery light, shining off her hair. The sense of peace overwhelmed him.

They walked in silence to his car.

"Thank you for tonight," she said. "I enjoyed it, and I hope we can do something again."

She wasn't shy about saying what she wanted, and Nick appreciated her directness. Even if he was slightly on edge that she might drop a question he wasn't ready to answer.

"I'd like that. Very much." Nick held open the car door for her, waiting until she was seated before closing it. Walking around the rear, he ran his fingertips along the trunk, smiling at the new feeling of happiness that flowed through him.

He owed it completely to Lizzie. He slid into his seat and started the engine. The throaty growl of the motor never failed to make his heart pick up a beat. He loved this car. He brought it out in good weather only and called it his fair-weather car.

"This is nice," Lizzie said, and ran her hand along the top of the door by the window.

"Thank you. It's fun." He'd bought the McLaren just after Ari died. Needing something to take his mind off what had happened. Its speed made him feel alive, and he had the tickets to prove it.

Nick pulled out of the parking space and headed back to Bicker Beach. The cockpit lights glowed on her face. He glanced at her often, unable to get enough of looking at her. What was she thinking? He couldn't even guess.

"I like it here. In Savage Cove," she commented.

He didn't think there was a reason to reply. As much as he wanted to say he enjoyed having her here, he hesitated. Tonight had been a big step for him. Going on a date and letting his guard down. It surprised him that he had been able to open up to Lizzie and tell her a little about Ari. He hadn't discussed his wife with anyone since she died. Not even his father.

A short while later, after a quiet but comfortable journey, Nick pulled into Lizzie's driveway. The house was dark, except for the porch light and the soft glow of a lamp behind a curtain.

Nick followed her up the path between the shrubbery to the front door. She unlocked it and pushed it open. He wasn't sure what he would say if she invited him in. For the first time that night, he felt an awkwardness between them.

Lizzie turned back and looked up at him. The sound of the ocean on the other side of the house, coupled with the breeze and chorus of night bugs, was like nature's symphony.

She lifted her hand and pointed with her thumb at the door. He knew what she meant. There was concern in her eyes, and she pulled her lip between her teeth. That moment told him she was feeling uncertain. Tonight was not the night. Relief mixed with regret, because he wasn't certain either.

"I enjoyed our time together," he said. "Thank you for agreeing to come."

"Of course I'd come. I liked it too. I should be thanking you." Her lips parted and her eyes grew wider.

The wind blew a strand of hair across her cheek. He reached out to tuck it behind her ear and allowed his fingers to linger. He stared down at her, so beautiful in the night. The hint of eyeliner accentuated her gorgeous eyes, which seemed to change depending on the light. Right now, they were dark, indigo, and so mysterious. He wanted to pull her into his arms.

Lizzie raised her hand and placed it over his, never looking away from him. He lowered his head closer to her, and placed his other hand on her cheek, brushing his thumb across her lips.

Nick's emotions boiled inside. They'd been non-existent for so long, he hadn't been sure if he'd ever feel again. He breathed deep, pulling in her essence. She had cracked the part of him he'd closed off after his wife's death. That glancing blow of realization was welcoming, even as it shook him to the core.

I looked up at Nick. The light played across his features under the overhang of the porch roof. He leaned down, and I held my breath. He was going to kiss me, and I wanted him to. I lifted my face. Our eyes remained locked on each other as his head came lower.

I was sure the pounding of my heart would be the death of me. My lips parted. He lowered his eyes, and I almost moaned as I waited for the touch of his mouth on mine.

He shifted slightly, his lips warm against my cheek. His gentle touch set me on fire. Heat rushed through my body like a flash. His mouth lingered on me and I raised my hand, touching his chest with my palm, feeling his heart race beneath it.

We were still for the briefest moment, staring at each other. The only sound was our breathing and the breeze rustling through the trees. Our special music, compliments of Mother Nature. I drew in a ragged breath, waiting for him. Waiting for what was to come. This was our first date, and I felt I had to be sensitive to him. He had shared a little about his wife, so I was aware of his conflict. I'd seen the heartbreak in the text that just might have been from him.

I sensed the importance of this moment. Nick appeared to be holding his breath, and then the slow smile took over his mouth and his eyes softened. It was okay. He was okay.

I cupped his cheeks and pulled him toward me. I lifted my face and whimpered when our lips touched. It was gentle, hot, and promised so much more. I wanted more. But did he?

"Nick." I whispered his name against his lips, inhaling the scent of him.

"Lizzie." He lifted his head, looking slightly dazed, and I was lost in his eyes. "I'm glad we did this."

"Me too." I couldn't make my voice any stronger.

We continued to gaze at each other, and then he said softly, "See you on the beach."

"Yes, on the beach." I nodded and stepped back to lean on the door jamb.

An unnamable feeling built in my chest when he turned and walked to his car. It was suffocating, and a surge of anxiety overtook me. I fisted my hands, and my nails cut into my palms. I didn't want him to leave, and yet I wasn't quite ready to have him stay. I was also very aware of his feelings, and I knew he wasn't ready either. I leaned my cheek on the edge of the door.

He stopped at the end of the path and turned around. My heart leaped. For the briefest moment, I thought he was going to come back.

"I'm leaving on a business trip for a few days, the day after tomorrow. Would you like to have lunch before I leave?"

"Yes, I would." My heart soared.

He smiled and nodded. "Great. How about I pick you up?"

"Okay." It was hard to contain the range of emotions I had racing through me.

"Tomorrow I have meetings, but I have a late flight the next day. We could do an early lunch and I'd have you back home before I need to leave for the airport. Pick you up around ten?"

I nodded. "Perfect. Looking forward to it."

Nick waved when he got in his car. I waved back, watching until the taillights of his car disappeared around the bend in the road and the roar of his engine faded.

I pressed my hand to my chest, took a deep breath, and stumbled over the threshold into the empty cottage. The door shut, and I leaned against it.

It was like he'd taken a part of me with him, and I was bereft.

Without turning on any lights, I walked through the dark to my bedroom, toed off my sandals, dropped my dress on the floor, and flopped on to the bed, pulling the comforter over me.

To my surprise, tears welled up, and I cried.

I cried for reasons I couldn't comprehend. I had no reason to cry. Things were fine. Right?

But cry I did, and with no energy to figure out why. It was cleansing. I'd been in a lot of turmoil, surrounded by grief over the past few years, and it was like it all came to a head tonight. I'd thought I was okay, but clearly I wasn't. Savage Cove held some kind of magic, or calm, a special something that was helping me begin to feel like my old self.

Free. Light. Optimistic.

So why was I crying now?

As the tears subsided and I closed my eyes, I thought of Nick. He was alive. Down the beach. And I was seeing him again.

Just before I drifted off to sleep, my last thought was that we should have exchanged phone numbers.

Chapter Fifteen

I pulled the AirPods from my ears when I entered the café. I loved Taylor Swift's song "Lover", and hummed the tune. I placed my stuff at a table to save the spot before ordering. It was busy again. But then, when was it ever not busy?

"It's good to see you again." The barista from the other day greeted me.

I glanced down at her tag to remind myself of her name. "Thanks, Wendy, I've fallen in love with the place." I shrugged and smiled. "Can't help it. Your food and coffee are my jam."

Wendy smiled, but I sensed it was robotic, as was her reply. "I'm glad to hear that. It's wonderful to get new customers who keep coming back. What can I get you?"

"I'll have whatever specialty coffee of the day you have going, please. And, mmm, let me see. Oh, that looks good." I pointed to a cupcake. My sweet tooth was in overdrive.

"Excellent choice. We tried something new. It's a take on red velvet, with a secret treat inside." She sounded as if she was reading off a script.

Wendy set one on a plate and placed it in front of me. She turned to make my coffee and glanced back over her shoulder. "Go sit down and I'll bring it to you. You want to keep it a surprise, don't you?"

"I don't want any trouble. But yes, I do like surprises." What woman didn't?

She shooed me with her hand. "Off you go, then."

I picked up the plate and carried it back to my table, moving my bag to the floor by the window. I settled in my seat, turning the plate to get a good look at my tempting treat. I'd wait to taste it until my coffee arrived. I absolutely needed to take a photo of it and post it on Insta. My followers seemed to love foodie pics.

I pulled out my new phone. I was thankful I'd increased my iCloud storage so I could take photos to my heart's content. But I still had to download some apps I needed.

"Excuse me."

I looked up and smiled when I saw it was the classy older woman from the other day. "Hi."

"Is anyone sitting here? Do you mind if I share the table?" she asked. "It seems everything else is taken."

I shook my head. "No, of course not. Please join me." I reached forward to move my stuff to the side of the table, and slid my chair close to the window.

"Let's move the table a bit to give you more room," I suggested. I pulled, and she pushed it. The legs made a horrendous screech on the wooden floor.

"Oof, that was loud." I winced and glanced around.

A few people looked our way, but there were no evil stares.

"It certainly was." She sat down, putting her bag on the floor beside her.

Wendy approached with my drink and a cup of something hot for my new companion.

"Hello, Claire. I'm surprised to see you.' Wendy stood back after placing the drinks on the table, and crossed her arms. Even though it was a casual move, it held a distinct air of aloofness.

Claire nodded her head, glanced at Wendy, then back down to the cup placed before her. "Thank you. Really? I tend to come in often. It's good to see you're busy."

"Hmm, well, I guess you come in when I'm not working." Wendy glanced around. "Yes, it's getting better all the time. I appreciate all the new customers. And those who continue to come back." She bobbed her head at both of us and then walked away.

What was that about? There seemed to be a strange tension between the two women. I glanced over at Wendy, who was watching our table.

Was it my imagination, or was there some underlying meaning to the exchange I'd just witnessed?

"I saw you the other day," Claire commented. She picked up her mug and inspected the contents before taking a sip.

"Um, yes, I've been here a few times. I've seen you before too, you were reading a book. I'm Lizzie."

"Hi, Lizzie. Yes, I usually come in on Monday and Tuesday mornings. The coffee is wonderful here, and I find it peaceful. Normally." I half expected to see her roll her eyes, or make some kind of face, but she didn't.

I thought it odd that she added "normally" to her sentence.

I took the fork and gently cut through the cupcake. "Would you like some? There's a treat inside." I used my fork and pushed aside some crumbs to expose a big chocolate-covered strawberry. "Oh, look at that. I can cut it in half so we can share."

Claire leaned forward and looked at it. "That does look interesting! Maybe just a piece? Thank you, that's very kind."

"Not at all." I broke off a piece and separated our cupcake portions on my plate.

Claire took hers, and I popped mine in my mouth.

"Oh, yum." It was delicious.

"I agree. I'll give her that. She has creativity where food is concerned."

"Wendy?"

Claire nodded.

Hmm, there was something there. Ever since I'd received that text, it seemed as if mystery surrounded me. "Well, that is just like a party in my mouth."

We laughed, and the tension in Claire's face eased.

"Have you moved to Savage Cove?" she asked me.

I shook my head, put my fingertips over my mouth, and swallowed the piece of cake I was chewing. "No, I'm just here till the end of July. Then I move on."

The image of Nick flashed through my mind, and the thought of leaving unsettled me.

"What brings you to our fair village?" Claire inquired, dabbing her lip with a napkin.

"Well, I'm kind of doing an eat, pray, love thing, if you will. But I'm mainly fulfilling a promise to my brother and trying to establish a new career."

Claire raised her eyebrows. "That sounds very intriguing. I'd like to know more, if you wish to share." She picked up her cup and looked at me with interest.

I had the strangest sensation in Claire's company. Almost as if she were a mother figure. Someone I was tempted to share things with. Heaviness filled my chest, and I glanced down at the crumb-littered plate.

"It's okay, you don't have to talk about it."

I looked up at her.

She leaned toward me. "I understand . . . and I'm a stranger, after all." Claire's eyes met mine, and I saw concern etched in their green depths.

I drew in a quick breath, and blinked. "Um . . ." There was something about her that reached deep inside and gave me the urge to be open with her. I lifted my cup and took a long drink. Putting it down, I held it between my fingers and glanced at her. "Rob, my brother, died eighteen months ago."

"My condolences." She reached over to touch my hand. "Was it sudden?"

I shook my head. "Thank you, and no. It wasn't, and it was quite awful. We were twins."

Claire's sharp gasp surprised me, and I glanced up at her.

"How tragic for you."

"The first few months were tough. Our parents had died years before, and it was only us. So it did feel like a part of me had been cut out, you know. Twin stuff."

"I've heard the connection of twins is unique. And for you to have lost your parents too. I'm so sorry."

I nodded. "Thank you. And yes, the twin thing is real, even though we were brother and sister, and not the same sex, we still had it. Twintuition." I sighed. "That part of me will be missing forever. But," I wagged my finger, "he made me promise not to give up on life once he was gone. To be adventurous and explore, live life to the fullest." I smiled and shrugged a shoulder. "So here I am."

A quiet moment stretched out between us.

Claire was first to speak. "I think that's wonderful. I'm sure it was extremely difficult. But as you said, here you are. Good for you. Do you have plans after your stay in Savage Cove?"

"Still deciding. I'm desperate to go to Indonesia. Bali, Thailand, and depending on how things go here . . ." I paused, and knew that meant with Nick. "I'll decide in a few weeks. But I have a flight booked. Have you been there?"

Claire looked like someone who would travel far and wide. She was intriguing, down-to-earth, tanned, and fit. I couldn't peg an age on her, and I wasn't going to ask. I decided I wanted to be her when I grew up.

"Funny you should ask, but yes. I did a lot of traveling until a few years ago. Then I came home to water my roots here." She tapped a long finger on the table.

"Are you from here?"

Claire nodded. "Yes, born and raised, but I had a terrible case of wanderlust."

I laughed. "You and me both! Although, I haven't done nearly as much as I'd like, hence my promise to Rob."

Claire leaned forward and fixed me with her very intense eyes. "Then feed that wanderlust. Go and do the things you want to do. Now, while you can. Don't settle. Days are long, but the years are short."

I sat back, at a loss for words. That came out of the blue, yet it struck a deep chord with me.

"Oh, um . . . that's sort of my plan, unless I get stuck along the way somehow."

Claire finished her coffee and gathered her bags, looking over her shoulder to the counter and then back at me.

"It's been delightful getting to know you, Lizzie. I hope we cross paths again, but I must be off. Places to go and people to see." Claire stood and touched me on the shoulder, then turned and left the café.

"Me too." I finally found my voice, but Claire was gone.

* * *

125

Nick liked visiting his dad at the boathouse. It was as if he was stepping into a different world, even if it was only down the path from his house and through the trees.

Dad's house had a feeling of being full. Which was kind of an odd thing to say, but it did. He'd renovated and decorated it with surprising taste. It was comfortable, welcoming, and reminded him a lot of when he was a kid. Maybe that's why he liked it here. The only person missing was Mom.

He looked over his shoulder to the kitchen. Dad had just lifted the kettle off the stove, silencing the piercing whistle. Nick smiled. His dad was quite the tea granny, a hangover from Mom, he supposed. She'd done a good job molding Dad to her liking.

"So, what's new, son?" Walter asked, the cups and saucers clattering on the tray. "Before you answer that, let's go outside and take the dogs."

On a table in the shade, Nick sat and watched the dogs jump and play, while Dad poured the tea.

He chuckled. "You do love your tea, don't you?" He shook his head with a smile, and took the cup and saucer his dad handed to him.

"I sure do. And as Mom always said, it tastes much better in a china cup. So, don't even get started on me about that," Walter said as he placed two cups and saucers from a bone-china teaset on the table.

"Don't worry, I won't." Nick chuckled, but he liked to see Dad using Mom's china.

"Okay, now you can answer."

"Answer what?" Nick teased him.

"My question, what's new?"

"Oh, nothing much really. Work mainly." He paused and decided there was no harm in telling Dad about Lizzie. "Houdini did his disappearing act last week. I found him way down the beach, catching sticks a woman was throwing for him."

His dad sat forward, teacup paused halfway to his mouth. "Oh? A woman?"

"Yes, a woman. I've seen her a few times. She's nice." That was about all he wanted to share for the time being.

"Does she have a name?"

"Yes, she does. Lizzie."

The dogs started to argue over a stick, and Nick took the moment to get up and sort out the squabble before he could be questioned any further. He'd seen his father's furrowed brow and knew a question would be forthcoming.

"Houdini, drop it!" Nick ran over and grabbed the stick.

Walter jumped up and pulled another one out of a pile, and gave it to Candy.

"There now, no fighting, you two," Walter instructed, giving both dogs a pat on the head. They flopped down, and each one chewed contentedly. "Come on, tea's getting cold." He held out a plate. "Have a cookie."

Nick took one. "Wow, when did you become so civilized? Tea and cookies." He smiled at his father

"You just haven't come around at tea time often enough."

"Tea time?" Nick raised his eyebrows and then nodded in agreement. He was relieved his dad didn't probe for more information about Lizzie, and finished his tea.

"Another cuppa?"

Nick grinned at his dad holding up the teapot.

"Sure." He held his teacup out for more.

Chapter Sixteen

I stood by the front door and looked between the blinds, waiting for Nick to drive up. I had checked myself in the mirror more than once. My hair was pulled back into a loose bun, and I'd decided minimal make-up was best. I never really used much to begin with, and walking on the beach had given me a tanned glow.

I'd put a subtle touch of eyeliner and mascara on my eyes, and some gloss on my lips, but I'd painted my toes and fingernails last night in a bright shade of coral. Now I worried it was too vibrant. I wrung my hands and told myself to own it.

My room appeared as if a cyclone had dropped out of the sky and left in a hurry, with clothes strewn over my bed, on the chair, and some on the floor. I needed the exact right outfit, and had pretty much ransacked my closet—not that there was a lot to choose from. But Cyclone Lizzie had left her mark.

One last look in the mirror by the front door and I nodded. Yes, this was perfect. A pair of turquoise shorts, an eyelet-lace white tank top, with a dove-grey sweater stuffed into my satchel. Good for warmth and sun. Today was sunny, but you never knew what kind of weather was around the corner.

I heard the thump of a car door, and my heart leaped into my throat. Why did it feel like I was going on my first date? I had to calm myself down, before Nick knocked on the front door.

I opened it, and knew I had a ridiculously big smile on my face.

"Hi. Please come in." My heart fluttered, and it was difficult to catch my breath. I wasn't expecting the hug, but it thrilled me when he swept me into his arms.

"Hi, yourself. Ready?" Nick's presence filled the room.

He let me go, and I grabbed my bag while completely aware of him next to me. His height and musculature made him even more attractive to me. I couldn't deny it was nice to be with a man who was taller than me.

"I am. Just a couple of things . . ." I grabbed a scarf hanging on the coat tree beside the door, and stuffed it into my bag. Then I remembered I had a sun visor in a bag hanging in the closet.

I locked the door behind us, and we walked around my SUV. He was parked behind it.

"Oh my. A different car." It surprised me that he'd arrived in a convertible.

He opened the passenger door for me. I hopped in, put my bag at my feet, and waited while he settled into the driver's seat.

"I was thinking it would be perfect for a drive along the coast. I have a few hours before I have to leave for the airport. We could stop on the way at a food truck, or whatever."

"I love the idea! I'll leave it up to you to take us wherever. It's a glorious day, and this is a perfect way to spend it. Very nice car, by the way. Great day for the top down."

"Exactly what I was thinking." He glanced at me with a smile. The roar of the car engine had nothing on the hopped-up beating of my heart.

"Just how many cars do you have?" I asked teasingly, taking in his appearance while he focused on the road ahead.

"A few." His smile made the dimple on his cheek pop. I hadn't noticed it before, and was enchanted. "A utility vehicle, this Range Rover, the car I picked you up in the other night, and my pride and joy." He gave me a sly smile.

"Your pride and joy? What kind of car would that be?" I inquired, now very curious.

"You'll see, one day. We'll keep it a surprise for now, how's that?" He stepped on the gas and the vehicle jump forward, pressing me back into the seat. My head fell back against the headrest and I laughed, raising my arms. We zoomed down the road, kicking up stones behind us.

"This is wonderful!" I yelled into the roar of the wind.

We drove along, under an endless blue sky, puffed with cottony clouds. It was the perfect day.

I rolled my head to look at him. Casually confident, driving with his elbow on the door, fingers on the steering wheel, and his bent knee resting against the side, his other hand looped at the bottom of the steering wheel. He wore a striped golf shirt which accentuated his chest, arms, and the tuft of dark hair in the V-neck. His shirt was tucked into grey golf shorts, his long legs were tanned, muscled, and he wore a pair of Sperry's. I wondered if he sailed. If he did, it could be one more piece of the puzzle. But I didn't want to think about it now, and refocused on us.

Together.

I was falling more and more under his spell. My imagination was running away with me, and it wasn't the sun that warmed me, it was intimate thoughts of the two of us.

The sun was bright, though. Reaching between us, he took a pair of sunglasses from the console and put them on. He turned to me with a big smile, his teeth even and white against his tanned face. The aviators reflected my image back at me.

"Have you had anything to eat yet?" he asked.

I nodded. "Yes, but just a yogurt parfait this morning." I rested my elbow on the door and watched the scenery flash by.

"I was thinking we'll stop at a fish shack. How does that sound?"

"I like that idea." Could this man get any more perfect? Our eyes caught, and I smiled.

He reached over and squeezed my hand, then laced his fingers with mine. That simple touch, coupled with my intimate thoughts a moment ago, completely unhinged me. I fought to keep my volcanic feelings buried, but the pressure was growing to an almost unbearable point. I breathed deep and looked up at the sky. This day was shaping up to be a highlight.

About an hour into the drive, Nick pulled up to a lunch shack on the side of the road with a view of the water. He'd heard this was a good place, but had never been.

"You're my guinea pig. We're going to taste test, and see if the reviews are correct." He pulled the vehicle under a shady tree, hopped out, and came around to Lizzie's side of the car to open the door. "Madam." He held out his hand and waited for her to place hers in his.

Just another casual reason for touching her.

He'd done a lot of thinking about them over the last couple of days. Kissing Lizzie had been a huge step for him. For the first time since Ari, he was actually connecting with a woman. More and more, he was warming to the idea of seeing where this would go with Lizzie. But there was still an element of wariness, not least the fact that she was leaving in just a few short weeks. They each had their own type of pain that had kept them in emotional turmoil, not wanting to be hurt again. Both had experienced very different types of grief, but grief nonetheless. It might have been easier to embark on a meaningless, time-limited fling, no emotions involved. But Nick realized he wasn't down for just a summer romance. It wasn't his style; it seemed he was an all-or-nothing kind of guy. He didn't know yet if Lizzie felt the same way about relationships.

Could he open his heart to someone again, though? It was a risk. He'd loved Ari, even if it hadn't been easy. She'd been alluring, a challenge, and could make life very difficult. But they'd also had some good times, exciting times, especially in the early days. It was as their marriage progressed that their differences had become ever more pronounced. Still, the ending had not been what he'd expected.

Nick shook off his thoughts of Ari, and turned his attention to the woman by his side.

Lizzie had appeared in his life so casually, softly, easily, materializing out of the mist that first day they met on the beach. If Houdini hadn't taken off that day, they wouldn't have met.

But, if you believed in destiny, then at some point they would have encountered each other. Nick wasn't a fan of putting the future in destiny's hands. He preferred to make his own path in life. Although others would argue that paths were put in front of you thanks to destiny.

He looked down at her. Her blonde hair was blowing like spun gold in the sunbeams. She'd brought so much light into his life already, when for so long, after Ari, he'd felt only darkness.

Nick frowned, feeling unsettled. If destiny were actually a

thing, then what happened with Ari was meant to be. He had a hard time accepting it.

"This is a wonderful view." Lizzie's voice sparkled with joy, and he embraced her light and energy.

Fingers entwined, they walked across the parking lot to the food truck. It was busy, and they fell into line.

She leaned closer to him and whispered, "There's too much choice." She pointed at the menu painted on the side of the Sea Snacks food truck. "I can't decide."

"Is this a habit of yours?" He gave her a teasing nudge.

"What do you mean?" She looked up at him.

She was stunning, and it took his breath away. Her eyes were now an almost translucent turquoise, like the clear waters of a tropical paradise.

He almost forgot what he'd said. "Ah, deciding what you want to eat. I think every time we've had a meal together, you can't decide.

"Of course I can't! I love food and want to eat it all, but obviously I mustn't."

"Okay, how about this, then. Whatever I get, you pick something else, and we can share it so you taste both," Nick suggested, and enjoyed the way her eyes danced.

"Great idea!"

"Good. We probably can't go wrong with pretty much anything on the board. Let's see what others are ordering as we get closer."

They moved up in the line, and the whole time, Lizzie held his hand. Nick liked the feel of her next to him, and he circled back to destiny. Did everything happen for a reason?

Nick was right; I hadn't realized how indecisive I was when it came to food. Why? I had no clue, but I just accepted it. He was also right about choosing the food, so I ordered the fisherman's platter, which was a sampler of everything, including French fries, which I was addicted to.

We walked down the path to the waterfront, carrying our food boxes, and picked a picnic table closer to the water.

"Mmm, this is nice." I put my box of food on the picnic table and stepped over the wooden seat to sit on the bench.

I was in the shade under the umbrella, Nick sat across from me, also in the shade. The sun was high and warm, and I felt a little crispy after the drive in the convertible with the sun beating down on us. The breeze coming off the water was refreshing.

"I agree." Nick pulled the tab on his can of soda, taking a long drink. "I was thirsty."

"You should have told me, I brought water."

"This did the trick." He put the can down and picked up a fork, stabbing at the fries in his box like he was playing whack-a-mole.

"Hungry too, I see," I teased and then dove into mine with the same gusto.

I didn't need all the fussiness of fine dining, white linen and silver. I wasn't opposed to being wined and dined, not at all, but I was just as happy with plastic forks, paper napkins, and yummy food in a box under an umbrella on a picnic table.

Nick let out a sigh.

I glanced at him. "Okay?" I asked.

He nodded, and lifted the can of soda. "I was hoping to avoid this business trip."

"It must be difficult to fly off regularly. Living out of a bag from day to day." Which was pretty much my life since honoring Rob's promise.

I wondered if there was more bothering him. Now and then,

I caught a thoughtful look on his face. I ripped open a salt package and sprinkled some on my fries.

We were silent as we doctored up our food. I squirted a pool of ketchup into the corner of the box, and my thoughts drifted to Marissa. After the conversation we'd had the other night, I was pretty confident my Marissa and his wife were the same woman, but I couldn't find a way to ask him outright afraid to ruin the mood or, more likely, afraid of the answer. I wondered if I could confirm it if I found out where she'd lived? If it was the same house, then I'd know for certain. Or be as sure as was possible. I scoffed quietly, never expecting to become such a sleuth. And all thanks to receiving that haunting text.

"Something up?" Nick asked.

I looked at him. "Mmm? What do you mean?"

"You made a snorty sound." He took a bite of his fish taco.

"A snorty sound?" I giggled and shook my head, pushing down the thought that this could be an opening to tell him more. "Just thinking of something. Where are you headed tonight?" I asked as I speared a fry and dragged it through some ketchup.

He tipped the can of soda, had a long drink before answering. "Staying in the country and on the red-eye to New York. Quick trip, this time."

"New York! Strangely enough, it's a place I've never been," I said as I picked through the scallops in my box and popped one in my mouth.

"A company I consult for is in New York. They have offices around the world, but their head office is there. The executive team is flying in for their annual board meeting. I'll be there for a couple of days and then home."

He smiled, and a sweet rush of heat swept through me.

"Oh, that reminds me. I finally have my new phone. I should

have given you the number days ago, but I kept forgetting. It took ages to get it, longer than they'd said. Initially, it was only to be a few days."

"What happened to your old phone?" He pushed his phone across the picnic table. "Here, put your number in my contacts, and I'll do the same to yours."

"I lost it and had to order a new one."

He held his hand out. I put my phone in his palm and picked up his.

I found his contacts and, before adding mine, I hesitated for the briefest moment to consider looking for Marissa's name, but I couldn't do it.

We took a moment to enter our info and then re-exchanged phones.

"That's too bad. You couldn't find it?"

I shook my head. "Ah, nope, I wasn't going to the bottom of the Strait of Juan de Fuca to get it.

"Really? How did you manage that?" I could see he was holding back laughter.

"Funny, not funny. Oh, I don't know. It just happened when I was taking pictures of a visiting whale and her baby."

"Lucky you. And you survived a week without a cell, imagine that." He gave me a wink and took another bite of his fish taco.

"Well, kind of. I bought an older phone to tide me over for emergencies. It was cheap. I couldn't even tell you the number." Okay, here we go. The topic was rearing its head. I was almost about to tell him the number must have belonged to someone else, because of the random text. But I just couldn't bring myself to. It concerned me that, if I did it now, it would lead to the bigger conversation I knew we had to have. But doing that before he left on a trip seemed like such bad timing.

Instead, I said, "Now if you would like to text me while you are away, you can." I smiled, doing my best not to feel like I'd missed an opportunity to fess up. Instead, I picked up my lemonade. Finding the straw with my tongue, I pulled it between my lips and sucked up a mouthful.

Nick watched me, and his eyes held mine for a beat until he cleared his throat and spoke. "I will. You can count on it." His voice was low and intimate, sending tingles along my spine.

I swallowed and put the cup down. The sexual tension between us was growing. At least I thought so, despite the moments of hesitation I'd sometimes sensed from him. But I understood. As a widower it must be so difficult to let go and move on.

"I'd like that." Heat flushed my cheeks. "A lot."

He reached over and touched my fingers. The tingles shifted into a sensual thumping.

A seagull squawked and flew in to land on the end of our picnic table, breaking the heated moment.

"Bird, poor timing." I threw a fry, and it took off, neatly catching it mid-air.

"Now we'll never get rid of him." Nick watched the seagull hover near our table before it flew off to a more interesting food stash, and then disappeared over the treetops.

Suddenly, the words tumbled out of my mouth. It just happened, and I supposed it was meant to.

"You know how we touched briefly on the tragedy in our lives? I hope you don't mind me asking." He glanced at me, and I shifted on the bench. "We share the loss of someone, and I didn't have anyone to talk to about it. Do you have anyone to talk to? Because I'm here and a great listener."

As I spoke the words, I knew my offer wasn't born just out of curiosity about Marissa. It came from my growing feelings for Nick, and my desire to understand him on a deeper level.

"Thank you. Maybe one day. I appreciate it, but it's a topic I prefer not to dwell on. A very dark place in my past."

"I understand." I was disappointed, but whatever this was between us needed patience. All my instincts were screaming it at me.

He picked up his fork and continued eating, which I took as closing down the conversation. So we ate. The mood shifted, as it did when the weather changed, a quiet chill before a storm. Only I hoped there wouldn't be one between us.

"How about you? Tell me more about your brother," he said while he finished his taco.

I shrugged and swirled my fork in the ketchup. "Just as you mentioned, a dark time in my past. We were twins, as you know. But we were very different. He called me the cautious one. He was the daring, adventurous one who dragged me along on his escapades. I tended to be all sunshiny and happy—so he said—even when we were busy getting in trouble. Nothing could get me down. Even though he was bold, daring, outgoing, he was the broody one, the thoughtful one." I hesitated and then lifted the corner of my mouth in a half-smile. I pointed my fork at Nick. "Almost like you."

He sat taller and put his hand on his chest. "Me? I'm not broody."

I laughed and nodded. "Oh, yes, you are. Not in a depressed, Eeyore kind of way. But you are a bit broody. I see it in your silences and when you're thinking. You're deep, solitary in whatever darkness you feel you are in. But you are such a thoughtful guy, and I'd hate to see you not be able to step out of that place."

I lifted my chin and gave him a cheeky smile, hoping to relieve any tension my words might cause. It pleased me when he returned the smile after a moment of hesitation.

"I don't know what to say to that, except I've never been compared to a donkey before. I'd like to know more about your broody brother." He deftly switched the subject, and I caught his tactic. He didn't like to talk about himself. I was disappointed, but hoped one day he would feel comfortable sharing.

"He was the best brother ever. I suppose I'm biased, since he was my twin. He was athletic, liked sports, and it drove me crazy. He always had sports on when we were growing up, or at his house, laser-focused on the NBA, NFL, and NHL drafts—and don't get me started about March Madness!" I rolled my eyes, and Nick laughed. "He always had a big Super Bowl party, if he wasn't attending it. Which kinda ticked me off, since our birthday is . . . was, well still is, February 2nd. And so many times it fell on our actual birthday, so he'd turn it into a huge celebration." My voice caught, and I went silent for a moment. "Ah damn, memories, right?" I cleared my throat. "Anyway, I went with him a couple of times."

As much as those things had annoyed me about my brother, thinking of Rob and voicing my thoughts out loud was more difficult than I expected.

"Ah, so you don't like sports. This is going to be a problem." Nick pressed his lips together and nodded his head.

I raised my finger and wagged it. "Now, I never said that, I just said he drove me nuts about it." I tried to shake the sadness off me as memories rushed like a movie in my brain.

"Now who's the broody one?" Nick said, and he stroked my knuckles.

He was perceptive.

"I was thinking how much I'd complained about his sports addiction." I looked at Nick. "Now I'd give anything in the world to have him back, sports and all."

He agreed with a nod. "Did he work in the sports industry?" he asked, and it helped me redirect my thoughts.

"Yeah, as a matter of fact he did. He was in entertainment law, but his focus was sports. He loved his job, which he said wasn't a job, it was his passion. How many of us are lucky enough to live our passions?"

"True enough. Don't you, though? Writing and travel?"

"I suppose. It's way better than a corporate gig." I sent a silent thank you to Rob for making it possible. "How about you? Do you enjoy what you do?"

"Sure, it keeps me busy and is rewarding. Business travel isn't all it's cracked up to be, though. Do you have any nieces and nephews?" Nick finished off the last of his food and scrunched up the napkin, putting it in the box and covering it with the empty soda can.

"No nieces and nephews. He was married to his work not a woman. I'm pretty sure he had his pick when he traveled, and there were lots of groupies hanging around the teams." I sat back, my belly stuffed, and then thought of something. "Oh! What if there are little Robs or Robettes running around out there?"

Nick raised his eyebrows. "Do you think so? I suppose that's a possibility."

"A rather upsetting one." I frowned.

"How so?"

Looking out to the water, I thought about it. "If he had kids, surely he would have told me. Or maybe he wasn't aware if there were any. It's upsetting, because there could be family out there. Somewhere. Meaning I'm not alone."

"But you're not alone. And I think if there were any kids, he'd have been aware and told you. Or wouldn't you have a twin sense or something?"

I laughed. "Twin sense? Hadn't thought about it when it comes to kids. But I think you're right. He would've known and told me. Okay, then, that topic gets pushed aside."

"Noted." Nick chuckled. "Finish up, I'd like to get on the road again."

I leaned forward and gobbled up the last few bites. "Okay, now I'm stuffed. But this was delicious." I groaned. "My eyes are bigger than my belly." I laughed and wiped my mouth, doing the same with the napkin and cup as he had done.

"I like to see a woman who enjoys her food. My wife—late wife—wasn't like that. Ari ate like a bird and was extremely picky."

Ari. His wife's name was Ari. Not Marissa.

I let out a sigh, feeling suddenly light-headed. I wasn't sure if I was disappointed or elated that there seemed to be no connection between him and Marissa. I wouldn't have to tell him about the text, after all. I looked up at the sky, wondering if it had just got sunnier, or if it was the burden of keeping the text a secret that had been such a dark cloud. Darker than I had realized. I was so relieved, I couldn't stop smiling. I didn't want to think about it here, now. I pulled myself back into the conversation.

"No fear, I have a hearty appetite, and there's pretty much nothing I won't eat, or at least try. I love food . . ." I paused, doing my best to move on. "Hmm, I think I'll have to do a series of foodie blogs about all these neat little places I, *we*, have discovered. Great idea, thanks."

Nick smiled. "You're welcome, although I don't know what I did to inspire you. But I'm happy to help."

He stood and picked up the boxes. I followed him and we fell into step after he put them in the trash.

"Shall we take off for another quick drive? I'd like to show you a nice spot not too far away that's kind of private." He checked his watch. "I still have time before I leave for the airport."

"I'd love it. Take me away," I teased, and batted my eyelashes at him.

Would he be receptive to a little more flirtation? I didn't know where this might lead, but I wasn't opposed to a summertime fling, and he made the idea very appealing.

If his work continued to cut into our time together, it might be difficult, though. The thought of not seeing him over the next couple of days knotted my stomach. I did my best to shake off the tension, determined not to put a damper on the rest of our time together. Even if I did only have a month or so left here. Time was going by so fast since we'd met—I mentally counted—twelve days ago.

We zoomed off down the road. It thrilled me to be by his side. A good, fun day out would leave him with a happy feeling, and I hoped he'd be eager to see me when he returned.

Chapter Seventeen

Nick was looking forward to showing Lizzie the small cove. He liked how she found pleasure from the simple things, and he was sure she would enjoy this beach. It was rather difficult to find if you didn't know where it was, and he hoped to have it all to themselves.

He slowed and pulled up on the shoulder, looking for the small opening between the trees. A tiny space that fit only a few cars. He picked his way through the trees and backed the convertible into a spot under the towering pines.

"Pretty tight in here," Lizzie commented as they squeezed out of the vehicle.

Nick rounded the front of the Range Rover. "It is, and we're lucky no one is here." He glanced down at her feet. "I think you should be fine with those sandals. It's not too rough, or too far to walk, but you can take my hand if you need to." He smiled at her, and she returned it.

Any time he was with Lizzie was good, but this is one of the first days he'd truly enjoyed in a long, long time. He whistled softly as they set off on the trail. She was just behind him, and rested her fingers on his back when they had to climb over a large rock.

Nick held his hand out, and she took it, jumping down to the path beside him. "Okay?" he asked.

"Yup, all good. It's lovely and hushed in the trees."

The path narrowed, and he had to let go of her hand. He let her go in front.

This was the perfect, relaxing way to spend the afternoon before going off on his trip.

Normally he didn't give travel a second thought. It was work, a necessity. It surprised him that he really didn't want to go. The only thing that usually held him here was his dad. But this time, he realized it was leaving Lizzie that sat like a stone in his stomach. Still, he'd be back in a couple of days.

Nick thought about his father, and how he'd spent the years since Mom died. As far as he knew, Dad hadn't dated or spent time with another woman. Nick didn't want that seclusion for him. He didn't want his father to be lonely in his twilight years.

But, knowing Dad, he'd feel guilty, as though he was betraying Mom. Nick looked up through the trees, their leaves dappled by the sun against the blue sky beyond the treetops. Grief. It was complex. When he thought of Ari, the sense of loss filled him, mixed with a good portion of guilt as well.

In front of him, Lizzie was watching her footing, the sun's rays between the leaves striking her hair a fiery gold. She was about as different from his late wife as you could get. He knew she'd been flirting with him earlier, and he enjoyed it, but his conscience prickled. How could he allow himself to be happy after what happened to Ari? He'd shouldered the blame and felt he'd let her down. He'd been content with his self-recrimination, but now these good emotions and hints of being wanted by someone made him feel conflicted. It also made him see what he was missing in life.

He'd thought he'd had that special closeness with Ari, originally. With her, it had always been a challenge. A life full of upheaval, drama. Her being so impetuous constantly kept him on edge, but the wild excitement and passion was addictive. Initially. He'd ultimately discovered she was good at concealment, and kept a veil between her real self and what she allowed others to see. Had he ever really gotten to know her?

He found himself comparing the two women. Comparison wasn't anyone's friend, but he did it nonetheless.

They were as different as chalk and cheese. He couldn't deny the sexual attraction growing between him and Lizzie. Nick wasn't sure where he wanted it to go, and her plans to leave had him holding back. He wasn't sure he would survive another heartbreak intact.

The trail widened, and they fell back into step, side by side. She didn't complain and, as far as he could tell, she was enjoying this as much as he was.

He couldn't deny being with Lizzie was having a profound effect on him, in a positive way. He resisted the urge to sweep her up into his arms, hold her, and kiss her until she was limp. He'd repressed his feelings for so long, he knew he was wading into deep water.

Of course, it led back to thoughts of Ari. The mysterious way that she'd disappeared. Nick had done his best to understand why she'd gone out on the boat alone. All the evidence pointed to suicide. What other explanation was there? That she'd simply gone for a sail and somehow fell off the boat? He worried she'd done it because of him. His chest tightened. It was a terrible row to hoe.

He'd tried to teach her the basics of sailing on his daysailer, but she never developed a love for the water and wind like he did. She'd lacked the skills, and was resistant on the few times he'd taken her out. She was nowhere near ready to go solo. He shook his head and wondered, for the millionth time, what on earth she'd been thinking. The last time he'd been on his Hunter was just before she died. Now what was left of it sat at dry dock, broken, untouched, and forlorn. Exactly how he'd felt when Ari had disappeared. He'd never had the boat repaired, and likely never would.

Nick drew in a deep breath. Grief and guilt had been his only companions for three years. All the if-onlys and what-ifs couldn't change what happened, or what people thought.

His shoulders loosened. It had taken meeting Lizzie for Nick to see how cloying and heavy those emotions were. It had taken today to understand how tormented he'd been.

He watched Lizzie in front of him. This willowy but strong woman was so fiercely independent, yet wasn't afraid to show a vulnerability that endeared him to her. It was a combination that made it a challenge to resist her. She was complex, a delight, and had a depth to her he wanted to explore.

"Not much longer," Nick told me as we bent under a branch.

"It's all good." I was a little winded, and kept my eyes on the rough ground.

I swear the air between us vibrated with energy. I felt him behind me as if we were touching. The more time I spent with him, the more the attraction grew. Like right now, I wanted to turn around and fling myself at him. But having witnessed Nick's hesitancy, patient was all I could be.

"Keep following this path between the trees, it'll get steep just up ahead."

I was at the top of the incline Nick just warned me about. It stepped down, with logs and rocks.

I turned to answer him, ungracefully caught my foot on a root, and stumbled. *This is gonna hurt.* I grappled for something to stop my fall . . . but there was nothing.

"Lizzie!" Nick shouted, and I heard him charge like a bull elephant on a rampage.

The next thing I knew, he had me. His arms were wrapped around my waist, and he yanked me back against his chest.

"Oh my God." I breathed and held on to his forearms, the hard planes of his chest against my back.

"You're okay," he murmured.

"See now how I could lose my phone? I wager I could trip over dust."

Nick chuckled and released me. "I'd like to see that."

"No, you wouldn't." I turned. "Thank you. That would not have been fun." I pointed down the path.

"Nope. It wouldn't. Want me to go first?" he asked.

I shook my head. "Only my pride is hurt. I can lead the charge."

"Lead away. Not far now, just around the bend at the bottom of the ridge."

"I can hear the ocean," I said when we got there. A breeze from the beach rushed up the path, and I pushed back strands of my hair that stuck to my lip gloss. "Here we are."

I was finally at the beach, and jumped down the little embankment. I couldn't contain myself and spun in a dizzy circle, twirling with my arms out, then stopped with my hands on my hips and looked up and down the beach.

"Wow. You were right. What an amazingly private spot. It's gorgeous." I pointed at the sand. "Footprints. People were here recently. It's not your secret place, after all."

He looked down at the tracks in the sand. "Ah well, I guess it's inevitable. Are there any undiscovered treasures? I hoped it would be empty for us today. And it is."

Nick looked happy, and it made me even happier.

"Yes, it is." I kicked off my sandals and ran down to the water, paddling up to my knees in the gentle waves.

Nick followed suit.

"Isn't this wonderful?" I took his hand.

"It certainly is."

We stood side by side, quiet, the water lapping around us. He put his arm around me, as if it were the most natural thing to do. I slid my arm around his waist, resting my head on him. This was just perfect.

"Cold?" Nick asked

"No, not at all, just happy. I could stand here all day with you." I glanced up at him.

His eyes were expressive, deep. The whirl of emotion I sensed was indescribable. I'd never felt like this before. I felt my lips part slightly and my breath cease when he turned to face me. My head tilted back to look up at him, my hair trickled down my back.

We stood like that for a moment, and I trembled when he ran his hands up my arms to grasp my shoulders.

I leaned into him, my arms finding their way around his neck when he dipped his head. I was desperate to taste him again.

He groaned and lifted me. One hand on my back, tangled in my hair, and the other under my bottom. I wrapped my legs around his hips and we molded together. His power and heat filled me to a blistering degree. I was so intimately pressed against him. I knew he felt the same.

Nick nuzzled my cheek until he found my mouth. My lips

parted under the pressure of his. The kiss started off tender, soft, but quickly dialed up, in an urgent, demanding exploration of one another.

Our tongues touched, and we breathed each other in as if our lives depended on it. Nick slid his hand up and cradled the back of my head. I tightened my thighs, increasing my hold on him, eliciting another deep grumble.

Then laughter from down the beach intruded on us.

"Damn," he murmured. Still holding me in his arms, with my legs around him, he walked us out of the water.

On the shore, he let me slide down his body until my feet touched the sand. I stayed close to him, both of us clinging to the significance of the moment.

My hands slid from his neck and down his arms. "It *is* a public beach."

"I know, but timing." I saw his jaw clench.

"Oh, but that was nice." I caught his fingers with mine.

"It was more than nice." Nick grinned.

We turned just as a crowd of people burst through the trees, laughing and shrieking. They ran into the surf, the guys tackling each other, and the serenity of the beach was shattered. They were having fun, their shouts echoing off the trees that ringed the cove.

Nick led us back to where we left our shoes. I found some rocks to sit on, and brushed the sand off my feet, watching the younger people romp around.

"Look at them, they're babies," I said. "It seems not that long ago I was their age."

"I know what you mean. But I'm not sure I'd want to be in my twenties again. Would you?"

I sat quietly for a beat before answering. "Knowing what I know now, at thirty-two, I would probably do things differently, but I agree. I wouldn't want to relive that age. It was way too angsty for me."

He laughed. "Agreed. At least we're pretty close in age."

I glanced up at him from my rock. "So how old are you, then?"

"Ancient. Thirty-six."

"Ah, yes, old and decrepit. You'll need a cane soon," I teased.

He took my hand and pulled me up. I slipped my arm around his waist, and he dropped his over my shoulder. Our hips brushed. The strangest sense of belonging draped over me. I looked up at him, and the rush of happiness nearly overcame me.

"Nick."

"Mm, yeah." The look in his eyes stole away all that I wanted to say to him. I couldn't pull my thoughts together, and only managed a soft, "Thank you. For everything."

His smile widened, and he looked very pleased with himself. "You don't have to thank me. I enjoyed these last few hours with you."

"What time do we have to head back?" I asked, knowing it would be way too soon.

He glanced at his watch. "Soon, I'm afraid."

"That's too bad, just when things were heating up—"

He silenced me by pulling me back into his arms and kissing me. It was so much more electric this time. Rather than satiate me, it did the total opposite. I craved more.

The kiss ended softly. Sweetly. But with a promise of what could lie ahead.

Chapter Eighteen

That night was the best sleep I'd had in . . . oh . . . forever. Waking up with the sun streaming in through my window, and the sound of the surf outside, filled me with utter contentment.

I stretched luxuriously in my bed. The silky sheets tangling around my legs. I flung my arm across the pillow beside me and imagined what it would be like if *he* was beside me. Sleepy, tousled, and warm after a night of lovemaking. I pressed my fingers to my chest when my heart fluttered.

I rolled on to my side and looked out the window. I relived yesterday. How Nick had brought me home. Walked me to the front door. I was so reluctant for our time together to end, as was he, and our kiss goodbye was the stuff dreams were made of.

I hugged myself, remembering his arms around me. The strength of him, the hardness of his chest against my own, his scent of sun, sea, and man. I missed him already.

The late afternoon sun had bathed us in a golden glow as we said our goodbyes. Our last kiss. Full of passion and promise. Even more so than the first real kiss we shared on the beach. It left me all tingly and excited for the rest of my day, which had spilled over into my dreams. Hot, erotic, and electric.

I checked my watch. It was just after 7 a.m. And I counted back . . . no . . . forward. He was on Eastern Time and I on Pacific, that's a three-hour difference. He was likely settled in his hotel by now and into his business meetings.

Which was a reminder that I had lots of work planned for today. Admittedly, it was going to be difficult to remain focused on my to-do list and not let my thoughts stray to Nick.

I swung my legs out of bed and pulled on the coral-colored satin robe laying over the back of the wicker chair, under the window facing the sea. I was feeling more and more comfortable here, and had sprinkled little bits of *me* throughout the cottage. I liked this place and could easily call it home.

I slid past, thinking too deeply about my time here coming to an end. Nope. Not now. Not for a while. I pushed the gloomy thought to the back of my mind.

I looked out the window to see dark clouds massed on the horizon, hinting at rain later. Padding into the kitchen, I was desperate for coffee, and brewed a pot. One thing was certain, coffee in this neck of the woods was excellent. I pulled out a tub of yogurt, scooped some into a bowl with blueberries, and chopped up some grapes, topping it off with granola.

I needed a real jolt today and filled a large mug, watching with satisfaction when the cream and black liquid swirled into the perfect caramel shade I liked. I inhaled the delicious aroma, and walked through to the living room.

Back at my desk by the window, I had my first sip of coffee. Why was the first sip of the day always the best? I closed my eyes, holding the mug close to my nose to breathe in the richness.

"Okay, enough making love to the coffee." I put the mug

down and opened my iPad and laptop. Time to check my social media and get busy.

Taking a spoonful of yogurt, I checked Instagram and let out a little squeal. I was closing in on 100,000 followers. Checking for messages, I made notes on the pad next to me, to reply later. I moved over to TikTok and was shocked the video I posted the other day, when I'd bought the fish and chips for supper, was closing in on 800,000 views.

"Wow, you just never know what's gonna hit," I mused. I leaned over the desk, sipping coffee and checking my stats.

A discovery I'd made during my promise journey to Rob was that, as well as thoroughly enjoying photography, I was kind of good at it. My photos received praise, regardless of the subject. I was thrilled, especially since I'd recently been approached about selling some of them. I'd need some legal advice over that, for sure.

One of my favorites was an image of a soft mist turning the rugged coast a hazy blue, with a wide beach and waves hit by shards of sunlight. The timing was perfect when four seagulls riding the wind entered the frame. My followers loved it too.

It had started as a video. Then I snapped some stills and put them together, which went viral.

My follower base had jumped to almost a million on TikTok and was climbing on Insta. I couldn't believe it. I'd made friends with other big creators and we'd done a lot of Snapchat brainstorming for content. It appeared I'd found my niche: food, and anything travel. Next, I opened my YouTube and was excited to see my subscribers had grown to almost 6,000—and I only had four videos. I jotted down some ideas for content. It was a platform I hadn't focused on too much in the past, but I was determined to build and hopefully monetize it.

A few travel companies and hotels had approached me, asking for me to showcase their properties, some even inviting me to stay, fully comped, and all I had to do was post from my accounts while there. Maybe I could get Nick to come along.

I sat back, the spoon in my mouth, and thought about it. Would we ever get to a place in our lives like that? After yesterday, I had the feeling that anything was possible.

But, either way, I was independent, and this was my baby. I needed this experience with social media to build my business. Needed it for me. I was excited at the challenge and adventure that was presenting itself. Not only could it be lucrative, it was crazy fun.

After finishing up my social media planning and my yogurt, I needed more coffee.

Rinsing out the bowl and spoon, I set them on the bamboo dish drainer and poured another cup. It was time to settle down and write a few posts, and plan a YouTube video. It took so much time due to the editing involved. I could always move a chair down to the beach and work there, or at least on the porch. Making notes, I lost myself in my work.

A little while later, I was satisfied with my progress and took a break. At the door, I paused beside the outdoor shower—I hadn't used it yet—where we'd watched the sunset on the day we first met, nearly two weeks ago. Which meant that my time here was marching along.

I'd have to plan for my departure soon. I'd been ready to keep moving on to my new destinations, before coming to Savage Cove. But then there was no Nick in the picture.

I touched my lips with my fingertips. Had he imprinted himself on me, and I on him? I could almost feel the warmth of his kiss. How would we end? Had we even started? I'd been open to a summer fling, but my feelings had taken a turn somewhere along the way. Maybe I wanted something more.

But what about Nick? What did he want? I didn't know.

I walked down to the surf and opened my notebook. I thought about Rob and my promise. I'd made it to him with no kind of hope for the future. It had seemed a good idea at the time, since I was solo, had no ties, and could work from anywhere. Plus, I'd thought it would be easier to be a nomad, rather than stick around, with constant reminders of what I'd lost.

The biggest surprise was finding my way to Savage Cove and meeting Nick.

Yet, despite my growing feelings, something was holding me back, something I almost didn't want to vocalize. It had to do with Nick's past. His reticence to open up about Ari made me wary. I sensed he had cared deeply about her and was living with his grief, and perhaps some guilt too. I wished he could talk to me about it.

I picked up a few stones and held them in my hand. One was flat and shaped like a heart. I rubbed my thumb across it and then slipped it into the pocket on the inside flap of my notebook. Was it a sign, or just a random stone? Thinking back, it seemed as if everything that had happened since my arrival was born out of curiosity. The Lady of the Sea . . . Marissa was in the center of it.

I puffed out a breath and tossed the other stones on to the sand. I didn't feel like going into town today, since yesterday had already taken me away from my work. Tomorrow, I would— and hopefully I'd see Claire again. She might shed some light. I decided to stay home and work, but afterwards, I was going for a drive.

* * *

In my latest research, I'd stumbled across a last known address for Marissa Wright. I built up the courage to take a drive out to the house.

Finding my way there, I came to a rather magnificent-looking gated entrance to a driveway.

The number on the gate matched what I had written down. There was also a sign . *Private property. No trespassing.*

Hmm. That meant I either buzzed the gate to go in, which I didn't feel comfortable doing, or I parked the car and went to the beach, and then walked along to see if I could find the house.

I felt I had to buzz first. I pulled up and took a deep breath before pressing the button.

I waited.

No reply.

Buzzed again.

Still nothing.

Satisfied I had tried, but to no avail, I turned my car around and drove to a spot on the road that had a wider shoulder. I saw a pathway through the trees that I bet dollars to donuts would take me out to the beach.

I got out and looked down the path, and then back over to the gates, and up to the sky. I felt somewhat like Lewis and Clark off on an adventure.

Getting my bearings, I stepped on to the path and disappeared into the trees. A short while later, I emerged on the beach. The house should be to my left, but I couldn't see anything. I struck off across the sand.

There wasn't a less than glorious view from anywhere on the seashore. I looked over the waves and appreciated the open vista for a few minutes, then glanced around, looking for the house.

I kept going to the left and must have trudged about a quarter-mile. Why was it so far, when the driveway from my car hadn't seemed so long? The beach was empty, and I passed what looked like a smaller house, tucked in the trees.

I toed off my sandals, bent to pick them up, and stepped into the gentle waves. I inhaled the air, tangy from the sea spray, and knew I was falling in love with being near the ocean.

After spotting the pretty agate stone the other day, I'd started watching where I was walking, always on the lookout for something to catch my eye. Another gentle curve of the beach, and I strolled along. I glanced up. I must be getting close by now.

I gasped, and my step faltered. There, through the trees, was a house. I shook my head, trying to process what was in front of me.

An incredible house loomed over the beach.

And it was Nick's.

I stared at it. My heart nearly exploded from my chest, and I thought I might throw up. I knew, deep in my soul, and I had to hold back the tears. This was the confirmation that I'd wanted but dreaded. I'd thought my suspicions allayed when Nick called his wife Ari. But it was only a nickname.

Marissa was his wife. His dead wife. And he'd been called in for questioning about her disappearance. My legs wobbled; I forced them to move, and they took me toward the house.

What was I going to do? Why was I being drawn there?

I needed to know.

But I do know!

It wasn't proof.

Yes, it is.

I heard my brother's voice in the back of my mind. "Just remember, curiosity killed the cat."

157

"I'm not a cat!" I squared my shoulders, walking across the sand to the pathway that led up to the house.

Then I stopped before the first rock slab that formed a step.

What was I thinking? That Marissa would be there? She was long gone, and Nick was in New York. There was nothing for me here. No discovery to be made. I was just torturing myself.

There were no lights on in the house. Houdini was probably with Nick's father. I turned around and looked through the trees. The house I'd passed was probably his dad's place.

What if he saw me here, snooping around? That would not be good. I hurried back down to the beach.

Occam's razor. The simplest explanation is usually the right one.

I sat in the car with my hands on the steering wheel, staring out the window at the gates ahead. Was it worth more research? I was thinking not. I'd taken it too far already, and now found myself in a situation that I didn't like.

At all.

I started the car, drove slowly past the gates, and looked up the long laneway. When Nick had driven me home, it had been so foggy, and that must be why I didn't recognize the road or gates.

I went home. This needed more thought.

My curious side pressed me to keep the old phone charged. Just in case more texts came in—though, so far, there had been nothing. I really wanted it to be a misdial. I hoped it was a misdial. It still could be, I supposed.

The odds were long, though, that Marissa—the intended recipient of the text—and Ari were not the same person. The relief I'd felt during our lunch by the sea seemed ages ago now. He simply had a nickname for her.

How was I going to tell Nick that I'd received his text? Did I need to tell him? If I didn't, he'd never know. Right?

But *I* would.

I twisted my fingers in my lap, knowing I'd nicely planted myself into a thorny conundrum. I should have told him so much sooner. Had I left it too late? If I told him now, it might look like I'd been withholding the text.

And did I have one hundred per cent proof he was the sender?

Chapter Nineteen

After a sleepless night, I needed to get away from the cottage and find somewhere to focus on writing. Of course, the café came to mind immediately. I packed up my gear and, a short while later, I was sitting at a table between the fireplace and window, behind a large potted plant, with a Breakfast Bomb and a large coffee.

Distractions were killing my productivity, and this spot was perfect. I set up my Mac and dove in, absently eating the pastry and sipping coffee.

I don't know how much time had passed when someone tapped my shoulder. I jumped and nearly knocked the mug over.

"I'm sorry, dear, I didn't mean to startle you." Claire was smiling down at me.

"Hey, how are you? It's okay, I was focused. Please sit." I moved my laptop aside and made room for her. "I'm surprised to see you here this morning. It's not a Monday or Tuesday."

She smiled and raised a delicate shoulder. "I've been known to be a rebel sometimes."

We laughed, and she put her travel mug on the table and sat, folding her hands together.

"Have I interrupted your work?" she asked tactfully.

I shook my head. "I've been trying to get stuff done, and it's distracting at the cottage. So I came here."

"I can sit elsewhere and leave you to your work," Claire offered.

"No, please stay." I leaned forward and captured her hand with mine. "Actually, Claire, I'm wondering if you'd mind if I talk to you about something?"

"Of course, dear, ask away, but it doesn't mean I'll answer," she said, not unkindly.

I gave a small laugh, suddenly nervous. "I understand, if it's something you don't want to talk about." I steeled myself and flicked the corner of my notebook with my finger. "I've been doing some research on the area, and I was wondering if you had any . . ." I paused. I couldn't quite bring myself to ask about Marissa, so I switched topics. "Suggestions that would make a suitable topic for my posts?"

"I'm pretty sure I could help you with that. What are you exactly looking for? Something nearby?" She lifted her cup and sipped, looking thoughtful.

Marissa Wright, what do you know about her?

"Anything fun and touristy, out of the way, off the beaten track. I'm planning on taking a short road trip tomorrow, and I'd like to explore a bit."

She nodded. "Hmm, goodness, depends how far you want to drive, what you want to see, and what your interests are. There's lots to do. Have you spent any time in Seattle?"

I shook my head. "No, except for driving through on my way here. I kind of wanted to stay out of the big city, you know?"

"Yes, I know what you mean. There is a vibrant Native

culture here you shouldn't miss. The art is exquisite. You can see a lot of this in Seattle, at museums and galleries. Even street names and public places. I would highly recommend learning more about the tribes. Then there are the whales, of course."

"Excellent idea about the Native culture. I agree with the art. It's stunning. And I know all about the whales." I shook my head and snorted.

"Oh? This sounds interesting. Tell me more." Claire leaned forward.

I looked into her grey eyes. "Well, you'll never guess what I did."

Claire shook her head. "How could I?"

"Somehow, I managed to toss my phone over the side of the ferry while trying to get a picture of a whale." I scowled, still angry with myself for being clumsy.

"You did not," Claire said, her voice edged with surprise.

"I totally did." Nodding, with my eyes wide, I told her the story. "I mean, really, how does somebody do that? Be so unco-ordinated, honestly."

"That must have been horrible."

"It was stupid. And then, this man grabbed me, thinking I was going to jump overboard after it. I wasn't, of course, but he thought so. I was embarrassed, and angry at myself." It still riled me to relive it.

"Oh my, you must have scared the daylights out of him. Did you get a new phone?"

I nodded. "Yes, as soon as the ferry docked, I came into town to look for somewhere to buy a phone. But there aren't many places here that sell them."

Claire chuckled. "No, you're right. Why didn't you just order online? Or go to a shop in a bigger town?"

I pulled a face and thought for a moment before I answered.

"Good question. I was still in shock, I think, and didn't want to drive anywhere. I just got here, after traveling across the country, and the last place I wanted to spend any more time was inside my SUV. I was in no mood to drive anywhere, so I just found that shop across the street." I pointed up the road to where I got the phone.

Claire turned and looked out the window. "Oh yes. Ackermans. They have a small selection."

"Small is not the word. They were ancient phones." I laughed and dug into my bag to show her. I still carried the old phone with me, just in case another text arrived. "See, look at this thing. It's from another century." I put it in her hand.

"Not quite a century, but close." Claire shook her head with a smile. "Good Lord, I haven't seen a phone like this in I don't know how long. But you made do." Her brow furrowed and she squinted at the screen. "Ah, there is a . . . here you go." She handed it back to me.

"It did the trick, and my new phone took forever to come in. But I finally have it now." I tapped my iPhone on the table. Claire looked pale and upset. I sat back, startled. What had happened? "Is everything okay?" I asked her, concerned.

"Yes, yes, fine." She swallowed, and slowly asked, "You said you got that from Ackermans?"

I nodded, worried now. "Yes, why? Is there a problem?" I looked at the screen. The first line of the text to Marissa was visible. Claire must have seen it.

I looked up at her, and we fell silent.

Now would be the perfect opportunity to ask her about Marissa. I steeled myself and figured, what did I have to lose?

"You saw that?" I pointed at the text.

Clare nodded. "Yes." She looked out the window, her lips drawn into a thin line.

I opened the text and handed her the phone so she could read it. "I have no idea who this is, who it came from, and why I got it."

I wasn't going to say anything about going to Nick's house.

Claire took my phone and read the message, her eyebrows scrunched together. "I'm not sure what you mean. The text came to your phone, and it's not for you? This is your phone, right?" She rubbed her cheek and glanced from the phone to me.

I took the phone from Claire and put it back in my purse.

"Yes, it's a refurbed phone with a recycled number. I got it from the store to use until my iPhone came."

Claire sat back in the seat and looked thoughtful. "Okay, that makes sense."

"What makes sense?" I asked her, getting the feeling that she knew something.

She closed her eyes and gave her head a slight shake.

"Do you know Marissa, or any Marissas? I've done a bit of research to see who this message might be intended for."

"You have? Why?" She pinned me with a direct look.

I sat back, my mouth dropping open at her tone. "Well, because, I just said, to try to find who it's for." I closed my laptop, feeling the urge to pack up and leave, to escape the strange vibes I was getting from Claire.

"What did you find?" she asked, and the intensity she'd expressed a moment ago melted away.

I raised my shoulders. "A woman named Marissa disappeared three years ago."

Claire was silent, and I watched her. She knew something; I was sure of it.

"Did you know anyone by that name?"

"Lots of people live around here. I don't know everybody. But I knew a Marissa once." It was all she offered.

I rested my arms on the table. "Can you tell me more? I know the woman who disappeared was Marissa Wright, and she was presumed drowned. Her husband was questioned about her disappearance. And I don't know if it's the same Marissa in that text."

There was no reason to mention Nick, or that I knew him. It was neither here nor there, as I'd never talked to Claire about him.

"Dear, I appreciate your interest in the text, but they probably sent it in error. A misdial."

"Obviously, it was sent to me by mistake. And if it was supposed to reach someone other than the dead Marissa, then they didn't get an important apology. My head spins when I think about it." I was getting frustrated. "I know she owned this café."

Claire blinked and nodded. "Yes, there was a Marissa who owned this café. That's who I was referring to."

"What happened to her?" I held my breath, wanting to know the answer. It could be the key that unlocked the mystery.

Claire remained silent, and I shook my head. Leaning back in the chair, I crossed my arms and looked out the window.

"I didn't know her well. It was a tragedy for the family— and, anyway, it wouldn't be my story to tell."

I gave her a hard stare.

"And really, it's the past. I'd put it out of my mind."

"I'm sorry, I didn't mean to pry or upset you. It's just something that has been driving me crazy since I got the text. My research turned up what I told you, and an old address."

Claire's head snapped up. "It did?"

I nodded. "Yes, I'm a bit of a research fiend—for my articles— and I'm pretty good at finding stuff, even if it's been buried deep. Unless, of course, it's been scrubbed and withheld. Much is public record, anyway."

Did I want to tell Claire that I had gone to the address and discovered it was Nick's house?

We fell silent, nursing our coffees, and awkwardness settled over us. I was sorry now I'd brought the subject up. It seemed to have changed things. But I couldn't take it back.

"I'm sorry, Claire."

"Why are you sorry?" She lifted her purse and set it on her knee to look inside.

"You seem bothered by the turn this conversation has taken."

Claire pulled out some money and laid it on the table. She looked up, with a smile. "It was a time that was unpleasant for many people. And, as I said, I don't know the details. I prefer not to get involved in any kind of conversation around it."

She pushed her chair back and stood, then leaned down and hugged me. "Don't fret, my dear. I'm fine. Do what you must about your story. Maybe you'll find your answers. Now I must be off, I'm meeting someone. It was nice to see you again."

"Thanks. You too, Claire. Take care." I watched her leave the café, feeling wired with emotion, and more than a little unsettled.

I was nearly asleep when my phone pinged, and I almost jumped out of my skin. Maybe it was another text to Marissa!

But it wasn't, it was my iPhone and not the old beater phone. Rubbing my eyes, I held up my phone to see who was messaging me.

Hope you had a great day. Thinking about you.

It was Nick. A thrill rushed through me. He was thinking about me while he was in New York.

I quickly typed back.

Wonderful to hear from you. Was a good day, got stuff done.

Nick replied immediately, and we fell into a sweet, easy conversation. I was surprised how difficult it was to stop texting. It was 2 a.m. for him, but we couldn't seem to say goodbye. I tried a final text.

Now off you go sleep. I'm putting my phone down now.

Okay, me too.

I didn't, and then sent another text.

You there?

Nope.

Me either x

This time, I did put the phone down, and snuggled into my cozy bed. I drifted off with thoughts of us walking on the beach, hand in hand.

Chapter Twenty

The sun wasn't even up yet, but I had to get a start on the day if I wanted to do the road trip I'd been thinking about.

I had moved a lovely oak table in front of the window that faced the beach. But the sea was still swallowed in darkness. It was the perfect location for my desk, and meant I didn't feel *stuck inside* while I was working. It was homey on a rainy day with a fire going in the fireplace to chase the chill away. Even in July.

I placed my Moleskine, maps (I was old school) and my calendar book on the desk, and set up my laptop. This morning, before I headed off on the trip, I wanted to organize the posts I planned. I had five posts I wanted to write, loosely plotted out.

If I was going to take this seriously and get to the next level, I had to let go of my willy-nilly approach and plan really logically. It was strange how my organized self had deteriorated into organized chaos. It wasn't like me, but since Rob's death, some things just hadn't seemed as important.

This was.

I owed it to Rob to make my new writing and travel life a success. And that meant being more dedicated to it.

I got out my Post-its, set up a plotting board. It leaned against the wall at one side of the desk so it was at a glance for me. I wrote my thoughts down and stuck them underneath the title topics.

Foodie Stuff
My Travel Highlights
Destinations
Nature
Random Stuff

I forced myself to become methodical. Having come from an orderly world, I needed to preserve this skill if I was going to keep my mind calm and focused. Particularly with all the distractions that had come my way since arriving in Savage Cove.

Especially one decidedly handsome distraction. I smiled, thinking of Nick.

Although I frequently fell down the rabbit hole, I fought hard to keep it together by being planned and orderly. Living out of a suitcase and traveling light had forced me to reassess the basic necessities.

I sat back, and watched my reflection in the dark window. Funny how I didn't miss anything. Maybe that meant I didn't need it.

At first, without a home base except for my vehicle, I'd found it fun and exciting, forcing me to be more efficient. But now, two weeks after arriving here in Savage Cove, I was questioning my nomadic lifestyle. Being on the road as long as I had suddenly started to weigh on me.

I felt like tiny little fibers of roots were growing under my feet. Would they take hold? I didn't know.

The six weeks I'd planned here had seemed to be more than enough. But now I wasn't so sure. With barely four weeks left, I was starting to feel a slight panic.

Why? For several reasons. First, it was beautiful here and spoke to my soul. Second, I loved the house located on the beach, and third . . . Nick. But I had to be careful I didn't make decisions based solely on him. I had to do what was right for me.

And, finally, my promise to Rob. I pressed my fingertips to my chin when it started quivering. How could I not fulfill my promise to take on the world?

I gave a ragged sigh and shook my head. I'd think about it later. Right now, I was eager to head out on the road and discover more about this area of America. It was beautiful, breathtaking, raw, and rugged. I needed to lose myself in that for a while. The more time I spent here, the more I fell in love. Claire crossed my mind, and I chewed on my thumbnail, reliving our conversation of the previous day.

I hoped to bump into her again and try to fix what I may have broken. I liked her, and I hated to think my budding friendship with this interesting woman could have been ruined.

I planned a full day's road trip today, and was determined to get some work done before I left. I pushed everything except my work out of my head, and buckled down.

A couple of hours later, I left for the café to grab some road trip goodies. I knew it opened early, and I planned to be on the road by 7 a.m. My navigation showed it was a little over three hours to Rialto Beach. Even someone as old school as I was appreciated the in-car nav at times—although I didn't totally trust it, having been directed to some sketchy places a few times. And that was why I kept my trusty maps handy.

With snacks, water and a thermos of coffee packed, up I was out the door, and at the café just after seven. I felt exhilarated to be out this early, and was glad I'd gotten a couple of hours' work done first. I was ready to tackle a day on the road.

The long drive ahead of me wasn't a deterrent, it would be the drive home that seemed to go on and on and on. I didn't want to think about that. But the sooner I got cracking, the better it would be.

I'd thought the café would be relatively empty, but it was still hopping.

Standing at the counter waiting for my drink and a bag of goodies, I turned when someone touched my shoulder.

It was Claire.

"Oh, good morning."

"Good morning, my dear." She smiled. "You're out early."

"I am. Off on my road trip today."

"I'm glad." She didn't appear to be holding on to any ill feeling from yesterday's conversation, and I breathed a sigh of relief.

"Where are you going?" Claire asked. "It's always good to let someone know where you'll be."

"Rialto Beach. I'm looking forward to it, but it's a long drive." I handed over the money to the barista.

"I think you'll really like it."

"I hope so. It's a research day, gathering info and photos for a travel blog series. I'm desperately behind on my deadlines, and I need a couple of days to catch up."

Without the tempting distraction of Nick.

"You've been busy, then?" She had a twinkle in her eye.

I tipped my head, wondering why she looked mischievous.

"Um, yes." I wasn't planning on mentioning Nick, but I was near to bursting to tell someone. I was intrigued at the amused look on her face. I much preferred it to her upset frown from yesterday, though. "Well, I met someone and we've gone out a few times. And my foodie and scenery posts did amazingly well, went viral, so now the pressure is on to keep the momentum up."

"They did! How interesting. I don't pay attention to social media and all those apps, as you call them." She pulled a book out of her purse. "I'm a bit of a dinosaur. Wait, back up a minute. You met someone?"

"I did. We met on the beach."

Claire's eyes widened and she beamed. "How nice. I hope you are enjoying yourself."

"We are. Nick is such a nice man. The only thing is, I'm leaving in a few weeks and . . ."

Claire put her hand on my arm. "Take it one day at a time. You don't know what the future holds."

"True, yes, that's good advice." It felt good telling someone about Nick. We were jostled by a group of teens as they excused themselves to pass through the line and find stools at the counter. The conversation paused, as I took my bag of snacks and coffee from the counter, then stepped aside when Claire placed her order.

"I was thinking, why don't we exchange numbers?" she suggested as she handed money to the barista.

"What a good idea." We did it quickly. "Well, I suppose I should get on the road. But I would enjoy sitting down with you again to chat." I walked with Claire to a chair by the window.

"I would like that as well, my dear. Enjoy your Nick." She

put her bag and coffee on the table. "Now, off you go, and be safe. Don't be traipsing around on lonely beaches, we don't want you to get lost."

"I'll be fine. See you again." It pleased me that there truly didn't seem to be any hangover from our conversation about Marissa yesterday. And now we had each other's phone number.

I pushed open the café door and got settled in my car. I took a sip of coffee and then stilled, holding it to my mouth. What did she mean, don't traipse around on lonely beaches? And who was *we*? I swiveled in my seat. Claire waved to me from the café window. I waved back and shrugged. Likely just a figure of speech.

I was entering Olympic National Park from Port Angeles for the drive to Rialto Beach, and it was rather foggy. I hoped it would lift soon. Driving through the city, I looked for the bilingual street signs that I'd read about. A linguistic revitalization project was the initiative behind the bilingual signs in both English and Klallam. I got a photo of the welcome sign to the park, where I discovered the S'Kallam Tribe, meaning the Strong People, were a Salish group with ties to tribes of British Columbia and Puget Sound.

Driving down the highway was freeing. The further inland I went, the more the fog lifted. The scenery took my breath away and reminded me of my trip with Nick. It had been such a good time. Too short, but nice.

And that kiss. That kiss! It still made me giggle, and heat radiate through my chest, when I relived it. I hadn't felt butterflies like this, ever.

I puffed out my cheeks and settled in for the long drive. Another song came on my playlist. The famous cover by

Disturbed of Simon & Garfunkel's "The Sound of Silence", and I choked up. Rob's favorite.

Damn, just when you think you've got it under control, a song comes on and knocks your feet out from under you. We would sing this together, but right now I just listened, sniffling and wiping away the tears that streamed down my cheeks.

When it ended, I switched playlists on my phone. No more soulful reminders of sad things. Only upbeat, happy songs.

I pressed my thumb on the volume button on the steering wheel and turned up the music. I groaned when Fergie's "Big Girls Don't Cry" came on. Was the universe trying to send me a message? I was no Fergie, but I did my best singing along to it with the windows and sunroof open.

My hair whipped around my head and, in the rear-view mirror, I saw it being sucked up to the sunroof opening.

Stopping to take a quick selfie, me laughing like hell, I sent it to Nick. I was very comfortable being on my own, but I was eager for him to come back. I put the phone down. There would be no next kiss if I didn't focus on my driving.

Finding the agate the other day had inspired me, and I was on a mission to do more beachcombing. Today I was going to do some rockhounding, and hopefully find some beach treasures, like sea glass. If I found enough of it, I might try my hand at something crafty.

I smirked, me being crafty? Who was I kidding? I wasn't crafty, and the extent of my creativity would be to put it all in a pretty bowl. Pinterest had beautiful images of crafts done with sea glass, I could look at them with appreciation.

I'd discovered several beaches where you could hunt for sea glass, and it was an added bonus that Rialto Beach, which I'd already picked to explore further, was one of them. The journey there would even take me through the town of Forks, the set-ting for the *Twilight* books.

If I had time, I was hoping to take a side trip to Hoh Rain Forest and visit the Hall of Mosses. It looked amazing in the photos I'd seen, and the old-growth forests were magical. It would add another two hours of driving, though, from Rialto Beach to the Hoh Rain Forest and back out to Forks. That didn't include the hike—and it was kind of out of my way, if I drove back the same way. It was the shortest route, and I was pretty sure by that time of day, I'd be eager to be home.

It seemed silly not to take the trip, since I was out this way, but that would make it the drive seven-plus hours.

"Ah well, play it by ear," I told myself.

I didn't have a convertible SUV like Nick, but my trusty Honda Pilot got me where I needed to be, safely. Plus, I'd used it a few times as a camper on my trip from NOLA to Seattle, and then on to Savage Cove. The back was large with the seats down, and even though I was tall it was easy to set up a cozy bed.

It surprised me how many people are, by choice, living in camper vans, SUVs, busses, while seeing the country. I'd seen many posts on social media, and used what I'd learned to keep myself safe. But I was really glad to find the cute beach cottage for rent in Savage Cove.

For today's trip, I'd plotted out on a map the places that I wanted—hoped—to see. Going further inland along the Cas-cades Loop would have to wait till another time. I'd wanted to visit some of the old mining towns, and I'd heard there were ghost towns, as well as spectacular scenery. Doing that trip couldn't be rushed, I'd have to carve out about four or five days. But I wasn't sure when to make that happen. I couldn't believe how quickly time was flying by.

I clenched the steering wheel. The days were passing way

too fast, and there was still so much I wanted to do while here. Especially with Nick.

The conversations with Claire yesterday and today had me thinking more about the mystery surrounding Marissa, especially after the way Claire reacted. I thought I'd exhausted the possibility of discovering anything new on my own to finally confirm the connection between Marissa and Nick.

I wasn't sure how to proceed, other than outright asking Nick. But was it too late for that? Maybe I should just let it all go—the text, everything about it—and finally accept that it was just a mistake. A misdial. But I couldn't shake the feeling I'd already found the answer, and the more I thought about it the crazier it made me. I had to stop thinking about it.

"Okay, done. Done and done. No more." I scolded myself for letting my thoughts drift off to la-la land gain. I turned up the music.

Damn, I'd wanted to use my dashcam to record my drive to the park. Finding a good place to pull over, I set it up. It would be an added feature to my YouTube channel. One of my research tricks was to find driving videos of locations so I could get the true feel of the area. I hoped to accomplish the same with this video.

Finally, it was sunny. Every bend and turn in the road afforded more spectacular views. I was oohing and ahhing to myself, with thoughts of what Rob would think had he been with me. I knew he'd been to Seattle many times to watch the Seahawks. I liked that name, it was cool. *Seahawk*. It had inspired me to find out if the sea hawk was an actual bird, and it was, better known as the osprey. I would keep my eyes peeled in case I saw one.

I was starting to get a little peckish. I still had some coffee left from the café, as well as donuts. I ate, and sipped, and drove.

My cooler contained a little more substantial food, and I was saving it for later. After the beach. I didn't need to stop for a break yet and was determined to make it through to Rialto Beach.

Everything I'd read about Rialto Beach had been amazing, and I was excited to finally get there. It, or La Push, were supposed to be locations in the *Twilight* movies, but they were actually filmed elsewhere, in Oregon and British Columbia.

I could pretend I was stepping into the realm of that world, which kind of excited me, because I'd been a bit of a Twilighter back in the day. Perhaps my desire to come to Washington was a subliminal fascination with vampires.

I'd passed Lake Crescent, which was stunning, and now I had to find a place to have a pit stop. Pee and stretch my legs. I was on the lookout for somewhere not too secluded. Up ahead, I saw a sign for The Hungry Bear. It had lots of cars parked out front and I pulled in, finding a spot off to the side.

I stumbled out of the vehicle. "Oof. Damn, I'm getting old."

My leg muscles must have molded to the car seat, and I hobbled a bit until they loosened up. I'd make this a quick stop and then get on the road.

I felt obligated to buy something in return for using the restroom, so I ordered some fries to go. It didn't take long for my order to arrive and I was soon back on the road, feeling refreshed and munching on my favorite food.

I drove into the town of Forks from where I had to make my turn toward the west, to head down to Rialto Beach.

The road out of town was winding and twisty. It was a challenge to drive because I rubbernecked to see the views. I gasped at the beauty; the mist hanging at the top of the mountains. One section of the road was like a tunnel, with pine trees arching like a canopy. There were some pull-offs along the way, but

I checked my time and as much as I'd have liked to stop for the view, I wanted to get to the beach.

Driving along this road was as if I was in an alternate reality. Breathtaking, and gorgeous, these smells coming in through the window were just beyond anything I'd ever encountered—sea, pine, wildness.

I'd been on the road for a while, and one thing was certain: I didn't want to do this drive at night. I was glad that I'd left as early as I did this morning.

A while later, a sign announced my arrival, and I turned into the parking lot. It was pretty busy, which surprised me. I finally found a parking spot and pulled in.

I puffed out a breath and turned off the dashcam. I sat for a minute to take in the view.

Simply extraordinary.

Oh, Rob, you would love this.

Chapter Twenty-one

I was in awe.

I got out of the vehicle, gathered up a bag I'd brought for keeping any treasure I found on the beach, plus my phone and my camera. I didn't want to go barefoot, so I wore hiking sandals. They could get wet, and I hoped to see the tide pools.

Part of the reason I wanted to come today was that low tide was midday-ish, which would make access to the tidal pools and Hole-in-the-Wall possible. I'd checked NOAA tide charts to be sure.

A wall of ancient downed trees, bleached and lined all along the beach in front of live trees, acted almost like a barrier. I was blown away by how many there were, and how huge some had grown. I could only imagine what it looked like when they were still tall and majestic, standing on the edge of the shore.

Climbing over the bleached bones of trees from eons ago, I came out on to a beautiful wide crescent beach and was surprised the sand was so dark, almost black. The wind was high and blew a light mist on to the beach, making it almost impossible to see anything in the distance. I couldn't take it all in. I wanted to record every minute while here. I took out my phone and held it up. Looking into the camera, I took a moment to organize my thoughts.

"I'm here on Rialto Beach, Washington. It is spectacular. There are no words that can adequately describe it." Walking down to the shoreline, picking my way through the driftwood, I continued my commentary.

I stopped and did a 360-degree turn, taking it all in. "The pictures I've seen do not do this justice."

I was sure my photos wouldn't, either. The wild beauty almost brought tears to my eyes, and I'm glad I had the phone turned around, rather than on me. I clicked it off.

There were other people on the beach, bent over and scavenging in the sand. It was strange, though; for all the cars in the parking lot, the beach was vast and people were spread out along the length, giving it a feeling of emptiness.

A beautiful emptiness.

I started taking photos. There were so many magnificent images to capture, I was like a kid in a candy store. I slowly made my way along the beach, completely enraptured by the experience. I could imagine being here with Rob or Nick. Both would have helped me search for sea glass, stones, and shells.

I continued on and picked up some nuggets along the way, I even found a couple of pieces of green sea glass.

The next thing I knew, an hour had passed. I'd seen some tidal pools, but the Hole-in-the-Wall was a bit too far to go. Plus, I worried about the tide coming in, so I turned around and worked my way back to the parking lot.

Nick hadn't replied to my text from the road yet. I wanted to send him another photo. I found a spot with a great background, held up the piece of sea glass, and snapped.

When I looked at the photo, there was something in the water behind me. Spinning around, I watched the water, and a few seconds later a whale surfaced in a graceful arc and slid back below the water.

"Oh God, wow. Did you see the whale?" I looked around, wanting to share the experience with someone, but no one was close by.

I plopped down on a large, gnarly piece of driftwood. "I can't believe there's a whale right there." I laughed in delight. "But you cannot have this phone!" I called to the whale and, as soon as I did, he sent up a spray as if to laugh at me.

This place simply enchanted me. It was incredible, wild, and it spoke to my soul. I wondered if it was just me or if others felt this way? A wave of sadness suddenly washed over me. This was an experience that needed to be shared, and I was here alone. I knew without a doubt Rob would have loved it. And now I understood why he made me promise. I needed to do these things for myself. To emerge from my grief and sadness, and realize the world was still out there. I could almost hear him say, *see, Lizzie, I told you so. Go off and see the world. Even though I'm gone, I'm still with you.*

A sob caught in my throat. Yes, he was right. I swept away the tears and rubbed my forehead, looking out across the waves and breathing in the wonderful sea air. Taking a precious moment to be *in* the moment.

I opened a text and quickly typed to Nick.

I made it to Rialto Beach. I am blown away. It made me think of Rob. You. And I wish you were here with me. Here's a picture for you x

I sent it and hoped he'd make the connection between the sea glass and the agate I'd found the other day.

A few moments later, my phone pinged.

I see you found some sea glass. I wish I was there too.

I smiled.

Yep, did a little road trip on my own. Research. Having a good day?

Typical business meetings. See you soon on the beach.

Safe travels, see you on the beach x

I hit send and then put my phone back in my pocket, deciding I'd rather enjoy the view live than from behind the camera. I walked closer to the shoreline, just far enough from the water's edge that the waves wouldn't reach my feet, and stood quietly, letting my arms hang loosely by my side and nature flow around me. The scent of the ocean, salty, tangy, and the damp sea air had a freshness I loved. It was rejuvenating.

I felt alive.

Clouds were rolling in and it started to rain. I sighed and took the hint. Time to go.

The rain came harder, and I jogged back to my car in the lot. I was absolutely drenched and rolled my eyes when I saw my forgotten raincoat on the back seat. Pulling open the door, I hopped inside and locked the doors.

I reached into the cargo area and pulled a duffle bag over the headrest. I'd gotten into the habit of keeping a fresh set of clothes in the bag. Nothing fancy, but something that would keep me warm and dry. Living in the vehicle while driving from place to place had taught me well.

I shed the wet clothes, which wasn't the easiest feat. Everything was sticking to me, but I finally hauled them off and shoved them in a plastic bag. The windows fogged up, which at least meant no one could see in. A chill had set in; goosebumps rose along my flesh, and my legs trembled. I lifted my butt and pulled on a cozy pair of fleece pants and a bulky sweater. I yanked on socks and my dry runners.

"Oooh, there we go. That feels much better." I wound my

hair up on my head. It was dripping, but I had some napkins I used to blot out the water.

Leaning forward, I started the car and turned the heat to full blast. I even turned the seat warmer on so my frozen butt could defrost. I gave a shiver of contentment when warmth filled the interior and spread through me.

I'd finished the fries long ago, but I took a sandwich from the cooler. I sure hoped my thermos of coffee was still hot.

Eating the sandwich, and sipping the warm coffee, I relaxed in the back seat and looked through the windshield streaming with rain.

I'd had the strangest sensation that the rain was cleansing me when I ran to the car, cleaning off residue from my past to be soaked up by the earth, absorbed, and allowing for renewal.

Overwhelmed, I sat quietly to allow these feelings in.

Waves crashed on to the beach and the rain grew more intense. The side windows were still steamed up, and I couldn't see much of anything around me. Even though I worried darkness may fall quicker with this weather, I had a sense of unbelievable peace.

I finished my snack, climbed over the console between the front seats, and settled into the now hot driver's seat. My bottom thanked it.

I turned the wipers on and took a last, long look before heading back. It was later than I expected, and too late for the side trip to Hoh Rain Forest. Truth be told, I wasn't up for that extra driving time, especially in the rain. While disappointed, I justified my decision. I was getting tired, both emotionally and physically, and eager to get home.

How I wished I could snap my fingers and be back at my cottage. I settled in for the long drive back, content, and still cradled in my newfound sense of peace.

Chapter Twenty-two

Finally, after what seemed like the Never-ending Drive, I was on the outskirts of Savage Cove and just about shattered. I needed food, watering, and a bathroom. I drove by a hamburger joint I wanted to try, but I needed the comfort food from the café. It was close, and I crossed my fingers, wishing hard for it to be open so I could stop in. I let out a little cheer when I saw the lights on, and parked in a spot I found right in front of Sol.

First, I ran to the restroom. Much relieved, I felt less stressed and went to the counter. I knew exactly what I wanted today, and my only intention was to grab some food and go. I'd eat at home.

Hardly able to keep my eyes open, I stood behind two couples and had to bite my tongue so I didn't rudely tell them to hurry up. I was bone tired and thought my brain was melting. My patience had evaporated and, to top it off, I was a grimy mess and needed a bath. I glanced around while I waited to see if I recognized anyone, and I was thankful I didn't. Not that I knew a lot of people here. If I could twinkle my nose like Samantha the witch, I'd transport myself right into a hot and bubbly bath. Do not pass Go. Do not collect $200.

Just go home.

Finally, the barista took my order, and moments later a bag with my boxed roast beef dinner was put in front of me, with a tall latte.

I'd all but finished my drink by the time I got home, and the aroma of the meal made my mouth water.

It was dark, and I'd missed the sunset. I was dragging my ass when I got out of the car. Not wanting to make two trips, I gathered all my bags to pack-mule into the house. Once inside, after struggling with the door, I dropped everything on the floor by the front door, except my satchel and dinner.

I walked through the dark house and turned on the kitchen light, eager to unpack my dinner. It had to be my exhaustion that disrupted my earlier sense of peace and now contributed to the smack of loneliness so intense my chest hurt. I leaned on the table, staring at the box of dinner.

One box.

One dinner.

One person.

Me.

I no longer had any family or close friends. Nick was on the other side of the continent, but we were too new to categorize us.

The darkened cottage embraced me. I was too tired to turn on the rest of the lights, and God knew how I'd even be able to draw a bath. I sighed and decided to sort through today's images and videos tomorrow.

I shuffled into the bathroom, ran the hot water, and added the rest of the bottle of bubbles. Back to the kitchen while the tub filled, I poured a glass of wine, washed my hands, and opened the box of dinner.

I carried the box and wine glass into the bathroom. Eating with my fingers, I leaned my hip against the vanity and watched the water rise in the tub. Unable to finish all the food—the café was very generous—I put the box in the fridge and topped up my wine.

The bath called me like a siren. After lighting candles and turning off the lights, I eased myself into the tub. Bubbles, sparkling like diamonds in the candlelight, swirled around me.

"Heaven at last," I said softly to myself.

The aroma of rosemary, eucalyptus and a touch of citrus, with the scent of the candles, surrounded me. I lay back, resting my head on a rolled-up towel, and balanced the wine glass on the edge of the tub with two fingers. My hair floated on the bubbles; it was stringy, dirty, and matted from being caught out in the rain. Taking a breath, I ducked below the surface and stayed under as long as I could. The silence of the water in my ears carried me to another dimension. I emerged and floated in the hot water, relaxed and calm.

I closed my eyes, feeling languorous. I tried to sip wine without sitting up and held the stem of the glass under the water. I tipped it just enough to get a mouthful, some spilling down my chin.

Starting to drift off, lulled by the water and wine, I was startled when the glass tipped into the water.

"Shoot." I sat up quickly. I practically ached to slide between the sheets.

I drained the tub, got my phone from my bag, and did the bare minimum to get ready for bed.

Dropping my phone on the comforter, I dug underneath the pillow for my sleeping shirt. I pulled it out, a pillow fell on the floor, and I threw it back on the bed, frustration taking over. Everything seemed to take forever to get done! I flung back the covers, and collapsed between the crisp sheets with a sigh.

Then I realized the old phone was in my bag in the kitchen. Deep down, I was still hoping for another text. "Damn, I'm not getting it." Snaking my arm out from the warmth of the covers, I plugged my new phone into the charger cord.

I looked at the pillow next to mine and imagined Nick laying there beside me. My breath quickened. I wondered if that would ever happen.

I checked my phone: no messages. I pulled up the app Bubble Pop! and played a few rounds until my eyes were almost crossing. My eyes drifted shut and dreams of waves, trees, and jumping whales came to life in my tired brain.

I wasn't sure if the ping from my phone was in my dream, or real. Eyes still closed. I felt the sheets, rummaging around. In my sleep-confused state I wondered if it was another text message to Marissa. Looking at the screen in the dark, a slow smile spread across my lips, and my heart nearly burst.

A text from Nick.

It instantly woke me up. So much better a text from Nick than one for Marissa.

Did you get back safely?

I replied straight away.

I did, thanks. It was a magical day.

I'm glad you enjoyed it. Good night x

Same to you. Hope your day was good. Sweet dreams x

The text from him was exactly what I needed to help me fall soundly asleep.

Chapter Twenty-three

I had a hard time containing my excitement. I felt like a school-girl again, waiting for my first boyfriend to show up and take me out in his car. But it was me who was going in the car to meet . . . my boyfriend?

I shook my head. I was too old to have a boyfriend. It sounded almost childish, but how else could you label it? I was going out to meet my man? Even that sounded weird.

Nick had arrived home from New York this morning and invited me to his house for a bonfire. It was a great idea and sounded wonderfully normal. I couldn't wait. We'd been apart three days, and it seemed an eternity. I was eager to see him again.

He'd offered to pick me up, but I wanted to drive for a change. He'd picked me up and dropped me off the last few times, and I didn't want to be overly reliant on him. He gave me the address. I didn't need it but wasn't ready to tell him that. It wasn't like I could say. "Hey, I know your address. I was at your house the other day, snooping around."

It was supposed to be cooler this evening. I dressed up warm and, while I was getting ready, I wondered what the evening ahead might bring.

It gave me an undeniable thrill. Hadn't I told myself I was open to a summer romance? I smiled ruefully at my mental change of *fling* to *romance*. Clearly, I'd gone past the stage of wanting it to only be a fling and had shifted to the romance category.

I had an hour to kill before I had to leave.

My stomach knotted with the secret knowledge I still carried. Somehow, I had to find a way to tell Nick about the text, and find out if it really was from him. I wondered if it would be easier now, because we'd gotten to know each other better. Maybe he'd be more understanding?

I shook my head. Nope, he wouldn't. I'd backed myself into a corner, and the only way out was the truth. A truth that could go either way.

I rummaged through the cupboards, picking some items I could take to have at the bonfire. I wondered if I should stop at the store on the way, to grab some marshmallows and graham crackers to add to the monster-size chocolate bar in my hand.

I was dying, watching the clock edge toward evening.

I caught my breath, suddenly anxious. It was a nervous excitement making me fidget. I needed to calm the heck down, so I walked to the beach. I checked my watch and sighed, seeing there was still some more time to kill before leaving. He'd said 6 p.m., and I planned to arrive right on time.

I shook my head. Enough, I told myself. I liked him, and from what I could tell he liked me. Enough of worrying about all the stupid things.

"Right then, time to go." Being early was no big deal.

Back at the house, I turned on a nightlight and locked the door behind me. The drive to the store didn't take that long, and I could get what I needed. Back on the road, about ten minutes later, I pulled up to the gates of his driveway. They were open, not closed like the last time I was here.

I drove up the laneway slowly. It twisted and turned so the house wasn't visible until you came out of the trees and into a beautifully tended landscape garden. It impressed me. To think he did most of this on his own, with only a little bit of help, told me what kind of a caring man he was. And I was getting to like him more and more.

I drove to the front entrance and pulled up just past the main door. I hadn't even turned the engine off before he was coming down the stairs from the front porch, taking them two at a time. He opened my car door.

"Hey." I got out and, to my surprise, he swung me into a big hug. I clung to him and laughed.

"Hey yourself." He set me back on my feet.

I hadn't expected such an effusive greeting, but I wasn't complaining.

"It's good to see you." I was reluctant to let Nick go. Being in his arms just felt right.

"You too. I'm glad you're here." The look in his eyes made my heart flutter.

We lingered for a moment longer, and then let each other go. I opened the rear door, and he reached in to grab the bags.

"You didn't need to bring anything."

"It's fine, I don't like to arrive empty-handed." I smiled up at him.

We walked side by side into the foyer of his house.

I hadn't seen this section last time I was here, and it was just as gorgeous as the rest. A beautiful timber staircase rose to the second floor, and a high vaulted ceiling gave a lot of light on both levels. "Wow, this is lovely."

"Thank you, it's almost too big for just me."

I gave him a quick look. "You wouldn't think of selling, would you?" I couldn't imagine selling such a wonderful home.

"It's crossed my mind several times but, as you know, my father also lives on the property, in his own house. So it wouldn't be as simple as just selling for me."

I followed him into the great room, and this is where things started to look familiar.

"It's been in the family for a lot of years," Nick explained. "It's hard to part with history."

"It sure is." I placed the bags on the counter island. "What made your dad decide to move out of this house?"

"He was being stubborn. He didn't want to live here."

"Why? There seems to be plenty of room." I was curious.

"The reason he didn't want to live in the house with me is because he's an older man."

"So? That doesn't matter, does it?" I couldn't comprehend that logic.

Nick slapped the counter. "Exactly what I tried to tell him, but he was adamant and didn't want to, in quotes, live with my son and cramp your style." He laughed and shook his head. "I hope maybe he didn't want *me* to cramp *his* style."

"That's funny. It sounds like he thinks you'll be busy entertaining and have a variety of women parading through the house." I found that humorous, but I think I was a little jealous of the possibility.

Nick shrugged his shoulders. "I guess. But he's wrong." He looked at me intently.

My mouth dried, and I licked my lips. That look was so hot it almost made me melt.

Even though I had no claim on him, I was feeling a touch possessive. Nick was a good-looking man in the prime of his life. Why wouldn't he have a parade of women in his life? All the same, I was glad to hear he didn't.

"Looks like this is a one-woman parade right now," he said, with a slow smile.

I placed my hand on the counter to steady myself.

Nick was ready for Lizzie. He hoped he knew her well enough at this point to feel confident that she would be happy with what he had planned. They seemed on the same wavelength, and he found it encouraging.

She was a take-it-as-it-comes kinda girl. That was very refreshing. The idea of having a bonfire out by the beach was perfect. It had inspired him to get the ingredients for a clambake, Pacific Northwest style.

It was years since he'd done one. He's picked up what he needed at the market earlier today: Dungeness crab, local mussels, clams, and some fragrant cedar, as well as potatoes, corn, onion, and sausage. And, of course, Lawry's seasoned salt.

He'd continued to check the fire and got the pot on a while ago so they could eat at a reasonable hour. He had enough food for an army, but his dad was coming over as well, and he had a very healthy appetite.

Seeing Lizzie in his kitchen, relaxed and smiling, Nick acknowledged to himself that he'd missed her. He picked her up and swung her into another big hug.

Her laugh was like music as she hugged him back. "Now that is my kind of welcome."

She was breathless when he put her down, and he was reluctant to let her go, liking the sensation the connection between them aroused in him.

"I'm glad you approve." It was difficult to pull his attention from her, but he did. They unpacked the grocery bag she'd brought, and he chuckled. "I can see what we'll be cooking around the bonfire. I have some wieners in the fridge too."

Lizzie's eyes sparkled in merriment. "I adore fine dining."

That's what he loved about her. He paused. Did he say love? That shook him, and he had to regroup his thoughts before he could speak again.

"A woman after my own heart," he said lightly, and liked the blush that rushed up to her cheeks.

She cleared her throat and sniffed. "What is that delicious smell?"

"It's a clambake."

Her eyebrows shot up. "Really? I thought that was an East Coast thing."

"It could be, I suppose, but we've done it for years, sourcing local ingredients."

He held up a bottle of white wine and one of red. She pointed to red.

"Well, why the hell not, I say?" She slid on to the stool.

He opened the wine and decanted it, then took out a small grazing board he'd made earlier, sliced some fresh bread, and put it on the island beside the wine glasses.

"You are hired." She was being playful today.

He relished how it made him feel. Until she exploded into his life, he hadn't realized that he'd been merely existing, coasting from day to day. With Lizzie he felt alive again.

He winked at her. "We'll have to negotiate the terms."

She'd been on his mind constantly while he was away. There were moments where he thought he'd be ready for the next step when he saw her again. Part of him wanted to ask her to stay the night with him, more than anything. He hadn't been with anyone since Ari. The realization that he was even entertaining the thought of Lizzie staying overnight was an enormous step for him. But to move their relationship a notch higher, to intimacy, was something they both had to agree on. If he was honest with himself, he just wasn't sure if he was ready to take that step.

Now, at last, they were together again, and all he wished for was for them to have a relaxed and enjoyable evening. But he couldn't deny his growing feelings; the desire he'd never imagined feeling again for a woman was awakening in her presence.

"You're smiling."

Her voice broke him out of his reverie. "Am I?"

She nodded. "You look happy."

He faced her. "I am. I'm glad you're here, Lizzie."

"Me too." She reached out and took his hand.

Nick held hers. He wanted nothing more than to kiss her right now. He gave her a gentle tug, pulling her toward him, and leaned down. Her head tilted back and he lowered his, brushing her lips with his own.

The kiss was gentle and soft, intensifying as they moved closer together. He held her close and tipped her back slightly, and she wound her arms around his neck.

It was perfect. He was breathless. The pounding of his heart echoed in his ears, along with the rush of blood through his veins. He deepened the kiss, and her scent wrapped around them. The stool turned, and he stepped between her knees, trapped between her thighs.

He pushed his fingers into her hair, cradling the back of her head, the silky strands of her hair sliding over his skin.

Their kiss consumed him, and he pulled her off the stool into his arms. Nick hadn't been this lost in a person, ever. He wanted to let himself go, but a shadow of underlying hesitancy warred within him. The part of him that had been hurt so deeply wasn't willing to open up.

Houdini barked, announcing someone was coming. If he hadn't interrupted them, how far would they have gone?

Chapter Twenty-four

Nick rested his forehead on Lizzie's. "Dad's arrived," he rasped, and he placed a hand on the side of her cheek.

She was panting, flushed, and her hair was mussed. "H-he has? Oh dear. Where's a powder room?"

"Through there." He pointed to the door beside the breeze-way, and Lizzie vanished inside.

Nick went behind the counter to conceal his erection and regain his normal breathing rhythm. He pushed around the groceries Lizzie'd brought.

"Hello, son." Walter entered the kitchen and went right to the fridge for a beer.

"Dad, glad you could come." Nick smiled at his father.

"When you told me what you were cooking, there's no way I'd be missing that. What's the occasion, anyway?" He twisted off the cap and took a long drink of the beer.

"No occasion," Nick replied casually.

Lizzie returned from the powder room. She was refreshed, still a little flushed, but gave no indication of their recent passion.

"Oh-ho, no occasion, you say? This is a big occasion. You have a woman in your house." Walter wasn't one to mince words.

Nick was used to it, and hoped Lizzie wouldn't be taken aback by his manner.

Lizzie hesitated a beat, before sliding back on to the stool. She looked at his father with an intensity that seemed a little strange.

"Hi."

"Dad, this is Lizzie. Lizzie, my dad, Walter." He made the introductions.

"I know you, I saw you on the beach." Walter nodded and glanced at Nick. "She was on the beach the other day."

"She's always on the beach," Nick answered, and winked at Lizzie.

"Walter. Walter *Charlton*?" Lizzie said, and looked between Nick and Walter.

"Yes, we do have the same last names," Walter chuckled, and then took a swig of his beer.

"Yes, of course you do." Lizzie looked a little flustered, as if she was trying to make sense of something. "I remember you now! It was that day you yelled at me, Nick." She pointed at Nick.

Nick watched his father as he glanced between him and Lizzie, a slow smile spreading on the older man's face. Nick knew exactly what his father was thinking, and he decided it best not to give him any fodder for the fire. Besides, there was nothing to say.

"He yelled at you? That's not like him at all." His dad looked shocked and gave Nick a stern glare.

"No, not like that. He was trying to get my attention, and I was way down the beach," Lizzie was quick to clarify.

"Well, okay then. That's better." Walter nodded, and wagged his finger at Nick.

"Dad. You know me better than that." Nick shook his head, but he was smiling. "It's a small world, isn't it?" he said, and raised his wine glass.

"So you guys have known each other for a little while?" Walter asked. A dog pushed up against his legs, sitting down and resting a chin against his knee.

"Not a long time, just a couple of weeks. I remember this beauty," Lizzie replied.

Walter played with the dog's ears. "This is Candy. My sweet girl."

"Aww, she definitely is."

"She's a senior lady, but still has the antics of a younger dog." The love for his dog came through in the tone of Walter's voice.

Nick remained silent, watching the easy interaction between them, and was pleased. It was the total opposite to his dad's relationship with Ari.

"Houdini seems to love her," Lizzie said.

"Oh, he does. He's infatuated, but she's the boss." Walter finished his beer and Nick got him another one.

"Okay, we should head outside. I've got a table set up under the arbor." Nick helped Lizzie off the stool. She didn't need the assistance but he wanted an excuse to touch her again.

He placed the glass and wine bottle on the table. His dad wandered over to the edge of the patio, beer in one hand, absently stroking Candy's head with the other.

"I could never tire of this view," he called over his shoulder.

Nick and Lizzie joined him.

"It is spectacular. Constantly changing," she noted.

"Where are you from?" Walter asked.

"DC."

He turned and looked at her. "Really? What brings you out west?"

Nick noticed her hesitation.

She glanced at Nick, then his dad. "Adventure, I guess. I'm also upholding a promise I made."

Walter pressed his lips together and nodded. "Hmm, maybe one day you'll tell me about it."

"Maybe." She smiled and glanced at Nick.

"It's time to dump the pot." Nick went over to the plastic-lined table.

"Dump the pot?" Lizzie asked.

She and Walter stood next to the table.

"Watch," Walter instructed her.

Nick tipped over the pot, and the contents spilled out across the table, caught from running over the side by the towels he'd rolled up and put under the edges of the plastic tablecloth.

"Oh my God!" Lizzie exclaimed. "Incredible."

Nick inhaled, and the aromas of the combined foods filled the air. "Dig in," he said.

"You don't have to tell me twice." Walter dove in.

"Where to start?" Lizzie tapped her chin.

He gave her a gentle nudge with his shoulder. "Anywhere you like."

She looked up at him through her lashes, then teasingly pursed her lips. Nick raised an eyebrow and nodded slightly. He would rather return to their interrupted kiss too.

The evening was going well, and they were sitting around the bonfire now. Nick enjoyed having his dad here and was thrilled to see how well he and Lizzie got along.

Walter slapped his thighs, making the dogs jump up. "Well, I'm off then." They all stood. "Mind if I pack up some leftovers?"

"Of course not," Nick told him. They'd cleaned up from dinner, and everything was in the kitchen. "Take as much as you want. I'd hate to see it go to waste."

"Great, thanks, we . . . um, I'll enjoy it." He kissed Lizzie on the cheek and shook Nick's hand. "You two stay here, I'll go pack up a container. Have a nice evening." He gave a wink before heading into the house, Candy at his heels.

Lizzie was laughing. "He's cute."

"He certainly is a character." Nick filled their wine glasses again. He watched his dad through the window, and waved when he lifted the container and left.

"You're very lucky to still have a parent," she said over the rim of her wine glass.

Nick nodded. "Yes, I am." A deeper emotion filled him. It was very powerful. "I dread the day he's not around anymore. And I can't imagine how you feel, not having your parents or your brother. I never had a sibling, so all I've got is my dad."

"You have no other family?"

He shook his head. "No, not really. Dad met Mom when she came over from England with her parents. They'd lost most everyone in the Blitz."

"How horrible. It's hard to imagine how long ago World War Two is now. It's something we can never forget."

"I agree." He raised his glass. "To all those we must never forget."

"Yes, to those no longer with us."

They gently touched the rim of their wine glasses together.

Lizzie snuggled down under the throw blanket and propped her feet on a log. She let out a big sigh. "This is heaven. How hard it must be for you to leave on business trips."

He reached over and tucked the corner of the blanket under

the cushion of her chair. He was rewarded with a soft smile. "Yes, you're right, it is. Truth be told, I am getting a little tired of it. There was a time when I didn't mind traveling so much, but now I find I want to be here more."

It was when Lizzie had dropped into his life that he'd begun to realize how much the trips away sucked the life out of him, keeping him from the things he found pleasure in. He was sick and tired of traveling, being alone on the road. He had enjoyed having someone to text when he was in New York, and it was like a shot of reality.

Nick sensed a change in the wind. He watched Lizzie stare into the fire and knew he had to decide. Did he want to make the change because of her, or because it was what he needed? After all, she'd be gone in another few weeks. Nick toyed with the idea of encouraging her to stay.

Even if it was only for a few days or weeks.

Nick had never felt so relaxed and . . . complete as he did with Lizzie. Knowing each other this short while, it didn't seem possible to feel so in tune with her. It was like he'd known her for years. And yet, the way the days were flying by, her departure date loomed ever closer. The thought of her being gone was so uncomfortable he fidgeted on the seat.

Being with Lizzie like this—contented and happy, with no drama—made him wonder what on earth he'd seen in Ari. It was like he'd been blind, deaf, and unable to see the real Ari beneath her dazzling veneered surface. He shook his head.

"What's wrong?" Lizzie asked him.

"What do you mean?"

"You were just shaking your head. And you looked kind of angry."

He saw she was genuinely concerned. He wasn't used to a woman being concerned about him. He was no longer walking on eggshells, being on his guard about everything he said. It was refreshing.

"I was thinking how this makes you happy."

"You mean the bonfire?" She faced him.

He nodded.

"Why wouldn't it make me happy? I love doing stuff like this, being outside, and with somebody I like. Getting cozy by a fire." She threw him a teasing look.

Nick thoroughly enjoyed Lizzie's company, and the night had been great. Introducing her to his father was no small thing. But the hesitation he still felt bugged the hell out of him. Was it time to stop listening to that voice in his head?

The fire was warm. I loved sitting out here under the stars with Nick. I'd had a few glasses of wine, and was relaxing nicely. Somehow I was able to push away the revelation that Nick's name was Charlton. I'd been careful not to show my surprise when I'd recognized Walter, but a lot had fallen into place at that moment. I didn't want it to take center stage tonight, though. I was so mellow, and to give thought to the complexity of emotions—shock, relief, concern, curiosity—would ruin our time together.

Nick stood, and I watched him poke the fire. It crackled and shot up a spray of sparks when he dropped a log on.

"Should I get another?" Nick asked, and held up the empty wine bottle.

I smiled and nodded, throwing caution to the wind.

"What the heck, I have nowhere to be. Dinner was delicious. Let me get dessert." I made a half-hearted attempt to move; I was so comfy, and Nick placed his hand on my shoulder.

"No, you stay here. I'll bring out your s'mores." He laughed. "They are one of my favorites."

"Me too, and hobo pies. I've even done pizza and grilled cheese on the fire."

"Really? Not me. Just wieners, marshmallows, and s'mores. Oh, and my mom liked to put potatoes in the fire. She called them jacket potatoes. They were great with lots of butter."

"Want to throw some on too?" I asked him. "They sound delish, and what we don't eat we can have for breakfast."

Nick turned and faced me as I realized what I'd just said.

"Uh, well, what I mean is—"

"You are more than welcome to stay. We've been drinking, and I wouldn't want you to drive."

I glanced out over the dark water to figure out how to reply. The words just fell out of me, as if it was a completely natural thing to say. A simmer of excitement sparked low inside me. I was ready to stay. I think I'd been ready for a while now. It was Nick who, I sensed, was holding back. I looked at his face, the glow of the fire reflecting on his features.

Oh, yes, I was ready.

"Okay, thank you. I didn't mean to invite myself." I pulled my lower lip between my teeth.

Nick held up his hand. "I was going to ask. If you want to go, I can call for a driver. But, Lizzie, I would like it if you decide to stay here with me."

I beamed, and that spark leaped to a little flame. "I'd like to stay with you."

With unspoken words, we both understood.

Tonight would be our first time together.

He came back to me and leaned down, kissing me until I felt boneless in the chair and lost all spatial awareness. The blanket dropped as I untangled my arm from it and slid my fingers around the back of his neck.

His warmth radiated up my arm, and I ached for him. His breathing was as ragged as my mine.

"What about the s'mores?" His voice was gravely.

"They can wait."

"Want to go in?" Nick's eyes reflected the firelight, and his words were low.

The moment had arrived.

I whispered, "Yes."

I let Nick's fingers take mine, and we walked quietly through his house, up the timber stairs, and down to the end of the hall. He stopped in front of wooden double doors.

He faced me, cupped my cheeks, and tipped my face up to his. I wasn't sure my knees would hold me up. The intensity in his eyes flooded me with warmth.

I held my breath.

"You're sure?" His question was simple.

I stared up at him and nodded. "Yes," I whispered again.

"I'm glad." He smiled and leaned down for a kiss.

I murmured against his lips, "Me too."

He nodded, and tilted his head. Our lips slid together as perfectly as if they were made for each other. I wound my arms around his neck. The heat from his body seared me through my clothes, and I melted against him. Nick broke the kiss and scorched a trail with his lips down my chin to the tender spot just below my ear.

My breath caught when he swung the doors open to the bedroom.

"Oh my." The room stunned me. It was huge. The décor was a mixture of sea and mountains, with Native art on the walls. And the windows . . . They were magnificent, looking out over the ocean. The massive bed was on the other side of a low stone wall, and faced the windows. Lying in it probably would feel like flying. A rustic fireplace rose from the highly glossed, wide-planked wooden floor to the vaulted ceiling. It was spectacular.

I looked at him. "I love this room. It takes my breath away."

"You take my breath away." His voice lowered, and goosebumps rippled along my flesh.

"Nick, oh . . . I'm—"

"I know. Me too."

I was speechless. So many emotions roared through me, I couldn't stop trembling. Nick scooped me up in his arms and carried me to the bed.

It was romantic, erotic, and I wanted him desperately. He rested his knee on the edge of the bed and lay me down. We didn't look away from each other as I plucked at the buttons on my blouse until they were all undone. His eyes dipped and the muscle in his jaw clenched. I watched him, my breath growing heavy as this amazingly sexy, gorgeous man stood before me.

I knew then I was at risk of falling for him more deeply than I could ever have imagined, and the racing of my pulse wasn't only because he excited me so. I reached up, needing to touch him, taste him, feel him.

His lips curved in a slow smile. His confidence and power radiated over me and swept me away to a place of comfort, safety, and glittering desire.

Chapter Twenty-five

The next morning, after a night of lovemaking, Nick was in the kitchen preparing coffee and Lizzie was sitting at the island. It was exactly how he'd pictured it would be. He wasn't sorry they had spent the night together—he had wanted it more than anything. But he knew it would complicate things, especially with her leaving to continue her quest.

He poured their coffee, the strong aroma filling the air. Nick paused and watched Lizzie for a moment. Her long hair was tousled and pulled over one shoulder, and seeing her in one of his T-shirts had more of an impact than anything else she could be wearing. Her chin cupped in her hand, she gazed out the window. He almost forgot how to breathe, and gave himself a shake.

Even though his reservations and guilt still clung to him, being with her, growing closer to her, continued to lighten his mood. He still had a lot of emotion to deal with that was directly related to his wife. That hurt was, amazingly, still raw.

He knew if they were to continue to be together, he'd have

to tell her the full story of Ari. It was just a matter of picking the right time. But when was there ever a right time?

He put the mug in front of her. "Here you go, my queen."

Lizzie looked at him with a bright smile. "Queen, I kinda like that. Isn't it the most beautiful morning?" She lifted the cup and took a long drink.

Nick looked out the window and scrunched his eyebrows in puzzlement. "It's raining."

"Huh? Oh, yeah, it is, but it's still beautiful."

"Are you hung-over?" he asked over the rim of his cup.

She shook her head and giggled. "Nope." Raising her shoulders, still smiling, she dropped them and let out a sigh. "Every morning you wake up is a beautiful day. And even more so after a night as wonderful as last night, thanks to you." She raised the mug. "Oh, and great coffee too."

He burst out laughing, and Houdini jumped to his feet barking. "Easy, boy. Lay down. I'm glad to be lumped into the joys of coffee and waking up."

"What can I say? Necessities of life. Between you and the café, I have definitely found my coffee haven."

Nick chuckled, and then paused. "Which café?"

"You know—the one I told you about before, Sol. The one that's on the road off Lincoln, remember?"

He pressed his lips together when he realized the café she was referring to. He hadn't expected their conversation to go there again. This was the opening he needed to tell her more about Ari. But he wasn't ready.

"Yeah, of course. I forgot."

Of course, he hadn't. He owned it. He'd bought it for Ari, to try to keep her grounded, happy, content. It obviously hadn't worked. He really needed to change the name of the café too.

Nick had no control over keeping Lizzie away from the café. The realization that she was so enamored of it made him unsettled, now they'd grown closer. If people started talking, and she learned more about him and his wife before he told her himself, that wouldn't be good. But it still didn't give him the push to talk about it now.

He watched her nibble on a piece of toast, and picked up his mug. He went to stand by the windows in the great room, now streaming with rain.

She followed him, and they sat at the table where they'd had breakfast the other day.

"I probably shouldn't stay too long," Lizzie commented. "Last night was amazing. And a bit of a surprise."

"For me too." Nick wanted to convey the meaning it had held for him too, but he couldn't find the words.

"Why don't you come over for dinner at my place tonight? Let me cook for you for a change. Invite your dad too," Lizzie suggested.

"Sounds like a great idea. I'm sure Dad would be thrilled to come over. What time do you want us?" Nick was touched she'd include his father, but he was already wondering how he could get Walter to drive himself, so the opportunity was there for Nick to spend the night. What had she done to him?

"How about just before sunset?" Lizzie suggested.

"You think there'll be one today?" Nick pointed out the window.

"Yes, I do. It will clear up and be beautiful." Lizzie pushed her shoulders back.

Nick glanced at the sky. "Well, there's no blue sky, and my mom used to say, if there's enough blue sky to patch a sailor's pants, it's going to be a nice day."

"Pff, there will be a blue sky." She waved her hand at him.

"You are irresistible." Nick pulled her chair beside his and kissed her.

"Mmm, you make me not want to go home. I have responsibilities, you know," she said against his lips, their eyes locked on each other.

"I have the same problem." He smiled and pulled her on to his lap. "You're not the only one with responsibilities."

They finished their coffee, all the while wrapped in the intimate bubble of each other.

Lizzie groaned and stood up. "Well, maybe I should go up and get ready." She dropped her head back, and her arms hung by her side. "But I don't wanna," she wailed.

"Then don't. Stay with me. We could go back to bed and watch the rain all day."

"You are tempting me, you evil man," she said, teasingly. "But I should get going. You know, deadlines, deadlines, deadlines." She curled her lip.

He followed her to the stairs.

"I appreciate you letting me wear your T-shirt," she said over her shoulder, a few steps up from him.

"Nothing looks sexier than you in one of my shirts." He appreciated the fine view of her trim, tanned legs, her delicate ankles, and he gave her a gentle swat on the bottom. He laughed when she yelped.

"Hey, I didn't think you were into that." Then she took off down the hall, Nick hot on her tail.

She dove on to the bed, laughing. Houdini had overtaken his master, and also launched himself on top of her. Nick followed both of them.

Howls of laughter and dog barks filled the room, before quieting down and being replaced by sounds of passion.

Chapter Twenty-six

I couldn't get over how quickly our relationship changed after our clambake night. The past few days, we'd spent time at each other's houses. It was good. Very good. And I refused to let the saying *it's too good to be true* darken my thoughts. Rather, I made sure to be present, in the moment, and enjoy every minute.

I hoped Nick was doing the same. He seemed to be, although I did catch moments when he was lost in thought. Did he think of his wife? It was natural, right? They had been married, had a life together before she died.

I'd shared some stories about Rob when we were younger. Nick would listen when I spoke of my parents, not saying anything, simply holding my hand while I talked.

He told me more about his mother. I was sad for Walter, because they seemed like true soulmates, and it made me wonder again if those who had experienced a great love could possibly have another? Was Ari Nick's great love? I wasn't sure I wanted to know.

I learned that Nick liked to sleep on his stomach, but not

before we cuddled after making love. I'd fall asleep with my head on his chest and his arm around me. If I woke in the night he was on his front. Keeping me in his arms until I fell asleep, before he found his own comfortable position.

I was still waiting for him to talk about his wife, Marissa . . . Ari . . . and it hung in the back of my mind. I'd made the decision to stop my research on her, and that led to me trying to forget about the text. I knew I was ignoring the issue, but I just couldn't bring myself to say anything yet. I felt if I continued the research, or even mentioned the text, it might jeopardize what we were building together. My departure date was fast approaching. I crossed my arms and looked out the window to the beach. Thinking of leaving made my chest hurt, and I gave myself a shake. I didn't want to think about it until absolutely necessary.

Nick was coming over later, after he checked his dad's place. Walter was away for a couple of days, and Nick looked in on the boathouse. He said he liked coming to my cottage rather than staying at his place. I wasn't sure why, really. Mine was smaller, more rustic; his had all the conveniences.

I only had a queen bed, as opposed to his king, and most nights Houdini took up almost half of it. I wanted to get him a dog bed. If I did leave at my planned departure date, he could keep the bed.

I'd never made it back to the market for the photos I wanted to take, to use in a blog post. So I decided to head over today to take some shots, and see what fresh seafood and vegetables were available.

Of course, going to the market also meant a stop at the café, and the chance of bumping into Claire. We had been chatting more since we'd exchanged phone numbers, and our friendship was growing despite our age difference.

I enjoyed spending time with her. But I still got the sense she was holding something back. I wasn't sure what it could be, but she had this secretive, happy air about her. Maybe she was in love. I hoped that was it. Everyone needs love.

Laden down with Dungeness crab, fresh oysters and clams, I made sure they were packed in ice so I had time to do a bit more shopping after getting a coffee at the café. No sign of Claire. I frowned and looked around. I wondered what she was up to. Wendy was behind the counter today, and I could ask her. But I'd come to understand that the two of them were like oil and water. So I decided it was best not to.

Juggling my bags, the desserts I'd caved in and bought, and my coffee mug, I pulled open the café door, lucky not to spill or drop anything.

Outside, I readjusted my load, and froze in the middle of taking a sip. A slow smile widened when I thought of a possibility.

Claire was away.

Walter was away.

Could it be? No, it must just be coincidence.

Did they even know each other? If they didn't then, I decided, we should have a dinner with the four of us. I thought they'd be the perfect cute couple and would suggest to Nick we should try setting them up.

I let out a contented sigh, and crossed the street. Savage Cove was really starting to feel like home to me. It would be easy to stay.

Nick and I avoided discussing my eventual departure. I think both of us preferred not to broach the subject, even though it hung over us like a cloud of doom.

I sighed and rubbed my forehead on the back of my hand. At this point, I could honestly admit I didn't want to leave. I wanted to stay. But I had a ticket booked, and car storage arranged.

And . . . the biggest reason of all.

I had promised Rob. He *made* me promise to live my life to the fullest. Get out and do things, travel, see the world, fly high and free.

Deathbed promises needed to be fulfilled. Right?

I was torn so deeply between Rob's promise and being with Nick, who had come into my world and knocked it right off its axis. What would Rob have told me? He probably would have said . . .

Oh . . . I didn't know what he would've said. Sometimes I knew exactly what Rob would think or say, and then there were other times when he just blew my mind with his thought patterns. Those were very un-twin moments. I wish I could call on twintuition now.

Either way, what I did in a few weeks' time should be completely up to me.

Nick would be a factor in whichever path I decided to take. But I was still cautious about making a decision without solid, clear, objective thought. I'd weigh it all up and then choose what seemed the best fit for me.

I had options, following my time in Hawaii. A few more places had invited me to come. I was stunned to think that hotels in Bora Bora, the South of France, Iceland and the Maldives all wanted to discuss collaboration—and all thanks to my travel blog. Of course I wanted to go. This week, a couple of brand deals had come in, which was completely unexpected and only complicated my decision. I'd started to think perhaps I needed an agent, or someone to vet the offers and handle the negotiations.

So many destinations were on my bucket list, and I definitely wanted to visit them. I wondered if Nick would be interested in traveling with me. He was busy with his own business travel, even though he'd like to cut back on it. I chewed my lip in thought. Going to these exotic locations was exciting. I knew I would meet people there, but deep inside I wanted to share my travels with Nick.

An ice cream truck was down by the waterfront, so I grabbed a soft cone and added it to my juggling act.

It was a bit of a misty day; it was funny how there'd be sun, and then the fog would roll in. I was getting used to the changing weather patterns here. The temperature seemed to hover somewhere around 75 degrees most of the days, except on rainy ones when it would dip into the 60s. Different weather from what I was used to on the East Coast, and it was a nice change.

My phone buzzed in my pocket. I panicked, not sure how to get at it with my hands full. Finding a bench looking out over the water, I put the bags down and pulled the phone out of my pocket, desperately licking the cone as ice cream dripped down the side.

It was Nick, checking in on our plans for tonight.

I replied, slipped my phone back into my purse, and spent a moment finishing my cone. Damn, I was happy. It was a good feeling. As long as I didn't think about leaving.

Chapter Twenty-seven

I adored fresh seafood. I kept it on ice after thoroughly washing the grit away. I'd bought horseradish, hot sauce, and seafood sauce to have with the fresh oysters. I didn't know what Nick liked best, but for me, it was seafood sauce with a touch of horseradish.

I checked the freezer and was glad to see I still had some shrimp. A friend of mine from college had a super easy recipe I'd make in a flash. I'd whip it up when Nick arrived. My mouth watered just thinking about it as I placed the fresh crusty bread I'd bought at the café on the counter. We'd use it to soak up the sauce.

Pulling out the drawers, I couldn't find an oyster shucker. I put my hands on my hips and pondered. Surely there would be something I could find to use that wouldn't rip open the palm of my hand?

All I had to do now was wait for Nick to arrive. In the meantime, I took a glass of wine to my desk by the window and got a bit of work done.

I closed some tabs on my desktop, did a bit of techie house-keeping, and then a screen jumped out at me. The image of Marissa stared back at me. I rested my elbow on the table and dropped my chin into my palm.

"What happened to you?" I whispered.

It was a search I'd done on Marissa a week or so back. I'd kept my promise to myself not to search for any more information about her. Anything new I learned had to come from Nick when he was ready.

For now, Nick seemed to be coming out of his gloominess. I could see a fun side to him that he had repressed. He was becoming more playful, and I adored that about him. Talking about Marissa would bring the clouds rolling back. I scrolled down; her picture was no longer looking back at me.

Nick was enjoying spending more time at Lizzie's house. It was cozy, and she had made it homey, even though she was only going to be here for another few weeks. His shoulders tightened and he gritted his teeth when he pushed open her door. He didn't want to think about her leaving, but it was something they had to deal with. The closer they became, the clearer it was that he needed to talk to her about Ari. It was just such a hard conversation to have.

He barely got the door open before Houdini was in like a shot, Candy following him. He chuckled and followed the dogs inside. Lizzie was bent over her laptop at the desk in front of the window. He admired her dedication to work. She was concentrating and didn't hear the commotion until the doored slammed shut behind him. Houdini ran to her, body-checking into her leg.

Rather than be mad and yell, which is what Ari would have done, Lizzie laughed and cuddled him.

The screen had text and photos on it too small for him to see clearly. She closed the laptop quickly. He glanced at it. Was it odd that she did that? A hint of unease tugged at him. Was it a big deal that she shut her computer as soon as he came in?

He didn't like this feeling at all. It was the same unease he'd felt with Ari, and he didn't want to go through that again.

"Nick!" She jumped up and wound her arms around him.

He caught hold of her, and tried to forget everything in Lizzie's kiss.

He lifted his head and rubbed the back of his knuckles along her cheek. "What were you working on?"

He felt her body tighten up slightly in his arms. "What do you mean?" she asked.

"You seemed engrossed in whatever it was you were doing. I can tell when you're down your rabbit hole now. You have a look." He let her go, picked up the grocery bag he'd put on the coffee table, and took it into the kitchen.

"I have a look?"

"Yep," he answered.

Lizzie followed him to the kitchen, Houdini and Candy hot on her heels.

"What is the look?"

"Oh, I can't tell you that."

"Come on. Tell me." She gave him a swat on the arm and then opened the paper bag with the tips of her fingers to peer in. "What did you bring?"

"I saw a great deal on some very fine, aged wine. I always keep my eye out for the good stuff." He pulled the bag toward him and lifted the bottles out.

"Four bottles? You think we'll drink four bottles of wine? Do you plan to take advantage of me, sir?" she teased, and slid into his arms again.

"I damn well hope so!" He hugged her and she sighed, resting her cheek on his chest. "What did you get from the market?"

Lizzie stepped out of his embrace. "Some Dungeness crabs, oysters, and clams. I've got shrimp ready to go, and some lovely crusty bread for dipping in the sauce."

"Sounds good," he said, and dropped another kiss on her forehead, then uncorked a bottle of wine. "Would you look at these oysters? What are your plans for them? On ice, or cook them?" Nick swirled the water around with his hand, doing his best to shake off the lingering feeling of suspicion. "Great job cleaning them up."

"Do you have a preference?" She stood beside him and rested her head on his shoulder.

"I like them both ways. Did you have something in mind?" He put his arm around her and pulled her in tight, liking the way she let her body mold into his.

"I was thinking a shuck and slurp. Or we could do oyster shots." She looked up at him and grinned.

"Oyster shots? That's not a bad idea. They'd go down real nice and smooth."

"But I bought all this as well." She went over to the fridge and took out all the sauces.

"Why don't we have it both ways? Looks like you got more than enough to feed an army. What about the clams?"

She shrugged her shoulders. "Dredging and tossing them in some hot oil?" She raised her eyebrows. "What do you think?"

"Perfect idea." Nick appreciated their simple conversation. It was easy and helped dispel his disquiet. This was how he'd envisioned a relationship would be. Effortless, relaxed.

"All right, then we'll shuck the oysters. I have flour over there in the cupboard, and some spices we can add in." She bent down and searched for a pot under the counter. "Aha! We can deep-fry the clams." She triumphantly held up an old and battered pot.

"That thing is ancient." Nick got the flour and put it on the counter.

"Pff, it's just one pot of food. And the hot oil will kill any cooties that might be released." She put the pot on the stove and poured oil in.

He drew in a deep breath and relished the feelings that filled him. The sense of home and belonging was powerful and pushed out the unease. He couldn't recall the last time he'd felt this kind of well-being and contentment—probably not since he was a kid. His chest swelled with happiness.

"Just give me a job, chef." He turned to the bottles on the counter. "But first, I'm decanting. We need wine as we prep and cook."

"Decant away, my man, and we can get this show on the road."

"Compliments to the chef," Nick said, after putting the last of the dinner dishes in the dishwasher.

"I'm glad you enjoyed it. And thank you for helping cook and clean."

"It's no problem at all."

I watched him as he easily uncorked more wine, his movements so fluid. I could watch him all day.

The evening had been lovely, though it had almost started in disaster. I'd became so engrossed with work that I'd jumped out of my skin when Nick had arrived, and Houdini raced in and pretty much jumped in my lap.

My laptop was still open to the tab about Marissa, and I'd slammed it shut. How would I have explained it if Nick noticed? I felt as if I'd been caught with my hand in the cookie jar.

It comforted me that he didn't appear to have noticed,

otherwise he would have said something, right? I chewed my lower lip. When would be the right time to discuss the text and Marissa? I just couldn't bring myself to do it tonight. Had too much time passed for me to raise it at all? I hoped not.

"You know they say oysters are an aphrodisiac." I waited to see what he was going to say.

"So I've heard. Here, hold these."

I took the wine glasses.

He scooped me up and carried me outside to the porch swing. We sat together, waiting for the sunset, sipping wine.

"Is that all you've got to say?" I looked up at him.

"About what?" He watched the horizon, and I could tell he was trying not to smile.

"You know."

I could see his lips tighten, and the corner of his eyes crinkle. He was trying not to laugh! I gave him a nudge.

"Hey, what's that about? It's not fight club." He dragged me on to his chest.

"Hey now, watch the wine." I held my glass out.

"There's always more where that came from.' He kissed me deeply.

I melted on to him with a sigh.

Nick broke the kiss. He lifted his head and peered out at the water. "Sunset. Watch."

"Rev a girl up and then leave her hanging? Not cool." But I wasn't mad, I was happily curled up in his lap and rested against his chest.

I let out a sigh of contentment. The swing rocked gently, with Nick pushing his toes against the sand. The gentle glide, back and forth, was hypnotic.

"Here we go, sun's almost down." His voice was soft and he held me tenderly.

Neither of us talked as we watched the ball of fire slowly descend below the horizon.

"If you listen carefully, my mom and dad used to say, you can almost hear the hiss when the sun touches the water," I whispered.

"Mmm."

We sat quietly, and memories flooded back—happy and painful ones. Tears pressed behind my eyes and I had to draw in a deep breath, feeling like a band was tightening around my chest.

I thought I'd dealt with all these emotions, but I was damned surprised they rose so unexpectedly.

Nick had his father, his mother was gone, and he had no siblings. I wonder if he ever felt the same despair that raced through me right now? It was suffocating. I drew in a ragged breath, my lungs fought against it. Panic flooded me. I'd never had a panic attack before, so why now?

I stiffened and sat up abruptly. Even though I was safe in Nick's arms, content, happy, watching the spectacular sunset, here I was on the verge of tears.

"Hey, are you okay?" Nick shifted, and I ducked my face into my hand and nodded.

I raised my hand, pointed to the sunset, and brought my finger to my mouth. "S-s-shh." It was all I could manage without giving away the fact that I was close to tears. And I felt ridiculous about it.

"It's all right. Sometimes nature can move you to such a degree that you become overwhelmed." Nick's voice, soft and caring, grounded me. He stroked my back and I let myself relax.

We were quiet again, watching the last of the sunset, and he held me. I told myself I was safe, even if my brain was thinking otherwise.

The rocking motion back and forth lulled me, and we sat with our arms around each other until the sun was gone and the sky purpled. Clouds and a mist rolled in, blanketing us in a chill.

I shivered.

"Let's go in, and I'll build a fire." Nick rose easily, with me in his arms, and we went inside.

"You don't have to carry me." I looped my arms around his neck, the empty wine glasses dangling from my fingers.

"I know, but it's nice to carry you." He smiled down at me, a tender expression on his face.

I felt so much better now. Inside, he put me down, and the dogs were right there, as usual. Nick built a fire, and I got some chocolate, put it on the coffee table in front of us, and we snuggled up on the couch.

He turned on the TV and clicked through the channels.

"Hmm, what do you feel like watching?" He kept changing channels and then stopped at a baseball game. "A-ha, here we go. Your favorite."

I looked at him and raised my eyebrows. "Seriously? If you're wanting to get a little something special tonight, you'd best move along in your channel surfing. Or we can do a puzzle."

He threw back his head and laughed. "Actually, I'd rather turn the TV off and make our own romance movie."

"Now that's my kind of show," I murmured.

And I pushed him back on the couch.

Chapter Twenty-eight

I was infatuated with Nick. Being with him was wonderful in so many ways. I felt special around him; it was how he treated me, listened to me, the fun we had, and the beautiful, intimate moments. The men who had come through my life in the past were not like him. Not just those I dated, but men in general. Of course, apart from Rob.

After one rather difficult relationship and break-up, I'd been convinced my man pick-ometer was broken. I just couldn't bear to pursue another relationship, much to the chagrin of my brother and the friends I socialized with in my past life. I'd had enough of being disappointed. Rob had hovered around me to make sure I was all right. He was adamant that I shouldn't judge all men on this bad experience—there were good men out there. But he'd also encouraged me not to tie myself down too soon, too quickly. This promise wasn't an easy thing to break.

With Nick, my thought patterns were changing, and on a positive upswing.

I ran my hands up his jean-clad thighs, loving the feel of his muscles beneath the fabric. Further on up, I slid them over his hips, taking care to teasingly avoid the enticing bulge. He groaned when I brushed my hands under his shirt, over his muscled abdomen, and up to his chest.

He grabbed me under the arms and gently pulled me over his body. I caught my breath, doubting I would ever tire of feeling his hard strength beneath me.

Pinned in his arms, he pulled me close and I sighed with delight.

Holding his head steady, we looked into each other's eyes and the expression in his, so soft and open, pierced me. They also reflected a sense of calm, and a new emotion that flooded me with warmth and happiness.

A slow smile spread across his lips. I was mesmerized, and I touched my fingertips to his mouth, tracing his smile. I stroked his cheek, the rasp of his stubble a delightful sensation on my skin. Gazing lower at his mouth, it was as if a magnetic charge arced between us. I lowered my head. My lips found the spot where my fingers had been moments before.

I sighed into him, our breath mingling. He held the back of my head, his strong fingers staying me. Ragged breaths and sweet moans embraced us.

Later, wrapped in his arms in front of the fire and cozy under the quilt, we lay quietly. Snaps and crackles from the fire, and the soft snores of the dogs, were our only music. His heart thumped, I felt it beneath my cheek, mine matching time with his. I put my leg over his and pulled him to me, needing to feel him close.

He drew in a big breath and let it out slowly. I was tucked between the back of the couch and his side, my arm over his chest. I'd never been more comfortable.

"Where have you been all my life?" His words were so faint, I wasn't sure I'd heard them.

I looked up, and his eyes were closed. Had I imagined it? He looked asleep, but his words hovered in my mind.

I wondered the same!

"Pardon?" I asked, wanting him to say them again.

His eyelids opened. I couldn't tell what he was thinking.

He smiled and kissed my forehead, not saying anything. He looked at the ceiling. I rested my cheek back on his chest. My intuition told me he had uttered the words. He didn't repeat them, but I knew it must be difficult for him. So I lay there, feeling content, knowing that when the time was right for him, he'd say it again.

I must have snoozed a bit because I jumped when he spoke, his mouth against my hair.

"I'm glad you came into my life so unexpectedly." He pressed a kiss to my temple. "I don't want to think of you leaving."

My heart jumped. It was the first time he'd said anything about my looming departure.

"I don't want to either," I murmured and looked up at him, trying to read his expression.

His eyes had that look of tenderness again, and a new emotion. One I hadn't seen before but which made my heart flutter.

"But you know my promise to Rob, and how much I need to honor it. I don't want to leave you either, I've grown to love it here, and being with you . . ."

He nodded, tightening his arm around me.

Such a sense of despair struck me at the thought of leaving, I felt ill. Squeezing my eyes shut, I stroked my fingers over his chest. The moment passed but left me shaken.

What was I going to do?

Chapter Twenty-nine

Fog rolled in overnight, so their morning walk on the beach was damp, silent, and dreary. Nick didn't mind. He was used to it, having grown up here, and he liked the way Lizzie didn't grumble about it. She accepted things as they came—and, of course, there's nothing you can do about the weather.

Candy and Houdini raced along the beach, jumping into the waves and back out to chase each other. It was nice. Peaceful. And he liked how Lizzie's hand fit perfectly in his.

Thinking of last night's lovemaking with Lizzie was enough to re-fire him. They had great chemistry. But there was more to them than the physical side. She was fun and unpredictable, light-hearted, and found pleasure in most everything. It was refreshing not to be with someone who constantly complained.

Of course, his thoughts went to Ari. He'd been doing a little more thinking, and shook his head. She'd changed so quickly once they were married. As if she'd done a Jekyll and Hyde. Her anger at him came out of the blue, and it stunned him. He'd like to think he hadn't changed, but she had.

He watched the dogs. She hadn't even liked Houdini, complaining about his wet footprints, or his hair. The crazy part was her being angry that Houdini wanted to be with her, by her side, and she'd send him away. It bothered Nick, this side to her, so gradually Houdini took refuge with him.

He got used to walking on eggshells, never knowing when she'd pick a fight and cause a scene. It certainly didn't help when he was called to be interviewed by the police. He gritted his teeth. That had been the worst experience of his life. Thank God he'd been away on business at the time she'd disappeared, and was able to prove it.

Not getting a sense of closure, without a body to bury, had been so difficult. He watched the waves and was gut-punched, imagining her lost in the deep indigo depths.

The sea doesn't always give up her dead.

The memorial service, without her body, and only a few photos . . . well, it only fed into his guilt. He shouldn't have left her alone as much as he did.

He'd known she was estranged from her family—at least that's what she'd told him. Even knowing that, the lack of people at the service haunted him. No . . . no real closure.

Nick's mindset had been self-destructive, falling into a pit of guilt, grief, and self-recrimination. If only he'd done things differently, if only he'd only been more patient, if only he'd found a way to help her, if only . . .

So many if-onlys.

He sighed, and Lizzie looked up at him.

"What's wrong?" She tugged his hand.

"Just thinking." He smiled down at her.

"About what?"

Now was as good a time as any to talk to her about everything. But while it might've been the right timing, and a natural segue into the conversation, it was still difficult. He worried if he told Lizzie everything about that time, she would feel he carried too much baggage. Possibly feel betrayed and leave. And if she'd already decided to move on to the next place on her promised journey, then the conversation wouldn't be necessary anyway. If she was going to stay, then that was a whole different kettle of fish.

He had to ask. "Have you been thinking about when you leave?"

She looked out over the ocean. "I can't believe how fast the days have flown by. And it's been wonderful spending time with you."

She said nothing about staying. Was she avoiding talking about it?

"Would you ever consider staying?" By asking, he'd opened up the possibility of hearing something he wasn't sure he wanted to hear.

"I have. I mean, you make me want to stay, that's for sure. But I made a promise and feel an obligation to honor that promise."

He wasn't sure how to respond to that without sounding heartless. "That's a heavy weight to carry," Nick said.

"It is. But he was my brother." Her voice cracked, but she held it together.

"I know he wanted you to live your best life. And you are respecting his wishes." He drew in a breath and continued softly, pulling her close. "But remember, he's gone, and you're here."

"I know. But, if I don't keep my promise, I feel like I'm letting him down. But it will be so hard to leave you."

This was a decision only she could make. By asking her, he was letting her know he'd like her to consider staying. Three years he'd been alone with his guilt and regret over Ari. Wasn't it time to consign it to the past?

She was quiet.

"You'll make the right decision for you," he reassured her. "How does your work schedule look?"

She puffed out air. "I have an article I need to submit to a new magazine for consideration. Their deadline is the end of the day. I've got the notes for it but I just have to write it. How about you, any work stuff?"

"There's always work stuff going on. I think I'm going to have to fly out in a couple of days."

"Where to, this time?"

He heard the disappointment in her voice. He hadn't arranged the flight yet. What if he asked her to join him? If the client wanted him there, he had a feeling it would be a last-minute thing. Only a night away, but he wondered if she'd like to come.

"Well, it's a rather quick trip, I think Miami, I'm still waiting for the client to let me know. It will be last minute, a pack and go kind of thing." He paused and then asked her. "I just wondered, would you like to come along?" He almost held his breath, waiting for her answer.

"Really? You're asking me to come along on a business trip?" Lizzie grabbed his arm and looked up at him.

Her eyes, those eyes that changed with the lighting and her mood. Now a muted blue, but they sparkled with excitement.

Her joy was infectious, and he was glad he'd taken the risk. "Yes, I'm asking you. What do you think? Can you work on the road? This time, it should be fun because they're sending a corporate jet."

"No way," she said with shock. "And a big ol' yes for working on the road!"

"Have you ever flown private before?" He desperately wanted her to come. He'd like to see her excitement. Maybe it would brush off on him a bit.

"Oh yeah, I fly private all the time, didn't I tell you?" She waved her hand and turned around to skip backward, laughing.

He laughed too. "Wow, I'm impressed." He knew she was teasing.

It was starting to drizzle, so they headed back to her cottage.

"So, what do you think? Can you carve out some time in your schedule to come along with me?" Nick was eager to hear her answer.

"Of course I can go. When do we leave? I've got bags to pack."

It thrilled him that she jumped at the chance. Nick knew her work was just as important to her as his was to him, and he was glad she could take it on the road. It gave him food for thought. If things went as he hoped they'd go, maybe this would be an opportunity for her to see that staying in Savage Cove could be a good thing.

"Anytime over the next week, I think. By Wednesday for sure, though."

"Then that's great. I'll be able to get a lot done over the weekend, and I'm happy to be on standby." She did a little twirl, and looked back at him, brushing a strand of damp hair from her cheek.

Nick nodded and grinned. "Great. I'm glad you're coming along."

"Me too." She looked up at the sky. "Think we need to hoof it."

"I agree."

They called the dogs, and jogged back to her cottage.

The rain was coming down when they ran up the path to her porch, whistling for the dogs. They just got under the overhang of her porch as the skies opened up. The dogs shook themselves, releasing a spray of salty water, soaking the adults more than the rain they'd just run through.

"Damn, that was good timing," Nick said, and shook the rain off his hands.

"It certainly was. Let me run in and get some towels so we can dry the dogs off before they come inside."

Nick sat on a chair and called the dogs over to him. He hung on to them. Even though they were wet, he let them press up against his bare legs, not wanting them to go out into the deluge.

Moments later, Lizzie came out with a pile of towels, and they quickly toweled off the dogs.

"I'm chilly, let's go in and get dry ourselves. I'll put on a pot of tea. Then we can talk about our adventure coming up," Lizzie suggested.

"Sounds like a plan." He followed her into the house and spread the towels on the kitchen floor for the dogs, then told them firmly to stay put.

"Here you go, puppers. A treat for both of you for being such good doggies." Lizzie gave them each a cookie and they were content, placing their heads on their paws, eyes watching the adults' every move.

Nick went into the living room to grab his phone; he'd put it on Lizzie's desk beside her computer. Seeing it reminded him of when he'd arrived yesterday, when she'd been busy on the laptop and quickly shut it. It struck him then as odd, but he'd forgotten about it until now. Was she hiding something from him? He shook his head; no, she wasn't secretive like Ari.

He certainly hoped not. What could she be secretive about? Obviously, Ari's lies still affected him. He hated that her deception bled into his relationship with Lizzie, who'd shown no signs of being anything other than forthcoming.

He'd discovered Ari had two phones. When he'd confronted her, she'd been flippant about it and said the second was an older phone she didn't use. He'd wanted to believe her, and he'd tried. But it hung like an anchor around his neck. That had been just before she died.

He looked out at the beach and drew in a deep breath. Damn, he hoped it wasn't happening again.

"Tea's ready," Lizzie called from the kitchen.

"Want to sit on the porch?" he asked, and slipped his phone into his back pocket.

"It's too rainy, and the dogs are drying. They'll want to be with us and will only get wet again."

He nodded, not liking the unsettled feeling growing in him. "Yeah. I'll light a fire to take the chill off."

"Great idea, just coming."

Nick heard the clink of china and the slam of a cupboard door closing. Moments later, she carried a tray into the living room, dogs following her. The smile on her face warmed his heart.

But a tiny seed of doubt had been planted.

"Come on, dogs, lay down here in front of the fire so you can dry off."

I'd brought a couple more cookies for them, so it wasn't hard to coax them to settle before the warm hearth. I rewarded them with their treat.

"Happy puppers." I gave each one a stroke on the head.

"When it rains, it sure can get chilly fast." I shivered and poured the tea,

Taking the two mugs, I went to Nick who was standing by the window, looking out. I handed him one. He seemed to have something weighing on his mind.

"Is everything okay?" I asked him and slipped my arm around his waist, sipping the hot tea and relishing the warmth.

I glanced up at him and saw an expression on his face that I could only describe as a look of concern, or worry.

He shrugged his shoulders. "Something on my mind."

"Is there anything I can help you with?" I took another sip. "Mmm, nothing like hot tea on a dreary day."

He shook his head. "Nope. Just stuff I have to figure out." He drank and looked out the window.

The fire crackled, and its warmth filled the room.

"I think we need to get you more wood. I'll bring some next time."

"Okay. And thanks." I hoped it was only work stuff weighing on him, but something had definitely shifted his mood.

This was a completely different Nick than the one of moments before. So many facets of a person, and it takes a long time to understand them all. Still, I wondered what had happened.

I thought back over what we had done in the last twenty-four hours, to see if something might have annoyed him, or given him cause for concern. He hadn't been like this yesterday or this morning. Everything had been fine, as far as I could tell. What had upset him? Had he received an email or text? And if so, who or what had upset him? I looked at my desk; he'd put his phone there last night. There was nothing to show my Marissa research, and I breathed a sigh of relief. Even so, he had subtly changed.

Of course, with my imagination, anything under the sun could be the culprit for swinging Nick's mood. I wasn't sure what to do; stand here with him at the window, or give him space.

I decided to give him space, and curled up on the couch. But I watched him stare out the window with a feeling of dread in the pit of my stomach.

Chapter Thirty

Nick was in his office when his dad hollered from the back door. Houdini jumped up, barking a greeting, and ran to meet his dad. Candy came in like a whirlwind.

"Getting ready to leave, son?" Walter asked. He lowered himself into a deep leather chair by the window, with a groan.

"Yep." Nick closed the files on his laptop and spun his chair to face his dad.

"Where to, this time?" Walter asked. Candy rested her chin on his knee, and he absently stroked her neck.

"Miami." Nick paused and decided to tell him he wasn't going alone. "I've asked Lizzie to come along."

He watched his father's expression; the momentary surprise was quickly shuttered. "Is that right? Well, I'm sure she'll enjoy that."

"She's excited about the trip." Nick smiled, knowing his father was doing his best not to hit him with a million questions.

"How about you? This is a pretty big step. I don't recall you ever taking anyone on a business trip."

"I haven't. Yes, it is a big step." Nick wanted to explain to his dad, without getting into too much detail, how he felt about things—especially where Lizzie was concerned.

"She's a nice girl. I'm glad you two met." His father caught his eye. "I think she's good for you, Nick. You seem more light-hearted than you have in years."

Nick nodded. "I am, Dad. Meeting her, and it being three years now . . ." He paused and continued, "Seems like it was perfect timing. She has some heavy baggage from the past, just like me, but somehow when we're together it doesn't seem as big as when we're apart."

A look of concern crossed his father's features. Nick didn't have to ask him what he was thinking, because he knew he would find out soon enough.

"When do you leave?"

"I changed the flight to later today, from early tomorrow morning. Are you okay to take Houdini early?"

"Of course I am. We're pals. He's my granddog, and I spoil him as if he were a grandchild. Speaking of which . . ." Walter gave Nick a knowing glance.

Nick laughed and raised his hand, waving the implied question away. "Not there yet, Pops. Just be patient. I hope, one day, to make you a grandpop."

Walter smiled. "I'm glad to see some of your disquiet has eased up. The last few years have been hell on wheels, there's no doubt about that. You deserve some happiness."

"Thanks, Dad. And you do too." Nick saw the ghost of a smile flicker across his father's mouth.

"We all do, son." Walter drew in a deep breath and then met Nick's gaze. "Just be cautious. I don't want you to get hurt again."

Nick had no response to that. He didn't want that either,

even though he knew Lizzie's plans were not to stay in Savage Cove. But he was tired of letting the past influence his future. Moving forward meant putting yourself out there, didn't it? And he was doing that with Lizzie.

The interior of the private jet was dream worthy. Cream-colored, butter-soft leather seats, furnished in soft and muted tones of sand, gold, and lavender, with black accents. It wasn't as big as I thought it would be, but it was still stunning.

A three-person divan against one wall, very comfy-looking club seats in groups, one with a table I was sure lowered into a bed. A full galley, and a lavatory with changing room.

I wasn't surprised there was no flight attendant on board, since it was just the two of us. But the galley was well stocked and likely as fine as any first-class flight. You just had to get it yourself. No biggie.

I guess you could say, this jet came very well equipped and had everything you could want on the flight.

After the disquiet of the other night, I got a sense that the strain had eased. I was glad and ready to take on the Miami adventure with Nick. I wasn't going to worry about anything while we were here.

I was excited and had every intention of having a good time. I'd packed for sun and heat; a different kind of beachwear from Savage Cove. A thought popped into my head that it might make a good blog post and made a mental note to remember. And a cocktail dress. Damn good thing I'd thrown one in my travel pack. You know, the quintessential little black dress. But no suitable shoes. I'm sure I could find something once we arrived.

Nick had decided to leave the evening before his meetings so he wasn't rushed. That meant two nights in Miami. We should land around 6 p.m. I wondered if we'd be wired or pooped, seeing as there was a three-hour time change.

Although he had meetings all the next day, I'd be happy walking along the beach and sunning by the pool while he was doing his thing. Plus, I had some work I'd brought along. Nothing wrong with writing poolside.

I'd join him later in the evening, with his associates, for dinner. Hence the cocktail dress. I was a little nervous about the dinner and wanted to look my best.

I held my hand out in front of me.

Ugh. I desperately needed a mani. And I *knew* my feet left much to be desired. Beach walking had done a number on them. I'd tackle that when we got to the hotel.

This certainly was a side trip I had not expected. Rather a shock, but wonderful nonetheless. I was thrilled he'd asked me to come along.

Nick had been working since we took off from Seattle, and I hoped he'd finish soon. I had an idea and would try to entice him to agree, as we still had about three hours to go.

It would be so easy to be lazy and not take advantage of the flight time. I pulled out my laptop and worked on sorting pictures I'd taken the other day on my drive to Rialto Beach. I needed to select the best ones for my next article. Ideas came to me while going through them, and I jotted down notes for the copy. I looked out the window at the clouds below. I knew once we were in Miami, ideas for a story would pop up. It usually happened that way for me. In the moment, feelings, emotions, sights, all blended together, resulting in words to express the story.

It was hard not being distracted, though. It wasn't every day that I got to fly in a private jet.

I watched Nick work and smiled at the intensity visible on

his face. I was almost overcome with happiness. I looked out the window again and swallowed the emotion that had just overtaken me. What the heck? I was so happy, I almost started blubbing.

I reached for the sparkling water and finished what was in my glass.

I had about two weeks left until I was supposed to leave. Time was ticking away. Putting the glass down, I decided that when we got home, I'd tell Nick everything. Tell him about the text, my research on Marissa—and hopefully he'd fill in the gaps.

I glanced at him again; his head was bent, reading. The afternoon sun came in the window and shone on his hair. Another swell of emotion took hold of me. He had obviously worked hard to get to a level where he was rewarded with this amazing treatment. It made me unbelievably proud.

I let out a contented sigh. Looking out the window, I tried to figure out our location by the landscape below. We were as high as a commercial airliner, which was another surprise for me. I thought 39,000 feet was just for the big planes. A layer of puffy clouds broke up now and then, so I could see the land below. But I had no idea where we were.

Multiple televisions were on the plane, so I could probably tune in the map, like they do on commercial flights. But I didn't want to know that badly. I wanted this flight to last forever.

I'd never been to Miami, and I was excited at the prospect of a new destination. Key West was on my bucket list, but I didn't think we'd be able to go. It was about a three-hour drive down US-1, and the turnaround on our flight was the day after tomorrow. Oh, well, perhaps another time.

Even so, I'd be in South Beach, toes in the sand and just doing whatever.

"Enjoying yourself?" Nick asked.

I turned from the window and nodded. "This is amazing. There are really no words. How spoiled are you to have clients that jet you around like this?"

I got up and went over to sit beside him.

"Don't think this happens all the time." He smiled and closed his book, stacking his papers to the side. "This was a last-minute trip I wasn't keen to do. I expressed my dissatisfaction, and that's why they flew me in the corporate jet. Better than traveling commercial."

"Would they have put you in business class?" I asked. Another goal on my bucket list.

"My contract specifies any flights over two hours must be business class." He smiled at me when my mouth dropped open.

"You mean you put that in the contract?"

He nodded. "Of course. If they want me, and my know-ledge, and what I offer, then they have to pay for it."

"Wow. That's pretty cool. I'm impressed." I nodded and looked around again. "This is not hard to take."

"No, it's not. It makes it easier when you arrive, because a lot of times you don't have jet lag. You can relax on the flight, and you're not going through the terminals, since smaller, private jets have a separate terminal."

"What do you prefer? Going commercial or on a private jet?" I asked him, because I wasn't sure how I would choose.

He pursed his lips and tipped his head to the side. "Well, that's a tricky question. On this flight, there's no flight attendant, we just take care of ourselves." He leaned over and whispered in my ear, making a delightful shiver rush up the backs of my legs. "We have it all to ourselves."

I drew in a soft breath.

He continued, "If you go business, they wait on you hand and foot, and some meals can be amazing. Of course, they have the lie-flat beds—and some even have private suites. So, I'd say they both have their advantages and disadvantages."

I swung my leg over his thighs and settled in his lap. Leaning on his chest, I whispered, "Are you a member of the mile-high club?" I nipped at his earlobe, and liked how he sucked in a sharp breath.

He looked at me, eyebrows raised. "Are you?"

"That's not fair, you don't answer a question with a question." I grinned at him and waited to see what he was going to say.

Would he be honest?

"Well, let me see." He glanced around and pinned me with a look that made my insides melt. "I'm not opposed to signing up for that membership sometime."

My lips parted and the breath ceased to move in and out of my lungs. He swiveled the chair, and I settled on him, drawing in a soft breath. "I think I'd like to join that club too."

"As much as I'd like to get the membership started today, I think we have to abstain." Nick gently let me down. "We could get caught."

I was suddenly feeling very daring and naughty. "Well, isn't that what makes things more exciting? The chance of being caught?"

"You are a wicked temptress." He leaned in close, kissing me as he whispered against my lips, "Of course, never in all my times flying private has a pilot left the cockpit."

"Wicked? I don't mind being the temptress, but not wicked. How about a tempting temptress?" I leaned down and nuzzled his neck. "Why do you think I wore a dress?" I leaned away from him.

He looked at me. A slow, amazingly sexy smile widened on his mouth. "Okay, a tempting temptress it is."

We shifted on the seats, and he put his arm around me. I leaned back on his chest, facing the window.

"But I do want the membership card," I whispered, and he laughed.

"Me too."

Chapter Thirty-one

Nick stopped before the hotel room door. I could tell he was eager to open it, and I couldn't wait. He was different away from home, and it made this trip even more exciting.

"Are you ready?" He looked down at me, and I loved how his eyes sparkled. He was happy, and warmth washed through my chest.

I nodded. "I can't believe we're here, staying at the Ritz-Carlton in South Beach. I mean, come on, Nick! This is just so unbelievable. I feel like I've fallen into a fairy tale." I threw my arms around his neck and went up on my toes to kiss him.

He lifted me off my feet and kissed me back. "Your happiness makes me happy," he said against my mouth. "Now, let's see the room."

He held the key card in front of the reader. The light was green and Nick pushed open the door, ushering me through first.

"Go check it out." He gave me a gentle nudge.

Inside, my mouth dropped open. I stood in the center of the living room.

"Oh my God, Nick. This is insane." I ran to the windows. It was coming up to dusk, so the neighborhood lights were on, and the sky was streaked with orange.

"Look at this view! I could sit here all day and just stare out the windows. Look, that must be a cruise ship out there." I pointed. It was incredible.

"Port of Miami isn't far from here," he said, and watched the lights out on the ocean. "There are a few ships out there."

I turned and looked around the living room. It was a lovely suite, with a powder room at the front entrance, a seating area with a big couch, a large flat screen, a table and four chairs, and a separate bedroom with a full bath. Very luxurious.

I dashed through the door into the bedroom, and gave a high-pitched squeal of delight. "Nick, Nick, come in here, you've just got to see this."

He came in, smiling and looking pleased as Punch. "I'm glad you like it."

"Oh, I do! Thank you."

A big, beautiful king-size bed was against one wall, opposite curved windows that faced out toward the beach and the ocean. It was quite incredible.

"This is something," he said, and came to stand beside me.

I rested my hands on the window ledge and took it all in. "I don't think I've ever seen anything this spectacular."

He put his arm around me and I sighed, resting my head on his shoulder. Feelings raced through me as we stood for a moment looking out the window.

"It's nice not traveling alone. It's one of my biggest peeves, always going away and being by myself. I'm okay on my own, of course, but having someone share this with me is a big change." He indicated the view.

"Did you ever travel with your wife?" I looked up at him.

He didn't answer right away. "No, I didn't."

He didn't want to talk about her, and I didn't either. The question had just popped out.

"I'm glad we flew in tonight," he said, "rather than tomorrow. It would have been a godawful early flight."

"Me too. I think I could stay here forever." I jumped on to the bed, arms and legs spread out like a starfish. "Oh, this bed. It's a cloud. Come on, Nick." I patted the bed beside me and rolled over to make room.

Nick joined me. "Yep, a damn good thing we came tonight rather than tomorrow. With you lounging in bed like this, I'd be hard pressed to leave you for meetings." He rolled over and pulled me into his arms.

"I totally agree," I giggled.

Nick pushed me back into the pillows and lowered his head. "I think I need a little taste before we head out."

"I thought we'd be eating in." I felt saucy, and my eyelids drooped seductively.

"We can do both," he murmured.

I smiled and reached for him, and Nick moved between my knees, lowering his mouth to mine.

By the time Nick got off the bed, the sky was dark and lights dotted the beachwalk and out to sea.

"Now, how about we go for a walk?" he suggested, watching Lizzie lying on the bed. "Are you sure you're not purring? You look like a very contented cat."

She looked at him, her arms above her head, breasts exposed, a tan leg tangled in the rumpled sheets and her hair spread out over the pillows in sexy waves. "Do I now? Well, maybe I am." She rolled on to her stomach, stretched her arms out in front of her, and watched him. "We could stay here if you like?"

It wouldn't take much for her to entice him to stay, except that he was starved. He'd last eaten when they'd just taken off from Seattle.

"As much as I'd like to oblige you, milady, I need food. Get that sexy butt out of bed."

She climbed from the bed and walked toward him, naked and glorious.

"Like I said on the jet, you're a temptress. I'm starved and need food."

Lizzie walked past him, running her fingertips along his chest. "Are you sure?"

"Yes, yes, I'm sure. Now get ready." He gave her a swat, and she bounced off to the bathroom.

The room filled with her laughter. Nick didn't think he'd ever felt so good, so happy. A sense of completeness seeped into him as he listened to her getting ready.

He put the suitcases on the luggage racks so they could unpack. She came out of the bathroom in a robe a short while later, looking refreshed and beautiful. He was in awe of her.

"Where do you want to go to eat?" Lizzie opened her overnight bag. "Do you want to hang up your work clothes? Stop them from getting wrinkled. I can iron if you need me to," she offered.

"I would never have you do that," Nick said, and took his garment bag out to hang in the closet.

"Why not? If I didn't want to, I wouldn't offer." She hung a garment bag beside his.

He raised his eyebrows. "And what is in there?"

"You will just have to wait and see." She spun on her toes and pulled more items out of her bag.

While he finished unpacking, Lizzie slipped into some very sexy undergarments. He smiled, appreciating the little fashion show she put on for him, before she pulled on a pair of white pants that came to her calves, and a turquoise, silky tank top that swung quite enticingly from her shoulders.

He took her hand. "You look terrific."

"You're not so bad yourself." She slung the shoulder strap of her bag over her head, and they left the room together.

The lobby was busy, and the aroma of food made my stomach grumble.

"Okay then. Are you hungry?" Nick asked.

"Did you just hear my stomach?"

We both laughed.

"Did you hear mine?" Nick led me through the lobby and out to the beach exit.

"We haven't eaten in so long, I think my stomach is eating itself." I followed him along the path to the beach.

"I was thinking the same thing. There's a lot of restaurants that set up tables along the sidewalk. It'll be packed. Rather than go along the street, I thought it would be nice to walk along Miami Beach Ocean Walk to Ocean Drive."

"That's the road that has the art deco and historic buildings, right?" I'd done a bit of research on it, a while ago, and remembered how lovely some of them looked. I hoped there would be time to get some architectural photos.

"Yes, that's right. It's unique."

"We might even see a celebrity or two." I was looking forward to this adventure.

"We might, you never know."

The Beach Ocean Walk was wide and well lit. Tall hedges on the ocean side obscured the view of the water, but you could hear the waves. We passed offshoot paths leading to the beach. They were lost in darkness as the glow of lights from Ocean

Walk faded; sparkles of light on the inky water were boats and cruise ships. I imagined what it would be like to be on one of those boats, looking back at the brightness of Miami splashed on the night horizon. I sighed and reached for Nick's hand.

Now we were on Ocean Drive, the noise, the swarm of people, cars, and music rather startled me. It was a sight to behold, and rather overwhelming.

I clutched on to Nick's hand and fell into step behind him. Nick being taller made it easier for him to cut through the crowds, and I was quite happy following up behind.

I couldn't believe how packed it was. We had to weave our way through the throng of people, sometimes stepping off the curb into the road, and around tables belonging to restaurants set out on the sidewalk. Only enough space for two people to walk side by side, in some places. Tables under umbrellas perched perilously close to the curb on one side and flush up to the buildings on the other. I'd seen nothing like it.

We didn't pass a single empty table as we made our way through the crush of people.

"I'm going to try to take some photos. This is unreal," I called over Nick's shoulder.

He nodded, and I used him as a shield while I took photos with my phone. I could see the post in my head already, and was feeling excited about it.

Restaurant staff hawked their menus, trying to get us to stop. I was glad to be behind Nick. The press of the crowds made me feel anxious. It was an overwhelming assault on the senses.

Delicious-looking plates of food made my mouth water. But some tables were so tightly packed in, the food was so close to those walking by, they could've touched it. I wasn't too fond of that.

People were selling their wares and going from table to table, trying to get people to buy flowers, trinkets, and even hot sauce!

The street sounds were incredibly loud. I pushed up to Nick's back and called over his shoulder. "This is really different."

He turned his head so I could hear him. "It sure is—it's something you need to experience. We can stop anywhere you want along here and grab something to eat, or just wander around and see what you fancy."

"You pick. You're taller and in front. How about the first free table you see?"

He nodded.

The crowd wasn't so thick at this point, and I could walk abreast with him. I hung on to his arm, because it was shocking how people just pushed through and obviously had no problem knocking you out of the way.

The next block, Nick saw a spot open up on the sidewalk beside the curb, and he pointed. "There's a table up there," he said. "You want it?"

I craned my neck to see. It was next to a palm tree, with a tall plant on the other side, so it was screened off on its own. "Sure, that's fine."

Half an hour later, we had some Cuban appetizers, Nick had a beer, and I had a fancy concoction with rum, juices, and who knew what all else. It was good, sweet and fruity, until I felt a fireball going down my throat.

"Aagh! What is in this?" The delayed reaction to the heat set my throat ablaze. I choked and reached for a glass of water. Chugging down half the glass, I blinked away the tears in my eyes. "What the hell? Hey, no laughing, mister." My voice croaked rather embarrassingly.

Nick was killing himself, and I grabbed the drinks list. What had I asked for? It was the special of the day, scribbled on the chalkboard; it was called Ghost Ship or something. Finding it on the list, I read the ingredients. Then looked at Nick. My jaw dropped open.

"What is it?" He took a swig of his beer but couldn't hide his mirth behind the glass.

"It's not funny. Freaking scorched my throat. You know what's in this?" I tapped the menu.

He shook his head, still trying to hold back his laughter.

"Ghost pepper! Can you believe it? Ghost frigging pepper." I blinked and took another drink of water, which cooled my fiery throat. "It needs a warning label, for crying out loud."

Nick pulled a menu over and looked. "Ah, see here?" He pointed to a chili pepper, and beside it the words . . .

Warning, watch for the pepper beside the item. Indicates extreme heat and spice. Don't get it if you can't handle it.

"I didn't even notice that." I opened my mouth and let my tongue hang out. I must have looked like a gaping fish out of water. At this point, I didn't care if I looked ridiculous.

"I'll get you a glass of milk. It should help."

"I hope so. Thank you."

"Maybe you could put that in one of your blogs," Nick suggested.

"An excellent idea!" I took a photo of me and the heat warning.

The milk calmed the fire, and we finished up our food.

"A walk back to the hotel?" Nick asked when I finished paying for the check.

"That would be nice." He helped me up, and we strolled back the way we'd come. "Um, can I ask you something?"

"Sure." The crowd had thinned a bit, and he put his arm around me.

"Why didn't you ever bring your wife on your trips?" I hoped it was okay to ask, since we'd touched on it earlier.

He was quiet for a moment before answering. "She didn't want to come."

I waited to see if he would say more, but he didn't. "Why? It would've been nice for you to be together." Saying the words and acknowledging the love in his past was rather painful to me. But I felt it was the right time and place to have the conversation.

"Well," he cleared his throat and lifted a shoulder. "She could have come with me. I understood the single nights away or day trips were a bit of a hassle, but these longer trips . . ." He squeezed me tighter. "It would have been good for us. She wouldn't have felt so alone."

I nodded. "It is a shame she didn't join you." I held on to his arm as we strolled along the sidewalk.

"Who knows how things would have played out if she had? But, honestly, I think we were doomed from the start."

I couldn't have been more surprised by his comment.

His voice held an element of regret, and I did my best to keep my emotions on an even keel. This was the most open he'd been about his wife.

"You've said very little about her, just bits here and there, but I'm sorry you went through what you did. Especially after she died." They must have loved each other once. I looked up at him. "It's horrible to go through the experience of a loved one dying."

"It is." Nick was thoughtful; I sensed he wanted to say something more but was hesitant. "I never thought I was the marrying kind. After seeing what Dad went through when Mom died, I'm afraid to admit that I didn't want that kind of heartache. I couldn't imagine losing the love of your life, and how empty your world would become. I worried about Dad. I watched him grow gaunt with his grief. He became a shell of a man. That's why I got him Candy. For company. To have a purpose again."

"He's doing so well now, though." My heart ached for both Nick and Walter.

"Yep, he is now. He seemed to bounce back around the time I got married. He'd long since finished renovating the boathouse, and had started antique picking. He also got back to his daily walks on the beach again. Like that morning you saw him." Nick looked down at me and smiled.

"Yes, it is a small world. To think I'd met your dad on the beach. The same way we met." I was glad to see he didn't appear as solemn as he had a few moments ago. "Do you think he's seeing anyone?" I asked.

"I don't know. He isn't the secretive sort. I have a feeling, though, if he was seeing someone he would keep it quiet. Private. I know my dad. And his grief was so raw for so long, he'd be full of guilt. It would take a special woman to break through his crusty exterior and find the heart of gold underneath."

"I don't think he's crusty," I answered.

"Oh, yes, he sure is. As crusty as stale bread."

"Nick, that's awful! How can you talk about your dad like that?" I was horrified.

"Oh, don't worry. I'm the first to tell him when he gets that way. He's an old sea dog, set in his ways. But I have seen him mellow over the last year or so."

I thought of Claire. "Hey, you know what? I have an idea."

"Oh, do I want to know?" He was teasing me, and it warmed my soul.

"Of course you do." I jumped right into it. "I met a nice woman at the café." I ignored how he stiffened when I mentioned the word *café*. "Her name is Claire, and she's about the same age as your dad. We should set them up."

Nick burst out laughing, and people turned to look at us.

"What? Why is that so funny?"

Nick turned us to the curb and looked both ways before we jogged across the street. He was still chuckling.

"Come on, tell me. I don't think it's funny."

"My dad? Set him up to go on a date? I can't even begin to imagine it."

"Hmm, I think it's a rather brilliant idea. Two people close in age, alone—what's the harm in trying?"

He laughed again and then stopped, turning to me. His laughter faded, and he looked thoughtful. "You know, you may have something there."

"There, see!" I felt triumphant.

He put his arm around my shoulder. "You come up with the darndest things, and this one just might be worth a shot."

I was thrilled. "Okay, we'll plan something. You bring your dad, and I'll invite Claire."

"Okay, my little matchmaker, we'll pick a day to do the deed."

We were in the hotel lobby now, and I'd barely noticed our walk. He had opened up to me about himself, his father, and a little about his wife. I was glad he had, but the woman he married still intrigued me, and my old curiosity got hold of me again.

"Now, then, can we refocus on ourselves, or is there anyone else you need to matchmake?" He ushered me on to the elevator and nuzzled my ear.

"I think I'm all matched out for now. Except, of course . . . for us." I turned in his arms, and he pulled me into a deep kiss.

253

Chapter Thirty-two

Nick came out of the bathroom wearing black boxer briefs, showered and shaved.

Lizzie was looking deliciously cozy and very sexy, wrapped up in the bedsheets. Damn, he'd rather stay here than go to his meeting.

He walked over to the bed and pulled her into his arms, wanting to feel her skin under his hands one more time before he had to go.

The sun was coming in the curved windows at the perfect angle, and caught her hair so that it was almost translucent. And her eyes. He couldn't get over her eyes. They were the most incredible turquoise, with the irises rimmed in a darker blue. Every time he looked into them, he felt a stab in his heart and was transfixed.

He pushed his hands into her hair and tipped her head back. "You know, you are the most beautiful woman I have ever seen."

She pulled her bottom lip between her teeth, and her eyes

glistened. "You're going to make me cry." She rested her forehead on his chest, and hugged him.

Nick wrapped his arms around her and dropped a kiss on the top of her head.

"I have to get going." He was reluctant to leave her, but he did.

"I know. I'll be fine. Don't you worry about me at all. I'll find lots to do while you're busy at your meetings today." She got out of bed, wrapped in the sheet, picked up his shirt and held it out for him.

Nick slid his arms into the sleeves and turned to her. She buttoned it up and then smoothed her hands down his arms. That simple action spoke volumes to him. Told him she cared for him. He wasn't used to that kind of display of affection, and it moved him.

"I know you will. Just be safe. Things can be a little sketchy around here, keep your phone handy and hang on to your purse if you go out. And if you do, just send me a text where you're going."

"I might go to Macy's, because I need a pair of shoes to wear tonight. I forgot."

"Let me know when you leave and when you're back." He walked to the door and turned. "Take a taxi, get the concierge to get one for you."

"Okay, I'll be fine, don't you worry. I'm used to traveling alone, remember? I can occupy myself in this amazing place."

He wrapped his arms around her and kissed her one more time.

Lizzie gave him a gentle shove. "Now go, or you'll be late."

Damn, this was unexpectedly hard. Leaving her for the day.

"If you're hungry, just order room service, anything you want; charge it to the room and don't worry about it. I will text you when I'm leaving. I'll find out about dinner later, and what time they're expecting us."

She gave him a quick salute with two fingers. "Yes, boss. Now quit worrying. I'm not a kid."

"I'm going, then." He paused, opened the door, and realized she was in full view should anyone walk past their room. He rushed out and she laughed, waving goodbye.

Riding the elevator down, Nick felt like he was floating on a cloud. This was a business trip unlike any other, and he knew it was because Lizzie was with him. He liked it.

A lot.

He was actually glad they'd talked a little about Ari last night. It wasn't as difficult as he'd thought it would be. It was a good start to cracking the wall he'd built around everything that had happened.

Her understanding during their conversation was another positive step, and helped him reach a decision. He was determined now to encourage her to stay a little longer. They needed more time together, to work out if they had any chance at a more committed relationship.

I was completely blown away by everything since we got on the plane yesterday. Not in a million years would I ever have imagined flying on a private jet or staying at the Ritz-Carlton. I wasn't prepared for all this glam, but I was going to soak up as much of this wonderfulness as I could.

The first thing on the agenda was going out to get shoes. Then the rest of the day was mine, to spend however I wanted. I thought of Nick, tied up in meetings. It would've been perfect if we had the day together.

Riding the elevator down to the lobby, I went over last night's conversation in my mind. He'd opened up about his wife at last, and I had a feeling it was a turning point. Perhaps it was time to let go of my worry over the text. I was glad, even though it was hard to hear what he had to say, knowing that if things had been different for him and his wife, Nick and I wouldn't be together today.

The elevator door opened. I walked to the concierge and inquired if there were shops close by. I was in luck. There was a little boutique just down the road. I'd go there first and hope I found what I needed. It would save a trip to Macy's.

The shop was just a block away. This early in the morning, it wasn't too busy, but it was hot. Super hot. I was looking forward to getting back to the pool. The boutique was open, and the collection of clothing and shoes displayed in the window was inspiring. I was sure I'd find something here and pushed through the door. Cool, refreshing air washed over me. The women inside were dressed to the nines, and friendly, greeting me when I came in.

"Can I help you?" A flaming redhead came over and asked me.

"Yes, actually, I'm looking for some shoes to go with a black cocktail dress." I glanced at the displays. There were so many choices.

"Okay, do you have a color in mind?" She walked over to a display and I followed her, bedazzled by the array of shoes.

"Oh, these are beautiful. I've seen nothing like them." I reached out to touch the toe of a black shimmery shoe and wondered if it would go well with my dress. Of course, black goes with black, but something held me back.

"I'm not sure I want to have a black shoe. I'd like something different, with a little pizzazz or bling. What would you suggest?"

"What about these?" She pointed to a pair on the shelves along the back wall.

I followed her to where a gorgeous pair sat, sparkling like royal gems under the lights. It took my breath away. They each had a wicked stiletto heel that looked like steel, with crystals on the strap that snaked from behind the heel, and across the top of the foot to a delicate toe covering that was also studded with bling.

"Oh wow, these are sensational." I ran my fingers over the crystals.

"They are, and one of a kind. You see the touch of the pewter coloring, where the crystals are set? Is your dress sparkly or sleek, swingy or pencil slim?"

"Well, it's low cut, front and back, and . . ." I paused and ran my hands down my sides. "It's form fitting, and has a little swing around the knees, kind of flared, you know? And there is a bit of jet sparkle, just in the shoulders, at the front where it pinches the fabric together."

"It sounds like a lovely dress. I think these shoes would be perfect. Are you size eight?"

I was shocked. "You're good."

The woman laughed. "I've been doing this a long time." She looked down at my feet and tapped her chin. "Yes, so an eight, and you're okay with a heel like this?"

"It's been a while, but I'm game." I chewed my lip, and hoped I didn't take a tumble off them at an inopportune moment. "Could I try them on?

"Of course." While I slipped them on, she continued to chat. "They look lovely on you, and accentuate your ankles and calves. I'd suggest when you get home to wear them, so you can get used to them. Are you walking far in the shoes?" she asked.

I thought for a moment. "I don't think so. I hope not." I raised my eyebrows and grimaced. "But I do love them."

She laughed. "The pain that we must endure to look good."

I looked down at the shoes and nodded. "You got that right."

I got the shoes, a matching handbag, and some lovely earrings and a necklace that complemented both. I was excited to get a little glammed up for a change. Nick was worth it. *I* was worth it. I couldn't remember the last time I'd treated myself, and I was looking forward to seeing Nick's reaction.

The walk back to the hotel didn't take long, and as much as I was curious to mooch around and investigate the other shops along the way, I wanted to enjoy the luxury of the hotel for the day. Back up in the room, I shook out my dress and hung it up. I held the shoes next to it and nodded. They were perfect.

And then I saw my feet.

They needed some serious help, as did my hands. I would indulgence myself in some spa treatments. I texted Nick and was glad for his swift reply. I needed to find out what time we were meeting for dinner so I could count backward for an appointment.

It was barely 10:30 and I had to be ready for 6:30, so I made my appointments at the spa for a mani and a pedi, and even thought I'd get my hair done.

That meant I had until 3:30 to enjoy the beach, pool, and whatever else I decided to do.

I hadn't eaten yet and was hungry. The outdoor restaurant by the pool next to the beach would be so much nicer than hanging out in the room. The overhanging trees shaded my table nicely, and a breeze off the ocean was refreshing. I went big and had a Cuban sandwich and fries with a beer.

I sat back on the chair and let it all sink in. Yesterday I was looking out over the Pacific Ocean, today the Atlantic Ocean.

What a crazy turn of events. I couldn't help thinking Rob would be proud to see me embracing these new experiences.

My phone pinged. It was Nick, and a warmth bloomed through me. He was only checking in to see how my day was going. I sighed happily and watched the activity on the beach, scanning the boats out on the ocean from under the brim of Rob's hat. Wearing it, and bringing it along on my adventures, was almost like having him here.

I was going to enjoy the rest of the day by the pool and then walk on the beach till it was spa time.

By early evening, make-up applied, and dressed for dinner, I was standing in front of the bathroom mirror, enjoying the full effect of my glam session.

The shoes matched perfectly, and I was so pleased with my hair. The stylist in the spa had swept it up into an artful messy-curly updo, gathered at the back, slightly off-center, and then falling in waves over my shoulder. She'd even had jewel-tipped bobby pins to anchor it all in place and give my hair some sparkle.

I'd gotten some sun today, which gave my skin a glow against the black dress, and the coral nail polish I'd chosen popped next to my skin and the dress. I'd even managed to create a sexy, smoky look with my eyes. The finishing touch was a nude lipstick.

It was 6:25 and I didn't want to be late, so I threw some necessities into my new handbag, and put on the earrings and necklace.

"I don't look like me." I spun slowly so I could see myself from the back. "I haven't been this polished in forever. It's kind of nice."

I was eager to see what Nick would say when he saw me. The

extent of my wardrobe over the past few weeks had been shorts, a bathing suit, and sweatpants—comfy, homey clothes. Other than the night at the Crab Stone, where I'd made more of an effort, I'd never dressed up like this.

My stomach was filled with butterflies when I stepped into the elevator. I did a final check of my make-up and lipstick in the compact mirror, satisfied everything was as it should be, before I stepped off the elevator and walked across the lobby.

Nick stood head and shoulders above the crowd, with his back to me. He was tall and so incredibly handsome that I forgot to breathe. He was still in his business suit but the tie was gone and his collar open. Other women noticed him too. He was talking with the concierge.

Then it was as if he sensed me. He turned and looked directly at me. His expression was what I had hoped it would be.

He smiled, his eyes widened, and he looked me up and down. It was as if I could *feel* his eyes roving over my flesh. Goosebumps rose along my arms under the weight of his stare. That he could make me feel this way with only a look!

He walked toward me and held out his hand, taking mine. "You look incredible. I am the luckiest man alive to have you on my arm tonight. Stunning all the stuffy business people will be the highlight of my day."

He leaned down and kissed me on the cheek, almost as if he knew I wouldn't want my lipstick smeared.

"You're not so bad either." I rested my palm on his chest.

"Then we're the perfect couple." He lifted his elbow, and I slipped my hand through it. "Come on, the car's waiting.

"The car?" I asked, still overwhelmed by the whirlwind of everything that had happened since jetting out of Seattle yesterday. When I saw the car he led me to, I nearly fainted.

*　*　*

"What did you think of the ride?" Nick asked me, and tucked my hand into the crook of his arm when we arrived at our destination.

"I'm not much of a car person, unlike you, but that was impressive. It's a classic, right?"

"Yes, an originally restored Rolls Royce Silver Cloud. And yes, I do like my cars." He guided me through the wide lobby of the hotel toward the restaurant where we were having dinner. "I think there could be about fifteen of us. Don't be nervous. You'll knock 'em dead," he assured me.

"I'll try not to be. I can usually hold my own, but these are your business associates, after all. I don't want to embarrass you." I glanced up at him and blushed at the way he was looking at me.

"You are wonderful. You could never embarrass me. And I know you can hold your own. Enjoy yourself."

I gripped his hand tighter, not so much for reassurance as to agree with him.

There was a crowd of people outside the restaurant, and Nick leaned down to tell me it was our group. I touched my hair and tried not to worry if my make-up was fine. I did my best to walk with confidence by his side.

Most of the assembled group were men, and there were three other women.

An older gentleman separated from the crowd and came toward us. He was tall, handsome, and had a thick mop of silver hair.

"Nick, Nick, good to see you." He reached out his hand and gave Nick's a solid shake. Then he turned to me and gave Nick a quizzical look. "Mrs Charlton?" he asked, but he looked a little confused.

That did it. My nerves just spiked. *Oh crap.*

I laughed, attempting to ease the moment of awkwardness. "No, no, we're . . ." I glanced at Nick, unsure how he wanted to introduce me, but answered in a rush, not wanting to put him on the spot. "Ah, friends." Although I must admit I wasn't the least bit offended at being called Mrs Charlton.

"I'm sorry. I thought you were Nick's wife, Marissa."

A chill raced down the backs of my legs. Oh my God, here we are.

Marissa.

That was the last thing I expected to hear—and on the other side of the country. I looked up at Nick, to see if I could read what he was thinking. He'd stiffened, so I knew he wasn't exactly okay about it.

"No, Jeff, this is Lizzie. Marissa died a while back." Nick didn't use Ari, nor did he elaborate, and the awkwardness grew.

"My condolences, Nick. I didn't know. And now I feel just horrible." He turned to me. "My apologies, Lizzie. I'm so sorry."

I shook my head and raised my shoulders. "Please don't worry about it."

Well, that was a way to start the evening with a bang.

Jeff held his hand out, indicating for us to join the crowd. "Please, come, we are about to sit down. And tonight is pleasure, no business if we can manage it." He smiled at Nick, then me. "We did all that today. And it was good. Thank you." He nodded at Nick.

"My pleasure. That's why you brought me here." I could tell by his curt response that Nick was annoyed.

Could Jeff read him as well as I could?

"Quite so, quite so," Jeff said, and he introduced us to the crowd, this time making sure I was not mistaken for Mrs Charlton.

But his slip-up reinforced the need for us to talk openly about the past.

Nick's mannerisms had subtly changed. I picked up on it right away, so I was going to tread lightly and see how this evening played out.

Nick placed his hand at the small of my back and guided me along behind the rest of the group. "Lizzie, I'm sorry about that."

I squeezed his arm. "It was an honest mistake."

He stopped and turned me to face him, holding my shoulders. "I know we have to continue what we talked about last night. But I don't want to do it here, if that's okay with you? I'd rather wait until we get home."

I nodded. "Yes, of course. When we get home."

"Thank you. But in the meantime . . ." He leaned down and kissed me. "Let's have fun."

Chapter Thirty-three

The trip to Miami had been amazing—something I would never forget. I was thankful Nick asked me to come away with him, and I felt we'd turned another corner in our relationship. Still, I was glad to get back to my little cottage by the sea. I was surprised by that, as well. Because who wouldn't want the glamorous lifestyle, sophistication, and beauty of the tropics like Miami? But Savage Cove was special. I was starting to feel as if I was coming home.

Coming home.

My heart swelled. Home. It had been a long time since I had a sense of home. It had to be before Mom and Dad died. I remember calling Rob and saying, *we're orphans now.*

He'd gone silent, and we'd sat there on the phone, quiet, then he'd whispered, *I guess we are.*

I could still hear his voice, the pain in it. Since then, we'd held each other together.

The reality hit me like a blow. I sat on the porch swing and looked out over the water. Such different water here than the ocean in Miami. It wasn't tropical blue, but a deep, mysterious indigo. The weather was dreary and drizzly—the more common pattern I had come to recognize, and even appreciate.

Now I let myself feel the emotion, not suppress it. I drew strength from the powerful sensation, recognizing my internal growth as time went by. It had helped me deal with my grief, even if I had felt homeless.

My vehicle had been my home since I began my journey after Rob died. And now I realized how alone I had been.

I reflected on my time here in Savage Cove, and the people I'd met. Nick and Walter. Wendy and Amanda. The locals were friendly and always ready with a hello. And, of course, Claire. I enjoyed being around her, and looked forward to throwing her together with Walter.

I hadn't been idle while I was here, and had done my best to stick to my promise, continuing to grow my alternative career path. The results so far encouraged me.

But meeting Nick had changed everything. Unexpected, incredible, unforgettable. It made my heart sing. I sighed, thinking of him.

I only had another ten days before I was due to leave. It was an increasingly unwelcome thought.

I curled one leg under me and pushed with my toe against sand, to rock the swing back and forth. The movement lulled me and let me declutter my mind. It was time to be open to possibilities.

Tonight, I was moving into Nick's house. We'd have a week and a half together.

It had been a big surprise when he'd asked me on our return from Miami, but I didn't need to give it much consideration. I said yes right away, because it meant we could be together, and I loved being with Nick.

I'd packed my bags and they waited by the front door. A thrill of anticipation tumbled through me. Although we'd spent many nights together at my cottage, this felt different. Tomorrow, I'd be waking up next to Nick in *his* house. He was welcoming me into his home, his life. But my excitement quickly dampened when I remembered it would be for just ten days.

If I leave.

My plan had been set in stone for so long. I had to keep my promise to Rob, to roam free and wild, to live in the moment, and not let go of that.

Now I was having a difficult time with it. What if the plan was wrong? What if the very thing I was about to let go of in order to live in the moment was what I needed to hold on to the tightest?

Nick was eager to finish the conference calls and get ready for Lizzie's arrival. He was smiling and whistling softly, while he put away the contract for the previous call, and got out what he needed for the next.

Goddamn, he was excited to have Lizzie come and stay with him for the remainder of her trip. She hadn't given up the cottage, though. She'd paid for the rental right through to her last day, and didn't think it was fair to ask for a rebate.

"And you never know," she'd said. "We could have a monstrous fight, or something bad could happen."

While he understood her reasoning, and respected her independent streak, he'd told her not to think like that. He wasn't suspicious, as a rule, but he didn't like how it made him feel.

Bringing Lizzie with him to Miami had been a polar shift for him. With Ari refusing to go with him, his business and personal lives had always been entirely separate. He hadn't been entirely sure how it would go when they merged. But Lizzie was so easy-going that he shouldn't have been surprised it had worked out well. Fantastically, in fact. He realized he didn't want to miss a moment with her, and so asking her to move in with him made complete sense.

He grinned to himself, thinking how much he'd enjoyed her company both in and out of their hotel room. For the first time on a business trip his mind had been elsewhere. Which wasn't the best approach, business wise, but it told him a lot about the growing relationship with Lizzie.

A growing relationship that had an end date in ten days. Yeah, he was counting them.

Nick frowned and pushed himself out of his chair. Houdini jumped up and started his Pepé Le Pew four-legged bounce routine, nearly knocking him over.

"Dog!" Nick lurched for the desk and grabbed the edge, to avoid falling on Houdini. He shook his head in fond exasperation. "You gotta watch yourself or I'll squash you."

Houdini sat and looked up at him with those big, sad, liquid brown eyes.

"You sure do know how to turn it on." Nick leaned down and kissed him on the head. "Wanna go for a walk?" Houdini jumped up and ran in circles. "Get your collar."

Houdini raced off and came back with his collar dangling in his mouth.

"Good boy. Sit." The dog did as he was commanded, and Nick put the leash on. He'd been giving him training on and off recently, and was pleased to see Houdini slowly learning. It's something he should have done years ago.

He stuck his phone in his pocket, in case Lizzie called or texted.

Having her move in for the rest of her trip seemed like the perfect opportunity for them to grow closer and learn more about each other. But if she still planned to leave, he knew it would make it even harder to say goodbye. Nick didn't want to think of the gaping hole she'd leave behind. It was as if she'd been in his life forever and not barely four weeks.

"Well, Houdini, time to go over and see Pops."

Houdini didn't need to be asked twice.

Nick was meeting his dad for a beer at the boathouse. They hadn't seen much of each other since the clam bake night.

Nick fully expected his dad would bring up Lizzie. He kept Houdini at his side, working on him paying attention and not taking off. It was training he should have been more vigilant about—but then he might not have met Lizzie. The path through the trees to the boathouse was narrow, easy to keep Houdini close, and was like walking into a different world.

The sound of chopping reached him. Nick smiled, knowing it was his dad. A day didn't go by when his dad wasn't outside doing something. He was good at keeping himself busy, and today it was firewood.

"Hey, son," Walter called, and raised his arm when Nick and Houdini came out of the trees.

"Dad. Busy again, I see." The yard was fenced around the boathouse, and he got Houdini inside with Candy. The two dogs took off, racing around entertaining each other.

"Idle hands and all that," Walter said, and gave a last swing with the axe so it bit into the log he was using as a chopping block. "How was the trip?" His dad pulled a handkerchief from his pocket and wiped his face. Yep, he was old school. A new handkerchief every day.

Nick was glad his dad was fit and active. It kept him sharp and healthy. He couldn't imagine a world without his father, just as he hadn't been able to imagine life without his mom. But here they were, without her, and just the two of them. They had an understanding. They would always be there for each other, but they also respected each other's space. They also didn't keep secrets. At least Nick didn't think they did.

"Trip was productive." He came over and started picking up pieces of wood to stack. "And yours?"

"My what?" Walter asked.

"Your trip? You haven't talked about it." Nick stood and watched his dad, noting that he seemed flustered.

"Fine, fine. Nothing much to say. It was good," his dad said, and he fidgeted a little.

Nick narrowed his eyes. "You okay?"

His dad was nodding and fussing about, putting tools back in his toolbox.

"Yes, I'm fine. Why do you ask?"

"You seem a bit nervous." Nick wondered why, and hoped his dad would talk about it.

"Ah, yeah, well, I'm not. It's all fine. Say, tell me about your trip. Did Lizzie enjoy Miami?" His voice cracked and he cleared his throat.

Yep, he was definitely flustered.

"Yes, she loved it. In fact, we had a great time together. I like being with her. Speaking of which, maybe you should think about meeting a woman, Dad." He watched his father's reaction and the flustering vanished, replaced with his damn good poker face.

"A woman!" He gave a nervous laugh. "Why would I want to do that, son?" He glanced at Nick and then refocused on the tools. The poker face slipped.

"Listen, Dad, I'm not going to pry. But you need to know that I want you to be happy, and if that means sharing your life with a woman, I'm fine with that. In fact, more than fine. And remember, Mom would want you to be happy too. Now, how about that beer?"

Relief softened his father's face, and Nick was glad he'd broached the subject. He didn't want his dad to be stressed about anything. Maybe he already had someone in his life. If so, Nick hoped this would encourage him to be more open about it.

"Here, let me get it for you." Nick grabbed a couple of cans from the beer fridge. His dad had made an outdoor barbecue and kitchen area, not that he ever used it—except for the beer fridge, of course.

He joined his dad, each sitting on a wood stump. They popped the tabs and drank in silence. Nick watched the dogs play, knowing it would tire them both out.

"So, when does Lizzie leave?" Walter asked him.

Nick drew in a deep breath and let it out slowly. "Only about ten days left."

"That's a shame. I like her. And you must too, if you took her on a business trip." Walter flicked the tab on the top of the can with his thumbnail, making it ping.

Nick tilted his head back and downed the rest of the beer. "Yup. I do. I asked her to stay with me in the house until then."

He stood and went to get another beer. Bringing one back for himself and one for his dad, he balanced it on a piece of wood.

"You did? Maybe that will be a good thing to help you both decide the next step. It's a conundrum, isn't it?" Walter asked.

"Yup, it is."

"Well, son, you two will sort it out. But I want you to know that I like seeing you happy. It's been far too long since you holed up and became the hermit. She's good for you."

"I'm not a hermit. And look who's talking," Nick pointed out.

"Ah, I'm an old man. You're not. I know your work keeps you busy, and I'm thankful for that. Yes, you went through a terrible time. Remember, I was there beside you all the way. I saw what her death did to you."

"And I've watched you with your grief after Mom died. It's been much longer with Mom than Ari."

Walter raised his hand. "Now, son, granted that's true. But I don't have many good years left. You have your whole life ahead of you. When I'm gone, I don't want you to be alone."

Nick glanced at his dad, reached out and touched his shoulder. "This is not the conversation I anticipated us having today."

They focused on their beer. Nick was quiet, trying to settle his stomach. He dreaded the thought of losing his dad . . . it was just too impossible to think about.

"Son, if you like Lizzie, let her know. Don't dance around it, just man up and do something about it, or your chance at happiness and companionship could pass you by. I don't want that for you."

Nick nodded his head and rested his elbows on his knees, looking down at the can in his hands. Then he turned to his father.

"I don't want that for you, either. You're right, Dad. We all need companionship. Even you." Nick gave him a slow smile, and was content at his dad's mischievous grin.

Walter lifted the can of beer. "To companionship."

Nick touched his can to his dad's. "Yes, to companionship."

Chapter Thirty-four

The next morning, Nick lay on his side and watched Lizzie sleep. She took his breath away. Her hair fanned out on the pillow, and her face was soft and relaxed. One arm was thrown over her head and she was murmuring in a dream. She rolled in her sleep, her hands under her chin, and her hair fell across her cheek.

Nick reached out and slid aside the strand of hair. She sighed and turned toward him. Her face tucked into his shoulder.

A combination of protectiveness and desire coursed through him. He'd never felt like this before. He wanted to pull her into his arms and never let her go. This woman he'd stumbled across on the beach only a few weeks ago had shone a new light into his life.

He didn't want her to leave; he wanted her to stay. Houdini was still fast asleep at the foot of the bed, and Nick had no real urge to get out of their warm and cozy nest. He'd rather stay here beside Lizzie, who had made such an amazing change in his life.

She opened her eyes, and he sucked in a breath. Those eyes. "How did you sleep?"

"Mmm, decidedly delightfully." She stretched her arms over her head, then looped them around his neck.

Houdini paced next to them.

"I think he needs to go out." Lizzie swung her legs out of the bed and pulled on her turquoise robe, which was on the floor, along with the rest of their clothes. "I'm going to make some coffee, but . . ." She held up her finger. "I'm not going to use your special pot or that fancy-dancy machine. It'll be plain old drip."

She blew him a kiss over her shoulder, and left the room. He rolled on to his back and clasped his hands behind his head, listening to her go down the stairs, talking to Houdini.

It was all so perfect. Too perfect.

"Want to go for a walkie?" I asked Houdini after I put the coffee on.

His ears popped up. He did a little woof and hopped on his front paws. I laughed at his excitement. Oh, to have such a simple life.

"Come on, boy. You be good and don't pull. I don't want to have to chase you down the beach, dressed like this. Let's be quick about it."

I clipped the leash on to his collar, and Houdini looked up at me as if I was his best person. His tongue lolled out, and his tail whipped back and forth.

After Houdini had done his business, I came back in and was greeted with Nick standing in the kitchen, shirtless, barefoot, and wearing a pair of shorts.

"I think I'm gonna like this arrangement." I smiled, leaned down, and unclipped the leash from Houdini's collar.

"I think I'm going to, as well. Seeing you traipse around in the trees, wearing your robe like a woodland fairy, is certainly a sight." He had poured the coffee, and the mugs were sitting on the island. "What's the plan for today?" he asked me.

"Same as usual, I suppose. My work. I guess you have work to do, as well?" I slid on to the stool and picked up a mug.

I didn't feel awkward about staying with Nick in his house. Quite the opposite, it seemed like the right thing. The next step. I was content, happy, and felt settled. The only time I felt anxious was when I let the prospect of leaving creep into my mind.

The departure date loomed over us, and it was too painful to think about it. I couldn't imagine leaving. But then, I couldn't imagine abandoning my promise to Rob. I sighed and pushed the worry from my mind when Nick answered.

"Yes, I still have work to do. And my office is in there, as you know. Feel free to set up anywhere you like. There's the spare room upstairs you could turn into an office for the next while."

We both looked at each other when he said *the next while*. Silence fell between us and lengthened. I put the mug down.

"I know. Nine days now. When I have to go."

"Do you *have* to go?" His voice was low.

"Yes, I think I do." I let out a sigh. "We haven't really talked, but I know you've been thinking about it too."

He nodded. "Yeah, it doesn't seem real." He paused for a beat. "Have you thought any more about staying longer?" He raised his eyebrows. "I'd like you to, if it's something you want to do."

My chest tightened. These damn decisions were tearing me up inside. "As you know, I never intended to stay. But it also wasn't my intention to meet you. Somehow, I feel we were destined to meet, which makes all this so unbelievably hard," I said and rested my palm on his cheek. "I can't imagine going without you, but . . . Rob . . ."

"I know. You must do what you feel you need to do. I didn't expect us to happen, either. We've had a wonderful time together."

"I know! This was all so unexpected." My eyes started to burn. "So wonderful and, a-and—"

"Shh, we don't have to discuss it now. It came up organically. Think about it and, in the meantime, what do you want for breakfast?"

I could tell he was trying to lighten our mood, and I loved him for that.

Love? Did I just say, love? Oh my God. My mouth went dry, and I licked my lips.

I was falling in love with him.

"Lizzie?"

"Mmm, oh yeah, what was that?"

I was falling in love with him.

"Breakfast? What would you like?"

My heart was nearly exploding, and I stammered. "U-uh, just something l-light. Um, do you have y-yogurt, granola, and fruit?"

He gave me a quizzical look, and I quickly tried to recover from my revelation.

"I do, I made sure I had some here just for you." He pulled open the fridge.

I slid off the stool, walked around the island to him, and linked my fingers behind his back, holding him tight. He wrapped his arms around me, and I melted into his embrace. I was overcome. Again, my eyes filled and burned, but I wouldn't let myself cry.

"We'll figure it out," I whispered, his chest hair soft against my cheek.

"I know we will." He stroked my back.

Don't let go. Rob's words echoed in my ears.

Now I was confused. Do I not let go of Nick, or of my promise to Rob?

I squeezed Nick tighter.

"Let's go out to the living room," he suggested.

I followed him and we sat at the table where we'd had our first breakfast. It had become one of my favorite places. Other than upstairs. It was a cozy corner surrounded by windows. And, of course, the view was amazing.

"I like this spot," I said, and curled my legs under me. I was still a bit strung out. Talking about leaving had made it all too real.

"I like it too. Kind of a solarium effect," he replied, and put his mug down. He sat across from me.

I smiled and looked around. "Yes, except for the plants. It desperately needs plants here."

He laughed and nodded. "I agree, but I do not have a green thumb." He gave me a thumbs up, then turned it to a thumbs down.

I had the urge to say something to segue into the conversation we still needed to have, and yet I hesitated. My mind was in turmoil, and then the next thing I knew, the words fell out of my mouth.

"Did Marissa have a green thumb?"

His head shot up, with a look of surprise. Then his shoulders drooped, and he sighed. "Marissa. Yes, we need to talk about her."

I held my breath and waited.

He drank a few more sips of coffee and then leaned forward,

with his elbows on the table and his fingers clasped. "We weren't married long. And she had captivated me."

He maintained eye contact with me, and I did my best not to show emotion when he said *she'd* captivated *him*. He reached over and took my hand. I swallowed, needing to hear more.

"She was different, she had a side to her that was compelling. I never knew if it was natural or intentional. She wasn't born and raised here, she just suddenly turned up one day and seemed to hook me. She told me she'd been in Canada, in Whistler, and got in her car and drove south, finding her way here."

"She didn't have any family?" I asked. "Why Whistler?"

He shook his head. "I don't know, skiing is all she told me. She said very little about her family, other than they were estranged."

He let go of me and sat back, turned to look out toward the water. We were silent for a few minutes and I nursed my coffee, waiting for him to continue.

"She was like a wanderer, and she had this air about her that made whoever she was around feel special. Like you never wanted to let her go. I fell under her spell." He looked at me and widened his eyes. "Against my better judgment. And next thing I knew, we were married."

"What was she like, though, how did she put you under a spell?" I raised my hands and wiggled my fingers, as if casting a spell, and smiled, trying to break the tension.

He gave a ghost of a smile. "What is that supposed to mean? And no, she wasn't a witch." Nick shook his head ruefully; it was clear the hurt went deep. "For the first little while, about four months, it was good." He frowned, looking up to the ceiling. "Then she decided she hated the water. Didn't like living near the sea. So, yeah, about four months, as they say, the honeymoon stage."

I gritted my teeth. Listening to him talk about his dead wife was important to our relationship, but it was damn hard. My stomach tightened, which I recognized as jealousy. Marissa had ruined him, in a way, and I wondered if he was emotionally traumatized as much by her actions as by her death.

"But then things changed. They say the real person reveals herself, eventually. And she did. I never knew what I'd come home to after work. It was a constant crapshoot. She hated it when I left for work, but eventually it became my place of refuge."

I was aghast at what he was telling me. But I kept quiet, suspecting he needed to unburden, and he was finally telling me what I needed to know.

"We drifted apart but continued to live here. Separately, though. And I felt guilty as hell, and responsible for her unhappiness." He stopped and looked at me. "And one day, I came home from a business trip and she was gone."

He looked at me, and the expression in his eyes broke my heart.

"I've never talked about it to anyone since it happened. For the last three years, I've tried to bury it and plow on. But the truth is, I couldn't."

"Oh, how awful. I'm so sorry." I meant it, I really did. I couldn't imagine what it was like to go through all that.

"It was the anniversary of her death a few weeks ago, and I realized I needed to find a way to let her go. And the next day, I met you."

I forced myself not to react as the words from the text swam before me.

I have to find a way to let you go.

We were quiet again for a couple of minutes, and though my head was spinning, I didn't want to interrupt Nick's thoughts.

I watched him closely. He had withdrawn into himself more than I'd seen him do before. When he drew in an audible breath, it startled me.

Nick lifted the coffee mug and finished it. "Want more?" he asked.

I nodded and was about to stand up.

He took my mug. "No, stay. I'll get it. Be right back."

I realized he might need a moment by himself to deal with what he'd just told me. I stayed in the seat and waited for him. My mind raced with chaotic thoughts.

When he didn't return after a few minutes, I started to worry.

"Nick," I called. "Everything okay?"

He didn't answer, so I got up and walked into the kitchen. He was standing at the stove holding his phone, and relief rushed through me.

"Didn't you hear me call you?" I stood beside him and rubbed his back.

He put his arm around my shoulder, and put his phone face down on the counter. "No, I was listening to voicemails and making you a proper cup of coffee."

I had to take what he said at face value, and he did have a pot of coffee going. I didn't feel this was the right time to tell him about the text. His revelations had been an emotional drain for him. I wouldn't put extra pressure on him now. One thing is certain, I knew now that the text was from him. How would he feel, knowing I'd seen it and not told him so?

"Thanks for telling me," was all I said, and I didn't expect him to continue talking.

He nodded and fussed about with his coffee pot and foamer. "Coffee is ready."

My heart swelled as I watched him. I wanted to take away

all his pain, his grief, his guilt. He'd been living with it all for three years, alone, never talked about it, and kept it bottled up inside.

Anger at that woman boiled inside of me. What Marissa had put him through! I didn't like to think ill of the dead, but seeing the pain she'd caused, it was impossible to feel anything else.

Chapter Thirty-five

I put my hands on my hips and looked around Nick's bedroom. I did love this room. My clothes were put away, and my bags stowed in the huge walk-in closet. I walked over to the bed, and fixed the corner of the duvet so it hung neatly. A very contented feeling of hominess washed over me. We were a few days into living together, and it was everything I hoped it would be.

I was happy.

He was happy.

We were having a great time, couldn't keep our hands off each other. We shared more about our lives, even though we delicately seemed to sidestep Marissa.

Nick was busy with meetings online today, so I was going into town. I hadn't seen Claire in a while, and I hoped she'd be at the café. It was Tuesday morning, so I crossed my fingers. I wanted to invite her to dinner so we could introduce her to Walter.

On the drive, I couldn't help the smile on my face when I thought about how Nick and I had settled in together.

He enjoyed reading. We'd lay on the couch in front of the

fire and he'd read to me. We liked similar music, and it played in the background most of the day.

I bought him a difficult puzzle and had it all set up as a surprise when he finished his business for the day and came out of his office. We worked on it for a few hours with wine, before heading to bed. I wasn't a puzzle person, but I soldiered on. I discovered he was fanatical when it came to finding the pieces, and it was hard to draw him away from the challenge.

It surprised him that I liked space and sci-fi shows. At first, he tolerated it when I turned on the newest season of the top space series. But he got hooked after a few episodes.

All was right with the world. I still couldn't believe our luck at stumbling into each other. How, if I looked back through the years, all the events that happened, both good and bad, had led me here.

To us.

I pulled on to Lincoln and was lucky to find a spot right out front of Sol. Sure enough, I saw through the front window that Claire was in her usual spot. I hurried out of the car with my bag, and she looked up at the same time as the bells hanging over the doorway jingled my arrival. Her face lit into a big smile. I went over to her table. She stood, and we hugged. A wave of affection washed over me.

"How good to see you, Lizzie." She sat and marked her page with a bookmark.

"And you too, gosh, it's been a while." I settled into the chair opposite.

"I know. And what have you been up to?" she asked, her eyes bright with curiosity.

"Well, I've moved in with Nick for the rest of my time here." I couldn't stop the smile, then bit my lip to contain my glee. "But I didn't let go of the cottage, just in case."

"Good for you. Maintain your sense of independence. Should anything go wrong, you always have someplace to go." She nodded, and tapped her fingers on the table with emphasis. "I've always said a woman must have mad money for emergencies tucked in her pocketbook, and enough money stashed away to care for herself should the need arise."

I thought about that. It was a pretty good rule of thumb. "Well, I hope it isn't going to happen with me. But I get that. However, we are enjoying being together."

"I'm glad." She broke off a piece of her pastry and nibbled on it.

"And you?" I asked her.

Claire's eyebrows rose. "And me? How so?"

"How are you doing?"

Claire stopped chewing and looked at me. "I'm fine. Why do you ask, my dear?" She picked another piece off the pastry.

"Well, I would like to invite you over for dinner soon."

She looked at me and seemed pleased.

"Will you come?"

"That would be lovely," Claire said, and there was a tiny lilt in her voice.

"Wonderful, we'll have so much fun."

Claire's eyebrows rose "We?"

I paused. Did I just let the cat out of the bag? "Ah, yes, we. Um, Nick will be there too. I'll check with him about a date."

Claire leaned back in the chair and dropped her hands in her lap. Her face fell, and suddenly I worried I'd either got it wrong or upset her.

"I'm sorry, is it a problem?" I wondered at her sudden change in mood.

Claire shook her head. "No, it's not a problem."

I let out a little squeal of delight and clapped my hands.

"However . . ." Claire paused, and I stilled. She let out a sigh and leaned forward in her seat. "Is Nick's father coming too?"

"Well, yes, he is. Do you know him?" It surprised me she asked, and I wondered if she already knew him, but then why wouldn't she? It's a small town.

"Yes, I do. We're only a few years apart, and both of us grew up here—"

We were interrupted by Amanda stopping at our table.

"Hi, Lizzie, can I get you anything today?"

"Hi, Amanda, yes, that would be lovely, thank you. Surprise me with a hot drink, and I think I'll have a . . ." I smiled at her. "Oh, tell you what, surprise me with a sweet treat too."

She laughed. "You're funny. What if you don't like it?"

"What's not to like here?" I swept my hand in the air, indicating the café.

"Okay, coming right up."

"Thanks, Amanda." I turned back to Claire. "I hope it's not a problem with Walter being there. We like to include him, so he's not lonely."

"Of course, it's fine, my dear. It's very sweet of you to ask me to come."

There was a twinkle in Claire's eye, and I was glad she seemed happy about the invitation. Amanda came back with a steaming drink and my favorite maple bacon donut.

"Oooh, thank you."

"Enjoy." And she was off serving another patron.

I took a bite and closed my eyes. "Mmm, this is wonderful. I love these. I think I've become a groupie." I laughed and wiped my fingertips on a napkin. "I'm so pleased you're coming to dinner. It will feel like a family gathering."

"A new family." Claire smiled.

Her words made me pause. I picked up my drink, and licked

off a bit of foam that stuck to my lip. Did I want to replace my lost family with a new one? I thought of Rob and my parents, and swallowed. I missed them so. But I was here, alive and living my best life, despite the hole in my heart created by their loss.

"Are you okay, Lizzie?" Claire asked, concern in her eyes.

I nodded. "Yes, I'm fine. Just thinking about Rob, and my parents too. I miss them. My family."

"Oh, I'm so sorry, it was insensitive of me." Claire covered my hand with hers.

I shook my head. "Reminders come out of the blue. It's just that my family is gone . . . and I can't, won't replace them—"

"That is not what I meant. I'm sorry to interrupt you, but please, dear, I wasn't meaning that at all." Claire looked upset.

I felt bad. "It's fine, and I know you didn't mean it that way. It's just the unexpected reminders that can knock you back." I took a sip of my coffee, swallowing back tears that suddenly threatened to flow.

"Here, have some of this pastry. It's huge." Claire pushed the plate closer to me.

I smiled. "I have this." And pointed at my donut. "You eat your pastry. It looks delicious."

"Are you sure you're okay? I do apologize."

"There's no need. I'm absolutely fine." I paused a moment, with a sudden thought that popped into my head. "There is something else I wanted to ask you, if you don't mind."

"What's that?" Claire straightened her collar and tucked a strand of silver hair behind her ears.

"Gosh, weeks ago, when we were sitting over by the fireplace, Wendy came over and you guys seemed to have some kind of moment. A tension-filled one. I was wondering what that was all about?" I asked. "I don't want you to think I'm being nosy, but it has been weighing on my mind, because you looked so upset and uncomfortable."

"Oh, well, how interesting you noticed." But Claire smiled, this time. I was relieved she didn't seem to be offended.

"I'm sorry. If you'd prefer not to say, I understand."

She laughed. Leaning forward, she crossed her arms and rested them on the table. "Okay, long story. Wendy was friends with the owner of the café. I'd been coming here, long before it changed to the new owners. I will admit the change of menu was a vast improvement, and I like to support local." I got the impression that Claire was watching her words carefully, and I wondered why. "I felt a sense of obligation to continue my patronage. Plus, I had a bit of a hand in the decor." She reached out and fingered the shiny steel plate that held the salt and pepper shaker.

It reminded me of the steel heart I bought at the market. I remained quiet, wanting Claire to tell me more.

"Then I noticed strange things began to happen—subtle, small things. I felt as if secrets were being kept, and I began to wonder if there was something underhanded going-on."

"Really?" I was surprised.

"Yes. One day, the owner vanished. And I heard a rumor of money being skimmed, so it was a rather peculiar situation. I don't know how much Wendy was a part of the caper, but they were thick as thieves. I don't trust Wendy, and she knows it. There's something about her that strikes me as sneaky. You know how you get a feeling about a person?"

"Yes, I suppose I do. And because of that, you and Wendy are at odds with each other?"

Claire nodded. "That we are."

I was fascinated by what Claire had told me, and needed to think about what it meant. I instinctively felt that I couldn't push her any further, though, so I leaned forward and changed the subject. "I've wondered what is up there." I pointed to the top of the stairs.

"You have, have you?" She smiled. "From what I know, it was a bordello many, many years ago, in the 1800s, and then it became a hotel, but I think working ladies still were available. After the stock market crash, it switched to rooms to let out. But during World War Two, it was closed up." She glanced up at the door on the landing. "I don't think it's used any longer. Perhaps as storage for the café."

"The history is so interesting." I glanced around and saw Wendy standing beside the coffee machine.

She was on the phone and staring at us. I got the oddest sensation from her. It chilled me. If looks could kill, we'd be long dead.

Chapter Thirty-six

"Nick!" I called. I was going to drop all these bags if he didn't come and help. "I need you."

I got through the front door and into the vestibule, but the wine bottles were precariously swinging in the bag hooked on to my baby finger. The weight of the grocery bags for tonight's dinner was getting too much, and it was all about to crash on to the floor.

"Nick!" I yelled.

"Hang on, I'll be right there," he shouted back.

I smiled and I held myself as still as I could.

"What did you do, buy the store out?" he said as he relieved me of most of my packages.

"You'd think so, but not really. I just grabbed everything rather awkwardly when I got out of my car."

He put the bags on the kitchen counter, and I unpacked them. I took my purse strap from around my shoulders and put it on the island.

"It was busy out there. I had to go to a few places to get everything you put on the list." I needed a glass of water.

"Atta girl." He separated the food items.

"Are you sure you want to go to all this trouble tonight? You know me, I'm happy with hotdogs on the bonfire."

"The bonfire is later. And this time, we're going to make those s'mores."

Nick wanted to do an Italian meal, which I was all for. I'd learned that anything he cooked was to die for.

Soon he had the sauce bubbling, butter and garlic simmering, and Italian loaves on the counter waiting to be doctored up with whatever he had on the menu. I had no clue what he was serving, but it was some kind of pasta thing with a creamy wine sauce and clams.

I watched him peel more garlic and get out a board for antipasto. I was mesmerized but then snapped out of my trance. "Give me something to do."

"Okay, thanks. Slice up these tomatoes, not too thin, and the mozzarella for the Caprese salad. Then slice this baguette on the angle for crostini."

"Oh, I love that salad." I swear my mouth was starting to water with all these great aromas. "Do you want me to do a topping for the bread?"

He put the container of tomatoes and onion in front of me. "Chop them up, please."

"I can do that." I got busy.

"Oh, you need garlic as well." He tossed me a couple of cloves, which I smashed, peeled, and chopped, as well as some basil that I stacked and rolled, making it easier to cut.

While Nick had everything prepared, I was still working on the tomatoes and onion. He opened a bottle of wine.

"There's nothing like cooking Italian food and drinking some fine Italian wine," he said, and put a glass in front of me.

I took a sip. I never really drank Italian wine, I mostly preferred French, but this was good.

"Okay, I think I'm finished here. What next?" I put the knife down and drank more wine, loving the warm, fuzzy buzz it was giving me.

"Drizzle some olive oil over the baguette, rub with garlic, and then toast it till golden."

"Another thing I can do. But first, I think we need some music, don't you?" I asked him as I wiped my hands.

"Great idea. I'll get something playing. I'm in a lull, prep wise." Nick left the room, and soon the soft notes of some whiskey blues came from the strategically placed and hidden speakers.

"Good?" he asked when he came back to the kitchen.

"Oh, yes." I loved blues, and swayed to the music while I got the bread ready for the oven.

A little while later, with everything ready, we sat out on the patio. It was a partly sunny day, so it was nice to be outside. When the sun came out, the temperature went up to about 78 degrees, I guessed.

"I'm understanding the weather patterns here. It's mainly overcast. Sunny days, I think, are treasures, are they not?"

"Yes, they are. But the weather is what it is. We get fog, and drizzle, and rain—and as we're on the western side of the Cascades, it's a little cooler. If we were on the other side, we'd have some higher temperatures."

"I'd like to go for a drive up into the mountains. You know, before I leave." Even as I said the words, I wished I hadn't. But the flow of conversation was so natural that they just . . . fell out.

I took a drink of wine, and so did he. We let it slide. I was glad, because even though we'd chatted about the possibility of me staying, I hadn't let myself think about it yet, so it was still all up in the air.

"It would be a beautiful drive on the Cascade Loop."

"I saw that, when I was planning my trip to Rialto Beach. It would take a couple of days, though, and I'm not sure I have time for it."

"You wouldn't get to see everything. More than a few days is usually best."

"Hmm, maybe I should try to go. It's one of those things you don't want to miss while here." I had a thought. "Would you like to come?"

"I would, but it depends on when my next calls are. The group from Miami will get in touch with me soon."

Walter shouted that he'd arrived.

I raised my eyebrows. "Oh, here we go."

Nick smiled. "I'm glad you're getting a kick out of this."

"I am, and I hope it works out."

Candy came roaring into the living room, and Houdini jumped to his feet barking. The two of them did their hello sniffs and then started a chase.

In came Walter and, behind him, was Claire, holding a bouquet of flowers.

"Look who I bumped into outside," Walter said, and went to the kitchen. "I didn't know it was a dinner party." He grabbed a beer from the fridge.

Claire came over and kissed me on the cheek, handing me the flowers.

"Thank you, they're lovely."

We all went into the kitchen. I slid on to a stool, Claire leaned against the island counter. Nick pulled some appetizers from the fridge and placed them beside Claire.

"Dig in," he said.

Walter was first to eat. I smiled, because I'd learned he loved his food.

"I understand you two know each other?" I said, smiling at Walter and Claire.

"We know each other," Walter said as he perused a shrimp, then stuffed it in his mouth. "We went to school together, different grades, but I knew of Claire."

I felt deflated. He didn't even look to acknowledge her. I glanced at Nick, and he shrugged. I guessed this wasn't going to work out all that well, after all. I only hoped dinner wouldn't be awkward.

"I barely remember him, to be honest," Claire commented, and took the glass of wine that Nick offered her. She put it down on the counter and leaned over to pick up a shrimp.

"What? I didn't leave an impression on you?" he asked, and sounded a bit annoyed.

Claire shook her head and looked up at Walter. She shrugged her shoulders.

"Well, I'll be damned," he said, and wiped his fingers.

I looked at Nick, who had a very uncomfortable expression etched on his face. I was suddenly sorry for thinking we could set them up. He picked up his wine and the plate of appetizers.

We walked into the great room. Music came from the speakers, and it eased the tension that had fallen over everyone.

Claire and Walter stood together, and it puzzled me when they looked at each other and smiled. I was stunned when he swept her into a hug and swooned her backward for a big kiss.

"W-w-hat?" I stammered. I looked at Nick, whose jaw was nearly on the floor.

"The hell?" he said.

Then Claire and Walter burst into laughter, and put their arms around each other.

"I think we beat you to the punch," Walter said, and he looked quite proud of himself.

I slowly smiled and glanced at Nick. He didn't look so stunned anymore.

"How long?" he asked, and he broke into a big grin.

They spoke at the same time.

"Over a year now," Claire said, and looked at Walter.

He nodded. "Yep, we started dating in May last year, and July 4 we decided to be exclusive."

"Oh, that's amazing." I clapped.

"She's right about that," Nick agreed with me. "But why didn't you say anything?"

Claire laughed, and patted Walter on the shoulder. "I told you."

The look on Walter's face made me giggle, and even Nick laughed. He looked like a forlorn little boy caught trying to hide something. "I was just thinking of you, Nick."

"Oh, don't give me that," Nick said. "It's not about me. I want you to be happy, and I told you that the other day."

Walter huffed out some air and shook his head. "You guys are ganging up on me. But yes, we are together."

"That's wonderful, Dad. I'm really happy for you both."

"But just for you to know. I'm not ready for the town to find out yet." He wagged his finger at us. It was cute when a blush stained his cheeks.

"Oh, so now that's the reason? You're worried about what other people are going to say?" Nick walked into the kitchen and we all followed him. "I was just going to open another bottle of wine. Claire, would you like a top up? Lizzie?"

"Red wine would be great, thank you." Claire stood beside Walter.

"Here we go." Nick topped up my glass and poured two fresh ones for Walter and Claire.

I knew I had a silly grin on my face, but I couldn't help it. They were so cute together. All this time I was working out how to set them up, and they'd already found each other. Serendipity. I thought about it for a moment. *Found each other.* Kind of like Nick and I. He was wiping down the counter when he looked at me, catching my eye. We lingered, connected, for the briefest moment, and the gentle smile on his lips made my heart swell.

"Ah, well, it's kind of nice out. Do you want to sit outside for a little while?" I asked everyone, letting my attention drift back to Nick before following everyone out to the patio table and chairs.

I made sure I clipped Houdini on to the long leash I'd tied around a post. We all settled under the umbrella, with contented sighs.

"Ah, relaxed at last," Walter said, and leaned back in his chair, sipping the wine.

Chapter Thirty-seven

After they'd left, we were in the kitchen tidying up.

"That was a wonderful dinner. You outdid yourself for sure." I slipped my arms around Nick's waist, and we slow danced to the soft blues playing on his hidden speakers.

"It went well, didn't it?" His hands ran up my back, and I shivered in delight.

I nodded. "Yes, wasn't that a wonderful surprise about your dad and Claire?"

"It was. The sneaky devil. But I'm glad. I've wanted him to have someone in his life."

Nick packed up the leftover food he hadn't put in a container for his dad. I wiped down the counter and licked my lips. They were dry and I needed to put on some moisturizer. Digging through my purse on the counter, I saw the old phone, which I hadn't checked for days. It had a blinking red light on it.

I gasped, and my heart just skyrocketed through the ceiling. There was a notification. I glanced at Nick, who was still putting lids on the containers. I pulled the phone out, desperate to read the message.

Dare I look?

He seemed well occupied, and I wanted to take a quick peek. I flipped the phone up and was just about to open the message when I heard Nick beside me. A chill raced down my spine and my mouth dried. *Oh God.* I quickly shut the phone and shoved it back in my bag.

"What was that?" he asked.

I fumbled for something to say. "Oh, n-nothing, I was just looking for my lip gloss." I pulled it out and held it up to show him, then spread some on my lips.

He stared at me, and I saw the same look in his eyes as that time his mood had suddenly changed at the cottage. I furrowed my brow.

"Are you sure that was nothing? It seemed like it was something to me." His voice held a sharp edge, and he stepped back.

I immediately felt defensive. Both my reaction and his suspicious tone upset me. "What? No, it wasn't a thing. Don't you trust me?"

"Well, I saw you with a phone, and you shoved it back in your purse. Why hide it?"

"I wasn't. You've seen my phone before."

His eyes narrowed. "It wasn't your normal phone, it was a different one."

He was getting angry, and I felt anger bubble up as well. I wasn't sure I was mad so much as I was confused, and worried. I think my spark of anger was a defense mechanism. Where would this go now? A fight? Oh, I hoped not. But I had a bad feeling that things were going to escalate.

Why hadn't I told him about the texts sooner?

"Are you hiding a second phone?" Nick demanded.

I didn't know what to say. My thoughts were scattered, and I felt pushed into a corner. My only reaction was to lash out and deny.

Nick paced the kitchen, looking at me with an expression that chilled me to the bone.

"Why are you looking at me like that?" I was determined not to let my emotions get out of control.

No crying!

"Why are we fighting . . . are you being serious?"

He scoffed. "You're keeping secrets.

I'd never seen him like this before. The thought flashed through my mind: did we really know each other at all?

"You have secrets too!" I shouted back at him, and left the kitchen.

"Please don't walk away." But he wasn't asking, he was demanding, and I ignored him.

"Don't tell me what to do." I was halfway up the stairs now, and ran down the hall to shove my things into my overnight bag.

We were having our first fight, and I couldn't deal with it. I didn't want to fight with him, and yet here we were.

I was conflicted, confused. I didn't know what to do, but I wasn't good at conflict. And the urge to run away was strong. We were angry at each other, and I didn't see any hope of sorting this out tonight.

"I'm going. We can talk later." I grabbed my purse. "I need time to think. So do you. Maybe this was too much of a rush, especially with me leaving soon."

"Lizzie, wait."

I turned around at the door. "Nick, think about everything. I know I will. This has all happened so fast. I just want to be alone tonight."

The look in his eyes nearly broke my heart. I hesitated and then ran to my car. I needed to think about my future. Would it be easier to make the break now?

I drove home. It was hard to keep the tears in check. I pulled into the driveway of the cottage, ran up the walk, and slammed the door shut behind me.

Exhaustion made my legs wobble, and I leaned against the door.

Now what?

I remembered the phone and the message that started our fight. I wanted to know what it said. But somehow, the thought of taking the phone out and reading it filled me with the strangest sensation. I couldn't describe it, except it felt like I was betraying somebody.

I had to know. Nick had obviously sent it. When did he send it? And why? I think part of me was afraid to read it. Afraid of what it might say.

I closed my eyes. I needed to settle down.

Just read the text and then you'll know what it's all about.

I opened the phone.

Marissa, I've met somebody new, and I don't know what to do. She's special, and I think I might be able to open my heart to her. But your death nearly destroyed me, and I'm still not healed.

I let out a sob and covered my mouth with my fingers. I walked to the kitchen and put the phone down on the counter, staring at the words.

Had I royally messed things up between us? Or did this mean he might never be able to be honest with me? If he'd felt hesitant about opening his heart, I'd sure helped make his decision much easier.

I shook my head, so angry at myself. If I'd only told him about the first text, before we'd grown this close.

I sighed. Honestly, now that I was in my cottage by myself, I didn't know if I wanted to be here in Savage Cove anymore.

Chapter Thirty-eight

Nick had tossed and turned all night. He hated that they'd argued. Just when things were going really well. All because of the damn phone.

Looking back on it now, perhaps he overreacted to it. Maybe it was all just as innocent as she said. But he couldn't help wondering what she was hiding. *If* she was hiding anything. Which threw him right back to the betrayal he'd felt with Marissa.

He wasn't sure what to do. He couldn't stop wondering how Lizzie was, and if she was thinking the same things. He already missed her. Nick looked out at the sky, which echoed how he felt. Dark and stormy. He groaned and rolled out of bed.

Even Houdini, following behind, seemed out of sorts. Nick shuffled down to the kitchen. Out of habit, he made coffee for two—and then remembered.

The house felt like a big, empty shell without her.

He took Houdini out front, clipped him to the long line

Lizzie had set up, let him do his business, while Nick sat at the table under the canopy at the back of the house.

His phone sat silently beside the mug. No new messages or calls, even though he'd tried calling and texting last night.

He typed another message to her. If she hadn't responded by the time he finished his coffee, he would drive over to her cottage.

Not only was he concerned about their fight, but he worried something may have happened to her.

Coffee finished, and still no reply. Nick was in his car a few minutes later and on his way to her place. He pulled into her driveway, and his stomach dropped when he saw her vehicle with the trunk up. Was she leaving?

He didn't even bother knocking, and just walked in. She had bags organized and ready by the front door, and fear trickled down his spine.

"Lizzie, what's going on here?" he asked when he found her in the bathroom packing up toiletries.

She didn't answer.

"Lizzie, what are you doing?"

She looked at him, then down at the sink. "I'm getting ready to go for a research trip."

Relief washed over him. She wasn't leaving Savage Cove early.

"When are you going?"

"As soon as possible. I told you I wanted to do a road trip, and asked if you wanted to come."

He could see she was still upset. As was he.

"Yes, I remember you telling me, but I can't come today, I have scheduled calls. Can you put it off and we can go later?" He stepped back when she walked past him out of the bathroom, and followed her to the front door.

"No, I can't put it off." She looked up at him. "I need to do this. You know, Nick, I have my own life and career. And I can't put things off because of your schedule."

He raised his eyebrows, a little shocked by her tone. Everything seemed so unbelievably strained between them now.

"Uh, yes, I understand that. I was simply asking if you could reschedule it. I'd like to come with you."

She was quiet and focused on zipping up the bag.

"Look, I'm sorry for getting so angry last night." He reached for her, and she stepped back. His heart sank.

"I know, I didn't like it either." She lifted her hands, palms facing him. "But I guess there's more going on here than we thought. This has been . . . so quick." She looked up at him.

Her eyes were sad and almost lifeless. He wanted to pull her into his arms, take the sadness away.

"Just let me go. I'm taking a drive up to that place we talked about." She rubbed her forehead with her fingers. "The circle."

"You mean the Cascade Loop? You're going up into the mountains?"

She nodded, then picked the bags off the floor and walked out to her car.

"Yes, I'm going up there." She put her gear in the cargo space and closed the hatch.

He followed her back to the house again. "I don't want you to go," Nick said. It was blunt and to the point.

She turned on him. Her eyebrows shot up, and he sighed. He knew she was about to do battle.

"Excuse me? You're telling me not to go. What is your problem?"

He was taken aback by her tone, and protested. "It's raining." And he lifted his hand to indicate the rain that had started to come down harder.

"Yeah, okay, so. It's just rain," she retorted and went into the cottage, got her keys, turned off the lights, and locked the door.

"Lizzie, please. In the mountains, it could be worse. You don't know what it can be like on the roads. There could be icy conditions. The forecast isn't great, and it can be treacherous." He hoped she would understand his concern and not go.

She got in her car, shut the door, and rolled down the driver's window. "I'm a big girl, I can take care of myself. Thanks for the warning, and I'll be careful."

She was determined, that was for sure. "When will you be back?" he asked.

"I haven't decided yet. I don't know if I'm going to come back tonight, or if I'm going to spend it somewhere—maybe even a couple of nights."

Nick frowned. "Please text me and let me know. Why don't you come back to my house after, okay? We need to talk."

She pinned him with a glare. "Yes, we do need to talk."

She started the car, and he took a step away.

Nick had a bad feeling about her leaving, and he didn't want her to go. But he also couldn't make her stay. He gave it one final try. "Lizzie, please wait. We can plan a trip for a few days and go together. Is there somewhere else you've wanted to see that's closer for today?"

"I'm going. I need some time to think. And, yes, when I get back I'll come to your place." He saw the way she was gripping the steering wheel. This stubborn streak was new.

"Okay, good. We do need to talk more, but I don't want you to leave like this." How could history be repeating itself? This was so much like the last time he'd said goodbye to Marissa. He felt sick to his stomach.

"I'll text you when I decide to come home."

He walked forward, placed his hands on the car door, and leaned down to the window. "Be careful."

She looked at him and her expression softened. She let go of the wheel and laid her hand over his. He sighed, feeling a little more settled when she did that.

"I will."

He leaned in and kissed her. She kissed him back, and they lingered, lips touching softly.

"Okay, I'll leave now so you can get out. But text me." He wagged his finger at her and tried to smile. Tried to ease the worry building inside him, and hoped her anger was fading. He hated angry goodbyes.

She nodded, and then rolled up the window.

Nick returned to his car, backed out and drove away, watching in his rear-view mirror. She didn't leave right after him, and he wondered if maybe she'd decided not to go, after all. He took his foot off the gas and coasted, waiting to see what she was going to do.

At the corner where he had to turn toward his house, he made the turn, and could no longer could see her through his rear window.

Nick had a sinking sensation in the pit of his stomach, and he hoped it wasn't a premonition of something to come.

I sat in the vehicle for a few minutes before I could compose myself enough to drive away. I'd originally hoped Nick would come with me when I made the trip, but after what had happened, I thought it was best that maybe he didn't. I needed to get away to think.

I wondered, though, if my determination to leave was thumbing my nose to . . . whoever . . . the world, the rain, I didn't know. What I did know was, I hated that we'd fought last night. It upset me tremendously, and something inside me shifted. Maybe a couple of days away doing research and driving around would be good for me.

I wasn't that enthusiastic about driving in the rain, but it was now or never. The more time that passed, the less opportunity there would be for me to go into the mountains.

I was trying to decide between a couple of places to visit: heading up into the North Cascades, or down to Mount St Helens. That fascinated me, especially after Nick told me about the volcanoes that day on the beach. It would've been nice to visit Johnston Ridge Observatory. But if it was raining like this all the way there, it would be poor visibility.

When I set the navigation for either of the locations I was considering, I felt discouraged to see it was at least a three- or four-hour trip each way.

"Damn, I don't want to drive that far," I whined.

Maybe I should just go back in the house and say, screw it, I'm not going anywhere, and just hole up and think things through.

Maybe Nick was right. Driving the Cascade Loop right now wasn't the best idea. And if we were able to patch things up, it would be a fantastic trip to do together.

But where could I go, if I didn't take the drive I'd made such a fuss about? I was too embarrassed to not do something now.

Suddenly, I felt both deflated and like a flake. I caused all that drama when Nick showed up because I was still angry. He was only concerned, and wanted to make amends. But I wouldn't have it. So, was I taking this trip out of spite or because I really wanted to go?

I knew what the answer was, but it was hard to admit it.

I would just take a drive. Cruise along the waterfront, maybe stop somewhere to eat, and then come back.

I wouldn't text Nick just yet—in case I changed my mind—but deep down, I felt better about this plan, rather than driving around aimlessly in poor conditions. My gut told me we needed this time apart, and I hoped it would give me some clarity. I had a big decision to make, and that decision wasn't going to be easy. No matter which choice I made, I'd be letting someone down, or hurting another.

Chapter Thirty-nine

A couple of hours into my drive, I texted Nick and told him I'd come by soon. I'd just been killing time, with no actual destination, and the weather was cruddy. It made little sense to drive aimlessly.

He replied immediately.

I'm relieved. See you then.

I took another road that I thought was a short cut. Of course, it wasn't, and there had been a crash that held up traffic for a while. Sitting here wasn't so bad, though. I could do a bit of work in the car, which was a bonus.

Finally, we were moving, and I felt better about going to Nick's. I grabbed my phone to text him about being late, but it was dead.

"For crying out loud!" I rummaged through my bags for a charger cord. I normally kept one in the car, but I had taken it out after the end broke off the one in the cottage, and in my emotional state I forgot to bring it. I felt under the seat, hoping one was stashed on the floor, but nothing. "Just great. He's going to be worried now. Exactly what we don't need, after everything that has happened."

His reaction last night was a new side to him. Realistically, there must be lots of things that we needed to learn about each other, over time, and I was hoping last night's anger wasn't the norm.

I finally reached his place, and let out a sigh of relief. It was a bad day to be out driving around. My stupid stubbornness could be a pain sometimes.

I found him sitting at the kitchen island. One look, and I knew we were in for another fight. What the hell!

"I was worried," he said bluntly.

"You shouldn't have been. I was fine." I leaned on the counter beside him.

"Yeah, but that was almost two hours ago."

I drew in my lower lip. His eyes reflected how deeply upset he was. I put myself in his shoes. I'd probably be worried and upset too. But two fights in twenty-four hours? That wasn't a good sign.

"There was an accident, and the traffic was at a standstill. There was nothing I could do."

"How about call and let me know you're okay?" He sat back on the stool and crossed his arms.

"My phone was dead, and I forgot to bring a charger. Don't you believe me?"

He looked at me and said nothing.

"You think I did this on purpose? I didn't." This was stupid. I didn't want to argue again.

"It's not that I don't believe you, it's just how things have played out in the last twenty-four hours. Like suddenly every-thing has changed," he countered.

The argument fell into stupidity by this point. I was in tears.

"Everything is falling apart!" I grabbed my bag, feeling the only place I could be right now was in my cottage.

"Lizzie, stop." He caught my arm.

I swiped tears from my eyes and tried to stop crying. I hated that I was in a mess in front of him like this. And I had to wonder where it was all coming from.

"Nick, I think I need another night." My emotions embarrassed me.

"Stay here, with me?" he asked, and pulled me into his arms.

I drew in a shaky breath, inhaling the scent of him. My arms crept around his waist, and we stood like that for what seemed like forever.

"Nick, we—I—have decisions to make. Big ones. I think it might be best if I do it at my place." I stepped out of his arms. "Please understand. Our future was never a sure thing. My stay here was temporary, as you know." The words were so hard to say, but they were honest.

My promise to Rob was never far from my mind when I thought of future plans. He was the reason I was on this adventure to begin with. There was so much I had to weigh up.

"I'll be here. Text me when you get home."

I looked up at him and nodded. "But, Nick, to give us both time to think, if we don't talk or text, it might make it easier all round."

Leaving like that was one of the hardest things I've ever done, but I knew I must. It would be so easy to stay with Nick, but I worried that what I needed to think about would slide away if I was with him. I had to decide, one way or the other.

Do I stay?

Do I go?

What about my promise?

On the road back home, I had to concentrate. The rain had

grown heavier, and the wipers barely kept the windshield clear. I finally pulled into my driveway and let go of the steering wheel. I'd gripped it so tightly my fingers cramped. I stretched them out to relax, and sat for a minute, the rain drumming on the car.

Why was I so upset?

It wasn't hard to come up with the answer. The other day, I'd recognized I was falling in love with him. But these fights made me realize I was already very much in love with him.

I cried. "Oh, for God's sake." I grabbed a napkin and wiped my eyes and nose. "This is ridiculous."

Had we broken up? Were we ever really a couple who had a future? I rested my hands on the top of the steering wheel and lay my forehead on them.

But did it matter if I loved him? Something had shifted in our dynamic, and I couldn't put my finger on it. I huffed, and wiped the tears from my eyes. The fights made my heart hurt, and I hated that we were having this confrontation. Why had we started fighting all of a sudden?

Deep in my heart, I knew why. We were both feeling the pressure of the unanswered question.

Would I stay or leave?

The next couple of days passed painfully slowly, and I'd gone through a few boxes of tissues from all my crying. I'd wake up, remember, and cry. Or be working, he'd cross my mind, and I'd cry.

I was a mess and hated it.

This all started because I tried to hide the phone, which led back to those damn texts. It was all my fault.

My window of being truthful had firmly closed, and I doubted he'd forgive me if I told him now.

I came to one conclusion. I had to leave Savage Cove. There was no point in staying. I had done most of my research and writing. Nick was the reason I had even considered staying longer.

I was going to stick with my departure plans, continue with my journey, and fulfill my promise to Rob. Although, I must admit, I felt differently about it now.

Oh, Rob, I'm sorry.

I couldn't blame Nick for almost stopping me from doing what I'm promised my twin. He'd helped me through my lingering grief, even if neither of us realized it. I could only hope that I'd also helped him.

I sighed and flopped on to the couch, gazing out the dark window. I would miss the view from my cottage and his house. I would miss Savage Cove, and the people I'd met.

I'd miss Nick.

I looked up at the ceiling. Damn it all to hell. I couldn't stop the tears, this time.

Nick was thunderous as he walked around his house. How could everything have gone off the rails so fast? If only he'd handled it differently. But it was learned behavior, he supposed. It was the way he'd dealt with it before, and he didn't realize how naturally suspicious he'd become.

He took Houdini out for a walk on the beach, even though the rain still poured down. Both of them were soaked when they got back.

The last couple of days without her here were awful. If only Lizzie had understood that his anger when she returned to his house was because he worried about her. It was like a throwback to Ari disappearing, and the thought of going through that again was devastating. She'd left in such a rush, he'd been stunned. He believed her when she said her phone was dead and there'd been no way she could text to say she was okay, but he'd said all the wrong things in the moment. Watching her leave again, and letting her have space, was the hardest thing he'd ever done.

He stayed out of the house in the rain, because he didn't want to feel its emptiness. Which was a complete reversal from how he used to be.

He'd welcomed its quietness then. It was his haven, his place of escape. But Lizzie had filled the house, had given it life again.

It had been a home when she'd been here. But now that she'd gone, it was empty again. He crawled into bed, after drying off Houdini and himself, and lay there staring at the ceiling. He knew he had handled the whole thing poorly, and he was at a crossroads about what to do.

He'd been called away on business again, which was terrible timing. He wanted to reach out to her, but he could still hear her voice, thick with tears, when she left, telling him to leave her alone.

He had respected her wishes, but he hoped she would come around. These two days had been the worst time in his life—right up there with the dark days after Marissa's death. He never expected another woman to come into his life, let alone leave it.

Marissa was gone.

He cared deeply for Lizzie, and now she was gone.

His mother was gone.

Everyone he cared for was gone. Except for his father.

Now that he'd lost Lizzie, he knew for certain he was falling in love with her. The realization was a gut punch, and he knew what he had to do.

Chapter Forty

I got up the nerve to drive over to tell Nick I had decided to leave Savage Cove. He at least deserved that. My stomach was in knots, and my heart raced, the entire way over. I didn't know how to break it to him, and psyched myself up on the drive.

When I was almost there, I couldn't hold back the tears. I'd been such a complete wreck. I hated the crying, the angst, the upset, and the broken heart. This is how I'd felt when Rob died, and I simply couldn't do it again.

I had to pull over on the side of the road to collect myself. I felt absolutely distraught. This decision hadn't been easy, but it was the right one. So why did it feel so unbelievably wrong?

Finally, after about fifteen minutes, I was composed enough, and drew in a ragged breath. I was still resisting the urge to run.

Just run away and not see Nick. Not tell him I'm leaving. Just go.

I couldn't do that to him. It wasn't fair. I couldn't do it to me, either.

The gates were closed, and I punched in the code. They

swung open, and I drove up to the house. Again, I sat for a minute or two in the car and watched the door, giving myself a pep talk. He didn't come out, which was unusual, because he normally greeted me.

I walked up to the door, then rang the bell. No barks from Houdini, and no answer. The house was dark and empty. I wondered if they were at Walter's house. I hadn't been there but knew it was through the trees. I turned around and found a path through the trees. I'd never been over to the boathouse, and the closer I got, the quicker my breathing became. Facing Nick and Walter wasn't going to be easy.

Walter was up on a ladder, doing something to the eaves trough. The dogs started barking and ran to the fence. Both of them put their paws on the top railing, happy to see me. I gave them hugs and pats.

Walter turned and saw me. His face lit up. "Hi, Lizzie, what are you doing here?"

"Well, I came to see Nick." I felt like I was talking with a mouth full of marbles. My throat went dry.

Walter backed down on the ladder and came over to the fence. "Nick is away. Didn't he tell you?" I saw the worry in Walter's eyes.

I shook my head. "No, he didn't." Had I missed the opportunity to talk to him, to say goodbye? It made me feel sick.

"Well, that sounds odd to me. But he shouldn't be gone long."

I realized how wide the rift between us had grown.

"Don't just stand there," Walter said. "Come on in here. I can make a cup of tea or coffee, or whatever you want." He pushed open the gate, and herded the dogs away from the opening so I could walk in.

"Water will be fine." I followed him.

"Coming right up." He headed to the boathouse, and then turned to look at me. "You've never been here, have you? Come on in, and see my pride and joy."

Walter was such an amazing man. He was always so happy and friendly, right from the first day I met him on the beach, weeks ago. He didn't ask why Nick hadn't told me he was going away. Did he even know that we'd argued? That we'd broken up?

Broken up.

God, that's awful. I reminded myself I'd been okay with the idea of a summer fling. Was that what we had? A fling? I shook my head, and fisted my hands to keep them from shaking. No. It had been more than that.

So much more.

"See, this is called the boathouse, but it never really housed any boats. My grandpop called it a boathouse, all those years ago, and maybe he kept boats in it, but I don't remember. Let me tell you! The crap in here I had to clean out. Ridiculous. All boating stuff too. Pretty sure some of it was antique."

"What did you do with it all?" I asked, grateful to have something else to think about.

"Ah, most of it I threw out, but I kept some things." He looked around, a wistful gleam in his eye, and I could see how much this building meant to him.

It didn't look like a boathouse at all. It was a lovely little cottage. Tidy, neat, colorful, cozy. There was no inkling it had ever been the mess Walter said.

"I would've liked to see the items you kept."

"Some are on the wall back there, in the hall. Those lanterns, on the shelf there by the door, and the glass buoys are old as dirt. Nick has some in his house, and I donated loads to the museum. Actually, I had them come by to see if anything had value."

"That was a good idea. I enjoy antiquing but don't get to do it much." The history of this building reminded me of the café. "So much history."

Walter nodded. "Yes, there is. I spent the years after Doris died cleaning it out, renovating, and finally was able to move in about seven years ago. Before Nick met . . ." He paused and looked at me.

"I know about Marissa." I gently touched what looked like old wooden fishing floats.

His eyebrows shot up. "You do? Well then, that's interesting."

"Why would that be interesting?" I asked him, curious now.

He lifted his hand and waved it. "Nick doesn't talk about her much. It was kind of a bad time for him. He rarely brings her up. It just surprises me he did. He must be very comfortable with you to mention that part of his life. Sit." He pointed to a chair at the table, and got me a glass of water. "What brings you to my humble home?"

I took a shaky breath, then a drink of water. "I came to say goodbye."

This time, his mouth dropped open. His eyes nearly bugged out of his head when his face contorted in bewilderment. I couldn't contain a wry laugh, he looked so funny.

"You're what? Why? What did I miss?" He dropped into a chair at the table.

He kept staring at me, completely dumbfounded. Evidently, Nick hadn't told him we'd been arguing and I'd gone back to the cottage.

I nodded. "Yeah, I'm leaving. Things kind of went south with us over the last few days, so I decided I'm going to leave, as planned."

I took a big gulp of the water and then finished the glass. My mouth was as parched as a desert no amount of water would help. Walter took the glass, filled it up, then came back, put it on the table, and sat down again.

"What in hell happened?" He slapped the table, making me jump. "Nick has been a different man since you've been around. I swear. I thought things were going good with you two?"

I nodded, and took another drink. "Well, they were, and then the other night—actually, it was the night you guys had dinner with us—we had an awful row."

"I'm sorry to hear that." He shook his head and sat back in the chair. "What did you fight about?" Then he put his hand up, palm facing me. "Nope, no, I don't need to know. That's between you two. But I want you to seriously think twice about leaving. Like I said a minute ago, he has changed with you. If you know about Marissa, you need to be aware of a couple of things. One, he doesn't talk about her to anyone. Second, you know she drowned?" I nodded, and he continued, "That was a horrible day."

"I can't even imagine. I had an idea, though, after I stumbled across some information. I wasn't entirely sure it was connected to Nick, but after a while, I learned it was. I wasn't sure at first, because of their different last names."

Walter was nodding. "Yup. She wouldn't take his name, kept her own name, and Nick didn't care. But I thought that was a bad way to start a life together."

I smiled. Walter was so old-fashioned.

"What happened?" I wanted to hear the story from Walter's perspective.

"Well, she died, as you know. Drowned. Some thought it was suicide, but others thought Nick had, well, I don't even like to say it, but they suspected Nick. You know the significant other is usually the prime suspect."

My heart tightened for Nick. "I was wondering about that,

because the article I read said that there was insufficient evidence. I had a moment when I wondered if he might have had some involvement in it." I realized I shouldn't have said that. I knew now there was no truth in it, but in the beginning, there was that question.

The look Walter gave me was intense. "He would never have hurt Marissa. If you don't know by now that Nick is not a violent man, then you don't know him at all. And maybe you *should* just go. He needs no more fickle women to abandon him in the night."

Walter's bluntness hurt me. But it also relieved me that he was so certain—even though he was Nick's father and would never assume the worst about his own child.

"But you have to understand, I *need* to hear this, all of it, from Nick. I appreciate you opening up to me, but he needs to tell me himself. And, no, I don't think Nick is the kind of man who would do that. But was she the type to commit suicide?"

He shrugged his shoulders. "Who really knows what's going on inside a person's head? She became very unhappy and angry. Nick tried hard. He loved her, in the beginning."

He looked at me, and I smiled. "It's okay, we all had lives before now. I don't think he would have married her without loving her to some degree."

Walter pointed at me. "Yes, that's it. To some degree. I think she bedazzled him when they met. I don't believe she was the love of his life by any stretch of the imagination. Not when he really got to know her. But he was a good husband, and he cared for her. What he did for her to try to keep her happy . . ." Walter shook his head. "I would have preferred he not have married her. But he was a grown man, able to make his own decisions. And mistakes."

I felt sad for Nick, hearing that he had worked so hard for something that was clearly doomed from the beginning.

"When will he be back?" I asked, and finished off my glass of water.

"I don't know exactly, but I think sometime tonight. Why don't you text him?" I grimaced, and he laughed. "Are you afraid?"

"What? Hmm, kind of, I guess. We had two fights within twenty-four hours. I told him I needed time to think, and asked him not to get in touch with me until I got back to him. I guess he's taking that literally." I dropped my shoulders.

"Okay, now, don't go getting all maudlin. Here's my suggestion, you can take it or leave it—it's up to you." Walter leaned forward and looked me in the eye. "Don't go without seeing him. See if you can patch things up." He covered my hands with his. "Please." The earnest expression on his face made it difficult for me not to do as he asked.

"I suppose. But I'm not optimistic."

Walter sat back and tipped the chair on to its two rear legs, a big smile on his face, nodding. "That's my girl. You stay, and then you guys have your talk."

I bit my lower lip. I could feel the nerves fluttering in my belly. "O-okay, I will."

Decision made. I did owe it to both of us to try to clear up what had happened. Whether the outcome was good or bad.

He smiled, and in that grin I saw a glimmer of affection.

I let out a long and ragged sigh, feeling as if the dark cloud hanging over me had moved along a little bit.

Chapter Forty-one

I don't think I'd ever felt so emotionally exhausted as I did just then. With so many thoughts roaring around inside my head, I needed to talk it over with someone I could trust.

I texted Claire, to ask her if she'd meet me at the café. Now that I knew about her and Walter, I felt I could be open with her and maybe ask a few more of the burning questions about Marissa and Nick that I couldn't get out of my mind.

My phone pinged, and Claire texted back that she could meet me in half an hour.

I arrived at the café before her, and grabbed the corner table, out of the way, so we could talk without being interrupted. For once, the place wasn't packed.

A couple of minutes later, she came in the door with a smile on her face and walked right over to me. I stood up, and she gave me a big hug, which made me feel warm inside. Yes, there was something special about Claire, and I was beginning to look at her as a wise woman. A friend who always knew the right thing to say.

"It's so good to see you, my dear."

Claire sat down, and I did as well.

"It seems like forever since our dinner."

She nodded, and put her purse on the window ledge. "It certainly does, though it's only been a few days. Gosh, I'm losing track of the time."

"You and me both."

Amanda came over and took our order. I glanced up, and caught Wendy giving us an evil glare from behind the counter.

I was shocked and looked at her, unable to hide my confusion. She looked abruptly away. What was wrong with that woman?

"What's up?" Claire asked, and turned to see. "Hmm. What happened?"

"Well, nothing, I don't think. Wendy was giving us the evil eye."

Claire laughed. "The evil eye. I don't recall the last time I've heard anyone say that. If it was evil, it was coming from an evil person." She said that with such determination that I swung my head to look at her, surprised.

"Claire, that's the first time I've heard you say anything remotely negative about somebody else."

"I don't often, you're right. But," she sighed and shook her head, "there is something not right there."

"Wow, that's caught me off guard."

I watched Wendy, trying to be inconspicuous. She walked past the coffee maker and my gaze fell on Marissa's photo. Damn, the more I learned about that woman, the madder she made me, and I had to unclench my teeth. I narrowed my eyes and stared at that photo. I wanted some kind of message to come from it, even if it now filled me with anger rather than curiosity. But, of course, I felt nothing. Photos only held moments captured in time, rarely giving away any secrets.

"Now it's my turn to ask what's going on with you. Why that look?"

Amanda came up with our order. She placed a tea before Claire, and a lovely, creamy coffee drink with whip cream, and a ham and Swiss on sourdough with coleslaw, in front of me. Claire had an egg salad on brown.

"Thanks, Amanda." I put the napkin on my lap.

"Yes, thank you, Amanda dear." Claire smiled up at her.

"You were saying? Sorry, I forgot," I asked Claire.

"The look on your face. I'm curious what that was all about?"

"Well," I drew in an enormous sigh. I wasn't sure exactly where to start. "This is long and convoluted, I think. Remember, we talked about the text message that I got?"

She nodded and held the string of her tea bag, dunking it in and out of the steaming water.

"I think—no, I know—it came from Nick. He sent her a second one, and it's left me so confused."

Claire paused, her hand hovering over her cup, and tea dripped from the tea bag. She lifted her eyes and met mine. I widened my eyes, nodding. Saying it out loud somehow gave me the confidence to go on.

"Tell me about Marissa's death?" I just dropped the question. I needed more. "I know you know about it. Nick and Walter have both told me a little, but I can't get my head around what happened, *how* it happened. After I got that text, I did a bit of digging and discovered some things, but I need to know more. What was her frame of mind when she disappeared? Would she really have committed suicide? No one will tell me. I'm sure Nick didn't have anything to do with whatever happened to her." The words rolled out of me, and I closed my eyes for a moment, holding my breath.

"Lizzie, dear, I don't know how much more I can say. My

relationship with Walter is important to me, and I felt the need to protect him and Nick. That's why I hadn't felt able to say more to you, earlier. Also, like I said before, it's not my story to tell. But I will say this." She lifted her teacup and took a sip slowly.

I was hanging on the edge of my seat!

Putting the cup down, she made eye contact with me and continued. "I don't think she drowned."

I gasped. "Oh my God, are you saying, did Nick—"

Claire raised her hand to stop me. "I also don't think she committed suicide."

I opened my mouth.

"Hold on, I'm not done. I'm confident Nick had nothing do with it—"

"What then? What do you think happened to Marissa?" I interrupted her.

She held her hand up again.

"Please, let me finish, or I might not be able to get it all out."

"I'm sorry. Please, carry on." I drummed my fingers on the table.

"I think she ran out on Nick." Claire just said it, like it was a normal thing to say.

I was stunned, not expecting that.

At.

All.

I fell back in my seat.

"*What!*" I practically shouted the words, and people turned to look at us.

"Shush, quiet. You don't want her to hear."

I shook my head, feeling frustrated. "Who? I don't want who to hear?"

Claire leaned forward and lowered her voice. "Wendy. I have a feeling she might know something about it."

"You can't be serious?" This was getting weirder and weirder. What the heck really happened?

"Quite serious. Those two were tighter than bark on a tree."

I made another noise of incredulity, and more people looked at us. Normally I wouldn't care, but this conversation was wild.

"That's just my take on it," Claire said. "I know nothing certain, it's just a feeling."

"So there's no evidence to support it?" I asked her.

Claire shook her head. "No, no physical evidence that I'm aware of. I overheard some chatter that didn't really make sense to me, at the time. If it was a set-up, they did a pretty good job of making it appear as if she'd drowned, or committed suicide."

I glanced at the photo of Marissa on the wall.

What did you do?

My feelings for Nick had deepened, and that was why I'd been so upset about our fight. But had he ever really fallen out of love with Marissa, and would he ever have room for me in his heart?

"Well then. This is just a drama, not a tragedy," I said, and felt deflated. Just when I thought some new, helpful information had been offered. Had Nick thought of it as a possibility?

"You know what?" I asked Claire, and gave the table a light swat with my fingertips.

"Of course, I don't, dear. What?" She took a bite from her sandwich, ate delicately, and then dabbed the corner of her mouth.

She was such a lady, but I had a feeling there was a wild side to her.

"I think I'm just gonna forget about it all now." I picked up my little bowl of coleslaw and dug around in it with a fork, then scooped some up. I stuck it in my mouth and chewed, thinking about what she had just said, and also trying to tell myself to let it go.

"That's probably the best thing to do. It's years ago. What does it matter now? People have moved on," Claire said absently, looking out the window and munching on her sandwich.

We fell into silence for a few minutes, eating. Her words went round in my head. Had everyone moved on?

The phone in my bag pinged. I put my sandwich down, to dig the phone out of my purse. It wasn't my new iPhone, it was the old one. I rocked slightly, and put the phone on the table.

Claire glanced at it. "Is that the phone the texts came in on?"

I nodded, my mouth suddenly parched and my stomach fluttering. I was afraid to look at it.

"Aren't you going to read it?" She leaned forward, just as intrigued as I was.

I chewed on my thumbnail and looked at the phone, trying to decide. "I don't know if I should."

"Of course, you should. You read the others, so why not this one?" Claire pointed out.

I said nothing for a beat. I stared at the phone, and said, "Because I might not like what it's going to say."

"Wouldn't it be better to know than not? You'll find out exactly where you stand." Claire's kind voice helped.

I nodded, gritted my teeth, and opened the message.

I read it.

Then read it again.

"What is it?" Claire asked.

I pushed the phone over to her so she could see.

Marissa, I need to tell you that I have fallen in love. I want to make a new life with Lizzie. She has brought light and joy into the cold darkness you left behind, and helped me understand

that life goes on. Maybe you've found the peace you were
searching for. This will be the last message I send.

Tears sprang into my eyes. My heart was beating almost out
of my chest, and I couldn't sit still. I had to speak to Nick. I
desperately wanted to reply—I had his number now, after all—
but these messages came from a withheld phone number. So if
I replied to Nick, he would know I'd seen them all, and this
wasn't the right way to find out.

"Oh, Claire, I'm in such a predicament. I don't know how
to explain what I know about the texts. I should have told him
a long time ago. Now what is he going to think? He got angry
at me the other day when I tried to hide this phone from him
and he thought I was being secretive." I let out a breath of
frustration. "I'm such an idiot. Now he'll never be able to
trust me."

Claire reached across the table and covered my hand with
hers. It was a motherly touch, and I looked at her through the
tears. I needed her right now, and my heart nearly burst with
emotion.

"Slow down and take a breath, you're getting ahead of yourself, my dear. If Nick means as much to you as you do to him,
then you owe it to yourself to try. Be brave. If he gets mad, you
deal with it. But if you don't try, you'll never know."

I thought about it, and wiped my eyes. My excitement grew.
"Thank you. You're right. Either way, I have to deal with it,
whether the outcome is good or bad." I pushed the remainder
of my food away. My mind was racing. "I have to go. Yes, I'll go
home and wait for Nick. I'm too wired to sit here in the café. I
hope you don't mind."

Claire patted my hand. "Of course I don't."

I gathered my belongings, and leaned down to give Claire a

kiss on the cheek. There was so much I would miss about Savage Cove, if I left.

Claire was right. She had helped me peel away the layers I'd piled on, enabling me to see how I was really feeling underneath. Nick was respecting my request for no contact. It was up to me to make amends. I had to text Nick.

Chapter Forty-two

The rain was really coming down outside, and I found myself extremely restless.

Nick might be home now. I'd finally gotten the courage to send a text asking him to reply, but I'd heard nothing. Was he still angry with me? Had I ruined everything?

I couldn't sleep. Tonight the rain and the wind had been joined by the occasional rumble of thunder and flashes of lightning, which, strangely enough, I had learned was not that common for this area. I sat in bed, with my book on my lap, but my attention was on the two phones.

All this upheaval in my life, thanks to technology, which started because of my own clumsiness.

I dozed, on and off, for the next couple of hours, until the wind picked up and the rain drummed against the cottage. I got out of bed and started pacing, thinking about Nick. I had to see him. I had the overpowering, driving need to see him *now*. I didn't know if he was home or not, but I decided I wanted . . . no, needed . . . to walk on the beach.

It was just after 11.30 p.m. and still raining. The wind moaned around the cottage. I dressed up in rain gear, slapped on Rob's hat, not bothering with an umbrella, and ran down the path.

Out on the beach, I was in the full fury of nature. The waves were loud, crashing on the shore. The wild weather matched my mood.

I trudged along, leaning into the wind that was whipping off the water. I stayed at the top part of the beach, away from the ferocious shoreline. In the distance, I saw a bobbing light. What idiot was out on a night like this? I wished I'd brought a flashlight with me. But I had left the back porch light on as a beacon.

I peered through the rain at the light and realized it must be a flashlight. My heart skipped a beat and raced into overdrive. I was the idiot—out here in the middle of a storm, in the middle of the night.

My heart pounded as the light got brighter. Alarm slithered along my spine, and suddenly I felt very foolish for coming out in this weather.

I turned around, catching hold of the hat when the wind tried to tear it off me. I wanted to get back to the cottage before whoever was on the beach saw me. I started to jog, then had to slow down to keep my footing on the rocks.

I heard a rushing sound and let out a gasp of fright. Something was running after me. I picked up my pace, the porch light not far off now. I ran for my life.

Something whooshed past me in the dark. I couldn't see it. Just as panic was setting in, a dog barked . . .

And Houdini was running around me.

I nearly cried with relief when he pushed up against my knees, wanting to be petted. Showing me all the attention that

I adored getting from him. He was soaked, and I wondered why on earth Nick would bring him out on a night like tonight.

But then who was I to question his reasons? Because I was doing the same.

Then Nick materialized out of the darkness in front of me. Life-size.

I launched myself at him, sobbing. "Nick! I thought I'd lost you!"

He wrapped his arms around me, crooning into my ear. "It's okay, I've got you now. I'll never let you go."

"I was so frightened." The rain swept away my tears.

I didn't care that we were out on a beach during a tempest. He had come to find me. I was in his arms and clinging to his neck. He held me tight. We seemed to stand that way for an eternity.

I finally moved so I could look at him, and cupped his cheeks with both hands. We were drenched and could barely see each other in the darkness. His hand slid up behind my head and pressed me to him. He nuzzled my neck, then found my mouth, and we kissed. In the rain. Water streamed down our faces, over our skin, inside our raincoats.

But it was a glorious rain.

A cleansing rain.

A rain to wash away the past.

A promising rain.

Nick's hands pressed my head closer to him. I tightened my arms around his neck. We fused together like sand struck by lightning. I sobbed in the middle of the kiss.

He lifted his head. "Baby, it's okay. Lizzie, we're going to be fine."

"Oh, Nick, I'm so sorry. I have so much to tell you. But I want to say this to you first, before anything else. I love you.

I've fallen in love with you. I love you, I love you, I love you!" I shouted it to the skies, then placed my hands on his cheeks again. The flashlight he'd dropped on the sand rolled in the wind, catching us in a spotlight.

His smile split his face wide. "Lizzie, I'm sorry for what happened. We have something. Something special and, yes, we need to talk it all out so we have no shadows of the past. We're closer to your house than mine. But first . . .I love you too."

I wasn't sure if I'd heard him correctly, with the howling of the wind, the crashing of the waves, and our raincoats snapping like flags around us. I drew my hand across my eyes and looked up at his face.

"Lizzie, I love you. Your loyalty, patience and trust have helped me understand you are unique, different. But I'm worried, if we don't get inside we'll catch our death."

I was struck dumb, unable to manage any words other than, "Oh, Nick. My darling Nick."

He released me and took my hand. "Come on, let's get inside."

We ran the short distance back to my cottage, and faced each other on the porch. We stripped off the rain gear, tossing it into the outdoor shower, along with my hat, so it wouldn't blow away.

"Why the hell are you out on a night like this?" Nick asked, and kicked off his shoes.

"I could ask you the same thing?"

We laughed, and burst into the cottage. The door slammed shut behind us, just after Houdini squeaked through. He shook himself, flopped down on the rag rug in front of the fireplace, and rolled around, rubbing his nose into the carpet.

"I'm f-f-f-freezing." I wished my chin would stop chattering, and I had my arms wrapped tightly around myself.

"We should have a shower. To warm up." He took my hand and led me into the bathroom.

We shed our clothes, and he started running a hot shower.

Unlike the tub at his house, this one wouldn't hold the both of us, and the shower would be a tight squeeze for two. But it would do. We stepped into the steaming water, and I raised my face to the stream.

"Oh, this is so much better than the icy rain," I murmured, resting my chin on his chest.

We stood, pressed together, his arms around me and mine tucked between us, until my shivering stopped.

"The water couldn't be hot enough right now." I gave a little shudder.

"I'll have you warmed up in no time." He tipped my head up, with his fingers under my chin.

"Promise?" I smiled through the steaming shower water, and ran my hands over his chest to his shoulders.

"I do."

The hot water and steam swirled around us, creating a misty haven that cocooned us in our own little world. It was just us, here, now, our wet bodies sliding together.

The water was cooling.

"We'd best get out before we get chilled again." Nick reached to turn off the taps. The cold air rushed into the shower when he opened the shower door.

"Brrr."

"Here." Nick took a thick, soft towel, wrapped it around me, and rubbed my shoulders and arms. He slung another one around his hips, and concentrated on drying me off. The friction of the towel helped.

"It's m-m-much w-w-warmer in b-b-bed." I looked up at him, my teeth chattering again.

He smiled. "Yes, it is."

He toweled himself off, and I took a dry towel to wrap my hair.

Nick swept me up in his arms and carried me into my bedroom. After pulling back the sheets and duvet, he lay me down and joined me. We burrowed under the bedding.

In his arms, my back to his chest, I pulled the covers up to my chin until warmth finally spread through me.

I heard Houdini come in and drop on the floor where his doggy bed was. Soon he was snoring.

We started to talk. In the dark. Cocooned in the covers. In each other's arms.

Chapter Forty-three

We lay quietly in the darkened room, the rain still pounding on the roof.

I felt his mouth against my ear.

"We married about eighteen months before she died. I'd known her about a year before that. I've told you she was captivating and very aloof. It intrigued me, and I found myself drawn to her and her mystery." Nick pulled me tighter, and I rolled to face him, resting my head on his chest.

I stayed quiet. He was going to talk, finally.

"I guess you could say I pursued her. I probably should've taken that as a foretaste of how things would play out down the road." He paused. "She finally agreed to go out with me. My career was taking off, and she bedazzled me."

I kept my body as quiet as possible, barely breathing so I didn't disturb his momentum. I had a feeling some of what he was saying would be like a spear into my heart.

But I had to hear it.

He had to say it.

"So, we dated, and then the next thing I knew, I asked her to marry me. To my surprise, she agreed. Based on the chase she gave me, I thought she'd be more evasive. In hindsight now, I think it was my status and income that may have been the attraction.

"We married, and as you know, things deteriorated. She loved that damn café in town. And I thought perhaps if I bought it for her, she would find fulfillment there. It would give her purpose, something to do. And it did, for a while. She seemed content running the café, but it didn't last for long. She turned over its management to the staff, letting Wendy assume most of the control. She wanted the café but not the running of it, and eventually distanced herself from everyone except Wendy."

He took a deep breath, and I heard Houdini giving little yips and growls in his sleep.

"She became restless and sometimes disappeared for hours at a time, not telling anyone where she went. To this day, I still don't know where. I bought Houdini for her. I thought perhaps he could give her some love. And be her pal while I was away on business. But she barely acknowledged his existence, so he became my dog—and then, of course, he was loved by my dad."

I realize my body had tightened up and I was holding my breath. I slowly let it out, and forced my body to relax. I rested my arm over his stomach and stroked his side. I knew what he was telling me wasn't easy. I also knew he needed to get it off his chest.

"I'd asked her to come on business trips with me. I told you that before. She had no interest. I was at a loss for how to keep her happy. And it got more and more difficult, to the point where I knew it couldn't continue. I didn't know what it was going to take to fix or destroy what we had. I tried teaching her sailing. Showed her around Washington. She wasn't from here.

She turned the café into a reflection of her and her rather bohemian style." He glanced at me. "Claire gave her a hand with some of the decor—she's very creative, as you know."

It all started to fall into place. Claire hadn't openly told me the details, but I had a sense she'd done some metalwork when she touched the little trays holding the salt and pepper, the other day.

He shifted and pulled me closer. I snuggled in.

"Nothing seemed to suit her. Looking back now, I can see in the months leading up to her death, she had completely disengaged. She barely talked to me, we were never in the same room together. And I knew we were approaching the end. I had planned to ask her for a divorce. It would free her from the tie of being here, and I just couldn't cope with her drama any longer."

Nick paused. I could feel the tension in his body. I draped my arm over his waist, hugging him and hoping that my touch would help him to relax and continue to speak.

"I was going to tell her I wanted a divorce when I came home from the last business trip. But I never had the chance, because she died . . ." He fell silent.

I held my breath. It took me by complete surprise that he was going to ask her for a divorce.

"No one knew that's what I wanted. When she died, it seemed impossible to voice it. So, it became my deep secret. Only you know now." He held me tighter. "The guilt I felt at hiding that pretty much crippled me, and I've carried it these last years. Part of me always wondered if she knew what was coming, and it was too much for her to bear, so . . . she did what she did. I've never been able to shake the feeling I betrayed her somehow."

I wanted to reassure him, or say something to try to help, but he continued talking.

337

"When she disappeared, and they found the boat, it devastated me. I blamed myself for not being good enough, for not doing enough to keep her content and happy. Lord! That she felt the only way out was to go out on the sea, alone, and drown herself. I had a hard time accepting she committed suicide, but I'm sure she did. They didn't find any bags on the boat, and she'd left most of her stuff behind. They found the boat smashed on the rocks, but nothing of significance in it. It all came completely from left field." He closed his eyes and shook his head. "I felt she'd taken her life because of me, so the guilt I've carried is just enormous."

How could I ever take the pain away from him? It was so clear in his voice. But I couldn't. I could only be here for him. Let him know I wasn't Marissa.

"Nothing changed until I met you, and you showed me there is a way through the grief, the guilt. You found your way through the pain. When your heart, soul, and mind shatter into a million pieces, and you feel dead inside, how can you heal? Especially with this sense of responsibility, and the weight of that on your shoulders. How do you deal with it and try to move on?"

He stopped talking, and we lay there quietly in each other's arms, the soothing sound of the rain thrumming on the roof. The streams of water running down the window obscured the view beyond. We were cocooned in our own intimate little world, and I loved it.

I thought he had finished. I didn't want to interrupt his train of thought, but after a few minutes, when he was still silent, I drew in a soft breath.

It was my turn.

"Thank you." I rolled closer to him. "I know how hard it was to tell me. I do appreciate it." I glanced up at him, but couldn't see his face in the dark. Maybe that was for the best. "I need to tell you something. The raw honesty you shared was heart-wrenching for me. I can't imagine the guilt and grief you've carried, these past years. I'm so sorry and wish I could have done something more for you."

"But you have. You must see that. You are like a shining light that came into my life at a dark moment. I don't normally speak of Marissa. It was a very, very hard time. Especially when I was considered a suspect in her death."

I couldn't stop my body from stiffening. "How horrible. I can't even . . ."

He groaned. "Don't they always suspect the spouse first in a suspicious death? Plus, we'd been fighting. She would fight in public, in the café, in the store, on the street, so it looked like we were always at each other's throats. I would never fight back, and that made her even angrier."

"She must have been in real emotional distress," I mused.

"It was too horrifying. I felt it reflected upon my family, and on my dad. He didn't need that kind of conflict. I tried to deal with a lot of it on my own. I got a couple of good slaps from Marissa, and she would throw things."

"Oh, Nick, I'm just devastated for you. Did you ever call the police?"

"No, it never got that violent, but by the end, I had learned her trigger points and avoided them." He rubbed my shoulder. "Police would have been an even bigger embarrassment."

"I can't even imagine being in a relationship with somebody like that." I couldn't comprehend it.

"It definitely wasn't easy. I thought I was in love and, like I said, she had a mystique about her that was very enticing." He stroked my hair. "I know this must be hard for you to hear, but I think if we want to have any kind of future together, we have to know it all. Even if it hurts now."

"I agree. Which leads me to what I have to tell you." My heart pounded in my chest. I did not for the life of me know how I was going to broach the subject. "Can we turn on the light?" I wanted to see his face.

He flicked it on, and I blinked.

My eyes adjusted, and I smiled at him. "Hi."

He laughed. "Hi."

I hesitated and twisted the corner of the sheet in my fingers.

"Just do it. Just tell me," he said, reaching out to still my hand.

I nodded. "Okay, well, here goes. What you said to me, everything about Marissa and what happened to her, I kinda already knew, or at least suspected."

"What? You did? How?" He sat up and pushed a pillow behind his back. "Tell me."

His voice held an edge, and I was suddenly afraid to continue. But I had to, and plowed on.

"Yes. It was bizarre how it all started. You remember I lost my phone?"

He nodded.

"I went to the store but they didn't have what I needed, so I ordered one. In the meantime, I got a cheap refurbed phone, nothing special, just to have in case of emergency. The night I got the phone, a text came in."

"What?" His voice was soft, and he stared at me.

"Yeah. I can show it to you, because I still have the phone, but it was a message . . . for Marissa. From someone who said this would be the last message, because it was time to let her go." I was whispering now.

"I don't understand," he said.

I sat up and crossed my legs, pulling the sheet up to my chin, suddenly feeling quite vulnerable in front of him. This was going to be the do or die moment. His reaction would tell me how things would go from here.

"This message came in and, obviously, it wasn't for me. But it held such a deep rawness, I could almost feel the pain through the words. They haunted me all night, and for days after."

He was silent and focused on something behind me.

"Now I know it was the message you sent to her. But at the time I had no clue. Only that the pain I saw in those words moved me. I couldn't send a reply, as the number was withheld, but I had to find out more. Find out who Marissa was and who sent her the text. After I ordered the new phone, I found the café, your café, and had a drink in there. I saw all the photos, her photo, on the wall. I didn't know your connection to her until I dug up a newspaper article. I still didn't know for sure it was you, because of the different names."

I stopped talking. His face was unreadable and he was frowning.

"And you got the other messages too?" he asked quietly.

I nodded.

"And the other night, when you shoved the phone back in your purse, that's what it was?"

I nodded again.

"God, I thought you were cheating, keeping secrets. That's why I blew up, because the same thing happened with Marissa. I was terrified it was happening again."

I leaned forward and put my hands on his chest. "Oh, Nick, no, I would never do anything like that. Never!"

"When I came to your house and Houdini rushed in first, you quickly shut your laptop when I came up behind you. That was the first thing that concerned me."

"I was researching Marissa, and I didn't want you to know. Because, if you knew, it would lead to a whole bunch more questions, and I was so afraid that too much time had passed for me to tell you. That you'd be irate and think I was keeping secrets and, well, I felt I'd just shot myself in the foot by not telling you right off. I should've."

"I'm stunned," he said. "Absolutely stunned."

I felt like I was going to cry again and bit my lip. I had to stop all this crying!

Nick was still coming to terms with what I'd just told him. I stayed quiet and held my breath.

Then he took my hand. It shocked me to see that his face didn't express anger, or disgust. Instead, I saw love and tenderness.

"Lizzie, this is a lot to take in. But I'm not mad. A little embarrassed, perhaps. Sending the messages was a . . . a cleansing ritual, in a way. I first started sending them on the anniversary of her death. I'd kept so much to myself, I really had no other outlet, and I never expected anyone to read them."

He gave a low chuckle, and a lightness filled me. Maybe it was going to be all right.

"It's strange too. What are the odds that those messages, which represented an old relationship, would be received by a new love?"

I relaxed and blew out the breath I'd been holding. This time, I didn't care that I burst out crying and laughing, all at the same time.

He pulled me into his arms. "It's okay. We've told each other everything now. And you know what?"

I shook my head and sniffled. Answering him with a shaky voice. "What?"

"We found each other because of all that. And randomly, on a beach, of all things. I have done a lot of thinking about it, and I've never believed in destiny before. But how can all this be random? What are the odds of you losing a phone, getting one that is loaded with Ari's old number, and me sending a text the first day you have it, when you're newly arrived here? It's incredible, really. Doesn't that say something to you? Like we're two soulmates who have found each other and fallen in love."

His words rolled around in my brain. "Destiny," I whispered. "Oh, Nick, you have no idea how happy I am. I was so worried you would be angry, especially after our fight. I thought you'd kick me out, not want to see me again, and—"

Nick put his fingers over my lips to shush me. I curled my fingers around his wrist, and blinked away fresh tears.

"You could've done the same thing with me. I told you so little about Marissa. With all you learned, you could have said no to us. Right?"

We stayed in each other's arms for a few minutes until he sat me up. I held my breath, not sure what to expect now.

"Lizzie, would you consider staying longer, please? We need more time so we can get to know each other better. Would you do that?"

"Oh, Nick, yes. Yes! I will." I didn't even have to think about it.

He threw back his head and laughed, drawing me back into his embrace. "Good, we'll get all this settled tomorrow. And please come back and stay at my house."

"Of course I will! And just in time, too, I can't believe how fast the days have flown by since coming to Savage Cove. My lease is ending, and . . ." I trailed off, unable to voice the rioting thoughts about leaving Savage Cove, and Nick.

"Ah, yes. Because of your promise."

"Yes, the promise to my brother. You know, Nick, even if I stay with you, I do still have to find a way to honor that." I shook my head and raised my eyebrows, drawing in a breath. "How could I not?"

"Easy, easy now. Don't fret about it. I totally understand, and I'll never stand in your way."

"Thank you." It eased my mind to a degree, but not enough to fully be able to come to terms with my promise to Rob and the desire to be with Nick.

"You know, I could even come with you on some of the adventures, if they don't conflict with my work schedule."

"Really? You would? That would be fantastic! And maybe your dad and Claire might like to join us sometime." The nice thing was, I could write from anywhere.

"Perfect." He pulled me down, and flicked off the light.

We lay in each other's arms, listening to the drumming of the rain on the roof. Was finding love part of the adventure I'd set out on, based on a promise? I sighed. I was in the arms of the man I loved.

Nothing could change that, right?

Chapter Forty-four

"So how was your first day on the Cascade Loop trail?" Nick asked Lizzie as they snuggled on the leather sofa in front of the fireplace. He'd been lucky when he began looking for places to stay on this trip, and had found one that had availability for four adults and was also pet friendly. River Rock Springs had an opening for a night, and he jumped at it, booking it even before checking with Lizzie, Walter and Claire.

He knew Lizzie would be packed and ready at the drop of a hat, and he was thrilled his dad and Claire were free to come too. Now, the dogs were curled up on the floor, with their backs to each other, at the base of the stairs leading to the loft where he and Lizzie would sleep. Dad and Claire were busy organizing drinks in the cabin's kitchen.

His little family.

"Incredible. I didn't realize I had such a thing for waterfalls until I saw Wallace Falls. I mean, it's two hundred and forty-six meters high! I just can't believe how stunning everything is!" Her face was glowing, and her eyes reflected her excitement.

She dropped her head to look at her camera, and scrolled through the photographs she had taken today.

"It was wonderful of you to ask us to come along as well," Claire said as she brought in a bottle of wine, four glasses, and an appetizing cheese board. "It was very lucky you were able to get a cabin. This place is in demand." After putting the tray down on the knotty pine table, she walked over to the fireplace and touched the base of a metal fir tree statue.

"Is that one of yours?" Walter asked.

She shook her head and came to sit at the table beside him. "No, but it's a lovely piece."

Nick reached forward and filled the wine glasses, then stood to hand them around.

"Oh, look at this image." Lizzie jumped to her feet and showed the photo she was looking at.

"Hold on, I need my reading glasses," Walter said. He pulled out a pair from the chest pocket of his shirt and popped them on the end of his nose. "You're very good. That is an excellent photograph of the waterfall."

"It is, isn't it?" Nick watched Lizzie, who was very distracted as she scrolled through the photos. He realized he was proud of her. Even if her passion and career . . . and promise . . . took her away from him, nothing could take away what they'd shared.

"Do you know what your article will be about?" Claire asked her.

Lizzie sucked her bottom lip between her teeth. "Mmm, not sure yet."

Nick smiled. This was a special trip for Lizzie. She'd wanted to come here, but never made it. He didn't need reminding that the reason behind her not going on her trip, as originally planned, was because of their first fight. He wanted to do this for her, and try to make up for that rocky period. Give her something she both needed and wanted.

"I'd heard about this place. Lotsa history here." Walter took a drink of wine and made a grimace. "Did we get any beer?"

Everyone laughed, and Nick rose. "Yes, Dad, we did. You don't like the wine?"

He shook his head. "No, not really. It bites back."

He fetched his dad a beer, and grinned at Lizzie, who sipped her wine, giving him a smile over the rim of her glass.

"Oh! I keep forgetting to mention." Everyone looked at Claire, waiting for her to explain. "Lizzie, I hear you're staying!"

A smiled widened on Lizzie's mouth, and she glanced at Nick.

He nodded, and was surprised when his heart pounded a little faster.

"Yes, I am. Nick asked me to, so I'm going to stay a little longer. I still have things to figure out, but I'm so happy I'll be here for a while."

Claire gave a knowing smile. "I had a feeling you two were right together, weeks ago."

"What? How?"

"I saw you on the beach, back before we even started meeting up at the café. Nick was with you, but I didn't understand the connection until a bit later."

"On the beach." I thought back to when I'd seen someone other than Nick or Walter on the beach. "Oh, Bigfoot! It was you," I blurted.

"Bigfoot?" Claire looked mystified.

I laughed. "No, what I mean is, I thought I saw someone on the beach on the day you and I had breakfast," I said, turning to Nick. "But I tripped, and when I looked up, you had disappeared into the trees. I just laughed at myself for thinking I had a Bigfoot sighting."

"Well, my dear, I'm definitely not Bigfoot," Claire said, humor edging her voice.

"Damn straight, she's not." Walter winked and then nodded at Nick and Lizzie. "You two were dancing around it for too long. If you know, you know—and you both know," he said, with a finality that made everyone burst out laughing.

The dogs jumped up, barking at the hilarity.

Nick watched his people relaxing, chatting and enjoying the log cabin he had rented for them. He saw the flush of happiness on Lizzie's face. That, in itself, made this the best day ever. She was engrossed with her work. He definitely didn't begrudge her that. He knew he'd have her to himself all night long.

"This cabin is so beautiful," Lizzie commented as she moved around, taking photos. "I mean, just look at these pillars. They're the whole tree here, inside the room, holding up the roof. And that fireplace! I just can't take it all in. It would be a spectacular place for a wedding."

"I'd like to come here again sometime," Claire said as she watched Lizzie. "They've done a wonderful job with the décor. Rustic, yet comfortable and fresh."

"I think River Rock Springs has won a lot of awards," Nick said as he leaned back on the couch and crossed his ankle over his knee. His eyes followed Lizzie as she snapped away.

"Well, did you see the other cabins? Good God, bigger than my house, and yours!" Walter said.

"Even the original house, where the founders settled, remains standing and lived in," Nick commented.

"You are full of trivia today, Nick." Walter gave him a wink.

"I know how to do my research." He was happy, and grateful to be able to provide a worry-free getaway for the people who filled his life. He was truly starting to feel that the damn dark cloud he'd been laboring under the past three years was dissipating. His eyes followed Lizzie, knowing she had a big part to play in that.

"The view from here is stunning." Lizzie was leaning over the log railing, peering down from the loft where they would be sleeping. The stairs were easy for them, and he didn't want any potential night-time accidents with his father or Claire.

"Wave!" Lizzie called as she descended the stairs. Everyone turned around and hammed it up for her. "This might just go in the article, you know." Her laughter filled the cabin.

"I think we have to sign some kind of a disclaimer to allow you to use our image, correct?" Walter said, with a teasing tone in his voice.

Nick sighed and welcomed how relaxed he was. Tomorrow, they would head south, stop anywhere along the way they wanted to, and continue on down to Mount Rainier or Mount St Helens. Possibly both. He wanted to show Lizzie the volcano, and he hoped the observation area would be open and the weather clear. She'd mentioned going to Hoh Rain Forest, and he would do his best to fit it in.

"No one's in a hurry to get home, right?" he asked everyone.

A chorus of nopes was the reply.

After breakfast the next morning, the car was packed and they were on the road early. Lizzie and Claire in the back again, and Walter riding shotgun.

The chatter from the women in the back was non-stop, and every now and then he and his dad glanced at each other with a smile. Nick could tell his father was happy. It was what Nick had hoped for his father: the companionship and love he deserved. Nick's own heart was near to bursting. He thrummed his fingers on the steering wheel. Everything was perfect.

"We need to stop for gas," Nick announced a little while

later, and pulled off at the next gas station. "I could also use a coffee."

"My treat, and I'll pay for the gas too," Walter said.

He and Claire went into the convenience store.

"I'm going to run to the restroom and be right back." Lizzie gave Nick a kiss, and disappeared into the store as well.

He pumped the gas, waiting for everyone to return. Tall pines surrounded the gas station. There was something special about the mountains, no doubt about that.

A few minutes later, they all settled back in the car. Walter balanced a tray of coffees on his knees, which Claire promptly took from him with Nick's help.

"The last thing we need is you spilling coffee all over the place." She smiled at Walter, and gave him a loving pat on his shoulder.

"Sure, whatever. I have the box of donuts." He opened the lid and took an exaggerated sniff. "Smells great!"

"Off we go, then," Nick announced, and they were on the road again.

Nick reached back for the coffee that Claire held to him, and put it in the cup holder. "That's yours, Dad."

The next one was his, and he took a big gulp.

"Here you go." Walter handed Nick a donut, and passed the box to the women in the back.

"Thank you." Lizzie took the box and carefully selected one. "Well, these look all right, but not near as yummy as those at Sol."

Claire took a bite into a cruller and nodded. "They're pretty good. But no maple bacon." She smiled at Lizzie.

"Now that sounds like a great combination," Nick said. "Maybe one day I'll try one."

"You mean you haven't gone to the café?" Claire asked, surprise in her voice.

Nick shook his head. "Nope, and I don't plan to, either. There's no need. It seems to be running along fine, and the property manager keeps me up to speed on things through my lawyer."

"What a shame, it's a lovely spot, and you're not enjoying it," Claire mused, then continued. "But I do understand. I'm just surprised you kept Wendy on."

"Oh? Why?" Nick found that an odd thing to say, and glanced at Claire in the rear-view mirror.

She drew in a breath. Walter turned around expectantly, and she looked over at Lizzie. "She was a close friend of . . . of M-Mar—"

"It's okay to say her name, Claire." Nick's voice was gentle, and he heard Claire's soft sigh.

Claire nodded. "Marissa, she was a close friend with Wendy. And with everything that happened, perhaps it was a reminder that kept your wound open and festering."

Silence filled the vehicle.

Nick was surprised at Claire's insight, and wasn't sure what to say. "True . . . that could be true. But I've just never felt the need to go there." He paused, wondering why she had brought Wendy up. "Is there something I should be worried about where Wendy is concerned?"

He heard Claire sigh again. "I do have my suspicions."

"Can you elaborate on them?"

"They are just suspicions, Nick, so a little part of me feels like I'm telling tales out of school." Claire sounded hesitant, and in the mirror he saw her glance at Lizzie.

What was going on here?

"Please, Claire, enlighten me." He did his best to contain the frustration that was threatening his sense of contentment. But he also knew he needed to know what she was referring to.

The car was silent. Nick listened to Claire recounting her suspicions of Wendy being involved in the scandal around Ari's death, when money had gone missing.

At the time, it was the last thing he was worried about. And he'd left it to the lawyer to deal with the café since. So much was a blur, back then, that he'd totally forgotten about it—until Lizzie brought it up recently. With everything that happened to him after his wife's death, he'd been in no condition to give anything much thought. And as time passed, all he wanted to do was put it behind him. Never to speak of it again.

"Have you ever thought of the possibility that Marissa faked her death?" Claire asked softly.

He'd heard rumors but didn't believe them. It seemed just way too far-fetched. "No, I haven't."

Claire took a breath before speaking. "But what if you're still considered married? If she faked her death and you're still legally married—"

"Honestly, I never had any doubt about it. I'm not married, Ari is dead," he answered.

Claire finished up. "I'm sorry if I upset you. For what it's worth, I could be completely wrong."

Silence fell in the vehicle as Nick thought about what he'd just heard. He wasn't sure if he wanted to revisit the past, or let it lay. But what he did know was he didn't want to talk about it now, and ruin this trip.

"Okay, well, the open road is ahead of us. I have a couple of destinations up my sleeve." He held out his hand. "And now, I think I'd like another donut, please."

Chapter Forty-five

I had moved in most of my stuff from the cottage, but still had to get the rest and clean it up. We had time before I had to totally vacate.

The trip with Walter and Claire had been wonderful. The tense conversation about Wendy wasn't mentioned again. I did think it needed addressing, but letting it blow over on the trip was the right thing to do. If Nick felt he had to do something about it, I would be there to support him.

It was so great to get away, and create new memories. The visit to Hoh Rain Forest and Mount St Helens had been breathtaking.

We had just finished breakfast and were cleaning up together.

"I have a hankering to do some baking."

He paused and looked at me with a surprised expression. "Baking? I didn't know you baked." He reached for a glass to take some water with him to his office.

"Well, I've been known to cook now and then. Do you have something favorite that you like?"

"Well, let me see, I like brownies." He smiled, and took a drink of water.

"Brownies. Okay, do you like them with nuts, or with icing, or any other specific requests?"

"I like a creamy icing. And no nuts, I don't like nuts. And if you're going on a baking binge, some muffins would be nice too."

"Muffins are good."

"And cheese tea biscuits."

"Hey now, this isn't Sol—and I've never made biscuits before."

He stopped on his way to his office and turned around. "Always a first time." He winked and continued, "I don't know how much I have in the pantry. I'm not sure if you'll find everything you need."

"Don't worry about it, I'll see what you've got and work around it. Now off you go, and leave me to do my stuff."

He left, and his door closed. I looked for baking equipment and found it in a drawer in the island. He was right, there wasn't a whole lot, but I could make do. I put the bowls, measuring cups, and spoons on the counter. I didn't know any recipes off the top of my head, so pulled out my iPad and did a search.

Brownies seemed fairly easy to make. My fingers were crossed the pantry had what I needed. Everything was on a shelf that was too high for me to reach, and I wasn't about to climb up the shelves. I remembered there was a stepladder in the broom closet.

It was a bit of a mess, with bags hanging on hooks, cleaning supplies, brooms, and mops. I made a mental note to organize it. I shoved some things around so I could lift the stepladder down. It got caught on a coat—why was that in the broom closet?—I had to give it a yank, and it gave way. I fell back against the wall and banged my shoulder against a stud.

"Oww, that hurt." I rubbed my shoulder and turned to the offending piece of wood. There was some garbage littered around. I grimaced and swept dried-up coffee grounds, a petrified apple core, clumps of something indistinguishable, and a twist of paper into my hand. I opened a plastic bag and dumped the garbage in. The paper curled opened, and I could see there was faded writing on it. I turned my head to read it, but the lettering was too faint. I held it to the light that came in the closed door and . . .

I had the worst feeling, but couldn't keep myself from trying to decipher the words.

Then I heard my brother's voice whisper in my head. *Curiosity killed the cat.*

"Damn that cat," I said to myself, and leaned against the wall, my legs trembling. I took a deep breath and held up the note again. I had to read it twice, to fully comprehend what the words said. Then I'm pretty sure my eyes bugged out.

I read it again.

The paper was worn and yellowed, ripped down one side, and the pencil had faded. But the words on the paper jumped off the page like a neon sign. I pressed my hand to my chest, trying to steady my heart. I read the words yet again.

M,
It's arranged. They'll pick you up then you set the boat adrift.
Good luck. The money is waiting where you said.
W

I staggered away from the wall, and in the process knocked over a bucket and a broom, making a clatter that had Houdini race in to see what the matter was.

I rushed out of the closet, nearly slipping on the floor, and staggered into the kitchen. Close to hyperventilating, I put the paper on the counter under the dropped lighting. The words lit up like a spotlight was on them.

I croaked out Nick's name, then screamed louder. "Nick! Nick, get in here now." I was surprised by the shrill cut to my voice.

He came at a run. "What's the matter, Lizzie? Tell me what's wrong." He grabbed me by the shoulders.

I was unable to verbalize anything. My finger shook, pointing at the paper.

"It's a note—from Wendy to Marissa."

Nick let go of me to see it. I could have sworn he growled, when he placed his hands on either side of the paper and leaned over it. I held my breath. He was deathly silent, and it rather scared me.

He turned to me, and I'd never seen such a look of pain in his eyes before. It was a combination of anger and deep hurt. He'd been hurt, yet again, by this woman, this *dead* woman! I seethed, and could have spit nails, I was so furious.

"It's time we get to the bottom of it." He forced out the words.

I nodded. "It's time." So much for blowing over.

He took the note, my hand, and the keys to the car.

I knew where we were going, and I wasn't sure I wanted to be there when he confronted Wendy. Would he be able to contain himself when Wendy was standing in front of him? I, for one, wasn't sure I could be trusted when this confrontation happened. But again, that darn curious cat.

He took my hand, and my feet barely touched the floor. He raced down the hall and into the garage. Before I knew what was happening, I was seated in a gorgeous car. The garage door rose and we zipped under it. The tires squealed on the cement floor and spun on the stone of the driveway as we roared away.

This car was one I hadn't seen before, and must be what he referred to as his pride and joy. I wasn't about to ask now but sat, gritting my teeth, pushed into the seat by the speed of his acceleration. He wasn't a reckless driver, in fact he handled the vehicle like a pro, but he was going damn fast. I gripped the seat belt across my chest, gasping as the road was gobbled up in front of us and we sped toward town.

Nick gritted his teeth. His hands squeezed the steering wheel. That note had effectively shattered his world. The last three years had been a sham. He'd lived with that guilt all this time, feeling responsible for what Marissa had done to herself.

What I was put through!

He was absolutely beside himself with anger. And confused. Nick couldn't even comprehend what kind of a person could do such a thing. That Marissa had been so insidious rocked him to the core. He shook his head, bewildered, and still unable to believe she could plan such a thing—and with someone who worked at the café. *His café!* The worst thing was, he might never have known, and would have carried this guilt for the rest of his life.

Only one person could give him some kind of explanation.

He glanced over at Lizzie. She looked just as enraged as he felt. He held his hand out, and she put hers in it.

"I'm glad you found that note," he said.

"It was completely by chance. I needed the stepladder. I nearly fell in the broom closet, and saw this pile of rubbish, like a garbage bag had ripped open, and there it was."

Nick shook his head. "Unbelievable. If you hadn't found it, we'd never have known."

"Oh, Nick. I'm so sorry you're going through this. Just know, I'm here for you. All the way."

They found a parking spot in front of the café.

"You don't have to come in if you don't want to. But it's fine if you do. I'm going to confront Wendy. If I have to, I'll shut the place down."

"You can—after all, you own the café." Lizzie put the strap of her purse around her shoulders.

Nick smiled, and gave a wry laugh. "Yeah, I suppose I do. I bought it for her, but didn't put it in her name."

"What about the money the note mentioned?" Lizzie asked. "Will you pursue that? If it was really taken from the café, it's fraud. The police should be involved."

"Another thing I'll bring up with the lawyer." He ran his hand through his hair. "Let's go and see what Wendy says."

They got out of the car. Nick grasped Lizzie's hand, and they walked across the street together. He pushed the door ajar, and paused. "This is the first time I've been in here since she died." He stopped and looked through the window, then at Lizzie.

He was still holding her hand, and she squeezed it reassuringly.

Nick didn't recognize any of the staff, other than Wendy, who was behind the counter. He walked over and waited for her to turn around. When she did, her mouth dropped open. Her eyes flickered between Nick and Lizzie. Then she scrunched her eyebrows together and frowned.

"Nick. Wow, haven't seen you in years," she said, and carried on with what she was doing, as if dismissing the encounter.

"No, you haven't, have you? But now, we have to talk." He crossed his arms and stood, with his legs braced wide, in front of the counter.

"About what?" She didn't even give him the courtesy of

a glance, but turned her back on him to wipe the espresso machine.

Nick gritted his teeth. He bit back a harsh response that was on the tip of his tongue. "Wendy, I'm talking to you. And, remember, I own Sol."

Her wiping stopped and she tilted her head, as if on alert. "Okay, so you own Sol. Who's been managing it since you bailed out on the place?" Slowly Wendy turned around, and the look on her face wasn't pleasant.

"That's neither here nor there. The fact remains, the place is mine. The profits are mine. Everything within these walls is mine." Nick took a step forward.

Wendy blinked and looked at the ceiling. Nick furrowed his brow. He glanced up, and then across at Lizzie, by the door. She was looking up as well.

"We are going to have a talk."

"W-what do you mean, we're going to have a talk?" Wendy wasn't quite so belligerent now, and her eyes darted around.

"You need to tell me exactly what happened with Marissa." He got right to the point. Nick wanted to know what she'd say, and if she'd hang herself.

"What? She died . . . drowned." Wendy picked up a cloth and started wiping down the counter again. Her attitude was replaced by a nervousness she was trying to hide.

"Wendy. I know what you planned."

She froze, and flashed him a look. "What are you accusing me of? I had nothing to do with anything."

Her voice was starting to rise, and some patrons glanced over.

He turned to Lizzie. "Can you put the closed sign on the door, please, and lock it. Let people out as they go, but no new guests."

Lizzie nodded and went to the door. Slowly the customers filtered out, and soon there was nobody left except Nick, Wendy, and Lizzie.

"You have exactly ten seconds to tell me what happened. What was your involvement?" Nick's voice was hot and loud.

Wendy shook her head. "I don't know what you're talking about."

"Enough!" Nick shouted.

Wendy jumped. She was still shaking her head and denying any knowledge, until he slapped the note down on the counter in front of her.

She glanced at it. Her eyes widened. She covered her fingers with her mouth, and her eyes glistened. Nick felt not a lick of concern for her.

"Where did you get that?" she whispered.

"You had no involvement, eh? Then what's this?" he demanded, and pointed with his finger.

"I-I don't know what to say." She glanced around.

"How about the truth?" Nick took the note back and put it in his pocket.

Wendy drew in a ragged breath and let out a sigh. "Okay, yes, I helped her," was all she offered.

"Helped her how?" Nick demanded.

"I-I don't know . . . she asked me to do things, and I did."

"Things? What things?"

"I don't remember. It was a long time ago." Wendy looked highly uncomfortable, and her eyes continued to dart around.

Nick knew by her mannerisms she was trying to decide what to say.

"She hated this place and your marriage. She wanted to leave, and told me she didn't want to deal with the drama of a separation and a divorce because she was concerned about your reaction."

"What exactly does that mean? My reaction?" Nick took a step closer to the counter. She knew something, and he wanted her to say what it was.

Wendy shrugged. "That you wouldn't like it, and might not let her go."

"What? That's ridiculous."

"She said she had to leave, get away from Savage Cove, and you."

Nick sucked in a sharp breath. Leave? He shook his head, not believing where this was going. "She's dead. Drowned. What is this about leaving?"

Wendy shook her head, and took a step back until she bumped into the counter behind her. "Leave, left. Like *go*." She made a gesture with her hand to mimic flying off in a plane.

"She's alive?" Nick whispered. He glanced at Lizzie, who stood by the door with her fingers over her mouth and eyes wide, then back at Wendy. He was spinning.

Wendy smiled, but it didn't reach her eyes. She appeared to enjoy the effect of imparting this news on Nick. "Of course she's alive, you dolt."

"Where did she go?" Nick's voice boomed in the now empty café.

"I don't know where she went." Wendy was a little less smug now. "Marissa had planned it for a while." She gave Nick a narrow-eyed look and spat, "Like I said, she wanted to go, leave you, and Savage Cove."

"And you just went along with that? Why?" Lizzie walked over from the door.

"This is not your business." Wendy gave Lizzie a very nasty look.

"Seriously—"

"I can deal with this, thank you," Nick said softly to Lizzie, then turned back to Wendy. "Where is she now?" he snapped.

"I told you, I don't know. I've never known where she went. She just vanished after she got taken off your boat."

Nick sat down on the stool. It all felt surreal. How could he have been so gullible? Stupid. He'd been stupid not to see. He shook his head. Three years. Three years he'd grieved her, thinking she was dead. And the whole time, it had been for nothing. Marissa had set up the scheme.

This meant he was still married. Marissa was out there somewhere. Now he had to get a divorce. Unless there was a way around it. Nick let out a sigh. He needed to talk to his lawyer.

"Do you ever talk with her?" Nick asked, trying to contain his fury at Wendy.

She nodded. "Once in a while. Not all the time, and I have no idea where she is."

He shook his head. "This doesn't make sense. She left all her belongings at the house, didn't touch the bank accounts. I have a hard time believing she just up and left, without any money or clothes."

"She wasn't worried about it," Wendy said.

Lizzie leaned over and whispered, "Maybe she really was siphoning off money from the café."

Nick turned to look at Lizzie. He gave a small nod and rounded on Wendy.

"Right then, where's the money?"

Wendy's face went pale, and she didn't even try to deny it.

"H-how did you know about the money. We were so careful." Then she slapped her hand over her mouth. "No, I mean—"

"It doesn't matter what you mean. Clearly, you both were skimming. Marissa for her disappearance, and you as payment for helping her."

Wendy bent her head and stared at the floor. Gone was the defiance, replaced with trembling fear.

"You sicken me," he told Wendy. "Consider this your notice. You will no longer be employed here. Get your belongings, and I'll escort you out."

"What about all the food?" she asked.

"That's not your concern. Get out. Now." His voice held no room for argument.

Wendy seemed frozen for a moment, and then she grabbed her bag and was about to scurry out the door, when she paused. "Um, I have some stuff upstairs I'd like to get."

Nick stood and looked up the stairs. He hadn't been up there in years. It had been Marissa's private retreat when she needed a break from the busy café below, and her sanctuary when the rows between her and Nick became more frequent. He had left strict instructions it was not to be used, ever. "I'll go with you."

Lizzie followed them up the stairs and through the door on the landing. It was dark on the other side, but tidy. He half expected it to be full of cobwebs and dust. Strangely, it looked lived in.

Wendy opened the door to a room that was set up like a bedroom.

"What is this?" he demanded. "You had no right to be up here."

"I, um, it's just a room." She went to the armoire and pulled a few items of clothing off the shelf, plus a small duffle bag, and quickly stuffed them in it.

"Let me see that." Nick held out his hand.

The bag hung at Wendy's side. "Why? It's nothing special, just some spare clothes I leave here." Fear edged her voice.

"I need to check what's in there."

Wendy didn't budge. Lizzie quickly walked over and snatched the bag from her. She handed it to Nick.

"Hey!" Wendy shouted. "That's mine." She tried to retrieve the bag, but Nick turned his back to her.

Nick opened it and shuffled some woolen sweaters around until packets of money fell out of the sleeves. "What the hell?" His eyes met Lizzie's, which were wide as saucers.

"Oh, Nick. This could be the evidence—it's all the proof you need. Don't touch it."

Before he could confront Wendy, she bolted from the room and raced down the stairs. They were right behind her, but she got the front door unlocked and vanished outside. It was raining again, and the sky had darkened under the heavy clouds. They had no idea which way she had gone.

"I can't believe what just happened." Lizzie was breathless as she slowly locked the door, then leaned against it.

"It's unbelievable. I guess we'll have to call the police, as well as my lawyer." Nick looked in the bag again. "We'll have to keep this safe for the time being."

"It's like everything has come to a head all at once." Lizzie slipped her arm around his waist.

He drew her close. He needed to feel her body next to his. To ground him.

"Nick, we have a lot of food here. Why don't we just open up and finish selling it? It's awful to waste so much."

He nodded. "Good idea. Grab enough dinner for us. Give

the food away to whoever comes in and wants it. We'll tell them no sitting, only takeout."

"Okay, I will." She turned, and rested her hand on his chest. "Don't worry. It will be fine."

"I hope so."

But clearly, anything concerning Marissa was far from predictable.

Chapter Forty-six

So . . . now I was dating a married man. How the hell did that happen?

I couldn't be the *other woman*.

Nick was doing his best to reassure me, but every now and then I'd catch him staring off into space and knew he was burying his emotions. While everything felt so unsettled, I found myself withdrawing.

The drama with Wendy seemed to fizzle out once the police had taken statements and filed a report. She'd vanished, but I still had huge reservations.

With Marissa being alive, I was concerned about how it would change things between Nick and me. How he would feel about her if she came back? Oh, Lord, I couldn't even give that any thought. Walter and Claire didn't know we'd discovered Marissa was still alive. We both agreed there was no point stressing them with the news right now. Once Nick had some answers, he said he would inform his dad, and I had to respect that.

On a lighter note, I was pleased they were becoming braver about their relationship. We double dated one night over at the Crab Stone. It was a huge step for Walter, and we teased him that he lived to tell the tale. He assured us he'd be telling no tales at all.

But I was always on edge. Always watching for Wendy. And, of course, now Marissa. If Wendy told her Nick knew she was alive—how could we be sure it was even true?—I had no idea if that meant she'd come back, or stay away. It was starting to take a toll on me, which spilled over to Nick. I was frustrated that we were back to him not wanting to talk about Marissa. I couldn't understand why—and honestly, I was a little annoyed. This affected me too. But he had a meeting booked with his lawyer, to figure it all out, and until then he seemed determined to avoid the subject.

I hated that I was beginning to second-guess my decision to stay in Savage Cove. Had all this happened before I'd canceled my flight and let the cottage go, I questioned if I'd still be here.

But there was Nick. How could I leave him?

A few days after our confrontation with Wendy, we spent the evening sitting around the bonfire, drinking wine. Today, I was feeling a little more like my old self. I couldn't let this spoil what we had. I brought all the s'more fixings outside. We roasted marshmallows, built our tasty treats, and watched the stars. It was a lovely clear night.

"You seem relaxed tonight." Nick leaned over and filled my glass.

"I feel it," I told him. "It's been really hard since finding the note."

He held out a golden marshmallow, which I pulled off and

set on a piece of chocolate sandwiched between two graham crackers. He took my offering.

"Look, Lizzie, I've tried to reassure you everything will be fine."

I thought I heard a little bit of an edge to his voice, and searched his face in the firelight. He munched the s'more. I saw no indication he was upset, so maybe I was just being too sensitive.

"I'm trying to believe you, but I'm worried. I can't seem to shake it."

He sat back and sighed, his expression unreadable.

"Are you sorry you stayed?" he asked, but he didn't look at me. "Because you seem unhappy, and that is the last thing I want for you."

That was the question I'd dreaded. "Nick, Marissa's alive. Somewhere out there." I gestured toward the sea. "You're still married, and I have a very hard time with that."

"What can I do to help you?" When I was quiet, he pressed me. "Are you worried we'll reconcile?"

I faced him. "I-I don't know. Maybe."

He rose and went to the fire, poked it with a rod, and crouched down to tend the flames. "You shouldn't be worried about that. Marissa has been gone for three years. There's no reason for her to come back. She left—"

"Exactly. *She* left. Not you. You could still have feelings for her."

"No, I don't! You know what I went through with her. Do you really think I'd set myself up for that again?" He shook his head and jabbed the fire.

"Don't be mad." I put two more marshmallows on my roasting fork for us, though it was difficult to carry on with normal activities.

"I'm not mad. I'm sorry." Nick shifted so that he was in front of me on his knees, still holding the poker. "We can get through this. I couldn't be happier, except for one thing."

I looked at him. "What now? What's wrong?" I stuck the fork over the fire to distract myself.

"Nothing's wrong. But like I said, there's one thing I'm not happy about." He put the poker in the fire, and a burst of sparks spiraled up into the air.

"Hey, watch out for my marshmallows. You'll get them all covered in soot." I sat forward to move my fork.

"This is what I mean. This is what makes me unhappy."

I was totally confused right now. He looked very serious, and I was getting worried. "Nick, what are you saying?" I didn't know where to look, so I stared into the fire.

"What I'm saying is, the way you talk to me, giving the orders, and bossing me around."

"I don't—"

"Well, I'm not too happy about it."

I turned on him. "What do you mean? I don't boss you around. You're trying to tell me what I can and cannot say to you? I thought we were completely open about everything."

"I thought so too, but I think it's time that I tell you more. I had been keeping a secret from you that last couple of days. I think I need to come clean. I know we've only been together a little while, and you may find this . . . well, anyway, I need to talk about it." He paused.

My mouth dried up. "W-what do we need to talk about?" I had to force the words out, and I heard the croak in my voice. He was breaking up with me. It was really happening. The note. That damn note! He wanted to find Marissa.

I felt ill, and grabbed hold of the chair arm. I'd been so focused on myself and how the possibility of Marissa's reappearance made me feel, I'd not given enough thought to how this would make Nick feel.

"I don't want you to talk to me like that anymore . . . unless you're my wife." Nick held out his hand, with a ring box in the palm.

I blinked and shook my head. Was I hearing him right? I looked at him, the box in his hand, and then back at his face.

"I-is this real?" I whispered.

He nodded.

Slowly I came back to reality. He was asking me to marry him.

"What! Why?" I stammered. "I-I . . . oh, wow, this is the last thing I expected."

He laughed, and he walked forward on his knees until he was between mine.

"Lizzie, my beach nymph, I love you. I cannot imagine my life without you. We've come through so much in the short period of time that we've known each other. But I don't want to be with anybody else."

Tears streamed down my cheeks. My marshmallows flared up into huge flames. "Oh, they're burning." I flicked a fork out of the fire, and then turned back to Nick.

"I am burning for your answer." He still held his hand out, and now he opened the ring box.

"Oh my God." My hand flew to my mouth. I glanced up at Nick and then back down at the ring. "For me?"

He nodded. "Who else?"

Ice fire was reflected in the diamonds. A large, square-cut center stone, with two triangular ones on each side, ringed with a multitude of smaller stones that cascaded down the band.

"It's absolutely stunning."

"Nothing but the best for you, my love."

My mind was jumbled. I wanted to scream *yes! Yes, I'll marry you*. But could I? There were so many reasons to say yes. And other reasons that made it difficult.

I looked at him and chewed my lower lip.

"Lizzie?"

We were silent, and I watched the expression on his face shift from joy to concern.

"I don't know." My voice was soft.

He sat back on his heels. "What are you saying?"

"Oh, Nick. How can we get engaged when you're still married?"

Chapter Forty-seven

"Lizzie, please. Listen to me. It's going to be okay. I promise you."

"Oh, Nick, I want to believe you."

"Then believe me."

I looked into his eyes. Oh, how I wanted to.

"If I hadn't found that note, I would be jumping for joy. But it's all I can think of, and how it's hanging over our heads. It's like I'm waiting for the other shoe to drop."

"There are no more shoes." He smiled, and held the box up. "Lizzie, it's us. Remember? Destiny. Everything we've been through has brought us here. Together. Please think about it."

My thoughts swam. "I know what I want to say."

"Then say it." Nick took my hand.

It's what I needed. To feel our connection. I laced my fingers with his, and slid forward on the chair. I looked into his eyes. The eyes I'd grown to love, and trust.

I launched myself at him, my arms around his neck, showering kisses all over his face. He caught and held me tight.

"Yes, yes, yes, yes, yes."

His hands slid up my back. I felt the press of the ring box against my neck.

We laughed, and kissed, hugging each other, and all my fears and concerns melted away. There was nothing I could do. It was up to him, and he promised he had it under control.

"I think we need to make it official." He was still on his knees before me.

"But, Nick, are you sure? This is all so quick."

He took my hand and he slid the ring on my finger. "I'm absolutely sure."

"It fits perfectly." I was amazed.

"Of course it does. There's a lot about you imprinted on me, Lizzie. You have become such an integral part of my life, and of me, it's as if we can't tell where one of us ends and the other begins."

I turned my head sideways and didn't even try to stem the tears that were just flowing down my cheeks. "That's so romantic."

He laughed with delight. "Thanks to you. You've brought out the romantic in me and made me very happy."

I rested my palm on his cheek, the ring sparkling in the flickering light. "No, I'm the luckiest woman alive, to have a man like you love me. We belong together. Destiny worked hard to have us find each other."

I held out my hand, with my fingers up, so I could look at the stone. "That's pretty damn big."

"It's nothing compared to the size of my love for you," he said softly, and his kiss told me he meant every word.

We'd kept our news to ourselves for the moment, as I still wanted to be cautious. We had to clean out my cottage today— thankfully, the realtor was able to give us a week's grace period before requiring access to the cottage. With everything that had happened, plus our trip away with Walter and Claire, the pressure was now on. So we were up early, wanting to get the rooms emptied and cleaned as quickly as possible.

After a sunrise walk, I headed over to the cottage in my SUV, with Nick following behind in his Range Rover.

I pulled into the driveway and sat for a moment. I did love this cottage and would be sad to close it up. But Nick and I had something new. Together.

He was by my door and opened it. "Ready?"

I nodded. "Yup. I'm glad we got most of it moved out the other day."

"Yeah, between the two of us we'll have it cleaned in no time."

I led the way in, and Nick was behind. In my mind, I replayed the conversations we'd had about Marissa before I found the note. I shook my head. It was time to really let her go. She was gone. In the past.

We were here, and after what we'd been through— individually and as a couple—we were ready to begin our future. Officially, once Nick heard from the lawyers, and unofficially now.

Houdini had followed us to the house and raced inside when I unlocked the door.

"Oh," I said quietly.

Nick put his arm around me. "You really love this place, don't you?"

"Yes, I do. It's wonderful." I looked at him and looped my arms around his neck. "But I have you, and you don't live here."

He kissed me. "Yes, you do. Come hell or high water. You have me."

"Well, I guess we should get started. No point lingering around."

"Agreed."

The next couple of hours went by, and the cottage sparkled. We did a last check of all the closets and drawers. Unloaded the dishwasher and put everything away. It shone as much as a rustic cottage was able too.

"Did you look under the bed and the couches for any wayward belongings?" Nick asked.

"No, good idea. I'll check the bedroom." I went to the side of the bed and was on my knees when I heard Nick shout.

"Ha-ha! See, always have to check under the furniture."

Satisfied there was nothing hiding under the bed, I went to see Nick. "What did you find?"

He held up the metalwork heart.

"Oh, wow, I wondered where that had got to."

He put it in my hand, and I held it up to the light, between my thumb and forefinger. Sunlight sparked off the shiny surface.

"I found it at the market, after I'd lost my phone, way back when I first got here."

"It was you," Nick said in a low voice.

I turned to face him. "It was me what?" I asked.

"That day, I remember driving along Wharf and it was packed with people. The ferry had come in, and I was stopped in traffic by the market. I saw a woman holding something in her hand that flashed in the sun, and it looked like a heart. It was you."

"Wow, I'm stunned." I looked at the heart in my hand, and back at Nick. "You saw me? Back then. And to think we met the next day."

"Meant to be, I would say." Nick smiled down at me.

"I guess it was," I whispered, and curled my fingers around the heart. "I'm so glad you found it, I was worried I'd lost it, or packed it without paying attention."

We stood in the living room. The cottage was now empty. I blinked when I felt tears sting my eyes. My life had taken a significant shift while I lived within these walls. Growth, pain, letting go, and . . . love. I smiled. Another life chapter closed.

I gave myself a little shake to bring myself back to the present. Houdini had been very well behaved while we were busy. Maybe we could go for one last walk on the beach.

Houdini's head popped up. He rose to his feet and looked at me, ears perked, tail wagging.

"I swear he can read minds," I told Nick. "I was just thinking about him."

"I can't, so why don't you fill me in?"

"One last W-A-L-K on the beach?"

Houdini jumped around us.

"He can spell now?"

We laughed, and I rubbed his head.

"Come on then, let's go for a wa—"

Oh, yes, he knew the words. I didn't even finish saying "walkie" and he was standing at the door prancing.

"I think he wants something," Nick said.

He snapped the leash on Houdini, and I put on Rob's hat, winding my hair up under it.

"Funny that we know exactly what he wants, and he knows exactly what we were thinking."

Nick kept Houdini on the leash, and his manners today were testy. He wanted to be off and running at full pelt across the sand.

"I'm going to miss this beach," I said as we strolled along, holding hands.

"You'll have my beach," Nick reminded me.

"Yes, very true."

We wandered to where the waves could lick our feet, and I watched the gulls soar on the wind. They were so graceful and free.

We got to the rocks and stopped. "I don't feel like climbing over. This is where you took her picture, isn't it?"

"Mm-hm. I did. That's when I started to notice things were changing."

"I picked that up from the photo at the café. I think it should be taken down." I looked up at him.

"Already done." He squeezed my hand.

I nodded and smiled. Since he proposed, we'd been good. My fears and concerns still lingered, but they were not nearly as ripe as they had been. I was working at getting better, at not worrying so hard.

Nick looked at his watch. "Maybe we should head back, before it starts to rain again. Plus, I could use a nice hot drink."

"Hot chocolate?"

"Exactly what I was thinking."

The weather changed quickly and it was suddenly blowing a gale. Waves rose and crashed on the beach, the sky darkened, and rain started to slash at us.

"Oh, wow. Where did this come from?" I leaned into the wind and took Nick's hand.

"Come on, let's hoof it."

We picked up our pace, struggling against the onslaught of the weather. Rob's hat was ripped from my head and my hair whipped around my face.

"No!" I screamed, and raced after the hat that was tumbling down the beach toward the water.

"Lizzie!" Nick yelled behind me. Just as I was about to jump into the waves to get the hat, he pulled me back. "Let me, it's too rough."

I watched in horror as Nick fought against the surf, almost up to his waist, but the hat continued to blow further out to sea.

"Nick, Nick, no. Stop!" He didn't hear me, and a huge wave swallowed him up. "Noooo. Come back!"

He slapped at the waves, trying to push through them. Houdini was frantic on the shore, barking and running up and down. He was the smart one, and knew better than to brave the rough water.

Another wave crashed, and still I couldn't see Nick. I heard myself wailing. And then I was under the waves too. They were ruthless, churning and pulling me along the bottom.

Is this how it's going to end?

No. I couldn't let it.

I fought against the water. I found my footing and pushed myself up, blinking from the salt stinging my eyes. Fighting for every step, I battled toward the shore.

I looked around, frantically searching for Nick.

Relief flooded through me when I saw him stumble out of the waves. He saw me at the shoreline, and came racing. I reached for him. He pulled me from the water and we fell on the beach, tangled together, with Houdini barking and licking us.

Nick petted his wet fur and reassured him. "It's okay, boy." He was just as breathless as I was.

"Oh my God, Nick. I thought I'd lost you." I stared into his eyes, afraid to break contact.

"You don't think a little bit of rough water is going to tear me away from you, do you?" He smiled, and pulled me to my feet. "I'm sorry I couldn't get your hat. I know how much it meant to you."

I faced the ocean. The wind and nature had taken something from me that I treasured. The hat was gone. And Nick had risked his life to try and save it for me. In that moment, I realized that my brother had given me to Nick. Rob had let go of me. And I of him. The symbolism astounded me.

"It's okay." I looked at Nick, my heart swelling with love for him. "It's all okay."

I extended my hand, and he took it.

Nick put his arm around me. "Let me take you home."

"Yes, let's go home."

Chapter Forty-eight

With the last of my belongings in my SUV, I marveled at how much I'd collected over the last weeks, and it was a tight fit. The cottage no longer held any essence of me. We stood in the doorway on the front porch, and I gazed around the place I'd called home.

I changed here. Grew. Faced my past. Found myself. Well, almost. I still had a way to go. But now I had Nick. We had each other. He had his arm around my shoulder. I reached up and took his hand, holding him while I said a quiet final goodbye to my lovely little cottage.

"I'm sorry about your hat." He squeezed me gently.

I let out a gentle sigh. "It's okay, it wasn't your fault."

We were quiet for a moment, each lost in our own thoughts.

"Ready?" he asked.

I nodded. "Yes." My voice was soft, and I let the sentimental feelings have their way with me. The cottage deserved it. "I'm glad we took our time getting it ready to lock up."

"I think you needed to say goodbye to it."

We closed the door for the last time. I slid the key in the lock, turned it, and the click of the bolt paralleled the feeling of leaving the past behind me. Locked and secured. Putting the key in the lockbox, and spinning the dials, was symbolic.

No turning back. There was only forward.

"Let's get home before we catch pneumonia," I said, with a smile, while I pushed my hair off my face.

"Excellent idea."

We quickly got in the cars, as the drizzle got a little heavier. I followed Nick to his house, wipers going so I could see the road, and reflected on our conversations.

A short time later, Nick pulled into his laneway. I was right behind him. A car I didn't recognize was parked near the front steps, which would make unpacking difficult in this rain.

We backed up to the steps, side by side. Nick got out and looked at the other car. I joined him.

"Who's here?" I asked.

He shook his head. "Not sure. No one's in the car, they must be at Dad's. Let's get your stuff into the house."

He pushed open the front door, and we lined up the boxes along the wall.

I saw Nick glance around, and shrug. "No one here."

"Weird."

We went for another load, and Nick took the groceries into the kitchen. I went back out to the car and organized what was left to bring in. I was eager to get out of these clothes. Loud voices reached me. I glanced in the direction of Walter's house, but they weren't coming from there.

They were coming from Nick's house.

"Wha—?"

The yelling escalated, and I ran up the steps into the house to see what was happening.

Heated voices—one was clearly Nick's and the other one, yelling over him, was a woman.

Who on earth was shouting like that? Had Wendy come back to confront Nick?

I put down the boxes and walked to the kitchen, hesitating at the door, then I peered around the wall, careful to stay out of sight. Nick was silent now, leaning against the counter with his arms crossed. His face was red, and he looked furious.

A woman stood at the door to the breezeway, screaming at him. She was in such a state that she didn't see me come in. Nick did, and he shook his head slightly. I backed away. The woman's confrontation was relentless as she spewed a stream of incoherent words.

I had a really bad feeling about this and was pretty sure I knew who she was.

Marissa.

Why is she here? Why now?

I wasn't going to hide from her.

I walked into the kitchen and kept my eyes on her. My body tightened, fingers curled into fists, and I was ready to pounce. She looked different from the photo—older, and with shorter hair. A chill filled the room, and I had a terrible sense of doom. Marissa coming back was definitely not a good thing.

She suddenly noticed me and swiveled, pinning me with a hostile stare. I kept walking to Nick's side.

"Who the hell are you?" she demanded. She took a step toward me, looking me up and down.

I stood taller, knowing I looked like a drowned rat, but no way would I allow her to intimidate me.

That seemed to activate Nick. He positioned himself between us. "Marissa, you're not welcome here. You need to leave. Now." His voice was low and steely.

"You can't make me leave here," she said with a snort. "This is my house too."

"No, it's not. And yes, I can. You will leave." Nick didn't allow room for argument. He walked over to the counter where she had put her keys, picked them up, and removed one off the ring.

"What are you doing, Nick? You can't take that key." She advanced on him and snatched the keys out of his hand.

I could barely contain myself. All I wanted to do was scream and drag her out of Nick's house. His life. But this was between them.

"I can and I did. This is not your house, you have no right to be here. You need to leave. Now."

She was shaking her head, her short dark hair framing her face. It was damn hard to be objective when I looked at her, but I could see the allure others may have felt. She did have a very striking appearance, and I glanced at Nick to see his expression. There was nothing but distaste.

She turned back to me. "You never said who you are."

I took a step toward her, with my eyes narrowed. "Lizzie." I tilted my head, waiting to see her next move.

She returned my stare, with a hint of a sneer. "Lizzie? Well, who the hell are you, and why are you here in my house?"

"Not your house." It was all I could do not to yell at her.

"More mine than yours." She took a step closer to me.

I stood fast. This chick didn't scare me.

"All right, I've had about enough of this." Nick stood in between the two of us, probably expecting some kind of fight.

I was ready to take her on. After everything I'd learned about her and what she'd done? No way would I sit back, but for Nick's sake I backed down.

"You," he pointed to Marissa. "Out." He swung his arm, with his finger pointed to the doorway behind her.

"I'm not going anywhere." She jammed her fists on her hips and she sat on the stool.

"Oh my God," I whispered.

She flung me a glance, her mouth tightening into a snarl. I blinked and narrowed my eyes again, willing her to get off the stool and advance on me so I could slap her silly.

"You have about ten seconds to get the fuck out of my house, or I'm calling the police," Nick said to her.

She crossed her arms, looking away from him.

"I think you should quit being so childish, and leave," I said. "There's nothing left for you here any longer."

She slid off the stool. "You, shut up." She tried to look menacing. "You shouldn't be here."

I refused to back away. "It's you who shouldn't be here. No one wants you here," I said through gritted teeth. "You gave everything up when you did what you did. What could you possibly think you can achieve by coming back?"

"Patience, blondie, you'll find out soon enough."

"And so will you," I spat back at her.

I was about to say more, but Nick grabbed her, holding her tight by the elbow. "No, you shouldn't be here. You're out. Now." He led her out through the door and into the breezeway.

She swore and started screaming. I raced after them, so I could be a witness to back up Nick, should it be needed. I had my phone handy, to record their interaction.

"You have no right to be here. You've been gone for over three years. You faked your death. It's reprehensible. Get out and off the property. I'll be getting a restraining order if you don't comply."

Nick shut the door in her face and locked it. He spun around and put his arm around my shoulder. "Come on, let's go into the living room. She'll leave."

"Do you really think so? She doesn't look like the leaving kind of girl. If you hadn't pushed her out, I'm pretty sure she'd have refused to go. She seems so volatile."

I was really worried. If this was how she behaved when they were still married, my heart broke for Nick.

We heard the car start, and then the crunch of the gravel when she drove off.

"She's gone." I breathed a sigh of relief, and took Nick's hand. "I am so sorry that this is happening to you. But, Nick, I don't want to put you in a difficult position. I've been thinking that, until you get this settled, I should find somewhere else to stay. Give you time to think. If only I still had the cottage."

"No, I don't need time to think, I don't need you to go away. You're going to stay right here with me, and we are going to deal with this together." He pulled me into his arms and we sat on the couch. "Lizzie, I told you before that you are the new shining light in my life. All the dark clouds that weighed me down have lifted. The sun began to shine, that day we met on the beach. I won't allow Marissa back into my life. It took only minutes for her to be in this house to feel the oppressive weight of her. I didn't like it." He shook his head. "I still can't believe everything she's done."

"But she's so confrontational, she might make our lives miserable. Impossible, even."

"The easiest decision I've ever had to make is this one, right now. I will never forgive her for what she's done, and I don't even really want to know why she's come back. We're going to deal with it when we go to see my lawyer.

I nodded.

'Yes, and don't you worry. This changes nothing. Nothing at all."

Nick pulled me into his arms, but I wasn't convinced it would go as smoothly as he said.

Chapter Forty-nine

I'd been to the café and brought back a load of food. Nick had promoted Amanda, and she was doing an amazing job. He still had the management firm handling the business details, but he trusted Amanda to do the day-to-day running of the café, and report back to him should Marissa show up.

Amanda was thrilled with the promotion. Wendy had all but vanished, and I wondered if she would ever be held accountable for her part in the skimming scam she'd perpetrated with Marissa.

But Marissa—that was a whole other kettle of fish.

We'd invited Walter and Claire over for dinner, and I was determined to focus just on them. Nick and I decided it was time to let them know what had transpired over the last while. We were soldiering on, and being optimistic about the outcome, providing Marissa didn't do something stupid.

I unpacked the food I'd brought from the café and set it in the oven. Walter and Claire should be over at any time. I was giving Nick some space, so that he could deal with some business, as he might have to head back to Miami.

Marissa being alive and back in Nick's life still hung over me. It stunned me that this woman dared to return. I was glad she'd only made one unwelcome visit to the house. We had no idea where she was staying. It boggled me now that I'd been so obsessed with knowing what had happened to her, and who had sent the text messages.

My anger over what she'd done to Nick far outweighed the curiosity I'd once had about her. She'd thrown Nick into a different mental chaos than the guilt he'd been feeling all these years. Since she'd *supposedly* died and he'd mourned her. I felt my lips curl with disdain.

While we knew what we wanted our future to be, I felt it was still up in the air. This woman had faked her death, only to blow back into Nick's life like a hurricane. I simply couldn't grasp the reasoning. Why disappear in such a brutal way and then come back?

I heard Nick talking in his office, and I hoped everything was okay. I was worried he'd have to go away on a business trip before the drama with Marissa was resolved.

I dreaded telling Walter and Claire. How would they react? What would they say? I quickly set the table so we could eat when they arrived, and ran upstairs.

I lay down on the bed and stared at the ceiling, then flopped over to press my face into the pillow. For the thousandth time, I asked why this was happening. Would it have happened if I hadn't been here, or lost my phone, which had set all this in motion? Imagine, if I'd never come to Savage Cove at all.

My chest tightened, making it difficult to breathe. If I hadn't lost my phone, then I wouldn't have met my love. Through all this, I came to know that Nick was my great love, but maybe all great loves were intermingled with tragedy. Would there be a happily ever after for us?

I was *not* going to cry.

I rolled on to my side and stared out the window. The ocean was gray and unhappy, matching my mood.

The sound of barking dogs filtered up the stairs. Walter and Claire had arrived. I drew in a deep breath and got off the bed, dragging my feet to the bathroom. I looked at myself in the mirror. What a mess. I brushed my hair and twisted it up, then dabbed cool water under my eyes, hoping it would ease the puffiness, and put on some light make-up.

I went downstairs and plastered on a smile as best I could. Nick was with our guests in the living room, sitting around the fireplace.

When he saw me, he held out his hand. I went over and took it.

"Well, we've had a strange few days." Nick jumped right in.

I sat down beside him and clutched his hand.

"What's been going on, then?" Walter asked.

Claire turned to me and gave me a questioning look. I widened my eyes, unable to give her any kind of sign.

"Well, I think I'll start with some good news. Then there's bad news to follow."

I was quite happy to let Nick take the lead.

"I hate bad news," Claire said, frowning.

"Okay, give us the good news first, son," Walter said. He was looking at us, a highly concerned expression on his face.

"Okay, well, look at this." Nick held out my hand with the engagement ring. "She said yes!"

Nick turned to look at me, and his happy smile chased away my worries. I had to believe if he thought it was going to be okay, then it *was* going to be okay.

"Oh my God! Congratulations to you both." Claire jumped up and sat beside me. She took my hand from Nick and held it up so she could look at the ring. "That is gorgeous. It is so classic—and that's an excellent stone too."

"I love it." I held my hand out and moved it so the light caught the ring, making it sparkle.

"I'm stunned," Walter said. "But not in a bad way. In a good way. I'm glad you two sorted your issues out and that you're getting married. But I'm worried about your bad news. Don't leave us hanging."

Nick and I looked at each other, and I shrugged. He turned to his dad and then he looked at Claire, glanced down at my hand with the ring, and ran his thumb over it.

"I don't even know how to start. So I'm just going to say it." He looked at both of them. "Marissa is alive."

A deathly silence filled the living room.

Walter sat back and let out a groan. He whispered, "Fuck me."

"Walter." Claire's voice was stern, then she put her arm around me. "What does this mean?"

Nick ran his hand through his hair. "I guess that means I'm still married and I have to get a divorce. Unless there's another way around it." He sighed and stood up. "I don't know about you guys, but I need a drink. I'm having bourbon, anyone else?"

We all said yes, and Nick went into the other room to get the drinks.

"This is such a shock. And it was just a total fluke that we found out," I told them.

"How? When?" Walter asked, and he stood up and started pacing in front of the window.

"I wanted to do some baking and needed a stepladder to reach the top shelf in the pantry. I got the ladder from the broom closet and tidied up some old rubbish lying about. Mixed in was a note that opened the whole can of worms." I filled them in on the details.

Claire gasped, and covered her mouth with her hand. "I don't believe it."

Walter stopped his pacing. He stared at me, and then looked at Nick when he walked back into the room with the drinks.

"Oh, believe it," Nick said, putting the tray down on the coffee table. "We confronted Wendy, and she admitted she'd helped Marissa execute this, whatever you want to call it, great escape. Said that Marissa wanted everybody to think she was dead and to disappear."

"Hmm, I had my suspicions." Claire shook her head and pursed her lips.

"What the hell?" Walter said, and reached for a glass. He shot back the bourbon in one go. "I always knew she was nuts." He thumped the glass back down on the tray and picked up the bottle to pour more.

"I know, I know," Nick said, and dropped on to the couch with his glass in hand. "I was incredulous. I don't even know how to tell you. But I was furious."

"So, what's next?" Claire asked, and sipped on her drink.

"I . . . *we* have an appointment with the lawyer." He looked at Lizzie. "I'd like you to come with me too."

"Yes, of course I will." I took his hand.

"Hopefully, we'll be able to get some indication from him on how things will work."

"Well, good goddamn," Walter said again.

"Walter, please, your language," Claire said in a soft tone.

"The hell with my language. I can't even find words. Un-fucking-believable."

Nick and I smiled at each other.

We finished the last of our drinks in silence. It seemed we were all caught up in our thoughts.

"Why don't we have something to eat?" I suggested. "After all, you came for dinner."

Walter nodded, walked over to Claire, and helped her up. They wandered into the kitchen, taking the bottle of bourbon along with them.

Nick put his arm around me. He leaned down and whispered in my ear. "Just remember, I love you."

I looked up at him, and felt an edge of fear creep up on me again. "I love you too."

Nick and our guests helped me carry the food to the dining table.

"You brought café food home," Claire commented.

"Yes, I've been spending more time there, with Wendy gone. I know she did the lion's share of baking, and it's important not to let that slide." I selected some vegetables and put them on my plate.

"Why don't you run the place?" Walter asked, speaking around a mouthful of beef.

I shook my head. "No way. First, I have my work to focus on. And second, I just can't bring myself to follow in her footsteps."

"I promoted Amanda," Nick told them.

"Amanda? I don't recall her," Walter said, then tore off a piece of bun.

"Of course you do, dear," Claire corrected him.

He shrugged his shoulders and continued to eat.

"No one could follow in my footsteps." A woman's voice came from the hall.

I dropped my fork.

Nick shot to his feet, as did Walter. "What the hell?" he shouted.

Nick leaned down and whispered to me. "Call 911, and do it quietly. Say we have an intruder."

I got up and went into the kitchen, staring down Marissa as I passed. I kept watching what was happening in the other room while I dialed.

"How did you get in?" Nick demanded. "Why are you here, when I explicitly told you not to come back?"

"Well, I thought it was time to come back and claim my husband." She slid a glance my way and then back to Nick.

I nearly spluttered when she said that. I fought hard to contain my anger when I saw the way she trailed her fingers across Nick's chest as she walked by him into the great room.

She put her purse on the armchair. "Looks like I'm just in time for dinner."

"You are in time for nothing." Nick marched over to her. "It's laughable why you came back."

She stood her ground. "Aww, Nicky, don't be like that. After all we shared?" She walked over to the table and selected a piece of meat, holding it between her thumb and forefinger as she inspected it. Then nodded and delicately put it in her mouth. "The door was unlocked, and I don't need to ask your permission to come into my home."

I left the kitchen and came to stand beside Nick. She looked at me, and her gaze slid away. She was dismissing me as posing any kind of threat.

"It's nice to see you, Walter." Marissa made a move to sit down.

I slid into the seat, stopping her.

"Well, it's not nice to see you." Sometimes his bluntness was perfection. "You're not wanted here, and we're not asking nicely again."

"Nicely? When did you ask nicely?"

Marissa walked around the room, inspecting various items, casting glances at us as she moved about. She picked up the amber stone I'd put on the fireplace mantel.

"Still collecting I see. And look at this cute little heart." Her sarcastic tone grated on me.

I was pushed into action when she picked the stone up. It had meaning to us, and I didn't want her touch to taint it.

"They're mine." I walked forward and took the stone from her. "You're not welcome here."

She appeared surprised that I had the tenacity to stand up to her.

"What? Did you think I'd be a pushover?" I snarled. "Hardly. And I heard what you said—we told you, the last time you were here, this is not your house!"

She made a pfft sound and walked away from me. I heard her say in a low voice, "Oh, but it is."

My ears were hot, I was so angry.

"You need to leave. You have no business being here." Nick shepherded her toward the hall.

"That's where you're wrong," she said, and cast a glance over her shoulder at him, her hair swinging seductively around her neck.

I don't think I've ever felt such hatred for someone as I did for her in that moment. I balled my fists.

"I don't think so. But I will not debate it now with you. My lawyers are dealing with it." Nick opened the door to the front porch.

She didn't move. "Oh, you've lawyered up already? What a shame. I guess you want a war."

"Oh, there'll be no war. Don't you worry about that."

"I guess we'll wait and see, won't we?"

"You're forgetting something." Nick paused, and crossed his arms.

"Mmm, I don't think so." She touched her chin and shook her head.

Marissa was just so damn . . . I wanted to scream at her! I knew Nick was referring to the prenup she'd signed. He'd told me about it earlier.

Marissa cocked her head as if listening. The very faint tone of a siren could be heard through the night. She turned to Nick, her eyes narrowed. "You didn't—"

"I told you I would. You're running out of time, if you want to avoid a night in the lock-up." Nick pointed to the door.

"You called the police," she spat, her voice dripping with poison. "How dare you do that? I'm your wife."

He snorted. "Not for much longer. Time for you to go. And don't come back."

Nick moved past her and held the door open. She stomped out, leaving behind her a peal of bitter laughter that echoed off the walls.

Claire and Walter stood motionless, wide-eyed with shock, when we came back to the dining table. We all looked at each other, and it was Walter who broke the moment.

"Right. Who needs a drink?" he said.

"Maybe we should wait until the cops come," I suggested. "After they leave, I'm having a stiff one."

"Good idea," Claire agreed. "We don't want to appear inebriated while the police take yet another report."

"No kidding. I certainly hope this is the last one," Nick said.

He walked to the front door when the lights of the police cars flashed through the windows.

I shook my head, trying to make sense of the evening. "She's just horrible, savage." I was reminded of something. "You know, I've always wondered about the origin of the name Savage Cove, but other things kept cropping up for me to find out. But damn, what we've been through with *her* certainly has been savage."

"Savage Cove was named after the first settler, Benjamin Savage," Walter informed me.

"Well, darn, that's a bit of a let-down. Here was I, thinking it was something big and dramatic, ships crashing and sinking, people fighting . . . you know, general chaos." I made an exaggerated pout.

"Oh, yes, that happened too. But sorry to disappoint about the name," Walter chuckled.

The tension of moments before faded as we all broke out in laughter. And I knew that, whatever happened next, we were now a family, and nothing Marissa did could come between us.

Chapter Fifty

Nick's appointment with the lawyer was in a few minutes. It seemed like forever, since yesterday and the second confrontation with Marissa. Everything about her behavior still mystified me.

We were called into the office and sat in chairs across from his lawyer.

"Nick, good to see you," Charles said, and shook Nick's hand.

"Thanks for fitting us in." He leaned forward and slid Wendy's note and the police report across the desk to the lawyer. "Charles, this is Lizzie, my fiancée."

"Pleasure to meet you, Lizzie." Charles nodded at me.

"And you too," I replied.

Charles turned his attention to the note. He picked it up and read it, registering surprise with raised eyebrows and a glance at Nick, then me. He fingered the police report with the occurrence numbers. "Really?" He put the note down and steepled his fingers. "You had to call the police as well?

"Yes, we did. We discovered the note a few days ago, and then Marissa showed up twice. We assume her accomplice, who worked in the café, alerted her that we knew about their ruse." Nick left the note on the table.

I wondered if the lawyer would copy it for the file. They began discussing details, and I tried to keep focused on their conversation, but my thoughts kept drifting back to Marissa. How on earth would things play out?

"I have a question, if I may?" I ventured.

The two men looked at me.

"Go ahead, ask away. This involves you too," Nick told me.

"Marissa made a threat to me. I'm worried about what it could mean."

Nick and I both looked at the lawyer, who was contemplative, then he nodded.

"Well, aside from a physical threat, she was probably referring to a financial threat. But, of course, no one will know what it really is until she asserts it."

"Well, that's rather unsettling. So she will never go away?" I closed my eyes with dread. "She'll always be in the picture, with alimony or support."

Nick took my hand. "Lizzie, we don't know that." He turned to Charles.

"She might try to make things tricky for you, Nick, but you were smart to have her sign the prenup, and it's iron clad. She's been away three years, that's spousal abandonment. She abandoned you, faked and lied about her death—pseudocide. Not to mention the threats, and her showing up unwanted at your house. There is a lot stacked against her." He paused and tapped the police report. "We can move for a restraining order. Did she say why she came back?"

"Just that she was returning to claim her husband." Nick

grimaced. "Likely she wants money. She's delusional to think there would be any reconciliation. After what she's done, and even before that. I was on the verge of telling her I wanted a divorce, but was unable to, because it was then she disappeared. That said, I want to start the process to annul, divorce, or do whatever's required to end the marriage—and the quickest way possible, with the least amount of financial impact."

Charles nodded. "Fine. I'll get it started." He looked at me. "Don't worry, we'll have this all cleared up as quickly as we can."

I smiled. "Thank you." I was so glad that Nick was speaking to his lawyer. Now someone else could help carry the load, as well as ease our worry. Well . . . maybe.

"Thanks, Charles, keep me in the loop and let me know what I need to do." Nick rose, and offered me his hand.

"Will do." Charles was already typing on his computer as we left his office.

Out on the street, Nick drew in a deep breath and lifted his face to the sun. "Well, now that's out of the way. Let's put it out of our mind until we have to revisit it."

I had to admit, I felt a tiny bit better.

We strolled down to Wharf Street, hand in hand. He'd parked his Jaguar, which I learned was a vintage E-Type, along the waterfront. It really was a pride-and-joy car and garnered a lot of attention, which actually made me feel proud.

"I hope your lawyer can make it happen with no fuss."

"Trust me, he's good."

"I'm counting on it." I squeezed Nick's hand, to emphasize my words and remind myself we were together. "Feel like some ice cream?"

"As a matter of fact, I do. First let me put my briefcase in the car."

"It's such a gorgeous car," I said after he shut the car door.

"My favorite." He reached for my hand.

Another vehicle pulled into the spot beside his, nearly striking me if Nick hadn't whirled me aside.

"Hey," he shouted. "Watch your driving."

The driver's door opened. The windows were tinted so we couldn't see the driver until they stepped out of the car.

"You mean I missed?" Marissa slammed the door and stalked toward us. "Too bad."

I backed up to the curb, and Nick stepped in front of me.

"What the hell do you think you're doing?" His voice was gravelly and menacing.

"I should ask you the same thing. You've screwed me over, Nick."

I burst out laughing. This was all too much. "I mean really. He screwed *you* over? That's a stretch—"

"No one asked you." She all but snarled the words.

"You're like the friggin' Wicked Witch. Someone needs to drop a house on you." I planted my hands on my hips and faced her.

"That's a threat. I could have you arrested for death threats—"

"Marissa!" Nick's voice was sharp and it stopped her cold. "It's over. Accept it. Move on and go.

I leaned into Nick and said in a low voice, "A crowd is gathering."

Marissa looked around. She had to see she'd created enough of a commotion to cause a small crowd to gather. She stood her ground, and her mouth worked as if trying to find something to say.

With a shake of her head, she spat, "I've always hated Savage Cove, and wouldn't want to be stuck here like you are."

"I think it's a perfect place." I had to bite my tongue not to say *even more perfect without you in it.*

Marissa yanked open the driver's door and paused, before turning what she must have thought was a seductive smile in Nick's direction. "Sure you don't want to come with me, Nicky?"

I gasped at the gall of her, but I also knew she'd finally accepted that her coming back had been for nothing. All her threats and claims had failed.

Nick put his arm around me, and I raised my hand to hold his, which was draped over my shoulder. I saw her watch the movement and then her eyes widen. I'm sure she saw the glint of the diamond on my finger.

"Marissa," Nick answered her. "I have everything I could possibly want. Right here."

I looked up at him, and he leaned down to kiss me, then faced her again.

"Your threats have failed. There's nothing more for you here, so you'd best be on your way."

This time, she didn't say a thing when she turned and stomped away. The car door slammed, and she squealed out of the parking space, nearly hitting a vehicle behind her, then roared off down the road.

The crowd behind us clapped hands, and there were various shouts of "way to go", "well done", and other comments before the folks dispersed.

Nick laughed and lifted a hand in a wave, before taking mine.

"She's gone," he said.

"For good, I hope." There was a lot I could have said, but now wasn't the right time. I certainly did hope this was the end of her. "What was all that for, anyway? Why come back like that?"

"I don't understand her thinking at all. How could I, after what she'd done? All I know is, I want everything settled, for her to never come back, and . . ." He paused and looked down at me. "Ice cream."

We laughed.

"Come on then, this way," I said.

We got ice cream at the truck and found a bench facing the water by the ferry terminal.

I pointed. "See that boat?"

"Ferry," he corrected me.

I looked at him and rolled my eyes. "Ferry. It started it all." I licked my ice cream.

"So that's the one," he stated.

"Yup. That's the one." I laughed.

"Well, I'll be damned. I think I need to shout a thank you to that ferry." He glanced at me and smiled. "In the meantime, I don't think there's anything wrong with wedding planning."

The expression in his eyes gave me butterflies. I'd never been moved so deeply by the adoring looks he gave me as I was now.

"Are you sure? Nothing's settled yet." I held my breath.

"Yes, very sure. No matter what, we'll be together. The dissolution of the marriage cannot come soon enough." He looked happy saying the words.

Excitement flared in my chest, chasing away the worry that seemed to live there recently. "Nick, I will stand by you all the way."

"And I will stand by you too. I love you, Lizzie."

"I love you too." A new feeling of lightness filled me.

I was confident it would all work out now. Our love and dedication to each other was our power, our driving force. We would make it, no matter what was thrown in our path.

We leaned together, our shoulders touching, while we finished our cones.

The ferry docked. Gave a horn blast. I stood up to throw my napkin in the trash. Nick was right behind me.

He swung me up into his arms. We kissed, neither of us caring that we were in the middle of a swarm of people getting off a ferry. We were together and ready to fight for our future. Nick let me slide down his body, and we held hands, swinging them as we walked along. I was nearly bursting with love, and the sun came out from behind a cloud. I looked up, the heat from the sun on my face, and flock of birds soared on the breeze. It was a perfect day.

I skipped a couple of steps and turned, walking backward in front of him.

"Careful," he said, and checked the sidewalk behind me.

"Let's get some fish and chips for lunch," I suggested.

"I like that idea. The first lunch of the rest of our lives together." His smile was wide and infectious.

We laughed, and I turned, falling into step with him. I rested my head on his shoulder.

"The sun's out now," I said to him. "I'll take that as a good sign.

"I will too," he murmured against my hair.

We wandered along the waterfront to the fish and chip truck. I couldn't believe I'd had my first meal here when I arrived in Savage Cove, back in June. The time had flown and so much had happened.

It seemed fitting having lunch here. Starting anew now, with Nick, in the same place where it all began when I arrived here on my own. I'd had no idea what was going to happen to me. I came to Savage Cove to fulfill my deathbed promise to Rob. I'd thought my purpose was to see the world. Travel and not let go of life. Do well at launching my new career.

But, instead, it was to embrace the moment, and not let go

of life, the experiences, or the people that fit perfectly in your world.

I sighed, knowing my journey was complete. I had learned what I needed to through my driving force to honor Rob's dying wish.

I looked up at the blue sky and the birds flying higher in graceful arcs. I imagined Rob, as free as one of those birds, soaring up and away. I watched the birds through a sheen of tears, and sent him the last message before I truly let him go.

This is my life lesson, Rob. I am my own home. And home can be anywhere. I don't need someone to make a home, but I have found someone to share one with. Thank you for sending me on my path of discovery.

Acknowledgments

This book would not be possible without my powerful team behind me. My agent extraordinaire, Louise, my absolutely fabulous editor, Kate, hawk eye copy-editor, Shan Morley-Jones, and all the behind-the-scenes folks at Headline Eternal that were instrumental with the development of *The Last Message*. A shout out to my friend and beta reader, Cathy, she dropped everything when a new file landed in her inbox and her feedback was golden. *The Last Message* was a long time in coming: writing, tweaking, researching, editing, reading, and re-reading, and I'm thrilled to be able to share it with you, the reader. I'm forever grateful to Kate, who saw the glimmer of the idea buried in my brain for TLM and was just as excited as me to bring Lizzie and Nick's story to life.

HEADLINE
ETERNAL

FIND YOUR HEART'S DESIRE...

VISIT OUR WEBSITE: www.headlineeternal.com

FIND US ON FACEBOOK: facebook.com/eternalromance

CONNECT WITH US ON TWITTER: @eternal_books

FOLLOW US ON INSTAGRAM: @headlineeternal

EMAIL US: eternalromance@headline.co.uk